Village
AFFAIRS

ALSO BY CASSANDRA CHAN

The Young Widow

Village AFFAIRS

CASSANDRA CHAN

St. Martin's Minotaur
New York

VILLAGE AFFAIRS. Copyright © 2006 by Cassandra Chan. All rights reserved. Printed in the United States of America. No part of this book may be used or reproduced in any manner whatsoever without written permission except in the case of brief quotations embodied in critical articles or reviews. For information, address St. Martin's Press, 175 Fifth Avenue, New York, N.Y. 10010.

www.minotaurbooks.com

ISBN-13: 978-0-312-33750-6
ISBN-10: 0-312-33750-7

First Edition: November 2006

10 9 8 7 6 5 4 3 2 1

In memoriam
Edward E. Chan,
my father, who first introduced me to the delights of mystery novels. It has been one of the greatest gifts ever given to me and is just one of the many reasons I love him so much. Here's hoping he would have liked this one.

ACKNOWLEDGMENTS

Firstly to Kelley Ragland, who had to work extra-hard on this one, even while training a new assistant and then not having one at all (he probably quit because I was late, again). And also to Jennifer, without whom I would be utterly lost, and to my mother, whose store of encouragement is endless.

Thanks to Dr. Lawrence Watkins for suggesting Seconal, and to Steve Krull for explaining about it. And a huge debt of gratitude goes to Linda Pankhurst, Brit extraordinaire, who undertook the monumental task of replacing all the unintentional Americanisms with proper Britishisms. And a special thank you to Beth Knoche for volunteering to proof the manuscript and for calling to say she loved it.

I'm also very grateful for all the support the crew at the bookstore has shown me, both in doing their utmost to sell the first book, and in putting up with me while I wrote the second one.

Lastly, I'd like to extend my deep appreciation to Jack and Mary Dodge for author photos, drinks, and friendship.

Village

AFFAIRS

CHAPTER

1

*I*t was Marla's idea. Phillip Bethancourt himself was not entirely convinced that the best cure for a broken heart was to surround the afflicted with attractive members of the opposite sex. But Marla Tate, one of England's most in-demand fashion models, was not a woman known for her generous impulses and she was likely to turn sulky if this one was rebuffed. Or so Bethancourt judged.

"Just the thing," he said, putting as much enthusiasm into the words as he could. He succeeded so well that the large Borzoi hound at his feet pricked his ears and lifted his noble head. Bethancourt bent to stroke his pet. "It ought to cheer Jack right up," he continued. "I don't know why I didn't think of it myself."

Marla tossed her head, shaking a loose lock of copper hair off her forehead. "I don't know why you didn't, either," she agreed. "You've certainly been thinking of little else lately."

This was true. It was now more than a month since Bethancourt had returned home from a polo match to find his friend Jack Gibbons sitting on the front steps of his Chelsea flat, bearing the news that Annette Berowne had left him. It helped not at all that Bethancourt had seen it coming; he had been suspicious of Annette's feelings from the beginning and had at first tried to put Gibbons on his guard. But since Gibbons had spent the summer plotting the most romantic way to propose, his friend had stifled the alarm bells that rang in his mind and hoped that his own bleak outlook of the suit owed more to his distaste of Annette than to the true state of affairs. He was very sorry to have been proved right in the end.

Bethancourt had done all he could to see his friend through those first miserable days, but what now concerned him was the fact that Gibbons did not seem to have improved much. It would have been inaccurate to say he was developing a drinking problem since he was usually sober; still, the pint after work was now usually two or three, and on the occasions when he visited Bethancourt, the level in the malt whisky bottle seemed to drop more rapidly than it once had.

"So are you going to ring him up?" asked Marla impatiently.

"Yes, of course," answered Bethancourt.

But he paused in reaching for the phone, having caught a gleam in Marla's jade-green eyes. It occurred to him that there was more to this than a simple desire to dispel Gibbons's gloom. Marla had never liked Gibbons, mostly due to the fact that it was he who enabled Bethancourt to indulge in his hobby of amateur sleuthing, an activity that Marla abhorred. And it was undeniably true that during the summer of Gibbons's affair, Bethancourt had seen much less of him. He wondered who among Marla's friends she had earmarked for Gibbons.

"Right then," he said, capturing the phone. "Let's ring Scotland Yard."

Detective Sergeant Jack Gibbons sat at his desk, buried in paperwork. He did not much like the clerical side of his job, but one had to take the bad with the good in any job, and if he could just keep his mind on it all, he thought he could clear his desk by six, providing he was not sidetracked by chatting about other people's cases. That was far more distracting than paperwork, and he badly needed distraction. There had been no truly interesting cases since the summer, and these days, when time hung heavy on his hands, he found himself continually contemplating the wreck of his hopes.

He brightened when the telephone rang, but the gloom returned when he heard the light, clipped tones of his friend Bethancourt, and not the deep, raspy ones of the chief inspector summoning him to a case.

"I'm ringing to see if you fancied a day or two in the country," said Bethancourt. "Marla's got a fashion shoot in the Cotswolds and it turns out that the house they're using belongs to an old friend of my family. Quite a showplace it's supposed to be. So I'm going along and I thought you could come and keep me company while Marla's working."

Gibbons tried to rouse himself. "It sounds very nice," he said. "When is it to be?"

"Tuesday," answered Bethancourt.

"Tuesday?" repeated Gibbons incredulously. This, he thought to himself, was what came of having independently wealthy friends. "I work on Tuesdays," he said with exaggerated patience. "It's considered part of the working week, Tuesday is. Along with Mondays, Wednesdays, Thursdays, and Fridays. I think you'll find that the vast majority of people with jobs work on weekdays."

"I know that," said Bethancourt, unperturbed. "I thought perhaps you could get it off, if you weren't on a case. God knows you end up working enough weekends—they must give you some time off."

"I expect they must," said Gibbons. "But I'm due in court on Tuesday afternoon, so I am not destined to revel in the autumn countryside."

"What a pity," said Bethancourt, who was secretly rather relieved.

"Well, I'll be back at the end of the week—Marla and I are staying on for a day or two after the shoot. I'll ring you then and we'll see a matinee of something or go to dinner."

"That will be lovely," said Gibbons. "I've got to get back to work now, Phillip. I'll talk to you over the weekend."

He rang off and returned to the contemplation of his paperwork. He was, as it turned out, destined to see the autumn countryside, if not to revel in it. It was rather a pity that all the models were gone by the time he got there.

"And now," said Clarence Astley-Cooper, "I've got all these fashion people coming in."

It was Wednesday night and the Deer and Hounds was crowded after choir practice, the usual regulars relegated to a cramped space at one end of the bar while choristers and their companions congregated in groups across the old flagstone floor.

Astley-Cooper, having had quite enough of standing during practice, had ensconced himself at the largest table and stretched out his gammy knee. He had passed his fiftieth birthday over the summer and felt his advancing years were due some consideration.

The vicar and his wife had joined him there, also glad to sit down after their labors. Reverend Tothill was new to the parish by village standards and was largely responsible for this weekly crush at the pub, having set the example. It had been the cause of no few lifted brows, but after five years even the most entrenched of the villagers were beginning to accustom themselves to him and his odd ideas, one of which was that he counted everyone, not just the regular churchgoers, as part of his parish.

He was surveying his parishioners now, one hand around a pint of bitter and the other entwined with his wife's fingers, but turned at Astley-Cooper's pronouncement.

"Fashion people?" he inquired. He still wore his cassock, but had slipped a worn tweed jacket over it, and the two garments contrasted oddly together.

"Fashion people," said Astley-Cooper firmly. "From *Vogue* or some such."

"*Vogue*?" asked the vicar's wife, who was the possessor of a remarkably fine soprano voice. She was not dressed in a manner that indicated any familiarity with the magazine, but her blue eyes were interested. "Why are they coming to Stutely Manor? Surely you're not opening the place to the public?"

"No, no." Astley-Cooper looked affronted. "Certainly not. They're coming to shoot pictures in the house and grounds. Probably evening dress in the gallery—it's a very fine example of its period." The fineness of the gallery appeared to depress him, for he relapsed into silence and took a long draught from his pint.

"I see," said the vicar encouragingly. "And sports clothes in the garden perhaps?"

"Very likely," admitted Astley-Cooper. "Of course, it's rather a pity that the sheep got in there. Mr. Crocks was very upset. Still, they left the late roses. Too many thorns."

The vicar pressed his lips together as if to hide a smile.

"They can't have done much damage," said Charles Bingham consolingly. He was not a member of the choir—as his raspy voice attested—but he was a sociable man and had early on discovered the pleasures of a late Wednesday visit to the Deer and Hounds. "Surely your dog chased them out again like one o'clock."

"Whiff might have done," agreed Astley-Cooper, "if he hadn't been shut up in the house at the time."

"Oh, dear," said the vicar.

"Yes, it was rather awful."

"But why," persisted the vicar's wife, not to be deterred from the original subject, "are you letting the *Vogue* people in?"

Astley-Cooper looked surprised. "They paid me," he answered.

The others all laughed, although Astley-Cooper had not meant to be funny. He did not seem disturbed by their reaction, however, taking it in his stride as if used to being the cause of unexpected humor.

"Well," said Bingham, recovering, "then I expect you must put up with them."

"I didn't say I wouldn't," replied Astley-Cooper with dignity. "I just said it's a frightful bother."

"Are they staying at Stutely?"

"No, thank heavens. At least most of them aren't. It happens that I know the boyfriend of one of the models. Or, rather, his people know my people, and I've met him. I think I have, anyway. So I had to ask them to stay."

"Ah, yes," said the vicar, thoroughly confused.

"That's the beauty," said Bingham, "of not having any family. You never need put up with anyone you only think you've met."

"You have family," said the vicar's wife tartly, though her eyes were full of laughter. "You just want to be thought of as eccentric."

"I'm older than Clarence here," said Bingham complacently. "Once you've reached a certain age, you can take refuge in eccentricity. I find it saves me ever so much bother."

They were interrupted by a tall, middle-aged woman with a large nose and iron-gray hair. She had a kind smile, which she bestowed on the company as she approached.

"Hello, Mrs. Potts," said the vicar.

"Where are the twins tonight?" asked Bingham, nodding his welcome.

Mrs. Potts glanced vaguely about the crowded pub.

"They're here somewhere," she answered, setting her glass down on the table and idly twisting at the man's signet ring on her finger.

"Do sit down," urged the vicar's wife.

But Mrs. Potts shook her head. "I'm afraid," she said, as if confessing a great sin, "I wasn't at my best tonight."

6

"No," said the vicar's wife sympathetically, "your voice cracked a bit, I'm afraid. Something got caught in your throat?"

"That's just it," said Mrs. Potts tragically. "I seem to be catching a bit of a cold. It's nothing much," she went on hastily, in response to sympathetic murmurs, "but it seems to have got into my throat. I'm afraid I won't be able to sing on Sunday, not if it goes on as it's starting."

Everyone expressed regret at this news, while the vicar's wife recommended hot tea and lemon. Bingham objected to this, advising hot toddies. This began a heated debate, during which Bingham decided to eliminate the hot water altogether and just add the lemon to the whiskey, straight. The discussion was ended by Mrs. Potts inadvertently dropping her signet ring into her port glass and the publican calling time.

The crowd spilled out into the High Street of the village, all shuttered and silent at this time of night, the golden Cotswold limestone turned gray by the dark. Chipping Chedding was an old village, and although there were several modern buildings on its fringes, here at its heart the architecture was a pleasant mix of Jacobean and Georgian, evoking an earlier era.

People sorted themselves out and bade each other good night while the vicar and his wife looked on, paying particular attention to those who might have had a drop too much and be inclined toward belligerence.

"Where's Derek?" asked Bingham, appearing out of the throng. "We were walking back together and he's got the torch."

"He was talking to Julie Benson last I saw," said the vicar's wife, craning around to look. "She had him cornered over by the bar earlier."

"Dear God," said the vicar, "Julie's not the latest to fall victim to Derek's charms, is she? She's old enough to know better."

"Shh," said his wife, "don't let her hear that."

"Derek never takes advantage," protested Bingham in his friend's defense.

"That we know of," muttered the vicar.

"Richard!" said his wife, startled. "I thought you liked Derek."

"I do, I do," said Tothill hastily. "I just wish half the young women in Chipping Chedding would stop throwing themselves at him."

"Well, there he is with Mary Wilson, anyway. Oh, good night, Mrs. Stikes—get home safe."

Slowly the street began to clear and at last the Tothills, too, turned away, strolling arm in arm through the cobbled market square toward the vicarage.

"Dear old Charlie Bingham," said the vicar's wife. "He is so wrongheaded sometimes, but so sweet, really."

"He's a character," said the vicar.

"Well, I like characters."

"That, my dear, is because you are one yourself," said her husband fondly.

CHAPTER

2

$\mathcal{C}$larence Astley-Cooper was feeling relieved. While it was true that his house and grounds were swarming with models, photographers, and various other people whose purpose eluded him, and that his drawing room was liberally draped with clothes and accessories, everything seemed to be going smoothly. No one was bothering him and no one had remarked on the sheep-devastated part of the garden. Mr. Crocks, being only a jobbing gardener, was not there to complain about svelte young women draping themselves over the carefully trimmed hedges or picking the flowers. The models were all extremely attractive and seemed rather careless of how close they were standing to the windows when they changed.

On top of it all, young Bethancourt turned out to be a pleasant sort, not at all what Astley-Cooper had expected. He was tall and thin, with shaggy fair hair and horn-rimmed glasses; Astley-Cooper was at a loss to explain his attraction for the glamorous young woman whom he introduced as his girlfriend.

Bethancourt claimed to be a chess player and they were presently enjoying an amiable game on the terrace, where they could keep half an eye on both the activity in the garden and the celebrated mullioned and transomed windows of the house. At their feet, Astley-Cooper's dog, Whiff, had reached an accommodation with Bethancourt's dog, Cerberus, and the two canines now lay amicably on either side of the table. Between moves, Astley-Cooper voiced his usual woe about how much time, effort, and, most of all, money it took to keep up a Grade 1 listed house, and how impossible it was to do anything at all to it without a horde of inspectors descending upon one. Bethancourt sympathized with all this, leading Astley-Cooper to reflect on how clever he had been to invite such a delightful houseguest.

It was now late afternoon and the fashion people were abandoning the garden in favor of a fresh attack on the inside of the house. This involved a veritable beehive of activity on the part of all concerned. Astley-Cooper, idly watching the hustle-bustle while waiting for Bethancourt to make a move, was surprised by the sight of Constable Patricia Stikes making her way through the crowd. He waved at her and the constable, toiling toward the terrace steps, waved back.

"I wonder what she's come about," said Astley-Cooper. "I do hope there isn't some sort of law against fashion photography in listed houses."

"I shouldn't think so," responded Bethancourt, who was still studying the board.

"Good afternoon," said Constable Stikes, reaching the terrace at last. She was a tall, muscular young woman, fair-haired and ruddy-cheeked, with, at this moment, a sparkle in her pale blue eyes. "I did try the front door, sir, but there was no answer."

"No," said Astley-Cooper, "there wouldn't be. Mrs. Leggett's got her hands full inside."

"Just so, sir. I hope you don't mind my coming round the back."

"Not at all, Constable. Only thing to do, really. Have a seat. This is Phillip Bethancourt, by the way. Phillip, Constable Stikes."

Bethancourt looked up and offered a hand, which the Constable shook before lowering herself into a chair.

"I've come," she said, "about the death of Charles Bingham."

"Oh, yes, poor chap." Astley-Cooper nodded. "Vicar found him dead in his cottage on Monday," he added to Bethancourt. "He was new hereabouts. A delightful chap, if somewhat eccentric. Spent a lot of time in the Far East, I believe."

"And Africa," put in the constable.

"Yes, and Africa. Exploring, I gathered."

"Well, CID's rung up," said Stikes, her eyes darting curiously toward the drawing room windows where the models were changing. "They think Mr. Bingham was murdered."

"Murdered?" repeated Astley-Cooper in surprise.

Bethancourt abandoned his study of the chessboard. There was a gleam of interest in his hazel eyes behind their glasses.

"Yes, sir. At least, it looks very like it. They want me to check into everyone's movements on Sunday evening before Scotland Yard arrives."

"Scotland Yard?" asked Bethancourt. "Isn't Gloucestershire CID handling it?"

Constable Stikes shrugged. "They think he was murdered in London, sir," she answered. "And they're shorthanded, what with those murders in Cirencester and that spate of burglaries in Cheltenham. Chief Inspector Darren has both of those on his plate, and he's down by two detective inspectors at the moment."

"Two?" said Astley-Cooper. "I heard Greene was retiring, but who's the other?"

"Henry Farthet." Constable Stikes leaned back in her chair, notebook and pencil abandoned on the table in favor of a good gossip. "His old aunt died—you may remember her, sir, Mrs. Castleford over at Stroud."

"Yes, yes, of course," said Astley-Cooper. "Positively ancient, she was. I remember her when I was a child—I was scared to death of her. An old martinet, she was."

"Yes, sir. Well, she left everything to her nephew, and it turns out she was richer than anyone realized. Henry's retired as well, and taken his family off to the Riviera for a holiday."

"Well, well," said Astley-Cooper. "Who would have thought it?"

"And Detective Sergeant Colston's broken his leg, not twenty-fours hours after DS Pilcher left on his honeymoon. So you can see the chief constable's in a spot, and not likely to start looking into murders in London."

"Well, no."

Constable Stikes drew a deep breath and reached for her pencil. "In any case, sir, I've got to take details of everyone's movements, though I can't call to mind that anyone here was off to London last weekend. If you ask me, it'll be some old friend of Mr. Bingham's that he visited there."

She seemed a little disappointed at this prospect.

"I'm sure you'll be very helpful, Constable," said Astley-Cooper soothingly.

"I'll certainly try, sir. So could you just tell me what you were do-ing on Sunday evening?"

"I had supper here," replied Astley-Cooper promptly, "and then the vicar came over and we played chess. We always do on Sundays."

"So the vicar said, sir," said Stikes, laboriously noting the informa-tion down.

"Well, if the vicar had already told you, what was the point of coming 'round here?"

"To confirm the vicar's story," supplied Bethancourt.

"That's right, sir," said the constable, forestalling Astley-Cooper's outburst in defense of the vicar's honesty. "Now, about what time was all this?"

"Well, the vicar always comes up about seven. I expect I ate at six or so. And he must have left about ten, perhaps half-past."

"And you, Mr. Bethancourt?"

Bethancourt looked amused. "I was at home in London, Constable," he said. "I didn't know the deceased, and I've never been to Chipping Chedding before last night."

"Phillip's come up with the fashion crowd," put in Astley-Cooper. "One of the models is his girlfriend and, since I know his family, I invited them to stay."

"Ah." A light dawned in the constable's eyes. "I'd heard about that, sir, only I didn't expect there would be so much . . ." She waved a hand.

"Bustle," supplied Astley-Cooper. "No," he agreed, looking about a little dazedly, "neither did I."

"Fashion shoots are always a bit frantic," said Bethancourt. "I don't know why."

"Is that so, sir?" Constable Stikes glanced at him, taking in his solid county clothing, and obviously wondering how he had come to be involved with a fashion model. "Which is yours, sir?"

"My—? Oh, you mean Marla." Bethancourt looked about, and then pointed at the drawing room windows. "The redhead there with her back to us."

Marla's back was turned because she was engaged in stripping off the ensemble she had been posing in, but their glimpse of her nudity was brief, as she moved off into the room. Astley-Cooper stared and then hastily returned his gaze to the chessboard, flushing faintly.

"Ah," said Stikes politely. "She looks pretty."

Bethancourt grinned. "I think so," he said.

The Constable sighed and looked back at her notebook. "Well, I'd best get on," she said. "Could you tell me, Mr. Astley-Cooper, when was the last time you saw Mr. Bingham?"

Astley-Cooper frowned. "Well," he said, "he wasn't much of a churchgoer, so I couldn't have seen him on Sunday. That means it must have been Saturday night, at the Deer and Hounds. There was a darts competition that night. You were there yourself, Constable."

"Yes, sir. It's always best to have an eye on these things, I find. You never know when someone might have a bit too much to drink and take offense."

"Quite right."

"I saw Bingham myself, but I didn't take much note of him. Was he just as usual, sir?"

"Oh, yes. At least, nothing wrong that I noticed."

"Could you tell me what time he left?"

"I don't think so. I came away at half nine or ten and I think—I'm not sure, mind—he was still there then. I don't remember him leaving, in any case."

The constable noted this down and then closed her notebook. "That's all then, sir. Thank you very much."

"I don't suppose," said Astley-Cooper diffidently, "it's any good asking you what happened?"

"They haven't told me that, sir. Only that the circumstances are suspicious. Thank you again, sir."

"Well, isn't that extraordinary," said Astley-Cooper, watching her go.

Bethancourt agreed. "What exactly happened?" he asked.

"Nothing very alarming. The vicar went over on Monday morning to see about a subscription. There was no answer, but he noticed that the lights were on, and he thought that odd, so he went in. And there was old Bingham, sitting in his chair with a book and glass of whisky, quite dead. We all thought it was a heart attack—he'd had one already, you see. The vicar rang up Dr. Cross, waited 'til he came, and that was all. Perfectly straightforward."

"Yes, I see," said Bethancourt.

"I wonder what made them think it was murder."

"Probably something came up at the postmortem," answered Bethancourt. "Look here, Clarence, do you mind not mentioning this to Marla? She'll know soon enough, but I don't see why we shouldn't have at least one peaceful evening."

Astley-Cooper looked confused, but all he said was, "Of course, whatever you like."

They had a very pleasant evening. A few people from the shoot were staying over at the old coaching inn in Stow-on-the-Wold, so they all gathered there for dinner, Astley-Cooper charmed to be included in this exotic party. Carol Morwood, probably the most famous model there, seemed to take a positive delight in flirting with Astley-Cooper, and he was pink with pleasure by the time the main course was served.

Since there was really nothing known about the murder, Bethancourt was able to keep his mind on their party and not appear absentminded in the least. It was this that usually signaled to Marla that murder had once again raised its ugly head, for, far from being absentminded, Bethancourt was normally completely captivated by whatever circumstances he found himself in, and it was only when investigating a case that his thoughts tended to stray. He himself could not say where this fascination with murder came from, and it was looked on by his friends as merely one more eccentricity in a man who had a flat full of coffee tables (he was very fond of them) and chose to keep a large Borzoi in London. They had learned, however, that he was serious about this rather grubby hobby and that, when an investigation was in hand, all the other details of his life were tossed unheeding to the four winds.

But on this evening, there was not much to think about, beyond wondering if Gibbons would be assigned to the case and, if so, whether it would prove complicated enough to distract his friend from heartache. Before he had fallen in love with Annette Berowne, Gibbons's paramount interest had always been his career, and he had excelled at it, gaining promotion from detective constable to sergeant in record time. But since the breakup, Gibbons had merely been going through the motions, though to be fair, none of the cases to which he had been assigned had held much interest. Bethancourt had been praying for a really tough case for nearly a month now.

"He's a funny old thing, isn't he?" said Marla in a low voice. "I thought he must be gay, but now I'm not so sure."

Bethancourt turned to find her contemplating Astley-Cooper, across the table from them. He was chuckling at something Carol had whispered in his ear.

"Oh, I think not," said Bethancourt, eyeing their host. "Probably just terrified of women, or at least of sex."

"Do you think that's why he never married?" asked Marla. "He must be fifty if he's a day."

"About that, I believe—he's a year or two younger than my father. They were at school together. But he seems quite fussy in his habits, and relationships tend to be messy."

"Well, I like him anyway."

Bethancourt smiled. "So do I. Here, Tony," he added, raising his voice, "you might pass some of that champers this way."

CHAPTER

3

Eight o'clock on Wednesday morning found Detective Sergeant Jack Gibbons driving a police Rover along the M4, accompanied by Detective Chief Inspector Wallace Carmichael. The chief inspector was a large man with bushy white eyebrows, bright blue eyes, and a cigar. Having got this last going to his satisfaction, and having rolled down the window in deference to his subordinate's nonsmoking habits, he settled back and opened the case file on his lap.

"They haven't given us much," he remarked.

"No, sir."

"Of course, they only got the pathologist's report late on Monday, so forensics is just getting to work."

"On a scene of the crime that's been greatly tidied up," said Gibbons.

Carmichael sighed. "I know, lad. But there's no help for it. The pathologist found whisky and a good dose of strong sedative in the stomach. He says that with a weak heart, that was enough to do it."

"He could have taken the sedative himself," said Gibbons, guiding the Rover past a lorry. He did not see that there was much of interest about the case, and rather resented having to drive all the way out to Chipping Chedding just to prove it.

"So he could," agreed Carmichael. "But time of death was put at about seven P.M. on Sunday. Bingham's next door neighbor, a Mrs. Eberhart, says that he left in his car on Sunday afternoon at about three, and that the car was not back, nor were there any lights on in his cottage at nine thirty P.M. However, she did notice lights in the cottage at eleven, when she went to bed." Carmichael puffed reflectively for a moment. "They've had the local rural police officer gather statements from everyone in the village who was well-acquainted with the victim, but there's nothing obvious in any of them. In fact, no one admits to having left Chipping Chedding last Sunday at all."

"Well, they might not have, sir. Gloucestershire seems to think Bingham went to London to see someone, who murdered him there."

"True, true. It's no good theorizing ahead of our data, which apparently we're to gather from the constable, a Pat Stikes."

"Do you think he'll be any help, sir?"

"She," corrected Carmichael. "It's a woman, and Chief Inspector Darren seems to think highly of her. She grew up in Chipping Chedding and knows everyone. And I rather imagine she'll be eager to do what she can, if I know anything about these rural beats. Most of her duties will be dealing with tourists, and the season's over. If she's as bright as Darren says, she'll be bored with nothing on her plate and happy to give us a hand."

"I'm sure you're right, sir," said Gibbons glumly. He was not looking forward to dealing with a bright rural constable, and a woman at that. These days, he did not feel charitably toward women in general.

Carmichael was gazing thoughtfully out the window.

"Frankly," he said in a moment, "I think the chief constable has got ahead of himself on this one. There's no real evidence the man was murdered."

"No, sir," agreed Gibbons. "He might easily have had a heart attack elsewhere and whoever was with him panicked and decided he was better found in his own house. That's very possible if a woman was involved—we've known it to happen before."

"Even more possible if the lady was married." Carmichael paused, his eyes on the file. "They don't seem to know much about the victim down there. Charles Bingham, aged fifty-five, in residence at Chipping Chedding for just under a year, previous address unknown, but believed to have lived in China. London firm of solicitors."

"I looked him up, sir," said Gibbons. "He was an inventor. He invented a new flush contraption for toilets."

The white eyebrows went up. "Did he, indeed?"

"Yes, sir." Gibbons grinned. "It's not quite as silly as it sounds. It's made him a fortune. This was all some time ago—I've written down the dates—but he was in his twenties at the time. He was married about then, and had one daughter. His wife died in a car accident three years later. And he was still, at the time of his death, a partner in the firm that manufactures the flush device."

"What you're telling me, Gibbons, is that he was a very wealthy man."

"It would appear so, sir."

Carmichael carefully rolled the ash off his cigar into the ashtray and glanced sideways at his sergeant. There was more, he knew; Gibbons did his work thoroughly. "What else did you find out?" he asked.

"Well, he became interested in anthropology and went off to Africa a few years after his wife's death. Ever since then, he has seldom been resident in England. Africa occupied him for several years, but he seems to have spent most of the last ten years in the Far East. I've made notes of it all, but that's the essence."

"Good work, Gibbons."

"Oh, one other thing, sir. His daughter's Eve Bingham."

Carmichael frowned. "That sounds familiar."

"She's a socialite, sir. Occasionally makes the tabloids."

"Ah, yes, that's it. All those copies of *Hello* magazine my wife is always reading. Well, that certainly implies money."

Gibbons glanced sideways at his superior. Carmichael was ruffling through the brief reports in the case file and puffing contentedly on his cigar.

"I thought I ought to mention, sir—not that it has anything to do with the case—that Phillip Bethancourt is in Chipping Chedding. He went up for a couple of day's holiday on Monday."

"Did he indeed?" the chief inspector transferred his gaze to Gibbons, who kept his eyes firmly on the road. He sighed. "That's all right, Gibbons." It would have to be, with Bethancourt's father so friendly with the chief commissioner. "Still, I can't say I understand it, however. If he's so interested in our work, why doesn't he join the force?"

"He's really quite rich, sir," replied Gibbons.

"I know that, Sergeant."

Carmichael did not really mind Bethancourt's poking about. On several previous cases he had been quite helpful, and he always stayed in the background. But that the idle rich should spend their time involving themselves in police cases did not seem to him appropriate. Carmichael was an old-fashioned man who had worked his way up from the lowest rung of the ladder, but he liked to think himself adaptable. He had certainly adapted better than others to the idea of university-educated detectives, and he was good with his subordinates. He let them think for themselves and was credited with almost superhuman patience in listening to the sometimes absurd theories put forth by newly made detectives. For this reason, he was often saddled with mere sergeants as assistants, something he did not usually mind. He liked to think he could see the chief inspectors of tomorrow in them. Gibbons, for instance: Oxford-educated no less, but as respectful as the lowest constable; a bright lad and a hard worker who would almost certainly advance into the ranks of senior officers. Carmichael liked to see that sort of thing, which was why Bethancourt, who was no part of this grand tradition, bothered him.

He sighed. "Well," he said aloud, "there may not be much here for Bethancourt or any of us. I fancy it can be cleared up rather quickly, once we discover where Bingham spent Sunday afternoon. I hope to God they've had the wits to put forensics onto his car. We'll call in at the local station and then go out to the cottage. Probably we'll find Bethancourt waiting for us there."

"Probably, sir."

At that moment, Bethancourt was in bed, but by ten thirty he was at the cottage next door to Bingham's. A phone call from Gibbons the night before had alerted him to the imminent arrival of the detectives, and he might have sought out Pat Stikes at her office in the Stow-on-the-Wold police station, explaining that he was a friend of those about to arrive from Scotland Yard. But there was nothing like doing a bit of investigating on his own, and a chance remark of Astley-Cooper's about the local vet sent him on a different course.

He had neatly diverted Marla, who was still in blissful ignorance of the fact that there had been a suspicious death in the neighborhood, by explaining that Cerberus, the Borzoi, seemed to be off his food. With that as an excuse, he had bundled the dog into the Jaguar and ostensibly set off for the veterinary surgery in the village. Instead, he had driven to the vet's home, which happened to be the cottage next to Bingham's, and where the vet's wife and baby son were in residence.

It was a pretty place, a mile or so along the Chedworth road out of the village. The two cottages, standing side by side, were small, built of the golden Cotswold limestone, and late Georgian in appearance. The road swept around them, curving away to the left, and they were separated from it by a low hedge, neatly trimmed along the front of the cottages and growing to massive proportions as it disappeared around the bend.

Before the first cottage was parked an ancient Morris, which was mud-splattered and exhibited several dents. The second cottage had no car and it was here that Bethancourt eased his grey Jaguar to a halt, sniffing appreciatively at the brisk autumn air as he ushered his dog out of the backseat. He was thoroughly enjoying this visit to the country after a long summer in London, and a spot of detective work seemed just the thing to top it off.

Mrs. Eberhart answered the door with her baby on her hip, a plump young woman with dark brown hair scraped back into a wispy ponytail. A pack of dogs ranged around her legs, barking excitedly. Bethancourt ignored them and stooped to beam into the baby's face.

"What a charming little fellow," he said. "What's his name?"

"Er, Daniel," said the mother.

"Hullooo, Daniel," cooed Bethancourt, rescuing his glasses from a diminutive fist, but keeping his smile intact. Daniel grinned back at him and gurgled.

Mrs. Eberhart shushed the dogs and shifted her baby so that she could disengage his fingers from her visitor's hair.

"Can I help you, Mr.—?"

"Bethancourt," supplied Bethancourt, straightening and transferring his smile from the baby to his mother. "And this," he added, motioning toward the Borzoi at his side, "is Cerberus."

Mrs. Eberhart, not having been blessed with a classical education, passed over the odd name and reached out to fondle the dog's ears. Cerberus, who was intent on the Eberhart dogs, ignored this.

"He's a beautiful animal, Mr. Bethancourt," she said.

"Thank you." Bethancourt patted his dog's flank. "I'm very fond of him, of course, and I daresay it's nothing."

Mrs. Eberhart did not look enlightened.

"But Clarence said better safe than sorry and told me to come here."

Mrs. Eberhart seized on the one intelligible piece of information in this declaration.

"Would that be Clarence Astley-Cooper?" she asked, and then looked doubtfully at Bethancourt. "Are you a model, then?"

"Heavens, no," answered Bethancourt. "You must not read many fashion magazines. Oh, dear, I didn't mean that the way it sounded. You look quite lovely, I'm sure."

This elicited a smile.

"I *don't* read fashion magazines," said Mrs. Eberhart with a laugh. "Or much of anything else, lately," she added, jiggling her son.

"I can understand that," said Bethancourt. "How old is the little chap?"

"Almost six months—he's sleeping through the night now." She smiled. "Mostly."

"He looks a remarkably happy baby to me," said Bethancourt.

"Oh, he is," she said, shifting his weight to her other hip. "I'm sorry—did you say Mr. Astley-Cooper had sent you 'round?"

"That's right. My girlfriend and I are staying at the manor for a few days."

"Well, do come in," said Mrs. Eberhart. There was a doubtful tone in her voice which indicated she was not entirely sure why this man had shown up on her doorstep, but she was obviously tired of standing there. "Come through to the kitchen, if you don't mind. Would you like a cup of coffee?"

"Thanks very much," said Bethancourt promptly. "That would be just the thing."

He ushered Cerberus into the hallway and followed Mrs. Eberhart to the back of the house and the kitchen. A meal was in midpreparation there, and a pot of coffee was already made. Mrs. Eberhart took a moment to settle her son in his cot and then poured two cups, joining her guest at the table by the window.

"So what can I do for you, Mr. Bethancourt?" she asked.

"I expect it's your husband I want to see," said Bethancourt, feeling safe in this pronouncement now that he was comfortably en-sconced with a cup of coffee. "As I say, it's probably nothing, but Cer-berus has gone off his food. Not a usual thing for him at all."

Mrs. Eberhart laughed merrily, enlightened at last. "But this isn't the surgery," she said.

"It isn't?" said Bethancourt blankly. He glanced out the window at the second cottage. "Oh, dear, is that it over there? I did look, but it seemed quite deserted."

"No, no." Mrs. Eberhart was still amused. "The surgery's up the road, in one of the old barns. That's Charlie Bingham's cottage." Her face fell. "Or it was."

"Bingham?" asked Bethancourt. "Isn't that the fellow who was murdered? Astley-Cooper was telling me about it last night at dinner. Such a sad affair."

"It is," agreed Mrs. Eberhart with a sigh. "Although I don't know why they think it's murder. Charlie was a sweet man, even if he was as full of mischief as a monkey, but he was stubborn and it's a fact that he drank and smoked too much. The doctor recommended he give up both altogether, as he'd already survived one heart attack, but Charlie wouldn't hear of it. And the vicar says as how there was a glass of whisky at his elbow when he found him."

"You liked him, though?" asked Bethancourt.

"Oh, yes." Mrs. Eberhart chuckled. "He was awfully funny, made me laugh something terrible, he did. And he was a good neighbor. He was very sweet while I was pregnant, always coming 'round to see how I was, and helping me to keep the garden in order. And, of course, giv-ing me advice. Said I should never send the child away to school—he'd done that and now he hardly knew his own daughter. Not that I ever thought of such a thing—the school here is very good."

Bethancourt, who had himself been sent to public school at the age of eight, made no comment. Instead he said, "Astley-Cooper was wondering why it was classed as murder as well. Amateur sleuthing is a hobby of mine, but all I could tell him is that something must have come up at the postmortem. Did you see Mr. Bingham that Sunday?"

"Yes, I was in the garden in the afternoon when he came out, all dressed up and said he was off. I said, 'Where to this time?' and he said, 'Oh, just a little business trip to London,' and winked at me. I took that to mean he was going to see his lady friend."

Bethancourt looked up from his coffee with interest. Astley-Cooper had known nothing about a girlfriend.

"Who was that?" he asked.

"Heavens," she replied, "I don't know. He was very secretive about it, but I'm sure there was one. When he first moved in, he was always around, and then about six months ago he started taking these little trips. Every week or so, he'd be gone overnight, or sometimes two nights in a row. She's never been here, that I know. The cottages are close together and you can't miss that kind of thing."

"No," agreed Bethancourt, glancing out.

"But I expect I was mistaken about where he went," said Mrs. Eberhart, sighing a little. "You see, he came back that night, so he couldn't have been to see her, not unless they had a row or something."

"That's always possible," said Bethancourt feelingly. Marla was known for her mercurial temper. "Did you see him come back?"

Mrs. Eberhart shook her head. "No," she answered. "My husband was called out at half nine to a bad calving and I went out to see him off. Charlie's car was still gone and there wasn't a light in the place. I waited up 'til after eleven, but when Steve hadn't come back by then, I went to bed. It was when I was turning off the lamp that I noticed a light in Charlie's cottage, and when I looked out I could just see his car in the lane. I was surprised because, as I said, I thought he'd gone for the night, but I didn't think any more about it."

"Astley-Cooper says Scotland Yard has been called in," said Bethancourt. "I know a few of those chaps, so perhaps I'll be able to find out why they think it's murder."

25

"Well, you'll let me know, won't you?" asked Mrs. Eberhart. "I don't mind saying we're all very curious."

"By all means," promised Bethancourt. He swallowed the last of his coffee. "Well, I expect I should be getting along to the surgery. Thank you so much for being so hospitable—and I'm sorry for the mistake. I could have sworn Clarence said the vet was here."

"That's all right," said Mrs. Eberhart. "We've had a nice chat, and you've broken up the morning for me." She rose and then paused. "Now I wonder who that is?" she said.

Bethancourt joined her in craning out the window to view the lane. Two men were coming up toward Bingham's cottage. The younger man was a little stocky with reddish hair and led the way, while an older man with white eyebrows followed behind.

"Ah," said Bethancourt. "I think, Mrs. Eberhart, that Scotland Yard has arrived. I'll just run out and pass the time of day before I go to the surgery."

Neither Carmichael nor Gibbons was surprised to be greeted at the scene of the crime by an elegant Borzoi. Gibbons patted the dog affectionately and waited for Bethancourt, who emerged in company with a young woman.

"Hullo," he said cheerfully. "Mrs. Eberhart, may I introduce Detective Chief Inspector Carmichael and his able assistant, Detective Sergeant Gibbons. I'm awfully glad it was you they sent," he added to the two detectives.

"We rather thought we'd find you Johnny-on-the-spot," replied Carmichael. "Mrs. Eberhart, we'll want to speak to you shortly, but first we'd like to look over Mr. Bingham's cottage. Will you be at home?"

"Yes," she answered. "I'll be in the house, so just ring when you want me. I'll put on a fresh pot of coffee."

They took their leave of her and turned toward the other house, virtually a twin of the Eberharts'. Gibbons produced a key and let them in the front door, which led them into a hallway running the length of the house. They turned to the right and the sitting room, which was neat and tidy but very sparsely furnished. A large, over-stuffed armchair stood by the fireplace with a battered side table containing a lamp, a large glass ashtray, and a book. In front of the hearth was spread a small Oriental rug, and above the mantel was hung a very fine Chinese watercolor. On either side of the fireplace were ceiling-to-floor bookshelves, and these had been filled with a great variety of books and curios. Against the farther wall stood an oak desk, badly in need of refinishing, and another chair. Other than that, the room was empty of furniture. However, at the end of the room opposite the fireplace were stacked several packing crates, most of them opened, and a large, handsome teakwood chest.

"Well," said Carmichael, "it's not much, is it?"

"No," agreed Gibbons. "Not at all what I expected. Looks as if he never got 'round to unpacking."

"Not really surprising in an older bachelor," said Bethancourt. "Presumably he'd been roughing it in the Far East and had got used to a minimal existence."

Gibbons eyed him. "How do you know he wasn't living in the lap of luxury in the Far East?" he asked.

"That at least was not the impression my host, Astley-Cooper, had," replied Bethancourt. "He seems to have the idea that Bingham lived a more or less hand-to-mouth existence—a little smuggling here, an archeological expedition there, even a stint at farming, so I hear."

"He sounds rather eccentric," mused Carmichael.

"That seems certain," agreed Gibbons. "To live like this when he had millions."

"What?" asked Bethancourt sharply, abandoning his perusal of the bookshelves.

"He was a very wealthy man," said Gibbons. "Didn't you gather that in all your chatting?"

27

"No," replied Bethancourt. "If he was rich, it was not a well-known fact here. Astley-Cooper would surely have mentioned it and so would Mrs. Eberhart."

"That," said Carmichael, "is rather interesting. I wonder if it was deliberate on his part. Well, investigate first and then draw conclusions. Let's have a look at the rest of the house and then we can start going through things."

As in the Eberharts' house, the hallway led them to the kitchen. Here again there was nothing to mark it as a wealthy man's, with only the minimum of furniture and appliances. There was a red-painted table and four upright chairs set in front of the fireplace on the bare floorboards. Tabletop and counters were wiped clean and everything was neatly put away. An old-fashioned toaster sat on the counter and a single glass was upturned by the sink. Upon examination, the cupboards yielded a frugal collection of pots, pans, and china, but the refrigerator and pantry were well-stocked. There were dying roses arranged in a jar on the table.

From the kitchen, they trooped upstairs. There were two bedrooms and a bath, but one of the bedrooms was not in use. It contained only a few more packing crates, this time unopened. The other bedroom looked homey by comparison to the rest of the house. The bed frame was a modest affair of pine, but was well-polished and across it was spread a quilted, silken counterpane. The floor was nearly covered by a large Oriental carpet of exquisite design which Bethancourt, after several minutes' study, pronounced to be silk. In one corner was the twin of the teakwood chest downstairs and next to it stood an old-fashioned wardrobe. There was an African carving on one wall and, over the bed, a Chinese pen-and-ink.

"Not much here," said Gibbons, flipping open the wardrobe. "He hadn't many clothes, it seems. Half a mo—what's this?"

He pulled out what was clearly a woman's silk shirt and a pair of woolen trousers.

"That's very odd," said Bethancourt, hurrying over. "Yes, and

28

here's a woman's jacket. But Mrs. Eberhart was certain that Bingham's girlfriend was never here."

"What girlfriend?" asked Carmichael quickly.

Bethancourt repeated what he had learned from Mrs. Eberhart. "Obviously she was mistaken," he ended. "But the woman couldn't have been here often."

"No," said Carmichael, "but, whoever she was, she clearly meant to come back. And it's all beginning to come together. If they took so much care to keep it secret that Mrs. Eberhart believed the woman was never here, there must have been a reason. Possibly the lady is married. In any case, if he died at her house, it might have been very inconvenient for him to be found there. Inconvenient enough for her to move him."

Bethancourt looked up from the clothes, an inquiring look on his face. "Ah, yes," he said. "I almost forgot. Exactly why has this been classed as a suspicious death?"

"Because," explained Gibbons, getting a nod from Carmichael, "he died at seven P.M. and according to your Mrs. Eberhart, his car didn't arrive back here until after half nine. Also, the heart attack was induced by a combination of alcohol and a strong sedative. He could have taken that himself, of course, but he could hardly have driven himself home afterward."

Bethancourt frowned. "But why on earth should he be taking sedatives if he was about to spend the night with his girlfriend? I should think just the opposite effect would be desired."

Carmichael shrugged. "Possibly he mistook them for aspirin. Or he might have had a distressing experience—a car accident, for example—and taken something to calm himself." He paused and his eyebrows bristled. "Or, of course, he was given the drug deliberately. But at the moment, we just don't know."

Bethancourt nodded, and turned back to the jacket he still held. "I wonder," he said, "whether Bingham bought these for her. If not, it'll make the search easier."

"How so?" asked Gibbons.

"If she bought them herself, we're looking for a wealthy woman. These are casual clothes, and they're very expensive ones. An upper-middle-class woman may save enough to buy an expensive dress, but only wealthy people spend a lot on casual clothes. These are all designer things from fashionable boutiques."

"That's very helpful, Bethancourt," said Carmichael. "I wouldn't have noticed, myself."

Bethancourt grinned. "One of the benefits of dating a fashion model."

"She's pretty tall," added Gibbons, who was holding the trousers up to his own waist. "Only about two or three inches shorter than I am. Say five foot eight."

"And relatively slender," said Carmichael, eyeing the trousers against Gibbons's bulk.

"They're a size ten," put in Bethancourt helpfully.

"Well, put them aside, Gibbons, and we'll have the lab go over them and see if there's anything else to be learned. We'd best have a look at the bathroom and then start on the desk downstairs."

There was nothing of interest in the bathroom. Forensics had already removed all the pills for testing, including three unidentified ones that had been lying loose in one corner of the cabinet.

The desk in the living room yielded little beyond the usual bills and statements. There were a few letters, one from the dead man's daughter, two from archaeologists, and two more written in Chinese. None of them had any bearing on the present circumstances; there was the prospect of a new dig, the events of an ongoing one, and it was very pleasant in the Mediterranean that summer. The Chinese correspondence Carmichael took away to have translated.

"Well, that's that then," said Carmichael, grunting as he rose from the desk. "No note of any kind, nor any help on this mysterious woman. Well, I can't say I expected more. Let's have a look at the outside."

He led the way, pausing just outside the door to survey the well-tended garden and the freshly mown grass, and giving a cursory glance at the old Morris; the forensics report on the car was already in his case file.

"They found several nails scattered at the edge of the road," he said, pointing. "Constable Stikes thinks they were probably dropped by Bob Ambler, the local handyman, who put up some shelves for Mrs. Eberhart last week. She says he's a very reliable workman, but not very neat, and he's always dropping things off his van, or leaving his tools behind. In any case, there were four or five of them just about here, and forensics says one of the tires on the Morris has been recently patched."

"And here is where they found the bicycle marks," called Gibbons.

He had moved to the bottom of the property, by the hedge that ran along the road. There was a large lilac bush growing there and, although it had been trimmed, it still overhung the hedge in places. In the soft earth between the two were the marks of a bicycle tire.

"Some bright lad from forensics found these," Carmichael told Bethancourt as he moved to join his sergeant. "The marks are recent—it hasn't rained here since the weekend—and you can see the leaves that have been torn off are barely dead." He straightened and gave a last glance about. "We'd best get on. Let's have a chat with Mrs. Eberhart and this fellow Towser, if he's at home. Then we can head back to the village for lunch."

"Who's Towser?" asked Bethancourt.

"Derek Towser," supplied Gibbons as they made their way toward the Eberhart cottage. "He's a painter and is only a temporary resident. He's been staying in the third cottage. You can't see it from here—it's 'round the bend in the road, along the lane that leads up to the old farmhouse. Originally, this all belonged to the farm, and the cottages were for the farm hands and their families. Towser's, I understand, is newer than these."

"Is it still a working farm?"

"No, no. Twenty or thirty years ago the farmers sold it to Joan Bonnar, the actress. They kept the cottages for themselves, but they've since died and their heirs rent them out."

"Does Joan Bonnar still own the farmhouse?" asked Bethancourt, vaguely intrigued by this celebrity.

"Yes, but they say she's seldom here. Her children live there. We'll have to see them, too, of course, although it's doubtful that either they or Towser saw anything."

Carmichael was already knocking on the cottage door. Mrs. Eberhart appeared and ushered them in, serving up coffee in the kitchen as a matter of course. Bethancourt sipped his second cup appreciatively while he listened to Carmichael skillfully draw from Mrs. Eberhart all knowledge of Bingham and his habits, as well as the admission that she had picked up several nails in the lane after Ambler's visit the previous Saturday. Bethancourt could not help but notice how much more information the chief inspector elicited than he himself had done, and in less time. On the other hand, he thought, he had had a far more pleasant chat. It was yet another good reason for not getting a proper job on the police force.

CHAPTER

4

When they were done with Peg Eberhart, they went off to find the third cottage, which was done easily enough, but Derek Towser was not at home.

Bethancourt, increasingly nervous about the time, left the two detectives then, making a quick stop at the vet's surgery for verisimilitude before racing back to Stutely Manor to take Marla to lunch.

Carmichael and Gibbons returned to the village High Street where they had arranged to meet Constable Stikes for lunch. She had been rushing off when they arrived that morning, called out to see to a stray dog chasing a farmer's sheep, and had had no time to do anything but point out the way to Bingham's cottage.

Gibbons had been secretly relieved to find that the constable was not a flirtatious type, and perversely annoyed to see that she was very nearly his own height. She was also his senior by four or five years, but gave due respect to his superior rank, something that could not fail to impress him favorably.

She was waiting for them at the Deer and Hounds, the seventeenth-century pub at one end of the market square. It was as picturesque as the rest of Chipping Chedding, with flagstone floors and a low-beamed ceiling, its décor showing signs of recent renovation.

"The owners are new," Stikes told them. "Martin Winslow and his wife Maggie; they're good folks. They bought the place a couple of years ago and did it all up. *And* brought in a top-notch chef from London—the grub's real good these days."

Carmichael nodded as he settled himself at the table by the window.

"Can we stay here?" he asked. "We haven't booked into anywhere yet. DIC Darren said to speak to you."

Stikes smiled. "I'd already reserved you two rooms, sir," she said. "I just didn't get a chance to say so this morning."

"Ah, yes. How are the sheep, Constable?"

Stikes sighed. "The sheep are fine, sir. But the dog wasn't a stray, strictly speaking. It belongs to Mr. Gamham and there's been trouble over it before. I had a word with him, but it won't do any good. But you can't be interested in any of that." She straightened alertly. "What can I tell you, sir?"

Carmichael had set the case file beside his place setting, and now he opened it.

"I take it these people you interviewed are the ones who were closest to Bingham?" he asked.

"That's right, sir. He hadn't been here long, but he was already one of the village characters. People liked him, but his social life mostly revolved around the pub here, and the other regulars. Well, except for the Eberharts—they're not part of the pub crowd."

Carmichael raised an eyebrow. "But the vicar is?" he asked.

Stikes grinned. "Oh, yes sir. At least, he is since he got married. They're in every Wednesday night after choir practice, and they drop by at other times, too. They've had Mr. Bingham over for dinner a few times, even though he's not a regular churchgoer."

"Well, well," said Carmichael. "That's certainly unusual."

Stikes smiled slyly. "Changing times, sir. If it comes to that, I'm unusual myself. Not many women doing rural police officer duty."

Carmichael rubbed a hand over his mouth. "Well, no," he said.

"We were tactfully not mentioning it," put in Gibbons.

Stikes laughed. "That's all right, sir. Don't know as it would have worked if everyone hadn't already known me so well. Oh, here's Marcie to take our orders."

The ordering accomplished, Carmichael returned to the case file.

"Well, let's see about the rest of these people," he said. "It says Derek Towser is only a temporary resident?"

"That's right, sir. He's the one person I can't tell you much about—he's only been here three weeks or so. The only things I know about him are that he's a painter, he's incredibly handsome, and rumor has it he's quite a ladies' man."

"Only rumor?" asked Gibbons. "He's not chatted you up, then?"

Stikes looked amused. "No, sir, but I'm hardly the pick of the litter. Only he hasn't chatted up anyone else, either, at least not that I've heard about."

"But he was friendly with Mr. Bingham?" said Carmichael.

"Yes, sir. They struck up a friendship soon after Mr. Towser arrived. Started coming in to the pub together most evenings, had each other over for fry-ups occasionally. That sort of thing."

"All boys together?" suggested Gibbons.

"That's about the size of it, sir," agreed Stikes.

Carmichael perused his file. "James and Julie Benson," he read off. "Those are Joan Bonnar's children?"

"Yes, sir, and Martha Potts is their housekeeper. They're Wednesday night regulars here, too, though they don't come in much otherwise. They keep to themselves more than the rest of the villagers, but they got on with Mr. Bingham. He's been up to the old farmhouse for dinner a few times."

"But he and Mr. Benson aren't boys together, as the sergeant so eloquently puts it?"

"No." Stikes shook her head. "Mr. Benson doesn't make a move without his sister. They're joined at the hip, those two. Twins, you know."

Carmichael hadn't known, but he passed it over.

"Then there's Clarence Astley-Cooper," he said.

"I wouldn't call him a particular friend of Mr. Bingham's," said Stikes, "though they got on well enough whenever they met. But I don't think Mr. Astley-Cooper has ever invited Mr. Bingham up to the manor or anything like that. I mostly put him into the report because he verified the vicar's alibi."

Carmichael raised his brows. "And did you seriously suspect the vicar of having murdered Mr. Bingham?"

"I didn't figure it was my job to do the suspecting, sir," said Stikes with spirit.

"Neither is it, Constable," said Carmichael genially. "I just wondered, that's all. I think that's everyone you mentioned. Now, is there anyone you didn't put in the report?"

"There's Mr. and Mrs. Winslow," said Stikes at once, nodding toward the bar where the couple in question were working. "Mr. Bingham was quite friendly with them, as he spent so much time in the pub here. But they were here all evening, with plenty of people to witness it if it was needed."

Carmichael nodded his acceptance of this omission, but Stikes hesitated before going on.

"I don't know if you'd want to hear about rumors . . ." she said tentatively.

"Indeed I would, Constable."

"Then word has it Mr. Bingham had a girlfriend, but nobody knows who it might have been. I don't think it was anyone in the village—someone would have been bound to twig that. Only I can't make out where else he could have met her since he was seldom away. My best guess is that it was one of the tourists at the beginning of last summer, someone who didn't live here, but whom he kept up with after she left."

"That's a very clever idea, Constable," said Carmichael, exchanging glances with his sergeant. "Perhaps you'd be so good as to follow up on it by checking the Winslows' guest bookings for the period in question."

Stikes looked delighted with this assignment. "I'd be happy to, sir. Only, of course, she mightn't have been staying here. They only have the four rooms, and lots of people come through that are staying in one of the other villages."

"Start here," instructed Carmichael, "and then go on to wherever else you think is a likely spot. Don't overdo it, though—I don't want the guest list from every hotel and inn in the Cotswolds."

"No, sir."

Carmichael considered. "Would you have said," he asked, "that this mysterious girlfriend had ever stayed at Bingham's cottage?"

Stikes shook her head at once. "No, sir," she answered. "At least, not on a regular basis. The Eberharts would have been sure to notice, even if nobody else did."

"And yet we found a woman's outfit hanging in his closet."

"Really?" Stikes was surprised. "Well, I don't know what to say to that, sir, except it's very curious."

"Curiouser and curiouser," murmured Gibbons under his breath. "You haven't said," he added aloud, "if there was anyone in the village who bore Mr. Bingham any ill will. Any little disputes over Mr. Gamham's dog, perhaps?"

Stikes shook her head. "Truthfully, no, sir," she answered. "Mr. Bingham was an easygoing sort. He did like to tease—he had quite a devilish sense of humor—but I can't recall that anyone was ever offended. People thought he was a bit peculiar, but on the whole they liked him."

"Well, Gloucestershire seems to think he was murdered in London," said Carmichael, "and it may be they're right, although as far as I can make out their only reason for thinking so is that comment he made to Mrs. Eberhart. And, since he was clearly lying to her about the purpose of his trip, I can't see why we should take the destination on faith. In truth, Constable, I'm not entirely certain it was murder. It strikes me as far more likely that his lady friend is married and that he died in an inconvenient place. If we can lay hands on her, I think we can clear this up quickly."

"Yes, sir. I understand."

"Nevertheless," added Carmichael, "Gibbons and I will continue to interview these people on your list—you never can tell. But no matter—here's the food coming. Let's tuck in."

"Now, Marla," said Bethancourt placatingly into the telephone.

Stutely Manor had been deserted when he returned, and Mrs. Leggett could only tell him that Astley-Cooper and Marla had gone to lunch, she knew not where. Any hope Bethancourt had of this being simple miscommunication was crushed when he found Marla's mobile phone on the dresser in their room, left there deliberately, he was certain, to ensure he could not reach her and try to put matters right.

He elected to eat at the house in the hopes they would return, but when they had not done so by the time he was finished, he decided to rejoin the police investigation and just caught Carmichael and Gibbons at the end of their meal. They were planning to visit the vicarage next, and Bethancourt had slipped out to ring the manor one more time before they set out. He knew if Marla did not hear from him shortly after she returned, all might be lost. In fact, finding him waiting for her at the manor was the only thing guaranteed to make her happy, but he had persuaded himself a phone call would do.

He knew he had been mistaken as soon as he heard her voice and realized she now knew a murder investigation was in progress.

"Dear God," she said now, "it's like going out with Dracula—you just never know when another dead body is going to pop up."

"Marla—"

"I really don't want a relationship littered with corpses. Believe it or not, Phillip, most women do not find dead bodies romantic."

"Marla," Bethancourt tried again, "it's not my fault I ran into Jack and the chief inspector. And I'll be back in half an hour. I did look for you to have lunch."

"Looking is not the same as finding. And I doubt you looked very hard."

"Well, I was a little hampered by not knowing where to start. You might have left a note or taken your phone."

"Oh, I see. So now this is my fault?"

"Of course not. Did I say that? Look here, I'll be back shortly and we can have drinks and go somewhere lovely for dinner."

Marla gave in grudgingly. "Very well," she said. "But if you're not back here in half an hour, I shall be on the next train to London."

"I will be," he promised.

Bethancourt heaved a deep sigh and rang off just as Gibbons and Carmichael emerged from the pub.

"You can see the church from here," said Carmichael, pointing at the steeple that rose from among the trees. "The vicarage is just beyond it, I believe. We'll walk, Gibbons."

The vicarage was a large, late-Victorian house with a well-tended garden in front. They let themselves in at the gate, and walked up the path to ring the bell.

"Hullo?" came a voice from above them, and Carmichael hastily came out of the porch to look up at the first floor. A dark-haired man in his early thirties was hanging bare-chested out of an upstairs window. He looked a little startled not to recognize his visitors, but called amiably, "Were you looking for me?"

"We're looking for the vicar and his wife," replied Carmichael, shading his eyes against the sun. "I'm Detective Chief Inspector Carmichael from Scotland Yard."

"Oh!" said the man, pulling on a black T-shirt that someone in the room behind tossed at him. "I'm Richard Tothill. Is this about Charlie Bingham, then?"

"Yes, sir," said Carmichael. "If this is an inconvenient time—"

"No, no, not at all. We'll be right down."

He disappeared and Carmichael returned to the porch.

"We seem to have caught the vicar changing," he said.

But when the door opened, it was a woman who stood there. She was remarkably beautiful, her cornflower-blue eyes and ebony hair set off by a pale, creamy complexion. The sweater she wore fit closely enough to reveal a full bosom and slender waist, and her bare legs beneath the hem of her skirt were long and shapely. They paused, a little startled by this vision, and the thought popped into all their minds that perhaps the vicar had not been merely changing after all.

She smiled and held the door open for them.

"I'm Leandra Tothill," she said. "Richard will be right down—he's doing up his buttons. Do come in and sit down. Oh, what a beautiful dog."

"He's mine," said Bethancourt. "He can wait outside if you'd rather."

"No, of course not. I love dogs."

She ushered them into the front parlor, giving Cerberus a last pat before excusing herself to fetch some coffee.

"She doesn't look much like a vicar's wife," whispered Gibbons.

"No," agreed Carmichael. "She doesn't, does she?"

"Not like any vicar's wife I've ever seen," said Bethancourt. "I wonder what he's like—oh, here they come."

Richard Tothill, suitably attired in a worn black cassock, entered carrying the coffee tray with his wife bringing up the rear. He was a tall, thin man with a pleasant face and a quiet manner; there was nothing about him to indicate how he had come by such an extraordinary wife.

40

He and Leandra sat together on the sofa, and Bethancourt was struck by how natural they seemed with each other, as if they belonged together and knew it. It was clear, from the glances they exchanged, that they adored each other, and Bethancourt wondered how long they had been married.

"Yes, it was very distressing," the vicar was saying in a calm, deep voice that seemed made for the pulpit. "Charlie wasn't a churchgoer, but he was a sociable man and had become a friend. And he did like music—I was sure he'd be good for a subscription to our Christmas concert. So I went along there on Monday morning to ask him, but right away I knew something was wrong. I could see the sitting room lights were on as I came up the drive, which struck me as odd, the more so when I knocked and got no answer."

"So you entered the house?" asked Carmichael.

"Yes—the door was open. I saw him at once in the sitting room, slumped over in his chair, but he was quite cold when I felt for a pulse. I knew he was dead."

"You didn't, I understand, ring for an ambulance?"

Tothill looked surprised. "No," he answered. "Why should I have? There wasn't an emergency. I rang Dr. Cross—he'd been taking care of Charlie—and he said he'd be right over."

Carmichael nodded. "And then?"

"I didn't like to just leave him," said Tothill. "So I waited until the doctor came. I tidied up a bit—"

"Excuse me," interrupted Carmichael. In his voice was his deep dislike of tidying up murder scenes. "What exactly did you tidy?"

"Well, I washed up the glass of whisky he'd left, and looked to see what might spoil in the refrigerator. That was all, really."

"And emptied the ashtray," supplied Bethancourt helpfully.

The vicar did not immediately reply and his brown eyes looked reflective.

"No," he said finally, "I didn't. There was nothing in the ashtray and there should have been. The glass was less than half full and

Charlie was a heavy smoker. If he'd sat there and drunk off most of a glass of whisky, he would have been smoking. I never noticed at the time."

"That's it then, isn't it, Chief Inspector?" Leandra Tothill turned her clear eyes on Carmichael. "You don't think he died there, do you?"

"No," replied Carmichael. "It doesn't look like it. But please go on, Reverend."

"Where was I? Oh, yes, I washed up the glass, looked in the refrigerator, and then went out to the desk to look for his daughter's address. I found that and his solicitor's number and made a note of them, and then Dr. Cross arrived. He examined the body and rang the hospital. He said it looked like a heart attack, but there would have to be a postmortem. While we waited for the ambulance, we agreed that I would try and contact the daughter. I went back out to the kitchen and took the milk and cream over to Mrs. Eberhart and broke the news to her. She came back with me—she had a spare set of keys, you see—and shortly after that, the ambulance arrived and Dr. Cross went off with them. I tried to ring the daughter in Paris, but there was no answer, and then Mrs. Eberhart locked up and I left."

"I understand from the local police that you later succeeded in leaving a message at Miss Bingham's flat?"

"That was me," said Leandra.

"Lee's French is better than mine," said the vicar with an admiring look at his wife.

"I spoke to Miss Bingham's maid," continued Leandra. "Miss Bingham had left town for a few days and the maid wasn't sure when she'd be back. I didn't like to leave a message saying her father was dead, so I just left our number and said it concerned Charlie. But she hasn't rung back."

"I see," said Carmichael, glancing at Gibbons. Miss Bingham had not yet responded to the message left by the police, either. If they did not hear from her soon, they would have to go looking. Carmichael only hoped she was not as inveterate a traveller as her father. She could be in Bangkok by now.

"When was the last time you saw Mr. Bingham?" Carmichael continued.

"I saw him at Saturday's market," said Leandra. "But Richard wasn't with me then."

"Did he seem just as usual?"

"Oh, yes. We had a cuppa together, in fact. He was always very bright and cheery, with a sly sense of humor. I liked him enormously, even when he was playing devil's advocate. Which he did a good deal."

"He flirted shamelessly with you," said her husband, but not as though he minded.

Leandra smiled. "I suppose he did," she said. "But he never meant anything by it. It was only amusement for him." She looked at the detectives. "I don't mean to give you a wrong impression of him," she said. "He wasn't one of those older men who are always pinching girls' cheeks. He liked to banter and flirting was the way he did that with me. In a funny sort of way, he meant it. It would have tickled his fancy to be sleeping with the vicar's wife—it's the kind of thing that would have appealed to his sense of humor. On the other hand, he never actually expected it to happen. He knew it wasn't on."

"That was because he liked you as a person," said the vicar. "Which he wouldn't have done if you had slept with him. He could be perfectly scathing about anyone he didn't like."

"Was he generally popular?" asked Carmichael, who had been listening intently to these reminiscences.

"I'd say so," answered the vicar. "Of course, he was still the new man in town, so there was a lot of talk about him, but most of it was in his favor, I think. Don't you, Lee?"

"Yes," she agreed. "The Eberharts liked him, and that went a long way with people. They both grew up here, you see," she added to the policemen.

Carmichael nodded. "Were either of you aware that Mr. Bingham was rumored to have a secret girlfriend?"

Both the Tothills laughed.

"Oh, yes," said Tothill. "I never asked him about it, because, frankly, I rather thought the lady must be married. But it seems I was wrong."

"Oh?" Carmichael cocked his head, as alert as a pointer. "Why do you say that?"

"Because I did ask him about her," said Leandra. "I'm not absolutely sure she wasn't married, though."

"What did he say?"

Leandra smiled. "He wouldn't tell me a thing, although he didn't deny there was someone. All he said was to tell Richard there was nothing to concern him in his clerical capacity."

"Which I took to mean that the woman wasn't married after all," put in Tothill. "Surely that's what he meant."

"Probably," agreed Leandra. "It's only that I wouldn't put it past Charlie to lie to me, just so my conscience wouldn't be bothered. I don't think we can really tell the chief inspector that for sure."

Carmichael smiled. "I don't need sureties," he said. "Every little bit of information can help in a case like this. Now, one last question. Would you say he was a man of independent means?"

Tothill shrugged. "He was retired. I think everyone assumed he was living comfortably on his pension, within his means. He once told me he'd managed to put away a bit over the years."

"You would be surprised then to learn that he was a very wealthy man?"

Both the Tothills smiled. "Oh, yes," they agreed.

There was a pause while the implications of the question sank in, and then Leandra, with her eyes wide and the smile gone from her face, said,

"You mean he was?"

"Exceedingly," replied Carmichael.

Marla was somewhat appeased by Bethancourt's prompt appearance and the bouquet of autumn flowers he brought with him. Presents counted for a lot with Marla.

In an attempt to spark some tolerance of the case from her, Bethancourt announced that the dead man had been the father of the socialite Evelyn Bingham.

"Eve Bingham?" repeated Marla.

"Yes," answered Bethancourt. "I think we've seen her in clubs a time or two. You must remember."

"Of I course I do," said Marla. "I know her."

"You do?" said Bethancourt, nonplussed.

"Yes. When I went to Paris last year for the shows. She was hanging round with the lead singer of Who Else, and the drummer was seeing Carol, who was doing Lacroix with me. You remember Carol?"

Bethancourt thought so.

"Anyway," Marla went on, turning back to flower arranging, "I ended up seeing quite a bit of her. She was fun—rather high-spirited. She drank a lot."

"I doubt if she'll be much fun when she gets here," said Bethancourt.

"Not a very cheerful time for her," agreed Marla, stepping back to view her handiwork.

"Do you think you'd better rally 'round?" asked Bethancourt, hope dawning that Marla might actually take some interest in this case. Or at least be preoccupied while he was with Jack.

"I might," said Marla. "Depending on who's with her."

"What do you mean?"

"She's not the type that goes anywhere without an entourage," answered Marla.

"Oh," said Bethancourt, privately wondering who of the glitter crowd would be willing to bury themselves in the Cotwolds in October.

"Hullo," said Astley-Cooper, coming in. "Did you get yourselves a drink? No? Let me then." He paused on his way to the drinks cabinet and added, "Those are lovely flowers."

"I brought them for Marla," said Bethancourt. "As an apology for deserting the two of you today."

"We had a lovely time without you," said Marla, her jade eyes sparkling at Astley-Cooper. "Didn't we, Clarence?"

"Quite right," replied that gentleman, avoiding Bethancourt's eye and pouring the scotch liberally.

Bethancourt only grinned at him. He was quite used to Marla chatting up the nearest man whenever she felt herself neglected. The fact that this ploy seldom, if ever, succeeded in making Bethancourt jealous did not stop her from trying.

"I met the vicar and his wife today," said Bethancourt conversationally. "He's quite a young man, isn't he? Somehow one always thinks of vicars as older."

"So did everyone here," said Astley-Cooper, handing 'round the drinks. "Considering that the previous man was ninety if he was a day. There was quite a lot of objection to Richard Tothill when he first came, but people got over it. Lord knows he's much easier to get along with. Doesn't badger people, and if you go to him for advice, it's usually sensible, not a lot of muck about sinning or not sinning."

"That must make him popular."

"It does, but as I say, it took awhile. And then just as everyone was getting used to him, he went off and married Leandra. That caused quite a ruckus." Astley-Cooper appeared to savor this past sensation.

"What's wrong with her?" asked Marla. "Surely if he's young, people must have expected him to get married."

"First off, she's beautiful," said Astley-Cooper with relish. "Vicars' wives aren't supposed to be good-looking, they're supposed to be motherly. You, for instance, Marla, should never consider marrying a clergyman. You're far too lovely and nobody would ever like you. Secondly, Leandra's a woman with a past. She was a singer in London and ran, I gather, with a somewhat racy crowd. Well, musicians and all that. She met Richard when she was singing at a wedding. She's put new life into the choir, I can tell you that, and she's very active in the parish. But people looked askance at her when she first came."

"It doesn't sound so awful to me," said Marla.

"My dear, you don't have a village mentality. They would much have preferred her to be plain, and have been a nurse or something. Anyway, you'll meet her tonight if you come 'round after choir practice, and you can see for yourself. Do come, by the way. Everybody turns out for a drink at the pub on Wednesdays—it's one of our social nights. You can look over all the suspects, Phillip."

"Phillip," said Marla coolly, "has spent the whole day looking over suspects."

"That's right," said Astley-Cooper hastily. "You never did say, by the way, why the police think old Bingham was murdered."

"The body was moved after death," said Bethancourt.

"That's all?" asked Astley-Cooper. "That's not much. Whoever found him could have got the wind up about it and hauled him back to his house."

"And poured the corpse a glass of whisky?" retorted Bethancourt. "The only reason for doing that was if he died in a place where he wasn't supposed to be. Speaking of which, you don't happen to know who his girlfriend was, do you?"

"Didn't know he had one," replied Astley-Cooper promptly. "Never saw him about with anyone."

"Perhaps he was having an affair with the vicar's wife," suggested Marla.

Astley-Cooper laughed. "That's right," he said. "She was alone on Sunday night—the vicar was up here, playing chess."

"No," muttered Bethancourt. "She's the wrong size."

The others did not hear him.

੩੦ ੩੦ ੩੦

Forensics reported that Bingham's fingerprints in his car were overlaid by smudges. Translated, that meant gloved hands. The various medicine bottles found in his cabinet had contained heart medications, and the three loose tablets corresponded with the sedative found in Bingham's body at the postmortem. This was Seconal, a powerful sleeping pill, and one which forensics thought incompatible with the heart medications. Other than that, they had little to report.

"Do you want me to look into the sedative, sir?" asked Gibbons. "It looks rather as if he had borrowed them."

Carmichael sighed. "Yes," he replied, "you had better see Dr. Cross, however unlikely it seems that the Seconal was prescribed." He frowned. "I wonder why Bingham was using it."

"Forensics says it's mostly prescribed as a sleeping tablet."

"I don't mean that, Sergeant. I meant, why did he take it on the evening he died? It seems an odd thing to do if he was, as we've speculate, spending the night with his girlfriend."

"That's true, sir," agreed Gibbons, frowning as well. "Perhaps something upset him and he used it to calm down?"

"Yes," said Carmichael, a little doubtfully. "That's no doubt it."

"At least," added Gibbons, "we now know something about her."

Carmichael raised a bushy brow. "We do?" he asked.

"Yes, sir. We know she has trouble sleeping and has a prescription for Seconal."

Carmichael chuckled. "Probably true enough," he said. "Well, off you go, lad. I'll stay here at the station and try to get hold of the London solicitors. Even if this death is eventually ruled a misadventure, we don't want to leave any loose ends. And," he added appreciatively, "this is certainly a pretty part of the country in which to spend a few days."

He glanced out the window, though in fact Constable Stikes's office looked out on the car park, with only a hint of the hills to be seen above the tops of the buildings opposite.

"It is that, sir," said Gibbons, agreeing automatically. The beauties of the Cotswolds had not entirely escaped him, but in his current state of depression, he had paid them scant heed.

Dr. Cross's consulting rooms were also in Stow-on-the-Wold, not very far from the police station. Gibbons found them easily enough, but once arrived there he was forced to wait almost twenty minutes while the doctor finished seeing a patient. He attempted to pass the time by chatting with the nurse—a thin, middle-aged woman with a mouth like a slit—but she did not respond to his overtures. With a sigh, he settled back in his chair and fell to contemplating the perversity of women in general. He was really quite relieved when at last he was called into the doctor's inner sanctum.

Dr. Cross was a short man with white hair and a brisk manner. He was plainly appalled at the sedative mentioned by Gibbons.

"Certainly I did not prescribe it for him," he said tartly. "Do you think I would have kicked up such a fuss at the autopsy if I had? With his heart condition that sort of thing could kill him. In fact, it did."

"Was he aware of that, do you think?"

"He was aware of his heart condition. I don't believe I ever specifically warned him against Seconal, but why should I? So far as I am aware, he had no trouble sleeping. And that's something people usually tell their doctors."

"I understand," said Gibbons, trying a new tack, "that you had advised him to cut down on his smoking and drinking?"

"I advised him to give up both," answered the doctor dryly. "He'd had a previous heart attack while he was in China—in fact, I suspect he had two. I told him if he didn't give up smoking and drinking, it was only a matter of time before he would have a third, and possibly fatal, attack."

"So you weren't surprised when Reverend Tothill rang you on Monday?"

"Well, now, I wouldn't say that." Dr. Cross looked thoughtful. "He was, as I understand it, leading a very strenuous life in China, virtually without any medical attention at all. On the whole, I would have ex-

49

pected him to live for quite a while longer here, with the new prescriptions I'd given him, and without heaving a heavy backpack about. So I was rather surprised when the vicar rang up and said he was dead. In view of that, I thought we'd better have the postmortem, but I can't say I was expecting to find anything. Heart cases do sometimes pop off suddenly. And although I did advise him to change his vices, and so did Dr. Loomis, he certainly did no such thing."

"Dr. Loomis?" asked Gibbons.

"Dr. Preston Loomis," replied Dr. Cross. "He's a well-known cardiologist in London. Bingham consulted him directly upon his return to this country, before he came down here. He saw me after he'd been here two or three months and his prescriptions from Dr. Loomis had run out."

"Do you have Dr. Loomis's address?" asked Gibbons.

"Yes, my nurse can give it to you on your way out."

Gibbons thanked the doctor for his time and went out for a fresh attack on the grim-mouthed nurse.

CHAPTER

5

*B*other," said Leandra Tothill.

She was just leaving for choir practice, a sheaf of music that her husband had forgotten under her arm, when the telephone rang. She turned back to the parlor to answer it.

"Hello," said a high, rather imperious voice. "Is Mrs. Tothill there? This is Eve Bingham."

"Oh," said Leandra faintly, taken unawares. "This is Mrs. Tothill."

"I've had a message to ring you," Eve Bingham said crisply. "I've also had messages from Scotland Yard and my solicitors. What on earth is my father up to now? I know he's an absolute devil, but surely he hasn't managed to get himself arrested and excommunicated all at once?"

"No," said Leandra, rallying. "He's not in trouble exactly, Miss Bingham. I'm afraid it's rather bad news."

"Bad news?"

"Yes. Your father had a heart attack on Sunday. I'm afraid he passed away, Miss Bingham."

There was a long silence at the other end of the line.

"Miss Bingham?" said Leandra. "Are you all right?"

"Yes," she replied, almost fiercely. "On Sunday, you say?"

"My husband, the vicar, found him Monday morning."

Again there was silence. Then came the sound of a long, shuddering breath.

"Miss Bingham, I'm so terribly sorry."

"Yes. I mean, thank you." It was almost a whisper.

Another pause, but Leandra didn't like to break into it. Finally the voice came again, dully.

"What has Scotland Yard to do with it? Tilly said they rang after you did."

"There is some question about his death," answered Leandra, trying to put it gently. "They're not entirely satisfied it was a natural one."

"I see." But from the tone, Leandra doubted she had taken it in.

"Thank you for calling me, Mrs. Tothill. I'll come at once."

"If you like to let us know, my husband or I will be glad to meet you at the station."

"It's all right. I'll be driving myself."

"Well, if there's anything else you want, don't hesitate to ring."

"Thank you, Mrs. Tothill. You've been very kind."

Marla's good temper had been restored by dinner at a pleasant restaurant recommended by Astley-Cooper. She and Bethancourt were now strolling down the deserted High Street in the direction of the church. Chipping Chedding was a very picturesque village, which accounted for the number of disillusioned city dwellers who had retreated there, or at least taken a house for the summer. Chipping Chedding was their idea of the English countryside personified.

The church, toward which Bethancourt and Marla leisurely picked their way with Cerberus at their heels, was a solid example of the Perpendicular style like so many of the churches built by the highly profitable wool trade in the fifteenth century. Chipping Chedding's church was not, perhaps, a paradigm of the Perpendicular, but that did not stop the villagers from being very proud of it.

The church was set on a rise at the end of the High Street amid a pool of grass. Light glowed behind the colored panes of the windows and, as they approached, a low murmur of music could be heard.

"They're still at it," said Bethancourt. He peered at his watch. "It's half nine," he said. "Shall we go in and listen? They should be finished shortly."

"What about Cerberus?"

"He can come, too. We'll sit in the back and no one will notice."

It was dim in the church and peaceful, with the high Perpendicular nave arching away above them. They slipped into a shadowy pew and let the music wash over them. The choir was surprisingly good, although the organist left something to be desired, and the acoustics of the old church sent the sound clearly back to them.

"There's Clarence," whispered Marla, snuggling against him.

Bethancourt nodded and put his arm about her.

"I didn't know he had such a good voice," he said.

In ten minutes or so the rehearsal came to its end and the choir set down their music and began to collect their various belongings. The vicar's voice echoed back, reminding them of a few things for Sunday. Bethancourt and Marla remained seated, waiting for Astley-Cooper to detach himself.

Eventually, he came down the aisle toward them, accompanied by a tall woman with a long face and iron-gray hair.

"Hello," he said. "Did you hear us? This is Martha Potts, one of our altos. She's the housekeeper up at the Bonnar place. Martha, this is Phillip Bethancourt and Marla Tate. Marla's one of the models who came down to Stutely the other day."

"I thought you looked familiar," exclaimed Mrs. Potts, shaking hands. "I've often seen your picture in the magazines."

Marla accepted this accolade with a smile.

"Oh, and here's our vicar. Reverend Tothill, Marla Tate. I think you've already met Bethancourt here."

"Yes, of course. How lovely to meet you, Miss Tate. I hope all went well up at Stutely Manor for the shoot?"

"Oh, yes," answered Marla, flashing her famous smile. "Clarence is a perfect host."

"Well, we're very honored to have you here. There's my wife—Lee, come and meet Miss Tate. You remember Mr. Bethancourt."

More introductions ensued and gradually the party edged their way down the nave and out into the porch. Whether because of tact or a genuine liking for dogs, Tothill made no mention of the large Borzoi in his church.

They waited at the door while the vicar closed up, and then made their way down the street to the Deer and Hounds, following the stream of choristers already headed in that direction.

"I left a message at the police station," Leandra told Bethancourt as she fell in beside him. "Eve Bingham rang this evening. She said she's coming over at once."

"How did she take it?"

"She was naturally very distressed. I hated having to break the news over the phone."

"Of course, it was a shock for her. She did seem shocked, didn't she?"

"Yes, certainly. What a funny question."

"Not really." Bethancourt paused to light a cigarette. "One has to remember, you know, that she is now an heiress. A very wealthy one."

"But she was in Paris when Charlie died," protested Leandra.

"We only think she was," said Bethancourt. "Has she ever visited her father here?"

Leandra shook her head. "Never. Charlie talked about her from time to time—I think he was very fond of her in his way, and proud, too. But he never spoke of expecting to see her here and as far as I know, he didn't."

"Did you have the impression they were close?"

"How could they be? She lived in Europe and he spent most of the last twenty years in Africa and the Far East."

"Yes, I expect you're right there. Well, we will just have to wait until the lady arrives."

"But I rather thought," began Leandra, "that is, we got the impression from the chief inspector that he thought Charlie's death was probably an accident."

Bethancourt could hardly tell her he was hoping it was murder in order to cheer his friend Gibbons up.

"Very likely it was," said Bethancourt, smiling at her. "You must allow for an enthusiast's point of view. Amateur sleuthing is my hobby, so naturally I prefer there be something to investigate."

The Deer and Hounds was crowded with even more than the usual Wednesday night throng. Chipping Chedding had rarely had so newsy a day: the murder of Charlie Bingham, the arrival of Scotland Yard, the revelation that Bingham was rich, and, to top it all off, a famous fashion model in their midst. Everyone was very eager to discover if she was as beautiful in real life as she appeared in magazines. As usual on such occasions, opinion on this topic was widely divided, but Marla was nevertheless soon surrounded by a crowd of admirers.

It was not long before Bethancourt was separated from both his girlfriend and his host; Astley-Cooper was glued to Marla's side, clearly enjoying his role of host to the elite. Bethancourt, looking around, thought with amusement that tomorrow no one would even remember he had been present.

He found himself in a corner with Mrs. Potts, who was introducing him to her employers, James and Julie Benson. These, he remembered, were the children of the actress, Joan Bonnar. Like most children of famous people who are not famous in their own right, they were polite and somewhat reserved. Neither bore any particular resemblance to their mother beyond a fairness of complexion; certainly there was nothing about them that reflected Joan Bonnar's charisma and beauty. In their midtwenties, both were a little over-weight, pleasant-faced without being particularly attractive, a per-fectly ordinary example of English siblings. Julie's thick brown-blond hair was her chief beauty, and she had made all she could of it by growing it long; the single braid fell to her waist. Bethancourt privately thought that a shorter cut would have flattered her face better.

They greeted Mrs. Potts like a favorite aunt rather than a house-keeper, and she, having finished the introductions, waved Julie over and joined her on the bench with a sigh.

"That's better," she said. "Do sit down, Mr. Bethancourt. That chair will disappear if you don't take it."

Bethancourt did as he was bidden, setting his drink on the table, leaning back comfortably, and lighting a cigarette. Julie and Mrs. Potts already had their heads together, so he turned his attention to James.

"The choir is remarkably fine," he said. "I just caught the end of rehearsal. I take it you don't sing yourself?"

James gave a small smile. "No voice," he answered. "And not much ear, either, for all I've had Marty there singing 'round the house since I was small. But Julie and I do enjoy it on Sundays." He sipped at his pint. "Are you enjoying your visit to Chipping Chedding?" he asked politely. "It must be rather quiet after London."

"Pleasantly so," Bethancourt assured him. "It's a very pretty spot. Have you lived here long?"

"Almost all our lives," replied James. "Certainly long before it was 'discovered.' We've travelled a bit, and been to different schools, but this has always been home. It's really our mother's house, but she seldom comes here except to visit, and we think of it as our own."

"There you are." Leandra Tothill appeared out of the crowd, clutching a double scotch. "Hello, James, Julie. Tell me, is Derek anywhere in this mob?"

"No, he's not," responded James, smiling up at her. Julie's smile, Bethancourt noticed, was far cooler.

"We stopped by his place to see if he'd come," she said, "but he was painting furiously."

"Oh, well. I'll see him tomorrow or next day, I expect. You couldn't make room for me on that bench, could you, Martha? I'm exhausted after that rehearsal."

Mrs. Potts apologized and moved over.

"It's just as well Derek isn't here," said Julie mischievously. "He might steal Mr. Bethancourt's girlfriend. She's certainly pretty enough."

"Really?" said Bethancourt, interested. In her tone, he had suddenly caught a glimpse of what it must be like to be the plain daughter of a woman not only beautiful, but famed for that beauty throughout the world. He wondered if a resentment of beautiful women was the cause of her less than effusive welcome of Leandra Tothill.

Everyone was chuckling.

"Derek Towser came down from London with a bit of a reputation," explained Mrs. Potts. "Or so we heard."

"He's been most disappointing," said James. "So far as we can tell, not a single village maiden has suffered at his hands."

"The general consensus," said Leandra, "is that none of us here are good enough for him."

"Hardly fair, Leandra," said James. "You're the prettiest thing we've got and you're taken."

"Nonsense. He could have at least tried."

Bethancourt was watching Julie. Though she joined in the general mirth—this was obviously a running joke among them—her eyes were not amused. Their farmhouse, he remembered, was close to the painter's cottage, and he wondered if there was one village maiden who had suffered. Or perhaps she had only wished it so.

"Oh dear," said Leandra, "there's Richard calling me. Just as I'd got settled. Well, save my seat."

Her seat, however, was immediately taken by Astley-Cooper.

"There you are," he said to Bethancourt. "We lost you in the crowd, but I see Martha has taken care of you."

"Admirably so," said Bethancourt, smiling at her.

"Naturally," said Astley-Cooper, turning toward her gallantly. "Why, Martha, where's your ring? You haven't dropped it in the port again, I hope?"

"I've lost it," replied Mrs. Potts placidly. "I'm always losing it, though I can't think where it's gone this time. I know I had it on Sunday at church."

Julie laughed. "That's right. It dropped off in the collection plate, but James rescued it."

"Martha's ring is famous," Astley-Cooper informed Bethancourt. "She's always leaving it about or dropping it."

"Playing with it is a bad habit of mine," confessed Mrs. Potts. "It was my father's signet ring, you see, and it's really too big for me."

"We'll have a good look 'round the house for it when we get home," said Julie sympathetically. "You haven't seen it, have you, James?"

"What? I'm sorry, I wasn't listening."

"I've looked 'round the house," said Mrs. Potts. "I think it must have dropped off at my sister's."

"Oh, that's an idea."

Bethancourt managed to attract Astley-Cooper's attention and inquire as to Marla's whereabouts.

"I left her at the bar," he replied, "in the midst of an admiring throng of almost every man in the village. She's got them all twisted 'round her finger. Honestly, Phillip, I don't know how you cope with her. She's an extremely dangerous woman."

"In some ways," said Bethancourt absently. "I expect I'm safe for the moment—she's in her element."

He nevertheless looked around, trying to spot her in the crowd, and thus caught a glimpse of Constable Stikes, surveying the scene from the doorway. Behind her were Carmichael and Gibbons, also looking in, but in a moment they moved on, no doubt headed toward their rooms. Bethancourt considered nipping out to ask how things had gone at Bingham's solicitors, but decided against it.

"Were those the Scotland Yard men?" asked Martha Potts.

"Where?" demanded Julie, looking 'round alertly.

"Behind the constable. They're gone now."

"Yes," said Bethancourt. "That was Chief Inspector Carmichael and Sergeant Gibbons."

"That's right," said James. "We heard you knew them. Do they have any suspects yet?"

"Not yet," answered Bethancourt. "They only arrived this morning—it's still early days."

He decided not to mention the fact that the detectives were still uncertain that Bingham's death was in fact a murder; the others were so clearly enjoying their sensation, it would have been a pity to put a damper on the occasion.

"The most surprising thing to me," declared James, "was that he was rich. You must have seen his place, Mr. Bethancourt. Can you credit it?"

"He didn't even have a daily," put in Mrs. Potts. She sounded as if she were mildly affronted that this should be so. "I offered to find him someone, but he wouldn't have it. Said he was used to doing his own housework."

"But who would want to kill him?" asked Julie. "That's what I can't understand. Such a sweet man, really. A little eccentric, but not in a way that would prejudice anyone against him."

With this they all agreed, and a little silence fell as they contemplated the death of someone they had all known and liked.

"Well," said Mrs. Potts, setting down her empty port glass. "It's getting late and I'm for home. Are you two coming?"

"Yes, indeed," said James, swallowing the last of his pint. "Julie made me walk down, and I want a ride back."

"A little exercise does us good," said Julie. "But you're right—I don't fancy walking back, either."

They gathered up their belongings and bid the rest of the company good night, making their way slowly through the crowd toward the door. Bethancourt watched them go.

"Tell me," he said to Astley-Cooper, "you never said whether either of the Bensons had careers, or families of their own."

"No, they're both single," answered Astley-Cooper. "They've got friends among the county set, and Julie does a fair amount of riding, but neither of them has ever dated anyone for long. They keep to themselves mostly, so far as I know."

"Do you know them well?" asked Bethancourt.

Astley-Cooper shrugged. "Tolerably so," he said. "After all, they've lived here nearly all their lives. I well remember," he added, smiling at the recollection, "the day we found out the Batemans had sold the old farmhouse. My parents were still alive then and they were appalled, absolutely appalled, at the idea of a film star moving into the neighborhood. Said it would bring hordes of undesirables thronging 'round, though of course there was no question of our actually receiving Miss Bonnar. Oh, yes, my mother was quite eloquent on that subject. Of course, back then we didn't have the tourists we have today. The summer crowds these days probably have my parents spinning in their graves."

"And how about you?" asked Bethancourt. "Were you appalled as well?"

"Well, no," admitted Astley-Cooper. "I was rather intrigued. I was still a young man, you must remember, and back then Joan Bonnar was love's young dream."

"I know," said Bethancourt. "I've seen the films." He took the last sip of his scotch and added, "Speaking of love's young dream, I think I'd best go see how Marla's getting on. She'll never forgive me if I desert her tonight."

"I left her right over there," said Astley-Cooper, waving a hand in the direction of the bar.

Bethancourt made his way in that direction, but was stopped by

Leandra Tothill before he had got very far. In the heat of the crowd, she had shrugged her sweater off her shoulders, giving her a delightful suggestion of *en dishabille* as she peered through the crowd.

"Hullo," she said to him with a smile. "I've lost Richard again. How are you doing?"

Bethancourt smiled back. "I've lost Marla," he answered.

Leandra laughed. "She's over there," she said, pointing. "The only reason you can't see her is that she's surrounded."

Bethancourt surveyed the crowd. "She certainly seems to be," he agreed.

"You can't blame them," said Leandra fondly. "We don't get many celebrities here, despite all the crowds in the summer."

"But you used to live in London yourself," said Bethancourt.

"Yes, but I grew up in a village like this." She laughed, a musical peal that delighted his ear. "And I could hardly wait to leave—as soon as I was done with school, I was off to London like a shot."

"Didn't you like it once you got there?"

"Oh, I loved it," she answered. "I never thought I'd go back to a small place. But then I met Richard and, well . . ."

She shrugged and smiled.

"Bowled over, were you?" asked Bethancourt.

"Rather." She looked up at him, her eyes sparkling at the recollection. "I don't know if you've ever had the feeling, but we just seemed to fit together from the start. I really didn't want to leave London, but it wasn't as if I'd never lived in a village before. I knew I could manage, and Richard and I agreed I could always take the odd weekend in town—it's not that far. But somehow I never do actually go."

Her expression had turned thoughtful now, as if she were thinking over the wisdom of this choice, if choice it was.

"No doubt the parish keeps you busy here," suggested Bethancourt.

"Yes, it does."

They were interrupted by another woman whose name escaped Bethancourt, but whom he recognized from the choir.

"There you are, Mrs. Tothill," she said cheerfully. "The vicar's looking for you."

"And I'm looking for him. Where has he got to? You will excuse me, Mr. Bethancourt, won't you?"

Bethancourt acceded to this request and resumed his course toward the bar. He found Marla there, still surrounded by her crowd of admirers and clearly enjoying herself, her jade eyes dancing and her full lips parted in a dazzling smile. The sight stirred Bethancourt as he joined her and was greeted affectionately with a kiss and a hand run through his hair. Envy abruptly appeared in many of her admirers' eyes, but Bethancourt hardly noticed as he slipped an arm about her waist.

She was going to be angry with him in the morning, he reminded himself, when he planned to leave her to her own devices so that he might run off with Gibbons. He toyed with the idea of hinting at his plans tonight, so as to relieve some of the abruptness of a morning announcement, but he caught a whiff of her scent as she turned to smile at him and decided that, after all, he might as well leave the evening unblemished.

Upstairs, Carmichael and Gibbons were poring over an ordnance survey map spread open on the bed.

"If we could just get a line on where Bingham was going that day," said Carmichael, frowning fiercely. "It would give us a big clue as to where to look for this confounded woman."

"Yes, sir," said Gibbons. "If he was going to London, then he must have taken the A40."

"If that's where he was going," said Carmichael glumly. "And he needn't have taken the A40, even if he was. He might have picked up the M4 at Swindon."

"He might, of course," said Gibbons, "but Constable Stikes says most people use the A40. And," he continued hastily, before Carmichael could interrupt with yet another gloomy prognostication, "even if he wasn't actually going to London, he would still have taken the A40, since he'd told people he was going to London and it would have been remarked on if anyone had happened to see him off-course, so to speak."

"There is that," admitted Carmichael, somewhat reluctantly. He was in a foul mood, having arrived back too late to ring his wife before she went to bed. He sighed. "We could have this case cleared up in no time, if we could just get the facts straight. Before we heard of this mysterious girlfriend, I had hopes that whoever Bingham had gone to see would turn up, but there's not much chance of it now."

"No," agreed Gibbons, "and that does make it look like it was the girlfriend he went to see. I suppose," he said reflectively, "it's possible she killed him deliberately, and that's why he took a sleeping tablet before his dinner."

"Possible," agreed Carmichael, beginning to fold up the map. "We won't know until we find her. Well, we've got to finish up here, make sure none of these people know anything. I think I'll let you do that tomorrow, Gibbons, and I'll go have a word with Bingham's business partner—what's his name?"

"Sealingham, sir. Andrew Sealingham."

"That's it. You know, Bingham might equally well have been going to see him—the man lives in the London suburbs."

"That's true, sir."

"And in any case, he's got to be ticked off the list," grumbled Carmichael, finishing with the map and tossing it aside. "They've all got to be ticked off, though what good it will do us, I don't know. Oh, never mind me, Sergeant—you take yourself off and get some sleep. I'll be in a better frame of mind tomorrow."

"No doubt, sir," said Gibbons, rising with alacrity and making for the door. "Sleep well, sir."

Richard Tothill awoke from a sound sleep at two A.M. In the past, he had often been troubled with insomnia, but this malady had disappeared upon his marriage. In his few previous sexual encounters, he had always found the presence of a soundly sleeping person beside him an irritant rather than a cure for this condition, but from the moment Leandra had begun to share his bed, all sleeplessness had vanished.

He was fondly contemplating her recumbent form, barely to be made out in the dim light, when the front door knocker sounded from below. That was what had awakened him, then. He slid from the bed and grabbed his dressing gown, thinking mournfully that someone must be dying for him to called out at this time of night. He hoped it wasn't old Mrs. Cracy; she had looked a good deal better in church last Sunday. Or Mrs. Bosworth was due to have her baby any day now, and it had been a very difficult pregnancy. *Oh, God,* he thought, *don't let it be the baby.* He hurried down the stairs, deciding in a very unclergymanlike manner that better Mrs. Cracy than Mrs. Bosworth and the baby.

But the young woman on the doorstep was unknown to him. She was very pale, but fashionably turned out, even down to a small navy hat clinging to her fair hair.

"I'm sorry to knock you up like this," she began. "But I never dreamed this place was so small—there's not a single light on, much less anything open. Your wife did say to call if I needed anything. This is the vicarage, isn't it?"

Dazed, he nodded.

"Well, do you have a spare bed or even a spare couch? Oh, I'm sorry, I should have said—I'm Eve Bingham."

"Of course," he said, enlightened. "I'm so sorry I didn't realize who you were. Come in, please. We have plenty of rooms—this place is far too large for us." He shepherded her along to the parlor and turned on the lights. "Do you have a bag or anything?"

"It's in the car," she replied, looking about her.

"I'll fetch it in a moment," he said. "Can I get you anything?"

"Is there any brandy?" she asked doubtfully.

"Yes, of course."

Going to the glass-fronted cabinet, he poured out a goodly measure of cognac and handed it to her. "Please sit down," he said. "I'll just fetch in your bag and check on which bed my wife's made up. I'll be back in a moment."

"Thank you," she said, and sank down on the end of the sofa.

A dark, nondescript car was parked in the drive. In it, he found not one but two good-sized suitcases. In his frail, newly awakened state, they seemed inordinately heavy, but he hauled them up the stairs and into the guest room which Leandra kept perpetually prepared. He checked to make certain the bed was made up, though he knew it would be, and then descended again.

Eve Bingham had removed her jacket and was smoking, gazing abstractedly at the patterns the smoke made in lamplight. She roused herself at his entrance, however, and turned toward him. For just an instant, he thought her eyes held the pleading look of a lost dog.

"Everything's settled," he said gently. "Is there anything else you'd like? If you're hungry—"

"No," she said. "No, I'm not hungry. It's very good of you to bother."

"You came very quickly," he said, knowing somehow that to mention her father would be a mistake. "We didn't think you could arrive until tomorrow."

"I have a friend with a private plane. I got ahold of him and told him he'd have to fly me back to England." She frowned. "It took him a little while to find the airstrip closest to this place. I drove from there," she ended.

"Well, I'm very glad you thought to come here."

She shook her head, as if to clear it. "I'm keeping you up," she said, stubbing out her cigarette. "If you'll show me my room, I'll let you get back to sleep."

The vicar hesitated. It never did to push people, but she was such an unknown, he felt he had to offer. "If you'd prefer company," he said, "I'm really quite awake now."

"That's very kind of you," she said, rising, "but I'm afraid I'm the one who's tired."

"Of course," he said sympathetically. "This way, then."

CHAPTER

6

ingham's solicitors confirm that he was very wealthy indeed," said Gibbons. "They also say he made very little de-
mand on his income. Occasionally, he would ask them to
wire him a sum, which they assumed was for the financing of archeological expeditions. Other than that, he lived very frugally, mostly on
whatever he had in hand in the Far East. There were some expenses, of
course, when he returned to this country."

He and Bethancourt were strolling down the High Street toward
the vicarage, where Gibbons had been sent to meet the heiress.
Bethancourt was pleased to see his friend in such good spirits; it was
the cheeriest he'd been in more than a month, which Bethancourt put
down to the country air and hoped the change of scene would continue to work its wonders.

He was in excellent spirits himself; it was a perfect autumn day,
and in the morning sunshine the limestone was truly golden. It was
the kind of day that inhabitants of London dream of when they
dream of the country. On such a day, it seemed perfectly reasonable

that Carmichael should have sent Gibbons off on his own to interview a primary witness, and that Marla should unexpectedly agree to Bethancourt's accompanying his friend, apparently wanting him to make first contact with Eve Bingham.

"See how she is and who's with her," Marla had instructed him. "If you think I can do any good, let her know I'm available."

Bethancourt smiled as he recollected this, inhaling the fresh air deeply. Getting out of London for a few days had, he thought, been one of his better ideas.

He turned to Gibbons and asked, "I expect the daughter gets everything?"

"What there is to get," replied Gibbons. "All the patents are already in her name, as are most of the investments, and the bank accounts are joint ones. Bingham didn't figure on her paying any more in death duties than she had to. Mostly what she inherits is his stock in the company that manufactures his flushing invention. Bingham was still a full partner, although he hadn't anything to do with the business in years."

"So Eve Bingham has had a free hand with her father's pile for some time?"

"Yes, and her spending habits are the exact opposite of her father's. But the solicitors say that although she spends it as if she were the Princess of Wales, she's actually a very shrewd businesswoman. The impression we got from them is that she may like to pretend she hasn't a thought in her head beyond her newest dress, but that she's got a very able brain to use when it suits her."

"Interesting type," mused Bethancourt.

"You think all types are interesting."

"I suppose I do at that. Human nature is fascinating."

Eve Bingham was waiting for them in the vicarage parlor. She was a slender woman of about twenty-five, with straight blond hair cut simply in a bob. She appeared perfectly composed and was again very well turned out in a navy woolen sheath (which to Bethancourt smacked of Chanel) and a single strand of pearls (which Bethancourt estimated had cost her upward of £500). Dark smudges beneath her deep blues eyes denoted a sleepless night, but beyond that there was no sign of grief. Gibbons introduced himself and Bethancourt and conveyed his condolences on her father's death.

"Aren't you going to introduce him?" she asked, pointing to Cerberus, who was sitting patiently at his master's side.

"He's mine," said Bethancourt. "His name's Cerberus."

She raised an eyebrow at that, but Bethancourt merely smiled blandly at her and she returned her attention to Gibbons.

"Mrs. Tothill said my father died of a heart attack," she said. "Clearly the police wouldn't be interested if that were the case. How did he die, Inspector?"

"Sergeant, Miss," corrected Gibbons, but Bethancourt thought to himself that the mistake had been a deliberate one. Any man with a sergeant's rank has no objections to being taken for an inspector. But Bethancourt also knew that any flattery, no matter how subtle, would get her nowhere with his friend.

He paid scant attention while Gibbons outlined their reasons for being interested in Bingham's death and began to question her about her father's habits and possible liaisons. She answered readily enough, but finally grew impatient.

"Inspector—I mean, Sergeant—I tell you I haven't the faintest idea about any of this. My father and I were not close. We used to correspond occasionally, but he certainly did not send me the details of his love life. I saw him last year on his way back to England, and before that I hadn't seen him in five years. Good Lord, I was in London myself last weekend and it never even occurred to me to look him up." She paused suddenly. "I'm sorry about that now, of course," she murmured, half to herself. "But he'd been away for so long."

Gibbons, however, pricked up his ears, manifested to Bethancourt by a sharpened look in his blue eyes.

"How long were you in London, Miss?" he asked.

"Not long." She waved a hand. "Roy and I flew in for a party on Saturday. We meant to go back on Sunday, but Roy was feeling under the weather, so we waited and flew over on Monday instead."

"Your father was not aware of this visit?"

"Of course not. I've just finished telling you—look here, Sergeant, our lack of communication may seem strange to you, but if your father had been thousands of miles away for most of your life, it would take you more than a few months to get used to the idea that he was now just across the Channel."

"I only asked, Miss Bingham, because he obviously meant to visit someone on Sunday. If he knew of your trip, it might have been you. Tell me, did you stay in a hotel or with friends?"

"A hotel," she answered shortly. "St. Martin's Lane."

"And you were there on Sunday?"

"I was. Roy and I met for a late lunch, but apart from that I spent a quiet evening in my room with the telly and a magazine. So if my father had come to see me, he would have had no trouble finding me. Which only proves that he didn't."

"I see," said Gibbons, unmoved by her tone. "How was it that you didn't receive our message until yesterday?"

"Because we stopped in Normandy and spent two nights with friends there." She lit a cigarette, snapping the lighter closed with finality.

"Well," said Gibbons, making a show of looking over his notebook, "I think that's all for the moment, Miss. The keys to your father's cottage are at the police station—you'll have to sign for them. And we'd appreciate it if you could let us know whether you'll be staying there or elsewhere."

"Just a moment," she said. "You haven't told me—where is my father? I want to see him."

"His body is at the police mortuary in Stow," replied Gibbons. "That's in the market lane just off the High Street. They won't be releasing him just yet, but they will want your instructions for when the time comes."

"Yes, all right," she said. "I don't really know what he wanted. Perhaps in his will . . ."

Bethancourt broke in. "My girlfriend, Marla Tate, is staying at Stutely Manor. I believe you know each other. She didn't want to barge in on you, but if you'd like her to go with you to the mortuary, she'd be very happy to."

"You're Marla's boyfriend?" Eve asked, looking him over with new eyes.

"Yes. I can ring her and ask her to come into Chipping Chedding."

"No." She shook her head. "I want to go alone. But . . ." She hesitated. "I've got to return the car and rent another one. There was nothing open when I came in last night, so I bribed the weatherman at the airport to let me borrow his. I promised to have it back today. Maybe Marla would come with me to do that? I'll need a second person to drive from the rental agency to the airfield."

Bethancourt beamed. All of that, he estimated, would take several hours and keep Marla happy and out of the way.

"She'd love to," he said. "I'll have her ring you here and arrange it."

Outside the vicarage, Bethancourt pounded Gibbons enthusiastically on the back.

"You were brilliant, old boy, absolutely brilliant. Not a suspicion raised."

"She'll tumble to it soon enough," said Gibbons, grinning nevertheless. "She's sharp—it won't take her long to realize she has no alibi for her father's murder."

"Yes, but now we know it, too. And you even got the name of the hotel from her."

"We'll have to check there—and on whether she has a prescription for Seconal. But that can wait 'til Carmichael gets back tonight. After all, it's still far more likely he died at his girlfriend's. And Miss

Bingham hasn't much motive—most of the money was already hers."

"Nonsense," said Bethancourt, eager for any complication that would keep Gibbons distracted from his woes. "She's a dreadfully neglected and motherless child abandoned by her father. She's probably wanted to kill him for years, only she didn't fancy doing it in China or Tibet or wherever. Well, what next?"

"Next we go on to Derek Towser and the Bensons. And, since the Chief Inspector has taken the Rover, you can drive."

"All right. Just let me ring Marla first and let her know what's afoot."

Gibbons nodded, strolling on in order to give his friend some privacy while Bethancourt paused to dig out his mobile. But Bethancourt caught him up again after a very few moments. He was smiling happily.

"That's taken care of," he said with an air of satisfaction. "I suggested to Marla that she might want to give poor Eve some lunch while she was about it, and she took to the idea like a flash. She's to ring me when she gets back, but that won't be until much, much later. Here's the car—hop in."

Gibbons had known Bethancourt long enough not to quail at the idea of riding in a car driven by him. In fact, Gibbons had formed the opinion that his friend was not really an unsafe driver; erratic would be a better word. At times, when his eye was actually on the road, Bethancourt's driving was quite commendable. Unfortunately, Bethancourt very seldom had his eye on the road. He found a myriad of fascinating things to look at on either side and occasionally even behind the car. He usually slowed down—sometimes to a crawl—when something really captured his attention, but even at a crawl, the car often strayed slightly off the road. Between distractions, he tended to accelerate to alarming speeds, apparently in a hurry to reach whatever he had sighted up ahead. Gibbons found that things were usually all right so long as he himself kept an eye on the road and alerted his friend to sudden curves, telegraph poles, and, above all, when it was time to make a turn.

Thus they inched past the Bingham and Eberhart cottages, and then the Jaguar leapt forward.

"The turn's coming up," said Gibbons. "It's only a quarter of a mile or so. There, that lane off to the left."

"That?" Bethancourt stamped on the brakes and downshifted, slewing the car around. He was then forced to moderate his pace, as the lane had not been resurfaced in some years.

About fifty yards on, well-shielded by trees, was another cottage, but this one was not Georgian. It was a late-Victorian effort in red-brick, snug enough but lacking the graceful lines of the other cottages.

The drive led toward an old woodshed, now converted into a garage and presently sheltering a rather dirty Range Rover as well as an assortment of dilapidated sporting equipment, such as a bundle of rusted croquet hoops, a bicycle with a flat tire, and a much-weathered cricket bat sticking up among a motley collection of croquet mallets, one of which was missing its head.

"Well, at least he's home," said Gibbons, indicating the Range Rover as Bethancourt brought the Jaguar to a halt.

"He could be out painting somewhere nearby," said Bethancourt, to which Gibbons merely grunted.

But Derek Towser answered their knock promptly. He was a tall, lean man in his early thirties with dark, sensual good looks. Bethancourt could easily see how he had acquired his reputation, deserved or not; he was the kind of man women daydreamed about.

He greeted them quietly and invited them in. The sitting room was large and had been transformed into a studio, the original furniture all pushed back against one wall to allow for the introduction of an easel and a taboret. But otherwise the room was very tidy. Rolls of canvas were stacked neatly in a corner, and drawing pads and various supplies were arranged on the bookshelves. A few landscape oils were leaning against one wall, and there was another on the easel standing by the window. The taboret held a paint-smeared palette, a few cans of turpentine and dryer, and various vases, mugs, and old coffee cans, all filled with brushes. On the chair by the easel lay a large paint-covered rag, and there were various daubs decorating the chair and easel itself, but other than that there was no evidence of the chaos usually associated with the creative spirit.

The landscapes, to Bethancourt's eye, were rather uninspired, despite a very capable technique. But peeking out from behind one of the landscapes leaning against the wall was part of a face, so lively in its execution that he wished he could see the whole thing.

"Come through to the kitchen," said Towser. "I do most of my lounging there—as you can see, there's nowhere to sit in here."

The kitchen was roomy, and by the fireplace were two elderly armchairs. Towser waved his guests toward these, and brought up an upright wooden chair from the table for himself.

"Shocking about Charlie," he said. "I expect that's what you've come about."

Gibbons admitted that this was so.

"I didn't know him terribly well," said Towser. "I've only been here since September, but I liked him. He told a good story."

"I understand you're only here temporarily, Mr. Towser?" asked Gibbons.

"Yes. I've let this place 'til the end of the month. I have a studio in London, where I mostly paint portraits. I was getting stale, so I came down here to try my hand at landscapes. I waited 'til the end of summer to come so as to avoid all the rest of the artists."

"So you've painted no portraits since you came here?" asked Bethancourt.

"Well," said the artist, rubbing his chin thoughtfully, "I wouldn't exactly say that. I haven't done any proper portraits, but I've done sketches of people. I did one of Charlie, as a matter of fact. He had a very interesting face. Here, I'll show you."

He jumped up and trotted into the other room, returning in a moment with a small canvas.

"It's just a sketch," he said, propping it against the mantelpiece. "I hadn't really finished it or anything."

They peered at the portrait with interest. It was just a head, showing a man with twinkling blue eyes, his face tanned and lined from outdoor living, but still retaining a youthful expression. He had not been handsome, but the face was an attractive one.

"That's marvelously done," said Bethancourt, and Towser shrugged.

"You had never met him until you came here?" asked Gibbons.

"No. He was a friendly sort, though. It wasn't long before we were trooping off to the pub together."

"When was the last time you saw him?" asked Gibbons.

"Saturday night at the Deer and Hounds," he replied promptly. "We went down together after dinner and walked back after closing. I said good night to him at his place and came along home."

"I see," said Gibbons. "Now, can you tell me how you spent Sunday?"

The question seemed to surprise Towser, but he answered readily enough. "I went out early," he said, "and did a painting up in the hills. I can show it to you if you like, although there's nothing to prove it was done on Sunday. I got back here in the late afternoon and had an early supper and then went down to the pub. I did pass Charlie's place on the way, but his car was out, so I didn't stop."

"About what time was this?"

"Getting on for five o'clock, I should think. I came away at about half six and spent the evening working on the painting I'd done earlier. That's it, I'm afraid. I took a book to bed and went to sleep early."

"So you saw no one that evening?"

"Not after I left the pub. I can prove I was there—the landlord knows me, and I chatted for a bit with Leandra Tothill. She left just before I did." He said it matter-of-factly, not defensively at all.

"When you returned from the pub," continued Gibbons, "did you notice whether Mr. Bingham's car had returned?"

Towser thought for a moment. "I wasn't paying attention at the time," he said. "But I cut through his garden and, no, it wasn't there."

"You came through his garden" asked Gibbons, surprised. "You were on foot?"

"Why, yes, I nearly always walk. There's a footpath here that cuts through the woods and meets the road at Charlie's place. It's much shorter than going 'round by the road. It runs up to the old farmhouse at this end, meeting up with the towpath by the lake."

"Lake?"

"Well, I suppose it's more of a pond, really. It's just over the hill, up by the farmhouse."

"I see," said Gibbons. "Getting back to Mr. Bingham, sir, were you aware he had a girlfriend?"

Towser looked amused. "I rather suspected he did," he answered, "but I don't know who she was, if that's what you're asking."

"What made you think he was seeing someone then?"

"The way he'd go off every so often, without a word to anyone. If you asked where he'd been, he'd just say he'd had a little business in London to take care of. I suppose Peg Eberhart put it into my head, really. She's mentioned Charlie's mystery lady, but I don't think she knew who it was, either. All anybody knew was she wasn't in the neighborhood. He always took his car, you see, and if it had been anyone around here, someone would have been bound to spot it."

"That's so," agreed Gibbons. "Any idea about why he kept it so quiet?"

Towser grinned. "I can think up lots of reasons," he said. "Beginning with the fact that women are sometimes married, or not quite respectable, or much younger than oneself, or sensitive about their reputations. But as for which was true in Charlie's case, I haven't a clue. He simply wouldn't discuss it, and the only woman I ever heard him mention was his daughter."

Towser really had nothing more to tell them, and they took their leave, thanking him for his time.

"He wasn't very helpful," remarked Bethancourt as he slid behind the wheel of the Jaguar.

"We didn't expect him to be," answered Gibbons. "Still, you never know—he might have noticed something that night. And he might have moved Bingham's body, although he couldn't have fed him the Seconal, not if he didn't leave the pub 'til half six."

"Surely whoever did one did the other," said Bethancourt.

"Probably," admitted Gibbons. "Here, if we go on up the lane, we'll come out at the farmhouse."

Bethancourt obediently reversed the car and drove slowly up the hill. As they crested it, they could see the pond Towser had mentioned, below them and to the left. The meadow ran down to it from the lane, but on the farther side, trees grew close to the banks and Gibbons observed that the farm property probably stopped there.

The lane curved away from the pond, leaving the trees behind, and ran up to the farmhouse, standing on higher ground. It was a large, gracefully proportioned house, built like the cottages of limestone and dating, like them, from the eighteenth century. The lane ran past the front door and on to some barns visible in the distance. Bethancourt drew the Jaguar to a halt and the two men got out.

Mrs. Potts answered their knock at the front door and her kindly smile broke over her otherwise stern features.

"Hello," she said. "We thought you'd be here rather earlier, Sergeant Gibbons. And you've brought Mr. Bethancourt with you."

"I'm sorry," Gibbons apologized. "We had some other people to see first. Miss Bingham arrived last night."

"Did she, poor girl? Mr. Bethancourt, your dog won't chase the cat, will he?"

"Not a bit of it, Mrs. Potts," Bethancourt assured her. "But he can wait outside, if you'd rather."

"No, no, bring him in. We like animals here. So Miss Bingham's arrived, eh? It must have been a terrible shock to her, for all I gather they didn't see much of each other."

Gibbons replied that she seemed to be coping as well as could be expected.

"Well, I expect it's not as if he'd been a real father to her," said Mrs. Potts, looking stern again as she led them into the parlor. "It does make a difference, and nobody knows that better than me. My twins, they're fond enough of their mother, but they've never had much to do with her from the time they were small, and I don't suppose it's unfair to say that they'd be sorrier to see me go than her, for all we're no real relation."

"That's understandable," agreed Bethancourt, taking the seat she indicated with a hospitable wave of her hand, "since you took on the role of mother while Miss Bonnar was playing other parts."

Mrs. Potts smiled at him. "That's a clever way of putting it," she said, "and true enough. Miss Bonnar hired me when the children were just five. She'd been divorced about two years by then and they were getting too old to be dragged about with her all the time. Besides, she'd married Eugene Sinclair by then, and I don't think he was keen on children. At any rate, they never had any all those years they were married. And when I told her the twins needed to be settled somewhere regular, she was more than happy enough to pack us off down here." Mrs. Potts's long face had taken on a thoroughly disapproving expression. "Miss Bonnar is a lovely lady, and she's always been good to me, but she hasn't a maternal bone in her body, and what she ever meant by having children in the first place, I can't imagine."

"Did their father visit much?" asked Bethancourt, ignoring Gibbons's impatient look.

"No—he was dead by the time I came around. Committed suicide a year or so after Miss Bonnar left him. They say he couldn't live without her, but that's just romantic bilgewater from the tabloids."

"Hello!" Julie Benson was standing in the doorway, clad in jeans and a sweater with her long hair braided down her back. "I thought I heard voices. James!" she called, turning. "It *is* Scotland Yard this time. You'd better come down. We've been waiting for you all morning," she continued, coming into the room, "and running downstairs every time we heard someone coming. In a village like this, one doesn't get the opportunity of being grilled by Scotland Yard every day, you know."

Gibbons murmured apologies, while Mrs. Potts said, "Eve Bingham arrived last night, dear, and they stopped to see her first."

"Oh, she's come, has she?" asked Julie, sitting down. "Look, here's James."

He greeted them politely, albeit with less enthusiasm than the female members of the household, and seated himself next to his sister on the sofa.

"Well, we're all set, then," said Julie. "What can we tell you?"

"First of all," said Gibbons, "I'd like to know when you last saw Mr. Bingham."

"Saturday night at the Deer and Hounds," responded James. "I was playing darts there after supper and I saw him with Derek. We chatted a bit."

"Were you with your brother, Miss Benson?"

"No. I saw Charlie last Thursday or Friday when I was taking a walk about the lake. I'm really not sure which day it was—it's a walk I take fairly frequently."

"And I saw him at the market on Saturday," put in Mrs. Potts. "I didn't speak to him, but I saw him there."

Gibbons nodded. "Then if you could tell me how you all spent Sunday, just as a matter of form."

"We all went to church for a start," answered Julie. "Martha here had a bit of a cold, so she sat with us instead of with the choir. Afterward we came home for lunch, and then Martha took off in the Volvo for Somerset."

"To visit my sister," explained Mrs. Potts. "I go once a month or so, always on Sunday afternoon so as not to miss church."

"And when did you return?" asked Gibbons.

"Early Tuesday morning. I can give you my sister's address if you like."

Gibbons noted this information down and turned his attention back to the twins.

"We went riding in the afternoon," Julie told him. "It was a glorious day. We came back about five, had an early supper, and then played a game of Scrabble. Afterward, we felt the need of stimulation and adventure and went out to a pub. Not the Deer and Hounds—that was the adventure part—we went off to Lower Oddington and the Kestrel Inn."

"What time was that?"

"Oh, it must have been about eight, isn't that right, James? And we stayed 'til closing."

"So you didn't pass the cottages on your way back?"

"No—we came from the other direction."

Gibbons nodded. "That's clear," he said. "What did you think of Mr. Bingham?"

"He was pleasant enough," said Mrs. Potts. "A very friendly sort of man."

"He came to tea and things a few times," amplified Julie. "I always found him rather amusing."

"We all did," said Mrs. Potts. "He even got on with Miss Bonnar, which is unusual."

"That's right," agreed Julie. "We were a bit taken aback last spring when she arrived unexpectedly and then Charlie dropped 'round for a drink. But it all went off very well."

Bethancourt was leaning back in his chair and smoking, a little bored by this recitation of facts. It was quite unusual, he reflected, for a murdered man to be so generally well-liked. And yet he had thus far noticed nothing in anyone's manner that hinted at insincerity.

"When did you hear that Mr. Bingham had died?" Gibbons was asking.

"Not 'til Tuesday morning," answered Julie. "Quite behind the times, we were."

"It was because of going to look at a horse," explained James. "It was all the way up in the Lake District."

"It was supposed to be a good dressage prospect," said Julie. "Only it turned out to be nothing of the sort. A wasted trip, really. Anyway, we didn't get back until late and didn't get the news 'til Bob came up with the post the next morning. And of course Marty didn't hear until she came home in the afternoon."

"It was a shock," said Mrs. Potts. "And then of course Constable Stikes came 'round that afternoon and said it was murder, so we got a second shock."

"Very upsetting," murmured Gibbons. "I think that brings me to my last question. Were any of you aware that Mr. Bingham had a girlfriend?"

"Girlfriend?" repeated James. "Well, I must say it never crossed my mind, one way or another. Who was it?"

"We don't know at present," said Gibbons, "but there certainly was one. I take it you, Miss Benson, and you, Mrs. Potts, didn't suspect, either? Women are sometimes more sensitive to these things."

They both shook their heads.

"He used to chat up Leandra Tothill down at the pub," offered Julie.

Mrs. Potts was shocked. "Julie!" she said. "How dare you make such an insinuation about the vicar's wife?"

"Well, everybody knows the kind of life she led in London before—"

"Julie! I will not hear such talk."

Mrs. Potts's was the voice of command and Julie subsided.

"Whatever," Mrs. Potts went on more composedly, "Leandra may or may not have done in the past, she has behaved with perfect propriety since she came here. And done a lot of people a lot of good, too."

"Yes, of course," said Julie.

"To return to Mr. Bingham," said Gibbons, "none of you ever noticed that he sometimes went away overnight?"

"I suppose he was sometimes gone," said James. "But if I ever noticed, I didn't think anything of it. Lots of people run up to town for a day or two."

"He was new here, you see," said Julie. "If someone mentioned that he was away, I just thought he'd gone to visit friends."

"A natural assumption," said Gibbons. "Well, thank you all very much. You've been very helpful."

Outside, Bethancourt turned the Jaguar and started back down the lane.

"Where to now?" he asked.

"High time for lunch," grunted Gibbons.

"I suppose you have a particular place in mind? Like a pub called the Kestrel?"

"Well," said Gibbons, "we might as well get it over with. It's probably pointless, but these things have to be checked. After all, they've no alibi for the time of death, and only this pub visit for the moving of the body."

"Maybe they were in it together with Towser," said Bethancourt mischievously. "The Bensons doped him and then Towser drove the body home."

"It's perfectly possible," said Gibbons, "only there's no reason on earth any of them should. You want to turn left here, I think."

"There's a pub guide in the glove box," said Bethancourt. "Pull it out and see if this Kestrel place is in it. I warn you, if it's not, I'm not eating there, not unless it smells uncommonly good when we walk in."

"All right," grumbled Gibbons, opening the glove box and producing both the guide and an ordnance survey map. "I don't particularly want synthetic cottage pie for lunch, either, you know. No, we're safe after all—here it is."

"Are we going right?" asked Bethancourt, who was dawdling along the road while peering intently out of the window at the view to his right.

Gibbons consulted the map. "Yes," he said. "Lower Oddington is just past Stow." He glanced up and said sharply, "Phillip, you're going into the hedge."

"Am I? Sorry." Bethancourt peered in a surprised way through the windscreen and corrected this error. "There we are. We'll be in Stow in no time."

He had become accustomed, over the past weeks, to adding such pointless but upbeat remarks to his conversations with Gibbons. But now, glancing over at his friend, he was surprised to see he need not have bothered. Gibbons did not appear in need of cheering up; instead, he wore a thoughtful look as he said, "Didn't you think it was odd that the Bensons and Mrs. Potts hadn't heard of Bingham's mystery lady? There seems to have been quite a bit of speculation on the subject in the village, and gossip travels fast in a small place."

"A little odd," agreed Bethancourt, stepping on the gas and shifting into third gear. "Of course, it's less odd if they already knew all about it."

"What do you—Oh, no, you can't mean Martha Potts."

"Yes, I can. She's about the right size to fit into those clothes."

"But you said whoever bought them was rich."

"Joan Bonnar is rich—the clothes could have been a present from her or the twins. Or Bingham might have bought them for her himself."

"Possibly," admitted Gibbons. "She's pretty unattractive, though."

"And Bingham was an appealing fellow. There is that," agreed Bethancourt.

"But if it was Mrs. Potts," continued Gibbons, "what on earth would be the point of keeping it secret? She's not married."

"Perhaps they wanted to avoid village gossip. Anyway, it's only an idea."

Gibbons thought for a moment. "It would explain the clothes being there without anyone ever seeing the girlfriend. She could have come by the footpath with no one the wiser."

"That's why I thought of it in the first place," agreed Bethancourt. "But of course the whole notion is just a stab in the dark. It could be anybody. Jack," he added, changing up to fifth gear in a sudden burst of speed, "there's a roundabout coming up."

"Oh, Lord," said Gibbons, and bent over the map.

They ran into Lower Oddington without further difficulty, beyond a slight difference of opinion as to exactly where in Stow-on-the-Wold the A436 turned off. But once arrived, they found the Kestrel right on the High Street, housed in a venerable old building covered with ivy. It was clearly a prosperous business, with a recently redone interior, and a separate dining room in which there was plenty of customers despite its being the off-season.

Bethancourt, who as usual had eaten no breakfast, made a beeline for the dining room, leaving Gibbons to interview the landlord in the bar alone. This was an active-looking man of about forty-five who came over quickly to take Gibbons's order, but did not seem much put out when Gibbons showed his warrant card rather than asking for a pint.

"Ah," he said, "that business over in Chipping Chedding, is it?"

"That's right," answered Gibbons, tucking his wallet away. "It's only a matter of an alibi, if you can remember who was drinking here on the Sunday night."

The landlord immediately looked thoughtful. "Sundays are quiet," he said. "I doubt there were many here beyond my regulars. Now, let me see. Was that the night that couple came in? Or was that Monday?"

"Couple?" asked Gibbons. "What were they like?"

"Youngish and fairish," he answered at once. "The girl was putting on a bit of a show—bright red dress she had on, a bit too short and a bit too tight. And long hair, all the way down to her—well, below her waist." He grinned. "I remember that because she kept pushing it back behind her shoulders and it kept swinging back. She was doing her best, and her hair was nice, but she wasn't very pretty in truth."

"That sounds right," said Gibbons, leaning on the bar. "And the man with her?"

The landlord paused before he answered, frowning thoughtfully. "Fair chap, a little heavy," he said at last. "That's about all I noticed. I didn't see as much of him—it was the girl came up for the drinks."

Gibbons nodded. "Now," he said, "how sure are you that they were in on Sunday night?"

The publican eyed the ceiling thoughtfully. "It was a slow night, like I said," he replied, "but that could have been Monday. Wasn't last night or the night before, I know. No, it were Sunday right enough, I remember now. Because it was early closing night and Alf had one too many and wouldn't believe me when I called time. Them two left and I said to Alf, 'See, you're the only one here.'"

Gibbons thanked him and went to join Bethancourt in the dining room. He found his friend already well-launched into a filled baguette and a pint.

"You haven't wasted any time," said Gibbons reproachfully.

"I'm hungry. I did get you a pint of Hook Norton. It's very nice."

"Ta," said Gibbons, pulling out a chair and looking for the waitress. "What are you having?" he asked.

"Smoked chicken with rocket and tomato," answered Bethancourt around a mouthful. He chewed industriously and swallowed. "I highly recommend it."

"Good enough. Ah, there's the waitress."

Gibbons ordered and turned his attention to the pint of ale Bethancourt had got him, taking a long, deep pull.

"That is good," he said.

Bethancourt nodded agreement. "What happened in the bar?" he asked. "Did the landlord remember the Bensons?"

"He did indeed, and off his own bat, too, without any prompting from me," said Gibbons. "They were here until closing."

"Well, that's settled then." Bethancourt washed down a mouthful with his ale and dabbed at his lips with his napkin. "None of them up at the old farmhouse could have done it, not unless Martha Potts's sister is willing to lie for her."

"It's not very likely it was anyone in the village anyway," said Gibbons. "Although I admit I was hoping to get more of a line on exactly where Bingham went on Sunday and whom he might have seen. But unless the chief inspector comes up with something, it looks very much like I will be spending hours going over all the traffic photos taken on Sunday between here and London."

He sighed and took a glum swig from his pint.

"Well," said Bethancourt, seeing no way in which to make this prospect seem less deadly dull than in fact it was, "at least you don't have to do it yet. Where do we go from here?"

"Back to Stow-in-the-Wold," said Gibbons. "I want to stop at the station there and see if I can find Constable Stikes. And I must ring the chief inspector to tell him about Miss Bingham."

"Where is Carmichael today?"

"Went up to see Bingham's business partner. Name of Sealingham."

Andrew Sealingham was a large, prosperous-looking man of about sixty. He had a hearty, jovial manner, which, as he grew serious, turned into bluntness.

"Oh, yes," he confirmed, "Charlie was still a full partner, as his daughter is now. I haven't heard from Evie yet, though."

"She only arrived in England this morning," said Carmichael. "No doubt she'll contact you very soon. I take it you know her?"

"Haven't seen her since she was about fourteen," answered Sealingham. "But I knew her fairly well back then. She even spent a summer holiday or two with my family and me. We were close to the Binghams in those days."

Carmichael nodded. "You say Mr. Bingham was a full partner. But how much did he really have to do with the business?"

"Virtually nothing," said Sealingham cheerfully. "Never did, actually. This place was originally set up not only as a manufacturing plant, but as a place for Charlie to work on his inventions as well. Which he did, in the beginning. I was always the businessman—that's why Charlie hooked up with me to begin with. And, at the start, we pretty much pulled in double harness."

"But then he left the country."

"Exactly right." Sealingham paused, his eye falling on a photograph of a group of young children which was positioned prominently on his desk. "His wife's death hit him very hard. He stuck it out for a while, but then his sister convinced him to send Evie to that boarding school and after that there wasn't anything to hold him here. He was a brilliant man, you know. Could have turned his hand to anything, but he became interested in archaeology and off he went. He came back for Evie's school holidays at first, and we'd go over things together then. But the next thing I knew, instead of his coming back, she was going out, and we ended up communicating by telegram."

"That must have been frustrating for you."

"It certainly was. Most certainly was. Then Evie started growing up, Charlie went out east, and his response to my messages was 'Do as you think best.' So I did. For the last few years, I've been trying to buy him out, but he wouldn't have it. I don't know why. Then he turned up about a year ago, said he was coming back to England to live and thought he'd get involved in the business again. I wasn't half-pleased with that, I can tell you, not after so many years. But it never came to anything."

"Why was that?"

Sealingham chuckled. "Oh, I think it was clear enough. What's that book, *You Can't Never Go Home Again*? Well, it was like that. We were great friends in the old days, but I hardly recognized him when he showed up here. He came to our house for a weekend, but it didn't come off very well. We didn't know each other anymore, Chief Inspector, it's that plain and simple. Charlie wasn't a man to deceive himself; he saw it as clearly as I did."

Carmichael nodded. "Now that Eve Bingham has inherited her father's share in the company, will you try to buy her out?"

"Probably. I can't see her taking a real interest in the business."

"Well, that's all very clearly put, sir. I'm afraid I must ask you, just as a matter of routine, where you were last Sunday evening."

"At home," he replied with the air of a man whose life was an open book.

Upon Carmichael's asking for further details, however, he became rather blustery. People often did, Carmichael reflected, when the police showed an inclination to question even the most innocent parts of their private lives. But the chief inspector was far too old a hand to either offend or to come away without what he wanted. Gently, he extracted the information that Sealingham had spent the day playing golf, and had then returned home, eaten supper in front of the television and been in bed by ten thirty. There were no live-in servants, and his wife was away.

"Ann was down visiting Clara, one of our daughters. She's due to have her baby any day now. Clara, I mean, not Annie." He laughed.

Carmichael congratulated him on this forthcoming event, thanked him for his help, and departed.

He paused as he settled himself in the car, and pulled out his mobile phone. As expected, Gibbons had left a message while Carmichael had been speaking to Sealingham, and he punched in the sergeant's number as he started the car.

"How are you coming, lad?" he asked when Gibbons answered. "Finished with those interviews?"

"Yes, sir," answered Gibbons. "It's all much as we thought, except for one surprise. Eve Bingham was in London on Sunday night."

"What?"

"She had come over for a party on Saturday and didn't fly back 'til Monday. She spent Sunday night alone in her hotel room."

"My God, Gibbons."

"Yes, sir."

"I'm on my way back," said Carmichael. "We'll go over everything then."

"Right you are, sir," said Gibbons cheerfully.

Swearing, Carmichael rang off and started out with all possible speed for the motorway.

"Hold on," he said to himself, slacking his speed about a mile farther on. "What are you dashing about for, old man? Gibbons is a bright lad, and not one to get carried away. You should have faith in him to do his job. And," he added practically, "if I stop for lunch, I won't be descending on the poor lad all hungry and out of sorts."

There was, he remembered, a likely looking pub not too much farther on. He set out toward it at a moderate pace.

Gibbons returned to the police station to make some phone calls. It had been arranged that he could use Constable Stikes's office, which turned out to be little more than a cubbyhole furnished with a desk, complete with a phone and a computer, and two uncomfortable chairs. The window overlooked the car park.

Constable Stikes was out when they arrived, though the sergeant at the desk said she was expected back shortly.

"She's probably out detecting," said Gibbons gloomily, seating himself at the desk. "She's not a detective, but she seems quite taken with helping us out."

"Surely that's all to the good," said Bethancourt, shifting one of the hard, upright chairs so that he could sit with his feet propped up on the windowsill. Cerberus followed him, sitting and gazing out the window. "I mean, she knows everyone in the village."

"Yes, but she's overzealous if you ask me," said Gibbons, taking out his notebook and opening it on the desk.

"It's no good ringing St. Martin's Lane," he grumbled. "They'll never tell me over the phone whether Eve Bingham stayed there or not. I wonder if Carmichael will send me back—he seems determined to leave no stone unturned, although if you ask me it's all make-work until we find Bingham's girlfriend."

"I don't know about that," said Bethancourt, lighting a cigarette and exhaling slowly. "Doesn't it strike you that a case which appeared quite straightforward and hardly seemed to be a case at all is now getting more complicated with every fact we learn?"

Gibbons shrugged. "The simplest explanation is usually the right one," he reminded Bethancourt. "And if there's reason to keep a six-month affair quiet, there's probably a reason to kill to keep it so."

"There is that," agreed Bethancourt. "And yet, there is the money. When very rich men die, the money is so often the reason, and that's simple enough."

"True," sighed Gibbons. "And now that we know the heiress was in London on the night in question . . . well, I probably will have to go back and visit the hotel."

"If that's a hint that I should drive you, you can forget it," responded Bethancourt uncharitably. "Marla would have a fit. Oh, no, half a tic—I forgot."

"You forgot what?"

"She's got to go back tomorrow—she's flying out to Paris for another shoot. That's all right then. You can come with us, and I'll drive you back afterward."

"I don't know that Carmichael will send me yet," said Gibbons evasively. He had no desire to make a third with Bethancourt and Marla. The addition, he was certain, would not be welcome to her. "I'd better try the doctor again," he said, pulling the phone toward him. "I couldn't get him yesterday, or this morning."

"I thought you spoke to Dr. Cross."

"Not him," replied Gibbons, dialing. "This is the cardiologist Bingham saw in London, a Dr. Preston Loomis."

This time, he succeeded in actually speaking to the eminent doctor, who confirmed that Bingham had been a patient of his at one time and went on to refuse any further information, when in fact Gibbons had only been about to ask when the doctor would be available for an interview.

"You could be anybody," he said cheerfully, "anybody at all. You come 'round tomorrow with proper identification and I'll be happy to tell you all all about it. By then I may even remember it. Only," he added, "if it's going to take any time, you'd better come late, around five. Otherwise you'll put my appointments out, and I'll have patients howling at me all afternoon."

Gibbons promised that he or another policeman would be there tomorrow at five and rang off.

Bethancourt had abandoned his chair to perch on the windowsill and flick his cigarette ash out of the open casement. He had opened a small, leather-bound book and was smiling down at it.

"Marla's going to be in Paris for four days," he said.

"You keep her itinerary in your diary?" asked Gibbons.

"Yes. I started noting down when she would be gone last spring, after the charity ball debacle."

"What charity ball debacle?" said Gibbons.

"Oh, you remember." Bethancourt waved a hand. "I had taken tickets for the ball, only to find that Marla was spending that weekend working in Greece. Tickets to charity balls are expensive, so rather than waste them, I took my friend Claire. It was all perfectly innocent, but when Marla came back and found out about it, she was furious."

As far as Gibbons was concerned, Bethancourt and Marla were always having one row or another, and he had never bothered to keep track of them.

"Oh, yes," he said vaguely.

"In any case," continued Bethancourt, "I thought Marla, as she's going to be in Paris, might as well dig up what she can about Eve Bingham while she's there. Particularly anything about the visit Charlie paid her last year on his way home."

Gibbons stared at him incredulously. "And why would Marla do that?" he demanded. "She loathes murder investigations."

"Yes, but she's taken an interest in this one because of Eve," replied Bethancourt. "I think the idea that she might actually be acquainted with a murderer has been very unsettling for her. If I take the right tone, I'm sure I can get her to do it."

Gibbons shrugged. "Well, you needn't bother," he said. "The girlfriend is still our most likely suspect in any case. And Carmichael's already spoken to the Surete about Bingham's visit to his daughter."

"Not the same thing at all," said Bethancourt. "Nobody gossips to officers from the Surete. Whereas Marla might find out all sorts of interesting things. If you're wrong about the girlfriend and Eve did kill her father, then her relationship with him must be at the core of this case."

"*If* she killed him," said Gibbons, returning his attention to his list. "I suppose anything that sheds light on how she felt about him might give us a line to follow, but it won't prove anything one way or another."

"You can't solve a puzzle without all of the pieces," said Bethancourt, undeterred. He took a last puff of his cigarette and tossed the butt out the window. "Truly, I think we've become far too fixated on this mysterious woman. When you stop and think about it, nearly anyone might have killed him."

"Not anyone," protested Gibbons. "By all accounts, Bingham was well-liked in the community."

Bethancourt waved away this detail. "What about other family members?" he asked. "Were there any?"

"Bingham had a sister," said Gibbons, crossing out an item on his list, "but she's dead. There's a nephew in Lincoln."

"It would also be interesting to know who Eve Bingham left her fortune to."

"On the chance we've got a serial killer on our hands?" asked Gibbons sarcastically. "Anyway, most of the money and investments are Eve's already."

"But our killer might not realize that," said Bethancourt. "And it doesn't have to be a serial killer—he could be planning to marry her."

"Marla might know if Eve is planning to get married," said Gibbons, retuning his attention to his notebook.

"She might at that," said Bethancourt. "Or at least she might find out while she's in Paris."

They were interrupted by the entrance of Constable Stikes, who smiled broadly when she saw them.

"There you are, sir," she said. "I've found that garage you wanted."

"Garage?" asked Gibbons.

"Yes, sir. Where Mr. Bingham got his tire repaired. The chief inspector mentioned it this morning."

"Oh, yes," said Gibbons, who had clearly had no idea she intended following up on this lead. "Well, that's good work, Constable. You'll have to write up a report for the case file, but you can just give me the gist now."

"Of course, sir," said the constable, leaning comfortably against the doorjamb. "It's a place out on the A40. Mike Nelson is the chap's name. He's closed Sundays, but his house is close by the garage, and Bingham pulled in before teatime on Sunday. Three thirty is as close as Nelson can come to the time, though I would put it a bit earlier if Bingham drove straight there."

Gibbons raised an eyebrow. "Even allowing time for him to discover the puncture, pull over, and have a look himself?"

"Yes, sir," said the constable, straightening just a little. "Not much earlier, mind you."

Gibbons nodded and waved a hand. "Go on then."

"Right, sir. There was a nail in the right front tire, and Nelson helped Bingham get it off and they patched it up together. There wasn't a spare. Nelson says he never saw Bingham before that, at least not that he can remember, but he was impressed with how he knew what to do. Bingham apologized for getting him out on a Sunday, and said he could fix it himself, if Nelson would just let him have the use of his tools, but Nelson's a careful bloke and stuck with him. Says it took them close on an hour from the time Bingham pulled in to when he left, maybe a bit less."

"That ties up beautifully," said Gibbons. "The scene-of-the-crime men found a few nails scattered in the road just at Bingham's cottage. He could easily have picked it up there. I don't suppose Nelson kept the nail?"

"No, sir."

"It might explain the bicycle, too," put in Bethancourt. "You know, the marks they found by the hedge. Someone could have picked up a nail in their bicycle tire, stashed the machine in the hedge, and gone on, picking the bike up again on their way back."

"That's true," said Gibbons thoughtfully. "We've been assuming that it was the murderer's—that he drove Bingham's car back and used the bicycle to get away. But you could certainly be right, and it might have nothing to do with the murder at all." He paused a moment and then retuned his attention to the constable. "You say Nelson's place is on the A40? That would mean Bingham was heading toward London, wouldn't it?"

"Yes, sir. That's the way most people take."

"Well, thank you very much, Constable. I'll let the chief inspector know as soon as I hear from him, and—" He broke off at the sound of the telephone. "That's probably him now."

Stikes nodded and, with considerable tact, wandered out again. She was clearly enjoying this departure from her daily routine, and Bethancourt was betting that she had stopped just outside the door, out of sight, but not out of earshot.

"Gibbons here . . . oh, Marla, hello." He raised inquiring eyebrows at Bethancourt, who jumped to his feet at the sound of his girlfriend's name and began to make hasty denial gestures, pointing repeatedly to the door. "No, I'm afraid he's left already," said Gibbons smoothly.

"I'll ring you later about tomorrow," hissed Bethancourt, edging toward the door.

"He said he was going back to the manor," said Gibbons into the phone. "He left a few minutes ago."

He nodded and waved at his friend as Bethancourt, calling his dog to heel, disappeared.

CHAPTER

7

*T*hursday nights in Chipping Chedding were reserved for the meetings of the Women's Institute. This meant that on Thursday night Astley-Cooper was forced to cook his own dinner, since both his cook, Mrs. Cummins, and his housekeeper, Mrs. Leggett, were stalwart members of the WI. Not that Astley-Cooper minded. Mrs. Cummins was an excellent cook, but confined herself to good, basic English food, while Astley-Cooper had occasional cravings for more exotic fare, a taste he had developed during his misspent youth in London. Thursdays, therefore, were his night for experimenting.

Tonight, in honor of his guests, he was experimenting with Beef Tenderloin en Chemise Strabougeoise, as his cookbook termed it, although, as he confided to his guests, he rather thought it was beef Wellington himself. Bethancourt, a fine cook in his own right, thought it was ambitious. Marla, eyeing the ingredients suspiciously, thought with resignation that one meal, however large, was hardly likely to spoil her figure. Marla's own cooking seldom advanced beyond scrambled eggs, but she had, in deference to the do-it-yourself atmosphere prevailing in the kitchen, tied a towel around her waist to protect her jade-green satin lounge suit.

Bethancourt poured out some of the fine wine he had purchased to augment this repast, while casting a dubious eye on Astley-Cooper's ministrations to the filet of beef with a brandy-soaked tea towel.

"Here you are, my love," he said, handing Marla her glass. "Uh, I'll just put yours over here, out of the way, Clarence," he added.

"Right!" said Astley-Cooper, cheerfully brandishing a large knife. "Thank you, Phillip. Now then, I'll just slice this lovely filet into six equal parts."

"You're cutting it up?" Bethancourt was alarmed.

"No, no; you don't slice all the way through," said Astley-Cooper confidently and obscurely. "Perhaps you and Marla wouldn't mind just spreading a little foie gras on that ham over there."

"Ham?" said Bethancourt wildly. He could not recollect ham ever having played a major part in the beef Wellingtons he had previously consumed.

"Ham," repeated Astley-Cooper firmly. "I'll need five thin slices."

"Oh, yes," said Bethancourt. Behind his glasses, his eyes looked doubtful. "I'll slice, Marla, and you can spread."

Marla, perfectly content that this was not beyond her culinary capacities, obediently joined him at the counter.

"How was Eve today?" asked Bethancourt, slicing capably.

"Fine," answered Marla. "Better than I expected, actually. Considering the circumstances, she seemed quite cheery."

"Well, I gather she and her father weren't close, which makes a difference. You were wrong, by the way; she came without an entourage."

"Yes," said Marla reflectively. "I was rather surprised about that."

"I do hope," said Astley-Cooper, "that you invited her to dinner. It must be difficult for her, all alone. Good job you happened to be here."

"I did invite her," said Marla, licking a pâté-smeared finger, "but she begged off. She was awfully tired, having been up most of last night."

"Is she staying in the cottage?"

Marla laughed. "It's hardly up to her standard, is it? Frankly, she was appalled. No, she's staying at a hotel over in Cheltenham."

"It's really quite a nice cottage," said Astley-Cooper, glancing about his own huge, seventeenth-century kitchen. The fireplace hood was considered particularly fine, and his gaze rested balefully upon it for a moment. "I'm ready for that ham any time."

"I suppose it is," said Marla, answering his first thought. "But Eve is one of those people who consider anything less than luxury in bad taste." She carefully picked up the ham slices, liberally smeared with foie gras, and transported them to her host.

"Thank you, my dear," he said absently. "Well, probably that's what it's like to be truly rich. Here, Marla, if you could just hold the filet while I wrestle this ham into the slits I've made."

"Phillip's truly rich," said Marla, "and he's not like that."

"I am not," replied Bethancourt, who was letting Cerberus lick the pâté off his fingers, "as rich as Eve Bingham. Nor do I find her sort of lifestyle very tempting." He leaned back with his wine and watched in fascination while Astley-Cooper recklessly hacked off the edges of the ham that were left exposed outside the filet.

Marla had backed away from Astley-Cooper and his knife, which was flailing rather dramatically. "And you must be rich yourself," she said to him, kneeling to let Cerberus have a turn at her fingers.

"Nonsense," replied Astley-Cooper. "Whatever gave you that idea?"

"Well, this house and all."

Astley-Cooper looked immediately depressed. "This house," he said, "would be a drain on anyone's resources. It's no wonder I haven't any money left. It's a miracle the bloody thing is still standing. 'Built to last,' indeed!" He snorted.

"You've missed a bit," said Bethancourt, pointing at the filet.

"Ah, yes." Astley-Cooper attacked the offending piece of ham, which seemed to restore his good cheer.

"Getting back to Eve Bingham," said Bethancourt, "is she seeing anyone, do you know, Marla?"

"Three or four that I've heard of."

"But no one serious? Not contemplating marriage or anything of that sort?"

"Goodness, no. She spreads her favors around where it amuses her, that's all. So far as I've heard, no one's managed to amuse her for very long."

"Running with the wrong crowd," remarked Astley-Cooper. "What people like that need is stability—oh, dear."

"What is it?" asked Bethancourt, moving forward.

Astley-Cooper had stepped back from the counter and was gazing dolefully at his creation. "They say to reshape the filet, but it won't reshape; it's gaping."

Gaping, Bethancourt thought, described it very well.

"String," he said succinctly.

"What a marvelous idea. I wonder where Mrs. Cummins keeps it."

This involved a rummaging through all the kitchen drawers, which were numerous. Bethancourt, glancing at his watch, decided that dinner could not possibly be ready before half ten, and was thankful that he had bought three bottles of wine. He poured himself another glass.

It was Marla who eventually found the string. Astley-Cooper cut off about four yards and proceeded to tie up the meat in as many directions as possible. Bethancourt, amazed, hovered nearby to watch.

"There!" exclaimed Astley-Cooper, surveying his handiwork. "Now, we'll just pop it in the oven for exactly . . ." he consulted his cookbook, "twelve minutes. It says to baste frequently. Phillip, can you take care of that while I just roll out this pastry dough? There's some beef stock in the refrigerator."

Bethancourt basted while Astley-Cooper exuberantly covered the counter in flour and began to roll out the dough. Once he glanced suspiciously at Bethancourt, who had sat down at the table and was lighting a cigarette.

"It says to baste frequently, Phillip," he said reproachfully.

"Frequently does not mean constantly," retorted Bethancourt. "Really, Clarence, if I don't leave it alone part of the time, it'll never cook properly."

"Yes, well, there is that, I suppose." Astley-Cooper flourished his rolling pin. "So," he said, rolling industriously, "why all the questions about Eve Bingham? Do you think she murdered her father?"

"I don't know," replied Bethancourt equably.

"Phillip," said Marla sharply, "you can't possibly think—why, he was her only family, for God's sake."

"By her own admission, she barely knew him," said Bethancourt.

"That doesn't mean she killed him."

"No, it doesn't. I didn't say that it did." He rose. "Twelve minutes are up."

"Perfect timing," said Astley-Cooper. "I've just finished the dough. My, doesn't it look lovely. Now, all we need do is slap a layer of foie gras over the filet and pop it into the dough."

"Um," said Bethancourt diffidently, "don't you think we'd better take the string off first?"

"Oh, yes—I'd forgotten it."

It took several minutes of silent struggle to remove the vast web of string, but at last it was done, with only minimal damage to the filet, and Astley-Copper and Bethancourt began coating it with the pate.

"I say," said Astley-Cooper after a moment, "it doesn't stick very well, does it?"

"It's supposed to be a thin layer," replied Bethancourt, doggedly spreading. "I think we just have to go more carefully."

Careful was not a term descriptive of Astley-Cooper's method of cookery. It was quite some time before the filet was appropriately coated. They shifted it over to where the dough lay, and Astley-Cooper began folding the pastry around it and muttering to himself.

"Phillip," whispered Marla, "what about things to go with? Vegetables, I mean."

"He's probably forgotten," Bethancourt whispered back. "I'll try and bring it up tactfully once the thing's in the oven."

Marla nodded. "I'm awfully hungry," she said wistfully.

"Have some more wine."

"Phillip," called Astley-Cooper, "do you think you could help with this? It doesn't seem to be going awfully well."

Bethancourt sighed. "I know absolutely nothing about wrapping beef in pastry," he said.

"Well, neither do I," retorted Astley-Cooper.

Bethancourt went to help.

"Perhaps," he said, picking gingerly at the dough, "Marla should start on the vegetables or whatever while we're working on this."

"Oh, Lord," said Astley-Cooper. "I always forget. Well, there's probably a packet of frozen peas in the freezer."

Marla pronounced herself capable of dealing with frozen peas. She cast an extremely doubtful eye at the dough-encased filet as it was conveyed to the oven. One slender eyebrow rose.

"I hope it's edible," she muttered.

In the event, it was not too bad. The pastry was, admittedly, rather soggy, but the beef itself was tasty enough, and Marla had done an admirable job with the frozen peas. Of course, they were all a little drunk by the time it was served which, as Bethancourt later remarked to Marla, probably helped.

Gibbons and Carmichael had a less elaborate but timelier meal at the pub.

"You did well today, lad," said the chief inspector. "Very well indeed. Tactfully handled."

"Thank you, sir," replied Gibbons, pleased. "I don't know as it really gets us much further forward, though."

"Well, now, I don't know about that, lad." Carmichael swallowed the last bite of his steak-and-kidney pie and pushed the plate aside. "It's true it looks more like accident than murder," he said thoughtfully. "And I won't be convinced it's not until we find Bingham's girlfriend with a cast-iron alibi."

"Just so, sir," said Gibbons.

"But," and Carmichael held up a cautionary finger, "my instincts are beginning to stir, Sergeant. I don't think this case is going to turn out to be as simple as we thought."

Gibbons considered this.

"It's true that the more we find out, the more complications there seem to be," he said.

Carmichael pulled out a cigar and bent to light it. He smoked meditatively for several minutes while Gibbons finished his meal and drank off the last of his pint.

"I think we had better do a bit of digging," Carmichael said at last. "Let's assume, for the moment, that Bingham was very cleverly murdered, the whole thing set up to look natural, or at least like an accident. We've no idea about the girlfriend, but Andrew Sealingham is nobody's fool, and according to her solicitors, neither is Eve Bingham."

He raised a brow in question.

"No, sir," agreed Gibbons. "She has brains, even if she sometimes seems not to use them."

Carmichael nodded, and paused a moment, thinking it through.

"Constable Stikes has finished compiling her list of possible tourists Bingham might be dating," he said.

"That was quick work, sir."

"Indeed. Very industrious, our constable. She's put the women who live in and around London at the top of the list. I'm thinking we can leave it to our colleagues at the Yard to check up on them while we tie up all the rest of the loose ends and see how our suspects look after that."

"Yes, sir," said Gibbons. "Will you want me to check up on St. Martin's Lane then?"

"I think so," answered Carmichael. He blew out a stream of smoke, aiming it toward the raftered ceiling. "But it might be a good idea to keep an eye on Miss Bingham in the meantime. She may have been estranged from her father, the money gives her a solid motive, and she certainly had the opportunity. I think, Sergeant, you might pay another visit to Miss Bingham tonight. Bethancourt's idea makes a good excuse; you can ask her who her beneficiary is and whether or not she's planning to marry. And meanwhile you can see if the penny's dropped about her lack of alibi, as well as putting her on notice that the police have their eye on her."

Gibbons was surprised.

"Certainly, sir. Won't you be coming along?"

Carmichael lit his cigar. "No, no, I think this has all worked out for the best. We can save the big, bad chief inspector for later if she turns into our prime suspect. Then I can go along and try to be intimidating."

"That makes sense," agreed Gibbons. "After all, we may find tomorrow that she's got a cast-iron alibi at that hotel in London."

"We may, we may. Have a coffee before you go, Gibbons. It's early yet."

So Gibbons had his coffee and then drove into Cheltenham alone. Queen's Hotel sat at the edge of the Imperial Gardens, a large, gracious building of Victorian vintage which Gibbons found without difficulty. He announced himself at the front desk and then ascended to Eve Bingham's suite, one on an upper floor with a view looking over the gardens. The curtains were open when Gibbons came in, but there was not much to see in the dark.

Eve's brisk, businesslike attitude of the morning had changed; she looked utterly weary, but invited him in politely enough.

"I'm having a nightcap," she told him. "Won't you join me?"

"Thank you," said Gibbons, divesting himself of his raincoat.

He followed her over to the windows where there was an arrangement of two easy chairs and a table. This room was the sitting room; the doorways to the bathroom and bedroom stood ajar on the farther wall.

Eve motioned to one of the chairs while she poured generously from a bottle of twenty-four-year-old single malt scotch. Gibbons sat and took up the glass she pushed toward him, waiting until she had seated herself before raising it and saying, "Cheers." He sipped judiciously and added, "That's very good."

Eve shrugged and set her own glass down, empty. She was wrapped in a heavy silk dressing gown and she smoothed the fabric over her knees, tracing the embroidered pattern over and over again with her fingers.

"I expect the fact that you're having a drink with me means you haven't come to arrest me?" she said, her attention still fastened on her knees.

Clearly, Gibbons thought, the penny had indeed dropped about her lack of alibi.

"No," he answered, "I haven't. I've only come to ask you one or two more questions."

"You keep long hours, Inspector." She poured another measure into her glass and this time sipped it. "Do you like good whisky, then?"

"I'm a sergeant, Miss. Yes, I do."

She glanced sideways at him, half-smiling. "But I suppose you can't afford it often?"

Gibbons's ears perked up; this sounded remarkably like the beginning of a bribe. "No," he said ruefully. "Only now and then, as a treat."

"And what would be your favorite?"

"I like the Islay malts. Lagavulin or Laphroaig," he answered, loyal to the whiskies to which Bethancourt had introduced him and which they often drank together. He waited for her to imply—subtly, of course—that in the near future he might be able to afford all the Lagavulin he liked.

She leaned back and lit a cigarette. "Laphroaig," she murmured. "Yes, that's very good. Rich and smoky, as I remember it."

"Yes, it has a distinctive taste."

He was still waiting, but she disappointed him.

"I'll have to try it again sometime," she said. Then, in a bitter tone as she glanced at the half-empty bottle on the table, "Maybe tomorrow. Bottles don't seem to be lasting very long these days."

Gibbons relaxed, realizing he had misread her. She was not about to bribe him, she was only making conversation, any sort of conversation, to avoid the topic he had come about. He had seen people do it many times before, had seen the understandable reluctance to have a tender spot touched, but he had not expected it of her. She had seemed so unmoved about her father's death that morning. Bethancourt, had he been there, would have told him that in the morning she had been prepared for their visit, whereas now she was not. Gibbons merely wondered if she had a different motive for avoiding the topic.

He drank a little more of the whisky and said, "Well, I don't want to keep you up, Miss. If you—"

"Keep me up?" she echoed. "I doubt I shall be sleeping any time soon, Sergeant."

"You might," he said gently, although in the back of his mind he was desperately curious as to whether it was guilt or grief that was keeping her up. "You try a hot bath after I've gone. That and a drink usually work."

"Perhaps," she answered listlessly. "You know, I've just been thinking how funny life is. We must be about the same age, and yet we couldn't be more different. You have a real job, a career, and I've never done anything at all."

"You didn't have to," replied Gibbons. "I might not have got a job, either, if I didn't need one."

"But you have an interest, you see. I mean, you must. You're not stupid—you could have done anything, but you chose the police. You must find the work interesting, or you wouldn't have chosen it. Whereas if I lost all my money tomorrow, I haven't a notion of what I might like to do."

Her mood was a curious one, and Gibbons was not certain how to respond to it. Her life was one of luxury and comfort and glamour; he did not think she could seriously be regretting it.

"It would be different," he said, "if you had grown up knowing you would have to earn your living, and support a family one day. You would have spent your time in school looking at careers, thinking about what would suit you best. It doesn't come on you all at once."

"I suppose not." She frowned a little.

"Now, then," said Gibbons in his best police manner. "I've only got a couple of questions here, Miss Bingham. The first is: how have you left your money?"

"Left it?" she asked, puzzled.

"Yes, in your will."

"Oh," she said, immediately losing interest. "Much as my father did, if I should predecease him."

"Could you tell me exactly how that is?"

She stabbed out her cigarette in the ashtray. "Well, let's see," she said. "The patents and most of the capital goes to Christopher."

"That would be Christopher Macklin?"

"Yes, my cousin—my father's sister's son."

"I see. Is he your only relative, by the way?"

"Yes," she said briefly. "My mother was an only child."

"And do you keep in touch with Mr. Macklin?"

She laughed and took another sip of her drink. "Not in years. I don't even have his address. In Lincoln somewhere, I think. The solicitors know."

"Very well. If you could go on with the other terms of the will, please."

"Hmmm." She refilled her glass. "The stocks and company profits go back to Uncle Andrew, of course."

"That would be your father's business partner?"

"Yes—and I haven't seen him in years, either. The rest goes to various charities and there are a few small bequests. I don't think I can rattle those off the top of my head, although I remember there are a couple to archeologists my father knew, and I've put in one for my maid."

"A large one?"

She shrugged. "Enough to make her comfortable. Five hundred thousand pounds or so."

"Do any of these people know about their bequests?"

"Oh, I don't think so. The archeologists aren't really likely to get anything unless I die very young—they're all much older than I. But they'll receive the bequests my father left them once his will goes through probate. I left them in my will because, well, I thought they might as well have it if I go early. My maid certainly doesn't know, although I'm sure she hopes. Even Christopher isn't sure what if anything he'll come in for. Uncle Andrew is the only one who knows what he'll get. He was very worried I might leave my shares to someone zany." A smile touched her lips.

"Thank you," said Gibbons. "That's very clear."

She looked at him curiously. "I can't see what it matters," she said. "Not unless you think someone's planned a double murder. Shall I hire a bodyguard, Sergeant?"

"I hardly think that will be necessary," said Gibbons with a smile. "But you'll understand that we have to investigate every possibility, no matter how remote."

"How dull for you," she remarked sympathetically.

"Sometimes," he replied. "The next few questions are rather personal, and I want to assure you your answers will be kept in confidence. Do you take any prescription medications?"

She lifted an eyebrow. "Like sleeping pills?" she said. "No, I don't.

If I had such a thing, I would hardly be resorting to this." And she waved a hand at the whisky bottle.

Gibbons smiled and nodded, though he had no intention of taking her word for it. "I'd also like to know," he continued, "if you are even remotely considering marriage to anyone?"

She laughed, truly amused. "Not unless you're going to ask me, Sergeant," she said.

Her humor fell flat, although Gibbons tried to hide it. He had, in fact, asked a murder suspect to marry him, and not so very long ago. It had not turned out well. He summoned up a rather anemic smile and said, "I think that would be most inappropriate under the circumstances."

"Yes, I thought you would. What's this other personal question?"

"It's one I really can't expect you to answer," he said earnestly, "but I can urge you to seriously consider it before you hide something. Is there anything at all in your past that anyone could possibly blackmail you about? Even something you think no one else knows? I can assure you," he added, "that even if this information led to the discovery of your father's killer, we would do our best to see it did not come out in open court."

"There's nothing," she said immediately, seriously. "Really and truly nothing, Sergeant. I admit I've done things in my life I'm ashamed of, but unfortunately those things are only too well known to a number of people. And there's nothing else. Nothing illegal, I assure you."

Gibbons had not thought there would be. Her life was only too well-covered by the tabloids. It would be a miracle if she had managed to keep anything really juicy from them.

"Thank you," he said. "You've been very helpful. I appreciate your seeing me at such a difficult time."

"You haven't finished your drink," she said. "There's really no reason to rush away, Sergeant. I won't be going to bed for hours."

"Thank you," he said again. "I'll be going home directly, so I will finish it if you don't mind."

"I've said I don't. I rather wanted to be alone before you came, but now I'm not sure but what company is better for me."

Gibbons forbore to say that the company of a police sergeant was not the best he could think of under the circumstances.

"I'm sure," he said, "if you feel the need of company, Marla or Phillip—"

"No," she said quickly and firmly. "I don't want sympathy. I want distraction. My father and I were not close, but, well, he was the only family I had. If ever I had needed family, I could have gone to him. Now I can't. It's like losing a crutch you didn't know you were leaning on." She frowned and tossed back half her whisky.

She must, thought Gibbons, be fairly drunk by now, but it did not show. Her speech was clear and she lit another cigarette with perfect dexterity.

"Tell me, Sergeant," she said, "if you thought you knew who had killed my father, you wouldn't possibly mention it to me, would you?"

"Probably not," he answered honestly. "But as we don't yet have any firm suspicions, it's pointless to speculate. It's still very early in the investigation, and the possibility that he died by accident is still very much alive." He paused. "I'm sorry. I expect you want it all resolved rather badly."

"I'm not sure that I do," she said, watching the cigarette smoke as it curled away toward the window. "You see," she continued, her tone uncertain now, "he's gone. In a way it doesn't matter how or why he went. We weren't close, we had no chance to be, but there's a hole where he used to be. When I saw him last year in Paris, I—" She broke off and shook her head. "I expect," she added, "that later I shall feel quite angry with whoever took him from me. But I haven't got as far as anger yet."

She seemed more vulnerable than Gibbons would ever have

thought her to be, but he was suspicious, too. Arousing sympathy in Scotland Yard was not the worst ploy a suspect could make, and he had fallen for it once. Never again, he promised himself.

He swallowed the last of the whisky in his glass and sat forward.

"That was a treat," he said. "Thank you. Might I use the toilet before I go?"

"Of course. Through there."

She waved a hand and Gibbons rose, making his way to the door indicated and closing it firmly behind him.

It was a large bathroom, with elaborate fixtures and large mirrors. Eve had not left much of a mark on it. Strewn over the counter were some cosmetics, as well as a toothbrush and toothpaste, while in the bath itself were arrayed bottles of shampoo, conditioner, and soap, all of French manufacture. Gibbons quickly inspected the depleted makeup bag on the counter, and then looked into the cabinet, but in neither place did he find medications of any kind, prescription or otherwise. The bedside table might be a more likely place to find a bottle of sleeping tablets, but he could not possibly look in there. So he contented himself with flushing the toilet and washing his hands, and emerging with a smile.

Eve still sat by the window; the glass beside her was empty again.

"Thanks," said Gibbons. "I'll wish you good night and be on my way."

She looked up and then rose. "You're welcome, Sergeant," she said, leading the way toward the door. "No doubt I'll be seeing you again soon."

"I'm afraid that will be unavoidable, Miss," said Gibbons, trying to interject a note of sympathy into the words. "I hope we won't have to bother you too much. Again, I'd like to offer my sympathies and thank you for bearing with us at such a difficult time."

"Yes, very good of you." She turned to collect his raincoat.

"Good night, then, Miss."

"Good night," she replied and, turning back to him, she leaned forward and reached up to kiss him.

Gibbons, taken completely by surprise, froze for a moment before recoiling in horror, catching her wrists more roughly than he meant to and pushing her away.

"Sorry," he said instantly. "Sorry—I didn't hurt you, did I?"

She was eyeing him with a mixture of curiosity and amusement. "No," she answered, rubbing her wrists. She continued to gaze at him for another moment, and he half-thought she would apologize. But she apparently felt no need to explain herself, for in the next moment she simply held out his raincoat with a small smile.

"Thank you," he said, seizing the coat and clutching it to him rather in the manner of a Victorian lady surprised *en dishabille*. "Good night again."

"Until next time," she said.

"Ah, yes, of course," he said, reaching for the door. "Er, certainly." And he was gone.

He strode rapidly down the hallway and found he was trembling. In the lift, he stood for a moment before pressing the lobby button, breathing deeply. He knew, of course, exactly why he was so distressed. Only last spring he had sat in another room with another attractive murder suspect who had also offered to kiss him. But he had already been deeply in love with Annette Berowne, something he now bitterly regretted. Eve Bingham's casual action had awoken nightmares in him.

All the same, he thought, frowning as he emerged from the hotel, feeling the evening air cool against his face, he needn't have behaved like such an idiot. Bethancourt would certainly never have been so gauche. Even now he could imagine the amused twinkle in the hazel eyes behind the horn-rimmed glasses, and hear that light, clipped voice saying, well, saying something suave and appropriately damping. But then, if Bethancourt had nightmares, they were not connected with the opposite sex.

As he started up the car, another thought occurred to him. He wondered if he hadn't after all received a kind of bribe.

Bethancourt had given him directions to Stutely Manor, and Gibbons decided to call in instead of phoning. He was too agitated to sleep and besides, it might be his last chance to see the Jacobean manor house. Glancing at his watch, he estimated he could make it there before eleven; a trifle late for a call, but not unduly so if one was a policeman in pursuit of his duties.

Like the Imperial Gardens in Cheltenham, Stutely Manor was not at its best in the dark, though there was light enough to make out the gabled front and the celebrated bay window. Gibbons let fall the massive knocker and in a few minutes a male servant opened the door and ushered him into the great hall, which was a very fine example of its period.

Gibbons had forgotten that Marla would be there, and less than pleased to see him. He could never quite tell if her antipathy was due entirely to his profession and the interest Bethancourt took in it or whether it was jealousy, stemming from an instinctive feeling that Bethancourt liked Gibbons better than he liked Marla, if in an entirely different way.

Bethancourt as usual handled everything smoothly. He greeted Gibbons with pleasure, introduced him to Astley-Cooper, and then said, "So you've come round to question Clarence, here, have you? I think I forgot to tell you, Clarence, that Jack might be dropping by if it wasn't too late."

Gibbons grasped at this deception eagerly; Marla was frowning at him from across the room.

"That's right," he said. "I hope you don't mind, Mr. Astley-Cooper. It won't take long—I'd just like to get your thoughts on a few matters."

"Phillip and I will leave you to it, then, shall we?" said Marla brightly, while Astley-Cooper, a little taken aback, mumbled that he would be delighted to help in any way he could.

"Don't forget your glass, Phillip," said Marla.

Bethancourt obediently fetched his port and followed her into the next room. He expected to have to placate her, but she closed the door behind them and said, "This looks well, don't you think, Phillip? I mean, if the police were absolutely set on Eve as their prime suspect, Jack wouldn't care about talking to Clarence. He's never met the woman."

"Darling," protested Bethancourt, "I've already told you that things are wide open at this point. Yes, Eve is a suspect, but so are any number of other people. Jack and the chief inspector are still in their collecting evidence mode."

"Yes, but I thought you were just trying to make me feel better." She wandered over to the sofa, sipping at her port and frowning. "Eve was different today," she said.

"Different?" asked Bethancourt.

"Yes. Much less scatterbrained than I've ever seen her." Marla sighed. "But then I've never known her well. I suppose . . . well, I suppose she could have killed her father. I just don't believe it. I don't know why."

"Woman's instinct," said Bethancourt, smiling. "Not to be lightly discounted. Here, once Jack's done with Clarence, I'll go find out how his interview with Eve went, shall I?"

Marla gave him a sharp look. "I thought you both spoke to her this morning."

"We did," said Bethancourt, "but Jack went back to follow up tonight. I imagine that's where he's come from now."

"Oh."

This seemed to disturb her, but in the next moment she sighed again.

"I don't like this," she said fretfully. "It's bad enough when all you can think about is murderers—it's worse when I might actually know one."

Bethancourt kissed the top of her head. "We'll be going home to-morrow," he said encouragingly.

She snorted. "As if that's going to stop you," she said.

"**I am here,**" **announced** Bethancourt, once Astley-Cooper's pointless interview had been concluded and he had trotted off to entertain Marla in Bethancourt's absence, "to assuage Marla's fears about her friend by grilling you on your chat with her tonight. You did see her, didn't you?"

"Oh, yes," said Gibbons ruefully.

"Here, don't guzzle the port that way," said Bethancourt. "It's very fine, very old, and was laid down by one of Clarence's ancestors—likely the one who built the house, to hear him tell it."

Gibbons snickered.

"So what happened?" asked Bethancourt, settling himself in a chair. "There must be some reason you came 'round."

Gibbons gave him a swift précis of the interview and its after-math. Bethancourt immediately looked concerned, but only said, "Well, I can see you would want a drink after that."

Gibbons stared into the fire. "It brought it all back," he said in a low voice. And then, plaintively, "Why the devil do female suspects keep trying to seduce me? I'm sure Carmichael never had this problem."

"I think it's just an unfortunate coincidence," said Bethancourt. "Marla says Eve is impulsive—the true madcap heiress. She's prob-ably never kissed a policeman before, and the notion amused her."

Gibbons smiled. "So I was a trophy?"

"That, or she truly wanted company and chose that way of per-suading you to stay. In any case, it was unfortunate." He shot his friend a sidelong glance. "Will you tell Carmichael?"

"Absolutely," said Gibbons firmly. "The more so because, well, I thought at the start she might be going to offer me a bribe."

"Yes, so you said," replied Bethancourt skeptically.

"Well, what happened might be looked at in that vein."

"But in that case, why should she waste her time with a lowly sergeant when there's a chief inspector away from his wife just a short distance away?"

"I suppose there is that. You think it's a washout then? That she's innocent?"

"Good Lord, no. Even if she is a murderer, she may quite likely not be happy with her own thoughts in the wee hours and wanted some distraction. And the same thing applies if she's innocent. Really, Jack, you have to remember that she's used to getting whatever she wants, and she has two ways of getting it: money and sex. She's young and she certainly leads a frivolous life; she may not yet have learned that peace of mind cannot be bought with either commodity." Bethancourt paused to light a cigarette.

"I'm overreacting," agreed Gibbons glumly.

"I wouldn't put it that way," said Bethancourt. "You've got good cause to be wary."

He looked at his friend and cursed inwardly. This case had looked to be the one that might take Gibbons's mind off his heartbreak, only now Eve Bingham had contrived, however innocently, to bring it all back to him.

"Well," said Gibbons, finishing off his port in one gulp, "I expect I should let you get back to Marla."

"True. It doesn't do to press one's luck. Are you going to be all right, Jack?"

"I'm fine," he answered, rising. His tone was resolute. "By the way, Carmichael's giving me the Rover to take to London tomorrow. He's got to stay here for the inquest."

Bethancourt looked startled. "But I thought you were riding up with us," he said. "Do you not want me along at the hotel? I didn't think it would matter."

"No, of course you can come along," said Gibbons. "You can meet me there after you drop Marla off, if you like. I'll ring you when I start."

"But what about this cousin in Lincoln?" persisted Bethancourt. "Surely Carmichael's going to tell you to stop and see him on your way back?"

"Lincoln is not on the way back to the Cotswolds from London," Gibbons pointed out dryly.

Bethancourt waved this consideration away. "It's another loose end to be tied up," he said. "And one can easily drive from here to London to Lincoln and back all in a day. I can follow you in the Jaguar, but I can't see why we should drive two cars over half of England. Think of the environment."

Gibbons sighed, beginning to feel, as he so often did with Bethancourt, that argument was futile.

"All right," he said. "I'll speak to Carmichael about it and ring you in the morning. Marla won't be happy, though."

"Nonsense," said Bethancourt. "It will give her an opportunity to persuade you that Eve Bingham is innocent. She'll jump at the chance."

Carmichael was still awake when Gibbons returned to the inn. The chief inspector had the case file spread out over his bed and was poring over it from a chair drawn up to the bedside. In the corner the television was on, but the volume was turned low, and Carmichael seemed to be paying it no attention.

"Come in, lad," he said, waving at the second chair in the room. "How was Miss Bingham?"

"Rather odd, sir," replied Gibbons, taking a seat.

Carmichael raised a bushy eyebrow and leaned back, settling his bulk more comfortably. "Odd?"

"I told you how cool she seemed this morning," said Gibbons, "but tonight she was quite different. Sad, it seemed to me, and a bit vulnerable. And then, when I left, she tried to kiss me."

He reddened as he said it, and both Carmichael's brows went up.

"Well, that's certainly odd," he said. A smile began to play about the corners of his mouth. "Not an interview technique I've heard of before, Sergeant."

"Sir!" protested Gibbons.

Carmichael merely grinned. "If you must have romantic interludes with murder suspects, you'd best accustom yourself to a spot of ribbing. Well, well. Suppose you tell me what led up to this kiss."

Gibbons obliged, happy to retreat to the mundane terms of Eve Bingham's will and his visit to her bathroom.

Carmichael frowned when he heard about the cousin from Lincoln. "That puts out my plans," he said. "I'd been thinking of sending you to London by train, so I could run down to Somerset after the inquest tomorrow and check on Martha Potts's alibi. I'd like to get all these loose ends tied up, but I hadn't counted on another one cropping up in Lincoln. I suppose you'll have to have the car after all."

"Phillip offered to drive me to London, sir," said Gibbons reluctantly. "I doubt he'd mind including Lincoln in the trip. You know how he is."

Carmichael brightened. "Then that's sorted," he said. "Having him around is a bit awkward, but every so often he does come in handy. What's he making of this case?"

Gibbons shrugged. "I think he's mostly curious as to who Bingham's mistress was, sir. He did say he thought Miss Bingham was only looking for distraction when she tried to kiss me tonight."

"He may be right," said Carmichael. "Did you think differently?"

"I didn't know what to think," admitted Gibbons. "I was quite startled, and the only thing that occurred to me was that it might be in the nature of a bribe. But it's rather an odd one for an extremely wealthy woman to offer."

"So it is," agreed Carmichael. "Well, we'll just tuck it away in the back of our minds for future reference. It may be she was merely overcome by your manly presence, Sergeant."

Gibbons regarded his chuckling superior resignedly.

"Oh, really, sir," he said.

CHAPTER

8

W e had better get up," said the vicar, glancing at the clock and reluctantly releasing his wife from his embrace.

Leandra groaned. "And I haven't yet done the breakfast dishes," she said. "Really, Richard, how you persuade me back to bed on the slightest of excuses . . ."

Her husband merely grinned and kissed her before flinging back the covers and sliding out of the bed. Leandra yelped as the colder air struck her and bent to reach for her discarded clothing.

"Anyway," she said, picking up their previous conversation, "I really don't think it's appropriate."

"It's quite clear it's inappropriate," said the vicar, drawing on his trousers.

"I don't care how much money one has," continued Leandra, "it is simply wrong to drive about in a white Rolls-Royce when your father has just died."

"White," said the vicar reflectively, "is the color of mourning in China."

"She is not Chinese, Richard. And don't go on about Charlie having spent so much time in China, because, however long he was there, he was not a Buddhist."

"I suppose not," agreed the vicar.

"If she wanted to get herself disliked in the village, she's certainly gone the right way about it." Leandra shook out her jumper with a sharp jerk before pulling it over her head. "Ah, that's warmer."

"You mean the Women's Institute last night," said Tothill.

"You should have heard the old cats," said Leandra, bending to retrieve a sock. "They feel, in some obscure way, that she's insulting them."

"You agreed with them?" asked Tothill, pausing in the act of donning his cassock.

"How could I? They feel strongly enough as it is. I said that she was burying him here and that could hardly be thought of as an insult."

"Thank God. I thought for a moment, my dear, that you'd gone quite provincial."

Leandra turned to him. "No," she said, "not yet. And I do know perfectly well that she probably didn't do it intentionally. She's used to fancy cars and that white Rolls was likely simply the best they had at the agency. Really, when you think about it, Charlie would have been quite amused."

"Yes," said the vicar, with a reminiscent smile, "he would be."

"But what do you think of her?" asked Leandra. "You haven't ventured an opinion at all."

Tothill considered while he did up his shoelaces. If Eve Bingham was grief-stricken, she certainly did not show it. On the other hand, he remembered a fleeting instant when she had looked at him with the eyes of a hurt and puzzled child. An instant, however, was nothing to go by; he could easily have been mistaken in what he thought he saw.

"I don't know," he replied at last. "I don't think I've seen enough of her to judge." He caught a frustrated look in his wife's eye and said, "Oh, dear. Your ladies last night have decided Eve murdered her father, haven't they?"

Leandra sighed. "It's no use trying to keep anything from you, is it?" she said. "Yes, you should have heard them. The scandal over the missing girlfriend has been completely forgotten."

They were interrupted by the doorbell. The vicar, buttoning up his cassock, said, "I'll answer it, my dear. Is there any coffee left?"

"Oh, yes," answered Leandra, pushing her hair out of her face. "There's nearly a full pot keeping warm. Let me know if you want it brought into the parlor."

"Righto."

They clattered down the stairs together and divided at the bottom, the vicar heading toward the front door and Leandra making for the kitchen. She rather expected to bring the coffee through to the parlor—those who knew the Tothills well generally used the back door—and was setting out a tray when her husband reappeared with Astley-Cooper's young friend in tow.

"Here's Phillip Bethancourt, dear," he said. "I've told him he's the very man we need to clear this up, as my parishioners seem to think driving a Rolls is indicative of a murderous nature. The police are still thinking misadventure, aren't they, Mr. Bethancourt?"

"Well," said Bethancourt cautiously, "not absolutely, you know. But," he added hastily as their faces fell, "they haven't settled on Eve Bingham. If it *was* murder, there are plenty of suspects. Take Derek Towser, for example. He's a stranger to the village and he lives conveniently close to Bingham's cottage. Perhaps they had crossed paths before."

Leandra looked horrified. "You can't mean they seriously suspect Derek?" she asked.

"At this point, they suspect anybody who hasn't got an alibi," he returned.

"But I haven't got one," said Leandra, a trifle nervously. "I did go to the pub that night, but I left early, and Richard wasn't here to say when I came in."

"Yes," said Bethancourt, "but it's rather difficult to make out a case for your having known Charlie before, since you were already living here when he returned to England. Whereas anything may have gone on between he and Towser before he ever moved here." Seeing that she still looked disturbed at the idea of Towser as the murderer, he added cheerfully, "But if you object to Towser as a suspect, how about Bingham's business partner, Andrew Sealingham? He lives near London, and perhaps Bingham went to see him that night. Or there's Mrs. Potts, up at the farmhouse. She's supposed to have gone off to visit her sister, but there's no confirmation of that yet."

Tothill was laughing. "Martha Potts?" he said. "Now that is absurd."

"I admit I like Towser or Sealingham better myself," said Bethancourt, "but you can see the field is wide open. Sergeant Gibbons is off this morning to interview an exceedingly sinister cousin of Miss Bingham's, with me as his chauffeur. I wanted to stop and ask a favor of you, though, before we left."

"Of course," said the vicar. "Anything we can do to help."

"What I want," said Bethancourt, "is for the two of you to try to remember anything Charlie Bingham said about his daughter. I don't expect you to think of everything right now, but perhaps I could drop by when I get back."

The Tothills looked surprised, but acquiesced willingly.

"Only," said the vicar, "I must warn you that he certainly never said anything very important about her. Lee and I would have remembered something like that."

"I don't expect that he did," said Bethancourt. "What I really want to know is how he felt about her and her life, how he thought she felt about him. That sort of thing. Try to remember as much as you can."

They promised to do their best and Bethancourt took his leave.

When he had gone, Leandra turned slowly back to the breakfast dishes while her husband sat thoughtfully at the table.

"I think we should write down what we can remember," he said. "And perhaps it would be best to try and start at the beginning, when we first met Charlie, and work our way forward. How does that strike you?"

"What?" said Leandra.

"I said—why, Lee, are you all right? You look rather pale."

He rose and went to put an arm around her.

"I'm fine," she said, although she did turn and lean her head against his shoulder. "Oh, Richard, I do love you."

"And I adore you," he responded, kissing the top of her head. "What's wrong, Lee?"

"Nothing," she answered. "Or, at least, it's just that I had never thought that the murderer might be one of us, here in the village. It's so peaceful here and people always seemed so, well, not all of them are nice exactly, but I thought they were quite normal."

"Dull, you mean," said Tothill with a grin. "But, Lee, it may not be true—they may all be as innocent as the day is long. It's not time yet to worry about that."

"You're right," she said, and hugged him fiercely.

Bethancourt stopped at the Eberharts' to repeat his request, and then went on to Towser's, his last stop before picking up his passengers and proceeding up to town. He rather expected Towser to be out painting in the early morning light, but he was at home.

"It's the inquest today," the painter explained. "They want Peg Eberhart to give evidence, so I said I'd drive her since Steve has his rounds to do. They really ought to get a second car now that Peg has the baby."

Bethancourt agreed with this point of view, and explained why he had come.

123

Towser scratched his head. "I suppose I can try," he said. "Offhand, I can't remember his saying much about her—oh, excuse me."

The telephone was ringing. Towser went to answer it, while Bethancourt studied the landscape painting on the easel.

"Really?" Towser's voice drifted back to him. He sounded surprised. "Well, I think you're getting the wind up. . . . of course I understand that, but I shouldn't worry now . . ."

A woman, Bethancourt decided idly, turning to another picture leaning against the wall, a woman was speaking at the other end of the phone. Men sounded different when they talked to each other than they did when talking to women. And both sexes sounded quite different from anything else when they talked to their families.

"Well, thank you," said Towser, "but, truly, I doubt it will come to that. . . . All right, I'll speak to you later."

"I must be off," said Bethancourt as Towser reentered the room. "I've still got to get up to town this morning."

"Very well," said Towser. "I'll give it some thought and let you know what I come up with."

Bethancourt thanked him and took his leave, glancing at his watch as he started up the Jaguar. He had timed it admirably, he thought. Marla had not finished packing by the time he was ready to leave, and experience had allowed him to translate her promise of "twenty more minutes" into an hour. By the time he picked up Jack and returned to Stutely Manor, she should be just about ready to go.

"Wake up, Jack."

Gibbons opened an eye. In fact, the nap he had been lulled into by the smooth ride of the Jaguar along the motorway had long since been broken by the stop-and-go London traffic, but he had decided feigning sleep was preferable to contributing to the discussion in the car. This had centered around Bethancourt's plan to have Marla pick up what gossip she could about Bingham's visit to his daughter in

Paris. When Gibbons had fallen asleep, Marla had still been hesitating, but by the amiable atmosphere in the car on his awakening, she had apparently acquiesced.

"We're here," announced Bethancourt.

Gibbons grunted and pushed himself into a sitting position. Cerberus, sitting beside him, leaned over to helpfully lick his face. Gibbons patted him and glanced out the window where the entrance to St. Martin's Lane Hotel sat beneath its canopy.

"All right, then," he said. "You'll meet me back here? You've got my bag in the boot."

"Never fear," Bethancourt assured him.

"Very well." Gibbons gave Cerberus a last pat and opened the door.

"Good heavens," said Marla. "You're not going in like that, are you?"

"Like what?" asked Gibbons, but she was already getting out of the car, calling to Bethancourt to open the boot.

"She'll set you right," said Bethancourt, waving him out. "I'll be back in half an hour."

Outside, Marla was rummaging in one of her bags, from which she eventually produced a lint roller.

"Here," she said, grabbing him by the arm and industriously sweeping down one side of his chest. "You've dog hair all over."

"Oh," said Gibbons. "I hadn't noticed. Thank you."

"People will never take you seriously as a police officer if you're covered in dog hair," she said, working her way down his left leg and then straightening to begin operations on his right side.

"Well, I do have the proper ID," he said.

Marla merely sniffed and continued her work.

"There," she said. "Your back's all right—Phillip must have brushed out the car this morning."

"Thanks again," said Gibbons. "I hope you enjoy Paris."

She waved at him as she went to return the roller to her bag and he turned toward the hotel.

St. Martin's Lane was the last word in fashionable hotels and Gibbons was rather glad Marla had noticed the dog hair as he entered the elegant lobby. He felt dowdy enough as it was.

The chic young woman behind the desk, informed of his identity and purpose, refused to deal with him at all, and instead summoned her manager. That gentleman looked slightly alarmed and ushered him quickly into an office as fashionably outfitted as the lobby. Gibbons explained his errand, adding, "I'll want to speak to anyone who was on duty that Sunday night—maids, waiters, lift operators."

"Of course, sir," said the manager, who then hesitated. "I'm afraid none of those people are here at the moment, it being the day shift."

It was what Gibbons had expected. He arranged to return in the evening for his interviews, after he had seen Dr. Loomis, and asked for a list of the night-shift staff. This being produced, he took his leave and then stood hesitating in the lobby. In the ordinary way of things he would have got himself a cup of coffee and settled down to wait for Bethancourt, but he felt distinctly out of place amid these surroundings and the people who inhabited them. Scotland Yard was not far away, and he could run his list of names through the computer there for anything that might crop up.

He made for the exit, digging out his mobile as he went to let Bethancourt know where to find him.

In the event, Bethancourt declined to accompany his friend that evening, opting instead to have drinks with the manager of a well-known art gallery where Bethancourt was an occasional patron.

They settled in comfortably at Atlantic, ordering dry martinis and chatting about a new gallery Max Merriman's onetime assistant had just opened in the East End.

"She did me proud," sighed Merriman, sipping at his drink. "I went to the opening, of course, and everything was spot-on. A really well-staged little show. And I've sent a few people her way—I'm really hoping she makes a go of it."

"I'll stop by there when I'm next in town," promised Bethancourt.

Merriman raised an eyebrow. "Next in town?" he asked. "Where are you now then?"

Bethancourt grinned. "I'm only here overnight," he answered. "I've been spending some time up in the Cotswolds. In fact, I ran into an artist up there that you must know of—Derek Towser?"

"Towser," Merriman mused. "Oh, yes, the portrait chap. Yes, that's right—he'd be off feeding his soul on landscapes just now. Does it every October unless he has something big on. I don't know him well, myself, but his work's very sound." He cocked an eyebrow. "Thinking of having your portrait done, Phillip?"

"Not at the moment," said Bethancourt. "I'm just curious about the man. He seems to have developed a reputation in the village up there as something of a ladies' man, and I can't make out if it's true, or just wishful thinking on the part of the womenfolk. He's certainly a handsome man."

Merriman chuckled. "That he is, and he doesn't hesitate to use it. Not that he's any worse than a lot of others, but of course that old scandal does cling to him."

"Ah," said Bethancourt, adjusting his glasses and regarding Merriman with a bright eye. "I love a good scandal, Max."

Merriman laughed again. "It's ancient history now," he said. "Well after Derek got his start, but before he was quite so well known. I don't know if you've met the Mayhews?"

Bethancourt sipped his drink and thought. "No," he said at last. "I don't believe I have."

"Well, no matter. Wealthy family with a pretty daughter named Lisa. She got herself engaged to Lord Wythens and everything was set for a big society wedding. Her parents had the bright idea of having her portrait done, and hired Towser for it—and he did a first-rate job, though that's by-the-way. He also seduced pretty little Lisa. Or maybe it was the other way 'round—you know how these things go."

"Indeed. I take it Towser was indiscreet?"

"Ah, that's the really fine bit in the whole affair—pardon the pun. No, Derek was the very soul of discretion, but Lisa couldn't resist telling her friends, and of course it got back to Wythens."

"Naturally. These things always do. Did he call off the wedding?"

"Oh, yes, in high dudgeon. As I say, it was quite the scandal at the time, and ever since then Derek's been suspected of sleeping with every woman he paints. It's not true, of course. Though if you're asking if he's likely to remain celibate for an entire month, I should say no. Not, at least, if there's anyone pretty enough up there—with his looks, he can afford to be particular and I hear he is."

Bethancourt sighed in satisfaction and drank his martini. "It's always nice to be in the know," he said. "Speaking of which, what do you think of his landscapes?"

"Never seen one," said Merriman. "He sells them over at Acton's, but I've never been interested enough to go and look. They don't make much of a splash. Not like his portraiture—really brilliant, that is. It's Danvers who's all the rage in landscapes these days. Have you seen his stuff?"

The conversation went on to other things, and after another half-hour the two men parted.

Bethancourt stood on the street outside the bar, hesitating for a moment before he shrugged as though casting fate to the winds, and turned toward Piccadilly Circus. He crossed Shaftesbury Avenue and walked briskly along Coventry until he came to Charing Cross. A few minutes later saw him descending the stairway leading down to Saint. The doorman, recognizing him, looked for Marla, but, failing to find her, returned his eyes to Bethancourt's face.

"Do you know if Spencer is here tonight?" Bethancourt asked him.

There was no need for a last name. There was only one Spencer in the fashion world.

"Came in a few minutes ago," said the doorman.

"Thanks," said Bethancourt, smiling, and made his way inside.

Spencer Kendrick, the noted fashion photographer, was standing at the bar. He was a tall, lanky man with an air of calm that the frenetic pace of his chosen profession rarely disturbed. He was several years older than Bethancourt, but the two men had got on well from their first meeting and had quickly become friends.

Kendrick, nursing an Irish whiskey and smoking languidly, smiled when his gaze fell on Bethancourt.

"Hullo, Phillip," he said. "I didn't think I'd see you tonight with Marla out of town. Or didn't she go?"

"She went," affirmed Bethancourt, leaning against the bar. "I was looking for you."

"And here I am, entirely at your disposal. I've nothing on tonight, beyond wanting dinner in a bit."

"I haven't eaten, either," said Bethancourt, signaling the barman and ordering another martini.

"Were you up in the Cotswolds?" asked Kendrick.

"Yes. In fact, I'm going back in the morning." Bethancourt, receiving his drink, settled himself more comfortably on his stool and lit a cigarette. "There's been a murder up there, you see."

"Ah," said Kendrick. "Does Marla know?"

"She could hardly avoid knowing—it was the talk of the village."

"Too bad," commiserated Kendrick, well aware of Marla's dislike of her boyfriend's hobby.

"Well, she didn't mind as much as usual," said Bethancourt. "A friend of hers is involved this time."

Kendrick looked startled. "There was a murder during the shoot?" he asked. "I hadn't heard anything. Although," he added thoughtfully, "I can well see how nearly anyone might want to murder Liz Randall. But she can't be dead—I'd certainly have heard that."

"No," said Bethancourt, smiling. "It didn't happen during the shoot. The murder was purely a village affair, but the victim happened to be Eve Bingham's father. Do you know her?"

"In a sense," replied Kendrick. "She's always somewhere about during the Paris shows. A couple of years ago, she had momentarily abandoned rock stars and was going in for photographers."

"I see," said Bethancourt.

"It was a nice weekend," continued Kendrick, "but I can't say we spent a lot of time getting to know each other."

"In that case, I don't suppose she mentioned her father."

"Well, no, but then very few women ever do mention their fathers to me. I can't think why. I mean, it's not as if I have anything against fathers. I'm quite fond of my own, for example."

"On the other hand," said Bethancourt, "you probably didn't mention him to Eve."

"Probably not," admitted Kendrick. "After all, the old fellow's principle interest these days is fishing, and while I'm a great fisherman myself, I don't find it goes down very well as a topic of conversation amongst the city-bred."

"No, I don't imagine it would."

Kendrick lit another cigarette. "I take it you think Eve killed her father?"

"I don't know," replied Bethancourt. "She's merely one of several suspects at the moment."

"That's good." Kendrick let out a stream of smoke with a sigh. "I should feel . . . odd, if it turned out she was a murderer."

"The most unlikely people are capable of murder, given the right circumstances," said Bethancourt.

"No doubt, but I do try to avoid sleeping with them," retorted Kendrick. "Oh, well."

He threw back the last of his whiskey with a shrug.

"Where do you want to eat?" he asked.

Bethancourt, when he arrived to pick up Gibbons the next morning, had brought coffee and Gibbons was grateful. He had risen later than he had meant to, decided he had no time to properly brew coffee, and had tried to make do with some instant coffee, only to find that the milk in his refrigerator had soured while he had been away. He settled himself in the passenger seat, patted Cerberus, and took the steaming latte thankfully.

"And so off to Lincoln," said Bethancourt cheerfully, edging his way out into the morning traffic.

"Mmm," said Gibbons, sipping. "Where did you get to last night?" he asked. "I thought you wanted to come to the hotel with me."

"I had drinks with Max Merriman," answered Bethancourt. "He manages a gallery in Cork Street, and I wanted to ask him about Derek Towser. I found out, by the way, why he has such a reputation with the ladies."

"You mean besides his looks?"

"That's right."

Bethancourt recounted the story of the scandal and Gibbons chuckled.

"I don't see that it has any bearing on the case, though," he said.

"No, as it turned out. I was only curious," said Bethancourt. "I really don't see that Towser could have had any previous connection with Bingham, not unless he painted a portrait of Eve. I asked Max, but he didn't know."

"I don't think he did," said Gibbons. "I spoke to his agent yesterday afternoon, and he claims not."

"And did the hotel staff give Eve Bingham an alibi?" asked Bethancourt.

"They did not," replied Gibbons. "She might have been there, but she equally well could have slipped out. They were, however, relatively certain that she had not had a visitor, particularly not one answering to Bingham's description. That doesn't mean anything, of course— she might have met him elsewhere."

"She must have, if she killed him—she couldn't possibly have smuggled the corpse out of St. Martin's. But it is difficult to see how she got back to London from the Cotswolds."

"I checked with all the major car rental agencies, and she hadn't rented a car that night, but that's not proof of anything, either."

"No," agreed Bethancourt. "How about those names you got from Pat Stikes? Any joy there?"

"Carmichael had me give them to DI Mathers," answered Gibbons. "He's already spoken to the first woman on the list—the one who stayed at the Deer and Hounds with a girlfriend. He rang me on the mobile to tell me about it." Gibbons was smiling.

"And?"

"Her girlfriend is literally just that," said Gibbons with a chuckle. "They've been living together for five years and have just adopted a baby—that's what the trip to the Cotswolds was, one last fling before they were tied down by parenthood."

"Oh, dear," said Bethancourt. "I wonder how Constable Stikes missed that."

"She probably never spoke to either woman herself."

"Probably," agreed Bethancourt. "Ah, here we go—the trunk road at last. The traffic will start thinning out now."

They drove on in silence for a bit, each lost in his own thoughts, until at last Gibbons said, "I wanted to ask you, Phillip—do you think my manner when I'm interviewing a witness is too friendly?"

Bethancourt's brows shot up over the rims of his glasses.

"Friendly?" he repeated.

"Yes, you know, when I'm trying to put someone at ease. Do you think I overdo it? I've watched Carmichael, and he always tries to make a connection with the witness and it works very well when it can be managed. I try to do the same, but I've been thinking that perhaps I go too far sometimes. What do you think?"

"That's nonsense," said Bethancourt, mildly exasperated. "Look here, Jack, I know you work hard at your career, but this kind of nit-picking is more likely to harm than help."

"It's not that," said Gibbons. "I was just thinking of Eve Bingham, and wondering what in my manner had led her to try it on like that. And even with Annette, at the beginning," he added in a lower voice.

"Oh." Bethancourt's exasperation vanished, replaced by a desire to strangle Eve Bingham. "They're two different things, Jack," he said more gently. "Annette came to care for you as she got to know you. Eve would have tried it on with anyone who was reasonably attractive that night. It had nothing to do with your manner."

"Annette didn't care much," said Gibbons bitterly.

"She did," said Bethancourt. "Just not enough."

He cursed silently, his thoughts returning to the hot August day when he had returned home from a polo match to find Gibbons sitting on his doorstep. He had been pleased at first, since he had seen much less of Gibbons that summer than was usual; between his job and his relationship with Annette Berowne, Gibbons had had little spare time. He had spent the spring and summer walking on air, having at last, he believed, found the woman he would marry. He had been head over heels in love.

Bethancourt had never taken such an optimistic view of the romance, feeling from the very start that Annette was not the right woman for his friend. He had tried to convince himself that this belief was merely a reaction to the fact that he did not find Annette attractive, but in his heart he had always had his doubts.

And on that hot August day, sweaty and smelling of horses, he had met Gibbons's eyes and known he had been right. It had been no consolation at all.

In the months since then, he had watched Gibbons struggle to mend the wound that had been torn in his sense of self-worth. It would have been easier if Annette had deliberately used and deceived him for her own ends, her true character only unmasked in the act of desertion, but in fact she had not meant to be cruel. Gibbons knew he had been deceived in nothing about her with the single exception of the depth of her feeling for himself. What it came down to, in the end, was the fact that she had not wanted him.

"Different people mean different things by love," said Bethancourt now, "and some are capable of a more profound feeling than others. Annette isn't, and ultimately you could never have been happy with her, because somewhere down the line, you would have felt the lack. But you're luckier than she is, because when you do find someone who means what you do by love, your relationship will be a greater one than Annette can ever have."

It was true, but he knew it did not help very much.

Christopher Macklin was at least ten years older than his cousin Eve, a thin, stoop-shouldered man with gray already speckling his fair hair.

They found him at Lincoln Park Grammar School, where he taught mathematics. He was surprised by their visit, but ushered them into his office with good grace. This was a small, windowless affair off his classroom, barely large enough to hold a desk, filing cabinet, and two chairs obviously borrowed from the classroom itself. Shelves ran along two of the walls and were crammed with books on higher mathematics, making the little room even more claustrophobic. Bethancourt leaned up against the filing cabinet while Gibbons took the chair usually reserved for students.

"I haven't heard a word from my uncle in years," said Macklin. "I didn't even know he was back in England until the solicitors rang to say he was dead. He'd left me a small legacy, you see. I thought it was rather kind of him, especially since we haven't had anything to do with each other in years."

It was certainly possible, thought Bethancourt, that this unassuming math teacher had plotted to murder his uncle and cousin for the fortune that would come to him. But it seemed wholly unlikely on the face of it. Macklin appeared genuinely grateful for the small remembrance Charles Bingham had left him.

"Did he keep in contact with your mother while she was alive?" asked Gibbons.

"Only very occasionally since Eve left school."

"What about Eve herself?"

Macklin shrugged. "I haven't seen her since she was a girl. She and Mother didn't get on very well. They were rather opposite characters—but I don't expect you want to hear about that."

"Yes, we do," put in Bethancourt.

Gibbons smiled. "We're interested in anything at all pertaining to your uncle and cousin. How were Eve and your mother different?"

Macklin was a little taken aback, but obligingly ransacked his memories. "Well," he said, "Eve as a girl was rather impulsive, even reckless at times. Uncle Charlie had a bit of the devil in him, too, but my mother missed that gene. She had a sense of humor, but she was strict and didn't approve of cheeky children. She tried to stand in for Eve's mother when she could, but it never worked out well. And then, of course, there was the money. My mother simply didn't know how to handle a child who could buy whatever she liked. My mother and uncle fought constantly about the amount of money he let Eve have. On Eve's side, I think she always blamed my mother for separating her from her father. Which was quite true."

"How so?" asked Gibbons.

"Well," said Macklin, "you have to understand that after her mother's death, Evie and Uncle Charlie were inseparable. He took her everywhere with him—if he went to the office, so did she, and if he went out to dinner, Eve was brought along. She had a nanny, of course, but Uncle Charlie was always giving her the evening off, or the afternoon, or even the whole day. It was Uncle Charlie who took care of her, and things went on that way for years."

"Until," said Gibbons, "Eve was old enough to go to school."

Macklin smiled at him, as if at a particularly bright pupil. "Exactly," he said, and then the smile faded. "I was about sixteen," he continued, "and although I was mostly interested in girls and getting a place at University, I do remember it was a difficult time. At first, Eve wasn't sent to school at all. My uncle hired various tutors, but none of them were very satisfactory, and of course Eve had very few playmates. At last, my mother absolutely insisted that Uncle Charlie settle down in one place—he had been travelling a good deal and so, of course, was Eve—and put her in a school. Uncle Charlie agreed and that was tried, but he was always taking her out for one thing or another. He had begun to get interested in archeology by then, and at the end of her first year, he took her out of school a month early to go to China with him."

"I suppose," said Gibbons, "it could be argued that that was another kind of education."

"I believe Uncle Charlie said something like that at the time," agreed Macklin. "My mother, needless to say, didn't see it in that light. I think it was about that time that she began to talk of boarding school. Uncle Charlie was going out to a different dig in Egypt that winter, and he planned to take Eve and hire another tutor. He and my mother had a tremendous row over that. Evie must have been about nine by then—at any rate, I think I was in my first year at Cambridge. Mother insisted that Uncle Charlie wasn't considering Eve at all and that it was high time he did so. Her point was that Eve might be enjoying herself, but she wasn't making friends her own age or learning to live in the world. She was quite right, I suppose."

"She convinced your uncle?"

"She was wearing him down. I believe he was coming to wonder if he was, in fact, being selfish where Eve was concerned. He'd had the same conservative upbringing as my mother, after all. In any case, something happened that summer—I forget now what it was, some quite small incident with another child—but it rather proved my mother's point. And the end of the whole thing was that Eve went into boarding school that fall and Uncle Charlie went to Africa without her."

Gibbons was silent a moment.

"I think it's a rather sad story," said Bethancourt.

"Yes." Macklin nodded. "I've always thought so myself. My mother meant well, she was truly trying to do her best for Evie, but I think now she was wrong. Eve was terribly traumatized by being separated from her father. And Uncle Charlie was never quite the same."

"But he would have had her with him during the holidays, wouldn't he?" asked Gibbons.

"At the beginning, yes," replied Macklin. "But they were living in different worlds, and it drove them apart. As you know, my uncle was a very wealthy man, but he didn't live like one. The money really meant nothing to him, beyond letting him do as he liked. He was off living in a tent in Egypt and Eve was at school where they made a lot of her because she was rich. And, of course, she was growing up. She adored her father, but there came a time when she didn't want to spend her vacations in the middle of nowhere; she wanted to have party dresses and meet boys with her friends. I don't really know what happened during that period, because by then I had finished school and moved away. I remember my mother mentioning one year that Eve was going to Italy with a friend's family for the summer holidays. Eve must have been well into her teens by then, but I don't remember precisely when it was."

"I see," said Gibbons meditatively. "Well, this has been a great help, Mr. Macklin. Thank you for speaking so freely."

"I didn't mind," answered Macklin. "Though it's beyond me how this sort of ancient history is a help to you."

"It's a matter of understanding people's characters," explained Gibbons. "People's relationships are often very illuminating."

"I suppose so." Macklin hesitated. "Sergeant," he said, "can you tell me if there is any truth to what I've been hearing? That you suspect my cousin of murdering her father?"

"She's only one suspect in a very wide field at this point," said Gibbons. "We're still getting it all sorted out at present. Speaking of which, could you tell me what you were doing on the Sunday evening your uncle died?"

Macklin was astonished. "Me?" he said. "But why in the world should I want to kill Uncle Charlie? I haven't heard from him in years. I didn't even know he was in England."

"I believe you, Mr. Macklin," said Gibbons. "It's just a routine question. You were related to the victim, after all, and there is the matter of the money."

"Money? You mean the bequest he left me?"

"That, and the fact that if anything had happened to Eve Bingham before her father's death, you would now be an exceedingly wealthy man."

"I would?" Macklin looked amazed. "Do you mean Uncle Charlie left it all to me if Eve died before him?" He shook his head. "That was awfully decent of him. I never knew . . ."

"So," prompted Gibbons, "you can see that I have to ask—"

"What? Oh, yes, quite. I don't really mind telling you; I was just surprised at your asking. My wife and I had some friends in to dinner on Sunday. They came at about seven and left at about eleven, or perhaps just a bit later. I expect you want their names?"

"It would be helpful."

Macklin produced a notebook and wrote down the names and addresses of his friends. He tore the page out and handed it to Gibbons.

"John Beltock," he said, indicating the first name, "is the biology teacher here. I think he has a class at the moment, but you can probably catch him afterward."

"Thank you," said Gibbons, rising. "You've been very helpful indeed, Mr. Macklin. I hope we won't have to trouble you again."

"I just hope Eve didn't do it," said Macklin.

"There's every possibility she will be cleared completely," Gibbons assured him. "Thank you again for your time."

"If he had anything to do with it, then I'm a blind fool," said Gibbons as they returned to the car.

"He seemed the very picture of innocence to me," agreed Bethancourt. "And his alibi holds up."

"At least as far as we've checked it," said Gibbons cautiously. "But I didn't see the point of tracking down all the rest of those people." He sighed. "Not that I ever thought it terribly likely a respectable, middle-aged math teacher had suddenly taken it into his head to kill his uncle, whom he hadn't seen in years. From all the accounts we have of Bingham, he would have given Macklin money if he'd needed it."

"True," agreed Bethancourt absently. "Where the devil is the A57? Get out the map, will you, Jack?"

"We're on the A57," replied Gibbons.

"We are? Well, how did that happen?"

"The school was just off it."

"Oh. Well, that's good, at any rate. And we must be heading west, as I turned right back there. All's well then."

CHAPTER

long day's work," grumbled Carmichael. "And nothing to show for it."

"No, sir," said Gibbons, stifling a yawn. It was late when he and Bethancourt had finally returned to the Cotswolds, and all he had wanted was his bed, but he had found the chief inspector waiting up for him in the darkened bar of the pub, a bottle of scotch thoughtfully purchased before time had been called. Gibbons could hardly refuse his superior's offer of a drink. "How did you make out?" he asked, though he thought he knew the answer; Carmichael looked distinctly disgruntled and a significant portion of the scotch bottle had been consumed before he arrived.

Carmichael grunted for reply and shifted in his chair. "Inquest was adjourned," he said shortly. "By the time it was over, it was raining, so I drove to Somerset and back in a downpour."

"Did you see Mrs. Potts's sister?"

"I saw more of her than I would have liked," answered Carmichael.

"She's an aggravating woman—very voluble without ever saying anything. It took me forty-five minutes to discover that when Mrs. Potts visits her, she's 'regular as clockwork,' inevitably arriving after lunch and before tea. No matter how I tried, I couldn't get her to be more specific, or to address herself to the particular Sunday in question."

Gibbons, having seen the skill with which the chief inspector was accustomed to winkle out information from the most unlikely witnesses, was surprised and sympathetic all at once.

"It must have been very frustrating for you, sir," he said.

Carmichael heaved a sigh. "Frustrating doesn't begin to express it," he said. "At least," he added, brightening, "I did manage to get her chemist to admit he has no customers with a regular prescription for Seconal."

Gibbons was surprised again. "That was good work, sir," he said. "How did you manage it?"

"It was easy enough to find out which chemist she used," Carmichael answered with a shrug. "As I say, the problem was not to get her talking, but to stem the flow. I only had to mention that I needed to call at a reliable chemist's to get the whole history of her medications. The chemist himself was a bit trickier, but since he does not, in fact, regularly fill a prescription for Seconal, he was willing to own up to that in the end."

"Well done, sir," said Gibbons, and then had to stifle another yawn; he had been sleepy to begin with and the scotch seemed to be making it worse. "So do you think we can rule Mrs. Potts out?"

"Tentatively, at least," said Carmichael. "There's no doubt in my mind her sister would lie for her, but I can't think where she would have laid hands on the Seconal."

"But so far we haven't found any Seconal anywhere," said Gibbons.

"True enough," agreed Carmichael, scowling. "And until we do, we're no closer to tying this up." He drained his glass and then sighed.

"I've just had a bad day, that's all. At my age, long drives in the rain are no treat, especially when there's nothing at the end of them. And then there were the reporters on top of that."

"Reporters?" asked Gibbons.

"Yes, the media has finally twigged to the fact that Charles Bingham, inventor, was the father of Eve Bingham, socialite. They're camped out at her hotel this minute, and they pestered me here until our landlord kicked them out."

"Maybe they'll find out who Bingham's mistress was," suggested Gibbons. "It's their line of country."

Carmichael laughed. "It is that, isn't it? Well, so long as somebody finds her, I won't complain. Because, even if we believe there was a murder committed here, we'll never get it to court until we've brought this mystery woman out into the light of day."

Astley-Cooper was also waiting up for his houseguest.

"It's awfully good of you to have me back, Clarence," said Bethancourt, stripping off his jacket in the entry. "I could have gone to a hotel, you know."

Astley-Cooper looked up from petting Cerberus and snorted. "Hotels are nonsense," he said. "Besides, how am I to find out anything if you're not here? Come into the sitting room—I was just having a brandy."

There was a fire burning in the sitting room, obliterating the chill of the October evening. Cerberus lay down before it while Bethancourt accepted a glass of cognac and then collapsed into the corner of the sofa.

"I can't think," he said, "why driving should always make one feel so grubby. The car's perfectly clean, after all."

"You look tired," said Astley-Cooper.

Bethancourt removed his glasses and rubbed at his eyes a moment before replacing them.

"It was a long day," he said.

Astley-Cooper, in contrast to his guest, was perched on the edge of his chair, his eyes bright with curiosity. "And was Eve Bingham's cousin a sinister fellow?" he asked.

"Not a bit of it," answered Bethancourt. "He was a perfectly ordinary math teacher with a solid alibi. I'm certain he had nothing to do with it."

Astley-Cooper looked disappointed and Bethancourt smiled.

"On the other hand," he said, "the hotel staff were unable to give Eve an alibi, so she's still in the running. And I did find out why Derek Towser has such a reputation as a womanizer. Apparently a woman whose portrait he painted had an affair with him, and her fiancé subsequently cancelled their wedding."

"I could have told you that," said Astley-Cooper. "Julie Benson heard the story from some friends of hers in London and that's how we got to know of it down here."

"Oh," said Bethancourt, rather crestfallen. "I never thought to ask you. By the way, is there any news this end?"

Astley-Cooper shook his head. "Martin Winslow barred Josh Landon from the Deer and Hounds last night," he replied, "and I ran into the Bensons this morning, who say Joan Bonnar will be visiting on Sunday, but that's all."

Bethancourt smiled. "That's not nothing," he said.

"Well, but it doesn't have to do with the subject in hand. Go on with what you were saying."

Bethancourt, unable to remember what that might have been, shrugged and said, "Anyway, I have several feelers out for information about Eve and her relationship with Charlie, so maybe one of them will bear fruit."

"Did Marla agree to nose around in Paris?"

"In the end," said Bethancourt wryly. "And I wouldn't call it 'nosing around' to her face if I were you."

"Well, she might find something anyway."

Bethancourt yawned. "There may be nothing to find," he said. "The girlfriend is still the best bet."

Astley-Cooper considered this. "What about the sleeping tablets?" he asked. "Have you found out where they came from?"

Bethancourt shook his head. "No. Presumably they came from the girlfriend, since nobody else seems to have access to Seconal."

"But mightn't he have borrowed them from a friend?" asked Astley-Cooper. "People do trade their prescriptions around, even though they're not supposed to. Yes, listen to this: supposing he'd had a near accident with his car that day, on the way to wherever it was. He might have been feeling jumpy and taken a pill to calm himself down."

"I should think," said Bethancourt, "he'd have been more inclined to have a drink."

"Well, he did do," said Astley-Cooper. "Perhaps it didn't do the trick, so he had a pill as well."

"I don't believe it," said Bethancourt. "I will admit that if one had trouble sleeping, one might borrow a pill from a friend, but I can't see anyone taking a sleeping tablet just to calm down. Especially not someone like Bingham, who'd spent the last fifteen years in the remoter areas of China. He can't have been terribly pill-conscious, so to speak."

"There you go," said Astley-Cooper, getting excited. "It comes back to that girlfriend of his. He goes to see her, and they have a drink. Then they, er, you know, but he can't sleep afterward. So she says, 'Have one of my sleeping pills.' And it does him in."

Bethancourt was amused. "But, Clarence," he said, "Bingham died before nine P.M. Even if he had been engaging in a romantic interlude, why should he have wanted to sleep so badly that he took a pill?"

"Oh," said Astley-Cooper sorrowfully, "I'd forgotten about the time. I don't seem to be very good at this kind of thing after all. I expect it can't have been an accident, then."

"I suppose," said Bethancourt slowly, "someone might have meant to just knock him out for a bit. But why should anyone want to do that? I'm an imaginative fellow, but I can't think of a reason. Not one that makes sense, anyhow."

"But there's not much more reason for anyone to want him dead," argued Astley-Cooper.

"There's the money," said Bethancourt.

"Yes, but no one knew he had it."

"Eve did."

"Oh, yes, she did, didn't she?" Astley-Cooper shook his head. "I can't keep it all straight. How on earth do you manage it?"

"Practice," said Bethancourt sleepily. "Next time you'll do better."

"I don't want there to be a next time," replied Astley-Cooper. "It's all very well to sit around the fire of an evening, speculating. But, well, old Charlie's dead, isn't he? And I liked Charlie, Phillip. We all did."

"Jack and the chief inspector will sort it out," said Bethancourt soothingly. "They always do."

Bethancourt woke late the next morning and found himself deserted. Gibbons and Carmichael, when he rang, had already left the pub, and Astley-Cooper had left him a somewhat incoherent note from which he deduced that his host had some sort of business in Cirencester.

Accordingly, he took Cerberus for a long walk around Stutely Manor's extensive park, and then drove into the village in search of lunch. He parked in the square and was just opening the back door for his dog when he caught sight of the vicar emerging from the newsagents. He was dressed as usual in his cassock, with a brown tweed jacket over it, and today had added a scarf knitted of brilliant blue, red, and yellow. Bethancourt assumed it had been a parishioner's gift.

He greeted Bethancourt cheerfully and bent to pat Cerberus.

"We've been wracking our brains," he announced, "trying to re-member bits and pieces of Charlie's conversation. It's made a wonder-ful change from writing my sermon."

"I'm sorry," said Bethancourt guiltily. "I didn't mean to put you off your sermon."

"Nonsense," said the vicar, "we've rather enjoyed it. And writing a sermon every week is one of the things I like least about being a clergyman."

"I suppose it must be rather tiresome," said Bethancourt. "Like having essays at school."

"Sometimes it's all right," said Tothill guardedly. "Sometimes, when I've been reading up some theology or something, it all comes together beautifully as soon as I sit down to write. But one can't expect that to happen every week, and mostly it's a bit of a struggle. Of course," he added, cheering, "it's better since I was married."

"Your wife helps you write your sermons?"

"Not exactly. But she gives me lots of ideas, inadvertently, as it were. Here, are you doing anything just now? Because, if not, you could come along to the vicarage with me, and we could tell you what we've thought of. Leandra's making lunch, but we can sit in the kitchen and she can talk while she cooks."

Bethancourt agreed to this proposition, and they turned together down the High Street. The sky was beginning to clear from the gray of the early morning, and they were bathed in shafts of golden light as they made their way toward the vicarage.

"It must be nice," said Bethancourt, thinking of Marla and the amount of persuasive charm he had had to use in order to secure her agreement to ask around about Eve and Charlie in Paris, "to have a wife who helps you in your work."

"Oh, yes," said Tothill, with positive enthusiasm. "Leandra's made an enormous difference in my life. I never thought, when I first met her, that she would ever take to being a country vicar's wife, but it suits her very well."

"I understand," said Bethancourt a little cautiously, "that she wasn't immediately accepted here, however?"

The vicar only laughed. "That's putting it mildly," he said. "Let's face it: when I first came here, about the only people who were happy to see me were the mothers with young daughters who thought it would be lovely if Sally could marry the vicar. They weren't at all pleased when I brought back a London woman with a wicked past. Of course, they didn't know about Lee's past, but they assumed it anyway."

"It must have been awfully rough going for you."

"Oh, we didn't mind so much, we were so happy together. Leandra positively delighted in thinking up little things to do that would bring people 'round. No, it was before I married that things were rough. I was seriously thinking of giving up the clergy then. I was so pleased about getting this living, you see, I suppose I looked forward to it too much."

"Everyone's guilty of that at some time or another," said Bethancourt. "I don't think there's anyone alive who hasn't spoiled a perfectly good thing by expecting too much of it. Of course, that doesn't make it any easier when it happens."

"No," agreed the vicar. "And I—who had always prided myself on being so pragmatic—wasn't sensible at all about this. I had some idea of just stepping into the role of vicar and having everything fall into place, and naturally it didn't happen that way at all. I was too young—at least, that's what everyone in the parish thought—and even if I'd been ninety, I was a different man from the one they'd been used to for the last thirty years."

"What changed it 'round for you?" asked Bethancourt.

"Leandra," answered Tothill. "I was really a very lonely man when I met her, although I didn't realize it. I certainly wasn't looking for anyone. Frankly, things never seemed to work out for me in that way and I'd more or less made up my mind to being a bachelor for the time being. But God was looking out for me, though I didn't know it until I met Lee. She made me so happy, I just plunged ahead, despite all my doubts. I kept looking at her and thinking, 'She's beautiful, but is she a vicar's wife?'"

"Presumably," said Bethancourt, pausing to light a cigarette, "she was more sure than you?"

"Oh, yes." The vicar grinned. "She said she didn't see why she wouldn't make a perfectly wonderful vicar's wife so long as the vicar in question was me."

Bethancourt smiled. "And she was right, in the end."

"Definitely. I've never been this happy, never enjoyed life so much. It's like a whole new life, really. And Leandra's happy, too. It's incredible, how fond we are of each other. Well, here we are. We might as well go 'round to the back door, if you don't mind."

Leandra Tothill, reflected Bethancourt, certainly looked happy. She greeted her husband with enthusiasm, and urged Bethancourt to make himself comfortable at the kitchen table. He took a chair and let his eyes travel over her, secretly amused. If the vicar's tweed jacket was incongruous with his cassock, his wife was just as eccentrically dressed. She had put on a gray sweater and wool skirt with a chef's apron tied over all, and had tied back her hair with a bit of shocking pink fabric that looked as if it might have come out of the ragbag. Her legs were bare, and she had pulled a pair of thick, oversized socks over her feet in lieu of slippers; they drooped about her ankles.

"Would you like a drop of beer?" asked the vicar. "It's ham sandwiches for lunch. You will have one, won't you?"

"Today's great idea," said Bethancourt happily. "Cerberus," he added, frowning, "leave Mrs. Tothill alone."

Leandra was standing at the counter, carving slices from a large ham, and Cerberus was glued to her side, tail wagging eagerly.

"Can't he have a bit?" asked Leandra, arresting the downward movement of her hand in which she held a sliver of ham.

"He can if you want to give it to him," said Bethancourt. "But he won't stop asking afterward."

"That's all right," said Leandra cheerfully, holding out the tidbit for the Borzoi. "He's really remarkably well-behaved. Did you train him yourself?"

"He was housebroken when he came to me. I got a book and did the rest myself. It took awhile." Bethancourt gazed fondly at his pet, who seemed to have taken to Leandra with a devotion not entirely explained by the ham.

"Richard wants a dog," said Leandra over her shoulder. "But he's afraid I should end up taking care of it."

"Well, you probably would," said the vicar.

"I don't know," she said, and shrugged. "Anyway, Steve Eberhart says those puppies of Mr. Powell's will be ready to leave home in a week or so. I told him maybe we'd take one."

"Oh, really, Lee." Tothill was laughing at her. "You always want me to have anything I fancy."

"What sort of dog is it?" asked Bethancourt.

"They're Kerry blue terriers, more or less," answered the vicar.

"Very appealing dogs," said Bethancourt.

"Well," said the vicar doubtfully, "we'll see." He set three bottles of Bass on the table and then sat down himself, reaching for a page of notes.

"Your sermon?" asked Bethancourt.

"No, no." Tothill produced a pair of half-glasses and peered at the paper. "Lee and I wrote down what we remembered Charlie saying about Eve," he said. "It's not very much, but you're welcome to it."

Bethancourt sampled his beer, lit a cigarette, and leaned back with a sigh of content to listen.

"We began," said the vicar, "by trying to remember everything we knew about Eve, and then to trace it all back to where we had heard it in the first place. We both remember when Charlie first came here, and meeting him in the Deer and Hounds, but neither of us remember when we first knew he had a daughter."

"We probably asked about his family," put in Leandra. "It's the sort of thing one does."

"Anyway," went on Tothill, "it was general knowledge that he was a widower and had a grown-up daughter living abroad. The next bit is that she was single—we've put that separately because Lee remembers it."

"Yes," she said. "I remember asking him if she had married a Frenchman and he said no, she had gone to a finishing school there, and that she was still single. And then he said that she travelled quite a bit, that she'd inherited the wanderlust from him. He seemed quite pleased about that, about sharing a trait with her."

"The other thing we remember," said Tothill, "is that whenever he spoke of her, it was as if she was on the other side of the world. That must have come from his being so far away for so long."

Eve Bingham, Bethancourt recalled, had said much the same thing.

"The next thing is much later, after we had got to know him. He mentioned one night being in Paris before he came back to England and I asked him why his daughter never visited, or why he didn't go to see her. He seemed very surprised at the question, but after a minute or two he said he supposed there wasn't any reason now that he was living in England, but that it was probably too late. I didn't press it, though it seemed to me there was a story there. He was a very private man in many ways, and I didn't like to pry. In my profession, curiosity is often viewed as meddling."

"As if," snorted Leandra, "you had to go looking for problems to solve."

"No," grinned Tothill, "I certainly don't. The trouble is usually to convince people that I can't solve their problems for them and that praying, although certainly admirable and uplifting, is rarely an answer in itself."

"People take comfort from it, though," said Bethancourt.

"Yes, but comfort isn't always what they need." Tothill looked rather stern. "If your husband is beating you, prayer may help you bear it, but it won't make him stop. God does not deal in magic."

"Oh, dear," said Leandra, coming over with the sandwiches. "I didn't know she had been to see you again."

"Yesterday," said the vicar briefly, with a look at their guest which suggested discussion of the subject would be better left until they were alone.

His wife took the hint smoothly, setting down the plates and taking her chair while she said, "I've put mustard on the sandwiches, Mr. Bethancourt. I do hope that's all right?"

"Brilliant," Bethancourt assured her. He took a bite and found that indeed it was. "This is very nice," he said. "Thank you so much."

"The ham came off the Brook farm," she answered. "They're marvelous with pigs. But we've got off the subject. What's next on the list, my love?"

Tothill looked back at his notes. "It's rather superficial," he said apologetically to Bethancourt. "But we thought you might as well have everything."

"Quite right," said Bethancourt.

"Charlie was talking about his wife one night," continued the vicar, "and mentioned that Eve looked very much like her. He said it had been a bit of a shock, when he saw her in Paris, to find his daughter looking the way he remembered his wife. I think it was in the same conversation that we gathered that his wife had died young and that he had raised Eve himself. But he didn't talk much about that part. As I say, it was really a conversation about his wife."

"It was rather touching," said Leandra. "He was obviously still so very sorry he had lost her."

"That's the worst of losing someone unexpectedly," said Bethancourt. "It's such a tragedy that you make a paragon of them and no one else can ever live up to that. I don't mean to imply that Bingham's marriage wasn't ideal; very likely it was."

"No, I agree with you," said the vicar. "Whether it was a perfect marriage or fraught with difficulties, losing one's partner practically guarantees that one's memory of it will be as perfect."

"Well, I think you're both callous," said Leandra. "I am sure Charlie loved his wife very much and was truly broken up over her death."

"Nobody's saying that's not true," said Tothill mildly.

She was peering over his shoulder.

"There's only one more thing," she said. "Fairly recently, when he got a letter from Eve. We asked how she was and he said she seemed to be doing very well, but that, as far as he could tell, he was no nearer to having a son-in-law."

"I gather he thought a son-in-law would be a good thing?" asked Bethancourt.

"Oh, yes," said Tothill. "The comment was certainly in that spirit. I think he was somewhat concerned about her being left alone when he died. I had the impression that the heart attack he'd had had truly frightened him, though he never spoke of it except as a joke."

"That's understandable," said Bethancourt. "Surely something like that would frighten anyone."

"Coming face to face with one's mortality usually does," agreed Tothill wryly.

Bethancourt took another bite of his sandwich, washed it down with beer, and asked, "So what was your overall impression? What would you say his attitude toward Eve was?"

They looked at each other for a moment.

"What any parent's is," replied Leandra, shrugging. "He was proud and obviously very fond of her."

That was all very well, thought Bethancourt to himself, but was she fond of him?

"Bloody hell," muttered Bethancourt, and carefully extricated himself from the hedge.

Upon leaving the Tothills, he had decided to go on to the Eberharts to see if their reminiscences matched the Tothills'. The day having cleared, he decided on the spur of the moment to walk, a decision both he and Cerberus had enjoyed.

The Eberharts had done their best, but they were less observant than the Tothills, and did not have much to add that was enlightening. Nevertheless, Bethancourt had a very pleasant chat with them, not regretting the time spent at all. At least, he hadn't until he had bade them good-bye and emerged from the cottage only to find the sun had set, and although there was a trace of light lingering in the western sky, the road, shadowed by the hedge, lay in inky blackness. He could barely make out a white gleam from Cerberus's coat, and, in making for the dog, he promptly tripped over a twig and fell into the hedge.

"Oh, damn," he said, examining himself and finding a tear in his trousers. He sighed and glanced up at Bingham's cottage, where a white Rolls-Royce was parked and a light shone in the window. According to the Eberharts, Eve had arrived earlier in the afternoon and had lately been joined by Derek Towser. Bethancourt, turning his back to the wind to light a cigarette, contemplated the wisdom of peeking in at the windows. Regretfully, he decided it would be impractical, particularly since the Eberharts would be almost sure to notice.

He turned back toward the village, groping his way past the hedge and sighing. It was going to be a long walk back, and the light jacket which had been just right for a walk in the sunshine was now beginning to feel inadequate. He thought wistfully of the torch tucked into the glove box of his car and sighed again.

"Come along, Cerberus," he said. "We had better get started."

It was late that evening when Gibbons arrived at Stutely Manor and found Astley-Cooper and Bethancourt sitting over a chess game and drinking cognac.

He was tired, and gratefully accepted a snifter of cognac, but refused to express much sympathy over the tear the fall into the hedge had put in Bethancourt's trousers.

"What were you doing in the hedge, anyway?" he asked. "You weren't spying on Bingham's cottage, were you?"

"Certainly not," replied Bethancourt, very glad now that he had ignored that impulse. "I was coming out of the Eberharts'. I walked up there from the village this afternoon, forgetting that it would be dark when I left."

"The Eberharts'? Oh, yes, you were trolling for information about Bingham and his daughter. Did you get anything?"

"Not really." Bethancourt leant back, stretching his legs out. "There was certainly nothing in Bingham's manner that led anybody to suspect he was displeased with her, or had any intention of disinheriting her. But money is not her only motive; she may well have been harboring a deep resentment against him for years. Of course, that isn't to say that in fact she was."

"No," agreed Gibbons, sighing. "There's nothing to prove anything. Nearly anybody could have done it, but why should they?"

"His mysterious girlfriend might have done it," suggested Astley-Cooper.

"We might know the answer to that if only we could find out who she was." Gibbons shook his head, frustrated. "We don't even know where he died. I never saw such a case. I'll never be promoted at this rate."

"Yes, you will," contradicted Bethancourt. "What were you and Carmichael doing all day?"

"Investigating Andrew Sealingham, Bingham's partner," answered Gibbons. He glanced at Astley-Cooper, and added before going on, "You understand this is not for publication, Mr. Astley-Cooper? We can't have the whole village discussing the police's innermost thoughts about the case."

"Of course, of course, my dear sir," said Astley-Cooper. "That's quite understood and I assure you I'll be as discreet as the grave." He hesitated, his face falling. "Or would you prefer I excuse myself? Probably the proper thing to do . . ."

"No, no," said Bethancourt, who understood how Astley-Cooper

154

felt from his own experiences in the early days of sitting in on discussions between Gibbons and Carmichael. "I think we can trust Clarence to keep this all to himself."

Gibbons nodded acceptance of this guarantee. "Well," he said, "as far as money goes, Andrew Sealingham had as much motive as Eve. But we got nothing today. If he was at all concerned about Bingham's return to England, he didn't mention it to anyone we could find. And there was nothing in his business dealings he might have wanted to conceal—our Andrew is squeaky clean."

"Does he have a prescription for Seconal?" asked Bethancourt.

Gibbons shook his head. "Not according to his doctor. But of course, the problem with that angle is that anyone might have borrowed a few tablets from a friend. Possibly not even with the friend's knowledge."

Astley-Cooper was frowning in thought. "It's terribly odd about Charlie's girlfriend," he said. "I can't see how it could have been anyone in the village, and yet he's not spent very much time away. Not enough to have met someone, I mean."

"What about that list of summer visitors that Pat Stikes made up?" asked Bethancourt. "Has anything come of that?"

Gibbons yawned and shook his head. "Not really," he answered. "Mathers has worked his way through them, but he's only got two possibles, and he's not very sanguine about either of them. But of course, Stikes concentrated on women from the London area, and for all we know, this woman could have lived almost anywhere."

Bethancourt frowned, thinking this over.

"It seems to me," he said slowly, "that if I were having a secret affair with a woman who lived anywhere nearby, I would hardly use London as an alibi. I would tell people I was heading into Cirencester, or perhaps Swindon. I think it's most likely the lady does live, if not in London itself, then at least a good piece of the way there."

"Probably," admitted Gibbons. "In any case, we've had another idea: that perhaps she could be a weekender. After all, this whole affair seems to have started in the spring, just the time one would open a summer cottage."

"Good thinking," said Bethancourt. "Clarence, can you think of anyone like that?"

Astley-Cooper shrugged. "Not really," he answered. "There's not much account taken of the summer people, truth to tell. Gerald Owens, the grocer, you know, he might know better."

Gibbons yawned again. "We'll have a go at him tomorrow," he said. "And we haven't asked the constable about it yet—it's her day off."

Bethancourt was regarding his friend rather severely.

"Jack," he said, "if you don't stop yawning, we shall take away your cognac and send you off to bed."

Gibbons grinned tiredly at him.

"I expect that's where I belong," he said. "It's very wearisome investigating a thing all day and getting nowhere."

"I daresay it must be," said Astley-Cooper sympathetically. "Rather like trying to find a good source of Stonesfield slate before the National Trust will let you repair your roof."

"Slate?" asked Gibbons. "Wouldn't there be a quarry?"

"There was—in 1640," said Astley-Cooper sadly. "I believe the last mine closed somewhere around the turn of the century."

"Oh," said Gibbons a little blankly. He tried to think of some appropriate comment, but instead merely yawned. "Oh, dear," he said. "I really am all in. I think I'd better say good night."

"I'll walk you to the car," said Bethancourt, rising. "Cheer up, old man. Maybe there will be a break in the case tomorrow."

"Maybe," said Gibbons doubtfully. "Good night, Mr. Astley-Cooper."

"Good night, my boy. Get a good rest."

CHAPTER

10

*B*ethancourt woke with a start, jolted to alertness by a hand
shaking his shoulder. Blinking, he peered up into the dark
to see a blurry face he thought must be Astley-Cooper's.

"Clarence?" he said, rolling over. "Is everything all right?"

"Tip-top, my boy," said Astley-Cooper. "I'm awfully sorry to wake
you, but I couldn't wait 'til morning."

Bethancourt rubbed his face blearily. It was dark in the room, but
a stream of light came in from the hall through the open doorway.

"That's all right," he said sleepily.

Cerberus was standing beside Astley-Cooper, apparently joining
in his excitement to judge from the wagging tail. The Borzoi, however, had what their host lacked: experience in waking his master. He
shoved a cold nose under Bethancourt's naked arm.

"Ow!" said Bethancourt. "Stop that, Cerberus."

He pushed himself into a sitting position and scraped the hair out
of his eyes.

"So sorry," said Astley-Cooper, not sounding sorry at all. "I truly would have burst if I had had to keep this to myself 'til morning."

"Of course," said Bethancourt vaguely, reaching for his glasses. "What time is it?"

Astley-Cooper peered at the clock, but failed to make it out in the dim light.

"Five-ish?" he suggested.

"Ah," said Bethancourt, adjusting his glasses and stretching out a hand to pet his dog. "So why are you up?"

"Couldn't sleep," replied Astley-Cooper, seating himself on the edge of the bed, his face shining with repressed excitement. "Phillip, I do believe I know who Bingham's girlfriend is."

"You do?" asked Bethancourt stupidly.

"I can't think how it never occurred to me before," went on Astley-Cooper. "But once it came to me, it was perfectly obvious. She's only here part of the time, she has a place in London, and she's certainly attractive."

"All right," said Bethancourt, making a heroic effort to wake up, "I'll bite. Who is it?"

"Joan Bonnar," announced Astley-Cooper with a flourish, and he bounced on the bed.

Bethancourt stared at him, his sluggish brain trying to make sense of this.

"I expect," continued Astley-Cooper, obviously pleased with himself, "I didn't think of her at once because she's so very seldom here. Only, of course, when I *did* think of her, I realized that she's been down here quite a lot recently—spent most of the summer at the farmhouse, really—and then it all made sense."

It was making sense to Bethancourt, too, even in his newly awakened state.

"Good God," he said, staring at the dim outline of Astley-Cooper's face in the dark. "Clarence, you're brilliant. Here, do you mind if we have the light on?"

He reached for the bedside lamp, cursing himself for not seeing the obvious, when it occurred to him just why he had never thought of this particular solution: Joan Bonnar was too firmly fixed in his mind as belonging to another world. She was starring in a play in London, her last film had come out in the summer, she was a legend and as such did not have affairs with everyday people.

Only it seemed that she did.

"Good grief," he muttered and switched on the lamp, blinking in the sudden light. He fell back against the pillows and gazed at his host in amazement.

"Joan Bonnar," he said. "It seems absolutely incredible."

"Doesn't it though?" agreed Astley-Cooper cheerfully. "You can see, though, how it all works out, can't you?"

Bethancourt, on the verge of replying that he did, realized in the nick of time that Astley-Cooper was panting to explain his thought process.

"It explains the secrecy," Astley-Cooper was saying, "because she'd naturally want to keep it out of the tabloids. And it explains the expensive clothes you found, because of course Joan Bonnar has pots of money. But most of all, it explains why Bingham was leaving to visit a lady friend on a Sunday afternoon—because the theaters are closed on Sunday."

"That's right," said Bethancourt. "Joan Bonnar's in a new play, isn't she? I remember seeing a review of it last month."

"Exactly." Astley-Cooper beamed at him. "I've got it right this time, haven't I?" he asked. "I've not muddled anything up this go 'round."

Bethancourt laughed. "No, Clarence, you certainly haven't," he said. "Though," he added, sobering, "it's hard to think of Joan Bonnar as a murderess."

Astley-Cooper shifted uneasily on the bed. "Perhaps she's not?" he suggested.

"Perhaps," said Bethancourt. "There are other suspects, after all.

Here, hand me my mobile, will you? We'll see what Scotland Yard says about it."

Astley-Cooper looked startled. "Now?" he faltered. "Don't you think, Phillip, you had better wait 'til morning to ring the police?"

"Nonsense," said Bethancourt, lighting a cigarette and carefully balancing the ashtray on his stomach. "If they wanted to sleep through the night, they should have thought of this themselves—as you said, Clarence, it's perfectly obvious. Hand over that phone."

Astley-Cooper did as requested.

As a policeman, having his night's sleep broken by the insistent ringing of the phone was second nature to Gibbons. He groped on the bedside table, found his mobile by touch, opened it, and held it to his ear, all without so much as opening his eyes.

"Hullo," he grunted, face still half-mashed into the pillows.

"Wake up," came Bethancourt's voice. "Clarence has figured out who the mystery lady is."

"Wha—?" Gibbons's eyes flew open. "Phillip?"

"That's right."

"Hold on a tic . . ."

Gibbons struggled into a sitting position and turned on the light. When he saw the time, he cursed his friend roundly.

"Are you drunk?" he demanded.

"Not at all," replied Bethancourt. "I am merely keeping the police informed in a timely manner. Have you happened to hear that Joan Bonnar is coming down to visit her children tomorrow?"

"Dear Lord." Gibbons flopped back down into the bed, squeezing his eyes tightly shut. "Please tell me you haven't woken me up to discuss village gossip."

"Apparently," persisted Bethancourt, "Miss Bonnar has been staying down here quite frequently over the past few months."

Gibbons's eyes opened again. "No," he said. "You can't be trying to tell me you think Joan Bonnar is a murderess."

"Possibly not," admitted Bethancourt. "But I do think she was Bingham's girlfriend. Think about it—it all fits."

Gibbons thought. "It does all fit," he agreed in another moment. "Why did we never think of her before? I rather had the impression that she was rarely here, and stayed holed up in the farmhouse when she was."

"I thought the same thing," said Bethancourt. "Which of course is why we didn't think of it. Are you going to tell Carmichael?"

"Of course," began Gibbons, and then caught himself. "You mean now? Don't be an idiot, Phillip, it's five o'clock in the morning. It can certainly wait another two or three hours—in fact, I don't know why you didn't wait to ring me. Surely you didn't think there was anything that could be done at this hour."

"I rang," retorted Bethancourt, "because we're all excited up here at the manor about finally getting a break in the case. Clarence is opening the champagne as we speak. I didn't want to leave you out of it."

"Thanks so much," said Gibbons dryly. "Since I'm in no position to share the champagne, I hope you don't mind if I ring off and go back to sleep."

"As you like," said Bethancourt cheerfully. "But don't blame me if Joan Bonnar is escaping at this very moment, only you're too sleepy to catch her."

"Good night, Phillip," said Gibbons and shut off his phone.

Carmichael, presented with this theory the next morning at breakfast, was equally struck by its merits. Upon consideration, however, he decided not to race directly off to the farmhouse and confront the Bensons and Mrs. Potts.

"Always assuming we're right about this," he told Gibbons, "I've no doubt we could get the Bensons to admit to it. But there would be no way of preventing them from alerting Miss Bonnar before she ever got here, and I'd rather take her by surprise, too. Much rather," he added thoughtfully. "No, since she's due here anyway, I think we'll wait to pay our visit to the farmhouse until after she's arrived."

Accordingly, Gibbons and Constable Stikes had taken it in turn to keep watch on the entrance to the farmhouse lane until at last, just before sunset, Stikes looked up and saw a black Mercedes saloon coming along the road toward her. She thought she recognized it, but waited until it had slowed and made the turn into the lane before she picked up her mobile and rang Gibbons.

At six o'clock Sunday evening, Leandra Tothill was bustling about her kitchen, just about to serve dinner. She was running late for a Sunday—it was the vicar's night to play chess with Astley-Cooper—but Eve Bingham had come over in the afternoon to discuss a few last-minute arrangements about the funeral tomorrow, and that had put her behind. Leandra frowned as she thought of her, as she had been doing ever since Eve had left. The young woman had been dry-eyed and businesslike, not at all Leandra's idea of a spoiled rich girl. She sighed and reminded herself that she had never known any spoiled rich girls before, and all her ideas were no doubt caricatures of reality. The fact that the woman did not choose to expose her innermost feelings had no bearing on whether or not she was a murderer.

"No bearing at all," muttered Leandra, slapping a pat of butter on the peas.

She surveyed her preparations and then glanced with some irritation out of the window, wondering where her husband was. He had gone across to check on the grave, and Leandra could only think that something must be wrong with it. Either that, or he'd fallen in; he'd left more than half an hour ago.

"Really," she said aloud, peering at the chicken, "if he wants dinner early, he could at least be here to eat it. *I've* got nothing on tonight."

At that moment, Tothill hove into view, trotting through the churchyard. Leandra waved, and began heaping peas onto the plates.

"I'm sorry, my love," he said as he came in. "Mrs. Cleppett caught me just as I was coming back. She had the most extraordinary news."

"Really?" said Leandra, busy at the stove. "What did she says?"

"It seems," said Tothill, leaning over his wife's shoulder and sniffing appreciatively, "that Joan Bonnar has come down."

"That's hardly news," said Leandra, scooping rice out of the pot. "She's often down these days. I think she's been having a maternal fit of late."

"Yes, but, Lee, apparently she's confessed to being Charlie's girl-friend!"

"No!" exclaimed Leandra, immediately losing interest in her dinner and turning to face him. "Charlie Bingham and Joan Bonnar?"

Tothill nodded. "Mrs. Cleppett had it from Mrs. Stikes," he said. "Pat told her when she came off duty today. I don't know how it happened, but Mrs. Cleppett says the chief inspector and Sergeant Gibbons have been waiting all day for Miss Bonnar to arrive, and as soon as she did, they were off to the farmhouse. They're there now evidently."

Leandra shook her head. "Who would have believed such a thing?" she said. Then she laughed. "And to think of Charlie, the sly old thing, keeping something like that dark. It's so like him."

Tothill reached 'round her to pick up a spatula and dish out the chicken.

"You'll probably hear more about it at the pub tonight," he said. "You're going over, aren't you?"

"Here, let me," said Leandra. "You get the wine. No, I wasn't going to the pub."

"I thought you usually did on Sundays."

"I do. I was just thinking I'd stay in tonight and read."

"Well," said Tothill, pouring the wine, "I must say I think you're picking the wrong night to have a change of pace."

Early Sunday dinners were the rule in Chipping Chedding and by seven o'clock the bar at the Deer and Hounds was packed. The news had spread swiftly from the Stikes's home throughout the village, and those who were not gathered at the pub were making use of their telephones. Everyone had long ago become inured to the comings and goings of the famous actress; now it was as if she had come among them for the first time.

The press, gathered for the funeral tomorrow, was electrified. This was the best bit of luck they had come across in a long time. Having been firmly repulsed at the farmhouse, and knowing in any case that they would get nothing there until after the police had gone, they had dropped back to annoy the Eberharts, who denied knowing anything about their famous neighbor. This established, the reporters repaired to the Deer and Hounds to pick up whatever they could and to await a statement from Joan Bonnar herself. She had been famous since she was nineteen, and she knew the rules. After the police had gone, she would make a statement.

It was Julie Benson who opened the door when the policemen arrived. Her long hair was pulled back from her face and hung in a single braid down her back. She looked decidedly depressed.

"Hello, Miss," said Carmichael. "We've come to see your mother."

That seemed to startle her, but in the next moment she shrugged.

"So you've twigged to it, have you?" she said. "I'm sorry we couldn't tell you before, but she'd forbidden us to tell anyone, and you don't know the fireworks there would have been if we had. Besides, we couldn't tell her Charlie was dead in the middle of a week of performances—she'd have had a fit."

"But surely she already knew," said Gibbons. "It's been in all the papers."

"Mother doesn't read papers."

"Do you mean to say," interrupted Carmichael, "that you deliberately lied to Sergeant Gibbons because you were afraid the news would upset your mother's performance?"

"Sounds mad, doesn't it?" she said. "But you don't know what she's like. Nothing, but nothing, is allowed to interfere with a performance. James and I learned that before we were eight. She's upset now, but at least she isn't screaming at us. And it's only delayed you a couple of days."

Carmichael's brow looked threatening, but Julie did not appear to notice it.

"So," he said, "you expect me to believe that you—and your mother—were always going to tell us the truth, just at a time of your own choosing?"

"It's true, whether you believe it or not," she answered. "None of us are stupid enough to think you wouldn't find out eventually. Hell, Mother even came down with her press agent so he can spin the story to the media. They're in the drawing room this minute, working up to ringing you."

"Then perhaps we'd better spare them the trouble," said Carmichael icily.

"Through there," said Julie, jerking her head. "I won't go in, if you don't mind. This is one performance I'd prefer to miss."

James Benson and Martha Potts seemed to share this feeling. At least, neither of them were present in the drawing room. Joan Bonnar sat in splendid isolation on the sofa. It was strange, thought Gibbons, to see her familiar features before him, just like anyone else's. Not blown up to several times their size on a movie screen, not reduced from being seen at a distance on a stage, not glossed over on the cover of a magazine.

She looked older, he noticed, than she did in photographs, but she was still beautiful. Her blond hair, probably tinted at her age, was carefully arranged, and her deep blue eyes were perfectly made up.

Her complexion had been restored to something resembling its youthful flawlessness with foundation and toner.

Gibbons was too young to remember her early successes on the London stage, or even the debuts of her first films, although these he had since seen on television. He did remember her turbulent marriage to the great Shakespearian actor, Eugene Sinclair. Presumably it was he she had left the twins' father for. She and Sinclair had been divorced at one point, remarried later, and were separated when he had died some six or seven years ago. She had subsequently married a well-to-do London barrister, but had divorced him after two years. Through it all, she had continued to perform brilliantly on both stage and screen.

She greeted them in a voice at once familiar and yet different; it was very odd, thought Gibbons, to have everything about her so familiar and still realize that one didn't know her at all.

There was a harried-looking, gray-haired man seated in the chair to her left, whom she introduced as Ned Watkinson, her press agent.

"Ned wanted to be here," she explained, "so that he can start working on a statement."

"Yes, that's right," said Watkinson. "Miss Bonnar understandably didn't wish to go over this twice, and it's as much of a surprise to me as it is to you, Chief Inspector."

"Is it indeed?" replied Carmichael, seating himself. "In that case, you would have had no reason to inform Miss Bonnar of Mr. Bingham's death."

"Just so," agreed Watkinson, shooting a resentful glance at his client.

She did not see it; her attention was focused on Carmichael.

"So when did you learn of his death, Miss Bonnar?" asked Carmichael.

She waved a hand. "Late last night. Julie rang after the show to tell me."

"You didn't see it in the papers, or hear it on the radio or television?" asked Carmichael in a tone of disbelief.

"No. I catch up on the news on Sunday and Monday. I never read the papers during the week while I'm performing. They so often have something upsetting about me." She was giving nothing away, her face and voice carefully schooled. Only in her eyes was there any sign of strain.

"I see," said Carmichael, leaving the topic. "How long had you known the deceased?"

"Six months or so."

"And you kept your relationship a secret?"

"Martha and the children knew." She hesitated. "Just recently, after we became engaged, we told a few other close friends."

"You were engaged to be married?" asked Carmichael, stunned.

The press agent looked grim.

"Yes," she answered. "He asked me a few weeks ago."

"But no one else knew of your affair until after that?" asked Carmichael. "Why was that?"

She looked astonished that he should ask. "To avoid the publicity, of course," she answered. "Having the tabloids speculate on your feelings puts a terrible strain on a relationship."

"I do hope you understand, Miss Bonnar," said Carmichael, "that anything you tell us will be held in confidence?"

"I do. That's very reassuring, Chief Inspector." But she did not sound reassured; it had been a stock reply.

"In that case, I must ask you to describe your relationship with Mr. Bingham."

"You mean, how we met and so forth?" Carmichael nodded, but she paused to light a cigarette before going on. "I can't see," she said at last, "how that is really pertinent, Chief Inspector, and I—"

"Joan," said Watkinson urgently, "the chief inspector is not a reporter and he knows best how to do his job."

She sighed and gave in at once. "We met here, last spring," she said, answering as if nothing had occurred between question and reply. "I spent a week here at the end of April. We got on well, and when I left, I invited him to the screening of my latest film. Well, that's how it all started. We saw a lot of each other over the summer—I was here quite frequently then. In August I began rehearsals for the play I'm in now, and Charlie started coming up to London more often. Then, about a month ago, he asked me to marry him and I said yes. We were planning to wait until the run of the play was over next summer, and then be married quietly down here and use the farmhouse as our home base. I'd keep the London townhouse, of course . . ."

Her eyes had begun to fill with tears as she spoke of their plans and now she abruptly stabbed the cigarette out and rose.

"Excuse me a moment," she said, and moved swiftly from the room.

There was silence when she had gone. Watkinson broke it.

"She'll be back in a moment," he said confidently. "As soon as she gets herself under control. She can be a prima donna with the best of them, but she's also a trouper."

Carmichael eyed him. He suspected it had been Watkinson who had convinced her of the necessity of revealing her relationship with Bingham before the police discovered it on their own.

"You've worked for Miss Bonnar for a long time?" he asked.

Watkinson grinned. "Getting on for twenty years," he said. "She's taking this awfully well, considering. At any rate, it's a lot better than when Gene Sinclair died."

"Understandably," said Carmichael. "Losing a husband of many years would naturally be more distressing than losing a fiancé."

"Well," said Watkinson, scratching his ear, "I expect that depends. In any case, she's not hysterical now and she'll cope."

Something in his tone caught Gibbons's ear, and he said, "You admire her?"

"Yes," said Watkinson firmly. "I do."

Miss Bonnar reappeared then, giving him a slight smile. Her eyes were red-rimmed and some of the makeup had been wiped away, but she was no longer crying. She apologized for the interruption graciously and seated herself again on the sofa.

"I'm sorry to have to disturb you at a time like this," said Carmichael. "We have just a few more questions. Since your play opened, was Mr. Bingham in the habit of visiting you on the days you have off?"

"Often he did," she answered. "Or sometimes I would come here."

"And last weekend?"

"No. We had no plans last weekend. That was a little unusual, but I had several things scheduled for Monday and, since we were keeping our engagement a secret, he couldn't very well come with me. At the last minute, Ned here scheduled an interview on Sunday, too, so I was solidly booked up."

Carmichael nodded, apparently digesting this information. "So you didn't see him last weekend," he said. "But you would have expected to hear from him during the ensuing week, would you not?"

"Yes, I was surprised he didn't ring," she answered. "We spoke on Saturday—he seemed just as usual then—and made plans for this weekend." She paused for a moment, biting her lip, but then went on, "I rang him on Tuesday and got no answer, and tried again on Thursday. I thought it strange he hadn't tried to contact me, but I never imagined anything was wrong. Charlie was, well, impulsive. If he had gone off to visit someone, or become involved in some project, he might not remember to ring me."

"You said your interview on Sunday was arranged at the last minute. Did Mr. Bingham know about it?"

A puzzled frown appeared between her brows. "Why, I don't know. I knew about it when I talked with him Saturday night, of course, but whether I mentioned it or not—well, I really can't say. It wasn't important."

"It would be useful," said Carmichael, "if you could try to remember, later on. It may make a difference. If he didn't know, and decided to surprise you with a visit on Sunday, then he might have arrived while you were out. What time did you return from your interview?"

"Oh, it must have been about eight thirty. Ned here came back with me and brought up an Indian take-away."

"And what time did you leave Miss Bonnar's flat?"

"Somewhere between half nine and ten," Watkinson said.

Carmichael was rapidly figuring times in his head. If Bingham had driven straight on to London after having his tire mended, he should have arrived there at about six or shortly thereafter.

"Suppose, Miss Bonnar," he asked, "that Mr. Bingham did arrive while you were out. Do you know where he might have gone to wait? Did he have any friends in London?"

"He knew an archaeologist at the university," she answered. "Max Dearfield is his name, I think. But, really, I should have expected him to let himself into the house to wait. He had a key."

"You found no sign that he had been there?"

She shook her head. "No. Of course, I wasn't looking for anything, but if he had been there, he would have left a note to let me know he was in town. As I said, I wasn't expecting him."

"Yes, that would be common sense," said Carmichael. "Let me ask you about something else. Had you met Mr. Bingham's daughter, Eve?"

"No." Tears appeared in her eyes again, but she blinked them away with an effort. "No, I hadn't."

"Do you know if he had informed her of your engagement?"

"I don't believe so. I asked him once, and he said there would be time enough later. We were really being very cautious that no word should leak out."

"Understandably," said Carmichael, who remembered the circus that had surrounded her first marriage to Eugene Sinclair. "Did Mr. Bingham ever talk to you about taking up his old job with Mr. Sealingham's company?"

"He mentioned it, I think," she said vaguely.

"Did you receive the impression that he really meant to do it?"

"I don't know." She made an impatient gesture. "Charlie was full of schemes. He just said once that after we were married, if I took another role, he could always go up to Andrew's place and tinker for a bit if he felt dull. I suppose he meant it. I don't really know."

"I see," said Carmichael. "Then there's just one last question, Miss Bonnar. Have you a prescription for sleeping tablets?"

"Why, yes," she replied, surprised.

"Did Mr. Bingham ever borrow one from you?"

"Heavens, no. Charlie never had the least problem sleeping." The import of the question suddenly struck her, and her eyes widened. "Chief Inspector, had he taken something?"

"Yes," replied Carmichael. "Taken, or was given. We found some sleeping tablets loose in his medicine cupboard. Did you ever leave any there? Or might he have borrowed some of yours without asking first?"

"Absolutely not," she said flatly. "I might have had the bottle in my purse when I stayed at the cottage, but I certainly never left any there. And if he had wanted some for any reason, he would have asked me."

Carmichael nodded slowly; he had been expecting a different answer, but adjusted smoothly nonetheless. "Might we have one of your tablets for analysis? It may have been something else altogether that he took."

"Of course," she said, rising. "I have an extra bottle that I keep here at the farmhouse—you can have that. I'll just go up and get it."

She obviously welcomed the opportunity to leave the room, but for all that, she returned quickly. She handed a small bottle to Carmichael, saying, "I'm afraid there only seem to be a couple left—I must have used more than I remembered."

Carmichael thanked her and, after glancing at the label, passed the bottle to Gibbons, whose heart took a leap when he saw it. It was Seconal.

"This is a rather old-fashioned medication," said Carmichael. "Is there some reason you take it, rather than one of the newer drugs?"

She shrugged. "I got the prescription years ago," she answered. "I've never used it every night or anything like that, just occasionally when I'm too wrought-up to sleep. My doctor has mentioned other sleeping medications, but this has always worked for me. I didn't want to change."

Carmichael nodded. "I see. And how do you take the pills?"

She stared at him as if he had gone mad. "I swallow them down with some water," she answered.

"I only ask," said Carmichael, smiling, "because some people have trouble swallowing tablets, and you might have needed to mix them up in something."

"Oh. No, I've never had difficulty that way."

"Well," said Carmichael, "I think that's all for the moment, then." He rose. "Thank you for your help, Miss Bonnar. We may have additional questions later, but we'll be off now."

He shook hands all round, collected Gibbons, and retreated.

"Well, said Watkinson brightly when the door had closed behind the policemen, "that's over."

"Thank God," she said. "I need a drink. A good, stiff one."

"All right," he said, moving to fetch it for her. "But don't forget there's still one hurdle to go, Joan."

"One hurdle? Oh, you mean the media."

"After that you can relax and drink all you want."

She grimaced. "Not if I don't want to be hungover at the funeral tomorrow," she said. "God, how I wish we could keep the press away from that. It's going to be bad enough as it is, with Eve there and never having met me."

Watkinson handed her a neat scotch. "It won't be so bad," he said reassuringly. "All you have to do is give her your condolences and wait through the ceremony. I'll have a car waiting to nip you away at the earliest opportunity. And you're bearing up beautifully, Joan. This will be easy as pie compared to some of the other things you've had to go through."

"You mean Gene," she said dully. She had gulped down half the whisky and seemed calmer. "That was different, Ned. He was . . . well, I've had one great love in my life and I'm old enough now to know that kind of thing only happens once. But Charlie had never really got over his first wife, so we were in the same boat. We thought we could be . . . comfortable together. I expect," she added bitterly, "that was foolish. Joan Bonnar is not a comfortable sort of person to be."

"You've had some rotten breaks, that's all," insisted Watkinson. He patted her arm and rose. "I had best go tell the reporters you'll speak to them in, say, an hour. I do think it's best to get it all over with at once, unless you really want to wait until later."

"No," she answered. "No, you're right, let's get it over with. You can come and tell me what I ought and ought not to say while I'm repairing my make-up. But, Ned," she added sharply, "I will not see them here."

"No, of course not," he said. "I'll make arrangements for somewhere in the village. We'll drive down. You just sit for a minute and collect yourself, and I'll be right back."

She nodded and he left her, sipping scotch and staring out the window.

Carmichael paused in the hallway, his eyebrows drawn together in a thoughtful frown. "On the face of it," he said, "it's difficult to see how Bingham could have taken the stuff by accident. But she could have murdered him deliberately, Gibbons."

"How do you figure that, sir?" asked Gibbons. "She was being interviewed at seven o'clock when he died."

"But she didn't need to be there," answered Carmichael. "She could have arranged to meet him at the townhouse after her interview, making certain she's late coming back. And in the meanwhile, she leaves out something he'll be sure to eat or drink while he's waiting for her, thoroughly lacing it with Seconal."

173

"But she couldn't be sure where she would find the body, sir," said Gibbons, like Carmichael keeping his voice low lest they be overheard. "What about Watkinson?"

"She said he brought up the food, lad. He probably stopped off for it while she went on to the house. It would give her enough time to drag the body into the bedroom, if it wasn't there already." Carmichael considered. "If Watkinson left her at half nine, she might just have made it here before Mrs. Eberhart saw the light in Bingham's cottage at eleven thirty." He frowned. "But then how would she get back? I can't see her coming over here, to three people who clearly don't like her, even if two of them are family."

"But we already know they'd lie for her," pointed out Gibbons. "They already have, when I asked about Bingham's girlfriend. And, remember, sir, only the twins were here. Mrs. Potts was at her sister's."

"That's true," said Carmichael. "Well, if she did come to them, they could have driven her back that night. Or she might have taken the train, if she were disguised. We'll have to find out when she was first seen on Monday—you can get that from the press agent. And we'll have to check out the parking situation around her flat."

Gibbons had been thinking. "There's no reason to think Watkinson is out of it," he said. "I don't mean for the actual murder, but what do you think a press agent's first reaction would be on encountering a dead body in his famous client's house?"

A slow smile spread over Carmichael's face. "To cover it up," he answered.

"Exactly, sir. She might even have counted on that. If he believed Bingham had had a heart attack, he might well have been willing to help her move the body and thus leave her name out of it. And he could have driven her back."

"That does leave us with those bicycle tracks, though," said Carmichael. "They wouldn't have needed the bike. On the other hand, we've never been sure the bicycle was connected with the murder."

"No, sir." Gibbons hesitated. "But do you think she did do it, sir?" he asked.

Carmichael gave him a wry smile. "I don't know," he answered. "It's the devil, having to deal with a professional actress. Well, we'd best finish up here. Mrs. Potts is probably in the kitchen—you look for her, and I'll find the twins. We need to find out whether or not they knew where Bingham was going on Sunday."

The kitchen was a large one with a blue-and-cream tiled floor and a good deal of highly polished copper hanging from the ceiling. A long butchers-block table ran down the middle of the room and Mrs. Potts was seated at it on a stool, looking over the paper and drinking a cup of coffee. She looked up as Gibbons came in and said, "I expect you've seen her then?"

There was no mistaking who she meant.

"Yes," answered Gibbons. "I've just come to put one or two questions to you."

She nodded, her long face somber. "Well," she said, "I'm sorry we couldn't tell you before, but there it is: she would have taken our heads off. Would you like a coffee?"

Gibbons said he would and seated himself on a second stool while she fetched it.

Mrs. Potts had left Chipping Chedding on Sunday before Bingham and so had no knowledge of his departure or plans. But she admitted that, had she known, she would have assumed he was going to visit Miss Bonnar. She paused and then added, "We all liked Charlie. There was a bit of constraint after he took up with Miss Bonnar—well, there was bound to be. The twins don't think much of anybody who would marry their mother and you can't blame them. Still, we all felt that if she had to get married again, Charlie was a good sort."

"But it must have been difficult, having her down here so much "more often than usual?" suggested Gibbons, accurately picking up on what she had left unsaid.

"Difficult isn't the word for it," she said grimly. "And the very idea that she'd move back here after they were married! I nearly had a fit and Julie almost fainted away. It may be her house, but it's been our home—the twins have always lived here, ever since they were babies. I confronted Charlie about that," she added, "and he was decent, I must say. Said as how he'd work something out."

"That was good of him."

"Yes. As I said, he was a good sort." She shrugged.

"So really," pursued Gibbons, "you had no objections to the marriage beyond that?"

"No. Why should I? It's no business of mine who she marries."

"But they seemed happy together?"

"Oh, yes. They were very affectionate and all that. Not," she added hastily, "that they were all over each other. They were a bit past that, it wouldn't have been seemly." She made a face. "Not that I think it's seemly at any time of life. We had all that with Mr. Sinclair—she couldn't take her eyes off him and he was the same. Tiresome, I call it. But it wasn't like that with Charlie."

"No rows?"

"None that I knew about. They were happy together in a quiet sort of way."

Gibbons paused and sipped his coffee, thinking. "Is the household here completely dependent on Miss Bonnar financially?" he asked.

Mrs. Potts didn't like the question, he could tell, but she answered gruffly, "More or less. The twins have what their father left them, but that's not much. Miss Bonnar pays my salary and gives them an allowance. It's generous, I'll give her that."

"Neither of the Bensons work then?"

She might have been a tigress whose cubs he was attacking.

"They do a lot of work in the parish," she said huffily. "And Julie takes care of the horses herself—up every morning at dawn, she is.

You can't call that nothing. They certainly don't sit about on their backsides—I didn't bring them up that way."

"Of course not," said Gibbons soothingly. "I was only wondering if they could have moved elsewhere if they'd had the inclination, or whether they were tied to jobs here."

She was placated, although there was still a dangerous glint in her eye. "They could move," she said. "But why should they want to? Or have to? Even if Miss Bonnar had moved in with Charlie, she wouldn't have stayed. She never does."

Gibbons hesitated. "She's impulsive, you mean?"

"That's right. She may have had some idea of living the quiet life down here with Charlie, but she'd have been bored soon enough. Not with Charlie, I don't mean, but with the reality of life in a small village. She'd have been off after a couple of months of it."

"So then it wouldn't have surprised you to hear that she'd had a change of heart and called the wedding off?" asked Gibbons.

Mrs. Potts looked taken aback. "Certainly it would have," she contradicted. "I've just finished telling you they were happy together. She can be impulsive, but that's not to say she always is. I don't think she agreed to marry Charlie on impulse. It wasn't a whirlwind romance kind of thing at all."

Which, reflected Gibbons, did not bode well for her having murdered him, if Mrs. Potts was right in her observations.

Carmichael was in the stables, watching Julie Benson currycomb a bay mare. He could not recollect ever having been in a stable before, and he found it much cleaner than he would have supposed. The floor of the aisle looked to have been recently scrubbed, and the smell of hay, horses, and saddle soap, while strong, was nevertheless a good, fresh smell.

He had found James Benson in the study, but he had seemed reluctant to speak to the chief inspector without his sister. Yet now they had found her, James did most of the talking, while Julie kept her attention on the mare and only occasionally contributed to the conversation.

"We didn't know Charlie had gone off on Sunday," said James in answer to Carmichael's query. "But if we had known, I would have assumed he'd gone to see Mother."

Julie nodded her agreement. "I don't think he often left Chipping Chedding except to see her," she added.

"Tell me," said Carmichael. "Did you like Charlie?"

"Oh, yes," said James. "We thought he was a bit of an ass for wanting to marry Mother, of course, but he was a good enough sort otherwise." He laughed. "We rather suspected that he had proposed more out of a desire for money than for connubial bliss, but obviously we were wrong about that."

"I don't know that I really believed that about the money," said Julie. "I just couldn't think of what else the attraction would be."

Carmichael thought that here they did their mother an injustice. She might not be much of a maternal figure, but she was an attractive and captivating woman by any man's standards.

"Then you were unaware that Mr. Bingham had money of his own?" he asked.

They both nodded. "It was a big shock when the news came out," said James. "We'd no idea. We'd been down to his cottage once or twice, and I still find it hard to believe."

"But your mother must have known?" pursued Carmichael.

James shrugged. "If she did, she never told us."

"Did you have any objections to the marriage apart from the money?" asked Carmichael.

"No, no," said James. "We didn't object to the marriage at all, even if he did want her money. I mean, they were happy together so far as I could see."

"It only would have mattered to us," said Julie, moving round to the horse's other side, "if Charlie had been truly odious, or if they were fighting all the time. You can't think how disruptive that sort of thing is. But they were quiet together, as James says."

"I understand Miss Bonnar has been visiting here regularly since she became involved with Mr. Bingham," said Carmichael. "Did she always let you know when she was coming?"

Both twins made a face at the mention of their mother's visits, and James replied dryly, "Oh, she'd always ring up and let us know. She likes to have everything ready for her."

"But you weren't expecting her last weekend?"

"No." James shook his head. "Not a peep out of her."

"You remember, James," said Julie. "She said she wouldn't be coming last weekend because of all the engagements she had on Monday. She moaned and groaned about missing Charlie."

"That's right," said James. "I'd forgotten."

"I see," said Carmichael. "By the way, I take it you've both been to your mother's house in London?" They looked surprised, but nodded. "Is there a usual place to park?"

"It depends on the time of day," said James. "I've been pretty lucky—I practically always find a place on the square. Or if Mother's got her car in the garage, one can use her space. Why do you ask?"

Carmichael smiled. "Just trying to put the odds and ends together," he answered. "If Charlie did go to see your mother last Sunday, I want to know where he left his car."

"Oh."

James lost interest, turning to watch his sister run a brush down her horse's flank. They both seemed perfectly at ease, and if they had helped their mother escape after she had killed her fiancé, Carmichael could not tell.

CHAPTER

11

*B*ethancourt spent Sunday glued to Astley-Cooper's side, worried that his gregarious friend might let the cat out of the bag before the police were ready to make their move. Astley-Cooper was clearly bursting with the news and his part in it, and Bethancourt was nearly certain he would at least have told the vicar at church that morning but for his own restraining influence.

Dinner at Stutely Manor was early on Sundays on account of Astley-Cooper's weekly chess game with the vicar, and it was after the meal that Bethancourt discovered a message from Gibbons informing him that Joan Bonnar had arrived and that he and Carmichael were setting out for the farmhouse. Reassured that loose tongues could no longer imperil the investigation, Bethancourt took Cerberus out to have a walk in the park and watch the sunset. The Cotswold Hills were peaceful in the gloaming and he breathed in the clean country air appreciatively, thinking that he really ought to get out of London more often.

He lingered until the first stars came out, shining brightly in the absence of city lights, and then he called to his dog and began to stroll back. Astley-Cooper had put on the outside lights and the old house looked truly grand. Bethancourt paused to drink in its aged beauty, resting a hand on Cerberus's head, before continuing on up the path, the great dog beside him.

He let himself in quietly, hanging his jacket on the old-fashioned coat rack and taking a moment to admire the linen-fold paneling of the great hall—a superb example of its kind—before going to see if the vicar had yet arrived.

He found Astley-Cooper and Tothill in the study, seated one on either side of a games table, and talking animatedly. A chessboard was set up between them, but most of the antique ivory pieces were still in their box to one side.

Tothill looked up and grinned at him as he came in.

"Is it true?" he asked. "Did Clarence here really find Charlie's mystery lady all on his own?"

"He did indeed," answered Bethancourt, smiling at his host.

Astley-Cooper attempted to look modest, but failed almost completely.

"Well, really," he said, "I might never have thought of it at all if I hadn't run into the Bensons the other morning. Julie happened to mention," he said to Tothill, who had not already heard the story several times during the course of the day, "that their mother was coming down today, and I just thought to myself, 'My, she's been down a lot lately—really, more than she's ever been since she bought the property all those years ago.'"

Bethancourt felt as though he ought to warn Tothill that nothing was confirmed as yet, but found he hadn't the heart to throw even the slightest amount of cold water on Astley-Cooper's accomplishment. Instead he went to help himself to a drink, half-listening to the two men's conversation as they continued to set up their chessboard, even though he had heard most of it before.

Mostly, he decided as he slumped into a chair and lit a cigarette, he was trying to contain his impatience. He knew it would be some time before he could expect to hear from Gibbons, but his curiosity was eating away at him. He settled himself comfortably in his chair and tried as best he could to resign himself to waiting.

Derek Towser heard the news at the Deer and Hounds. He entered to find a great many strangers at the bar, avidly questioning the locals, who seemed to welcome the attention. Towser ordered a pint and asked what had happened.

"Have they solved the case?" he inquired of the landlord.

"It's Joan Bonnar," the landlord replied, but he was called away to other customers before getting any further, leaving Towser with the impression that the commotion had to do with celebrity, not murder. He was still curious and looked around for someone who might fill him in. Neither Leandra Tothill nor Astley-Cooper appeared to be in the pub, though it was the right hour for one or the other of them to stop in. In Towser's opinion, one of the nicest things about Chipping Chedding was the casual way in which the inhabitants dropped by the pub to look for each other. The Tothills in particular seemed to use it as a meeting place, largely, Towser suspected, because it gave them a view on their parish they would not otherwise have had. But whatever the reason, he—and Bingham, too, before his death—had found this odd habit of the vicar and his wife to be most convenient, offering a fair chance of good company at the pub on many evenings.

But not tonight, it seemed. Towser, still in search of an information source, at last caught sight of Gerald Owens, who owned the grocer's shop in the High Street and was presently planted at the end of the bar.

Making his way through the crowd toward this goal, Towser was abruptly stopped by a voice saying, "That's Towser. He lives in the cottage next door."

He looked for the speaker, but before he could identify him, several of the strangers had turned to him and begun a barrage of questions whose import he did not understand.

"Did you know about the relationship, sir?"

"If so, why didn't you inform the police?"

"You do live on the farmhouse property, don't you?"

"You were the victim's best friend, isn't that so, sir?"

"I don't understand," said Towser. "What's it all about?"

They frowned at him.

"The news has only just broken," said one. "Joan Bonnar has confessed to being the murder victim's girlfriend."

"Really?" said Towser, astonished.

"But you lived right there, sir, you must have known."

"I didn't know anything," protested Towser. "And I don't know anything now," he added, as they opened their mouths with new queries.

After a few more such uncommunicative answers, the reporters left him alone and returned their attention to the other locals, who were leading them on in a shameful manner. Towser sat by himself, watching the show, and wishing Leandra would come in to keep him company. The pub seemed a lonely place without either her or Bingham, despite the influx of new people.

At about eight o'clock, somebody reported seeing the policemen's Rover driving through the village and the reporters hastily decamped, this evidently being the signal for a fresh onslaught on both the farmhouse and the station in Stow. Towser finished his second pint and reflected that, although he had only known Charlie Bingham for a month or so, he was not altogether surprised to find that he had nabbed the only celebrity in the neighborhood. Charlie had been that sort of person.

He decided against a third pint and left the pub. The stars were bright overhead and he walked briskly along the road. Towser liked walking at night and he seldom bothered with a torch even when the sky was overcast. He turned when he reached the cottages, but paused in the drive. Both houses were lit, and next to Steve Eberhart's mud-splattered Land Rover was parked a gleaming white Rolls-Royce. It occurred to Towser that there was one person in Chipping Chedding who might not have heard about Joan Bonnar, and who actually needed to know. He followed the path up to the first cottage and knocked at the door.

Carmichael had gone back to Chipping Chedding. He had dealt with the media, compared notes with his sergeant, and set a program for tomorrow, leaving Gibbons to type up a report at the police station. This Gibbons had finished, and now he was tired and very hungry. He was just about to ring Bethancourt and inform him that if he wanted to hear the latest, he would have to drive Gibbons to a restaurant when the telephone rang.

"Sergeant Gibbons?" said Eve Bingham.

Gibbons almost groaned aloud. "Yes, Miss?" he replied, stifling the groan.

"I'm about to leave my father's house," she said. "May I stop and see you on the way? I'll only take a moment of your time."

"Of course," said Gibbons, who felt a sudden qualm at the idea of a second tête-à-tête interview. Sternly he reminded himself that she was still a murder suspect and he was honor-bound to listen to what-ever she had to say.

"Thank you," she said. "I'll be there in ten minutes."

Gibbons replaced the receiver and sighed mightily. Then he dialed Stutely Manor.

"I'm starved," he told Bethancourt.

"We had dinner early," said his friend, "but I could do with a snack. Shall I pick you up? We could go to that pub Marla and I were at the other night. It's quite decent."

"Brilliant," said Gibbons. "Only don't come straightaway."

"Why ever not?" asked Bethancourt, surprised. "I thought you said you were starving."

"I am. But Eve Bingham rang to say she wanted to stop by. She said it wouldn't take long."

"Did she say what she wanted?"

"No, and I can't think what it could be. Normally, murder suspects don't offer to come down to the station."

"All right," said Bethancourt. "I'll drive down in a bit and wait for you outside in the car."

"Perfect," said Gibbons. "I'll be as quick as I can."

He rang off, slipped into his jacket and straightened his tie, and then sat back to wait nervously. He had only just settled himself, however, when Eve Bingham was shown in. He eyed her sharply, but she appeared cool and collected, if a little tired.

"They don't do you very well," she remarked, looking about the tiny office.

"I'll convey that to the chief constable," replied Gibbons before he could stop himself.

She seemed slightly taken aback and he apologized at once and asked her to be seated.

"It's just that I haven't had my dinner yet," he explained, and went on briskly, "Now then, what can I do for you?"

"It's about Joan Bonnar," she said. "I understand she was seeing my father."

"That's so," he said. "We spoke with Miss Bonnar this afternoon. You didn't know?"

She shook her head. "My father hadn't mentioned it in any of his letters."

Gibbons nodded. "You must understand, Miss Bingham, that no one else knew of the relationship, either. Miss Bonnar wished to avoid any publicity."

"Yes, I know." Eve toyed with the strap of her bag. "Were they— was it a serious relationship, do you know?"

Gibbons decided that there was no need to tell her that her father had planned to be married without letting her know.

"I believe so," he answered. "They had been seeing each other for about six months."

She looked up at him, surprised. "Oh," she said. Then she bit her lip. "I expect I'll meet her tomorrow then. I don't know how I feel about that. Was that where he was going on Sunday, then? To see her?"

"We don't know yet," said Gibbons. "It may have been."

"Then she wasn't expecting him?"

"Miss Bingham, I understand this news must come as a shock, but I really can't discuss the case with you," said Gibbons.

She met his eyes. "Can you tell me if you think she killed him?"

Gibbons spread his hands. "I simply don't know," he said. "We'll be looking into that, certainly, but at the moment she is no more a suspect than anyone else."

"Than me, you mean," said Eve bitterly.

"Anyone without an alibi is a suspect at present, Miss," said Gibbons evenly.

"Yes, of course," she said, recovering herself. "I suppose it was silly of me to bother you. I just thought . . ."

"Yes?"

"I thought you might have a feeling about it," she said.

"Even if I did," said Gibbons, trying to be patient, "you must see that it would be wrong of me to communicate it to you, to either prejudice you against Miss Bonnar or to give you confidence in her innocence. How would you feel if afterward I turned out to be wrong?"

"Then you do think you know?"

Gibbons sighed. There was just no reasoning with some people. "No, Miss Bingham," he said firmly, "I don't. After we've done some more investigating, I may have, but at the moment I honestly don't know. I'm very sorry I can't help you."

She nodded acceptance and rose. "Thank you anyway for seeing me," she said. "I expect I'm just on edge about the funeral tomorrow."

"That's perfectly understandable," said Gibbons, throwing his coat over his arm and holding the door for her. "I'll see you out."

He ushered her through the station and into the cool evening air. They paused on the steps, she to light a cigarette, he to look for Bethancourt's gray Jaguar.

"There you are," came Bethancourt's voice, and Gibbons turned to see his friend coming up the walk, Cerberus pacing sedately at his side. "Hullo, Eve. How are you holding up?"

She smiled and held out a hand to the dog. "As well as can be expected, I suppose," she answered. "I'm rather dreading the funeral tomorrow."

"A pity, that," said Bethancourt sympathetically. "After all, they say funerals are supposed to be for the comfort of those left behind."

"This one," said Eve dryly, "looks to be more for the comfort of the media."

"Do your best to thwart them," said Bethancourt. "Wear a veil."

She almost laughed. "It would serve them right if I did. Will you be coming?"

"Certainly," said Bethancourt. "Marla sends her regrets, but she already had a shoot scheduled in Paris and couldn't get out of it."

Eve waved this away. "She's already been kind enough. I'll see you there, then. Good night."

She walked down the steps toward her car, and they watched her go.

"I'm parked 'round the corner," said Bethancourt, starting off in the opposite direction. "We had better hurry if we want to catch them before they stop serving. Cerberus, heel."

The pub was a very old one, sitting in lonely splendor on the Cheltenham road. A large room off the bar was a modern addition and had been set up as a proper dining room. It was almost deserted at this hour. Bethancourt and Gibbons arrived just before the kitchen closed and long after most of the day's specials were sold out. They ordered steaks and pints of bitter instead and then Bethancourt lit a cigarette and leaned back while Gibbons, with half an eye on the kitchen door, demolished the rolls in the breadbasket and told him what they had learned from Joan Bonnar.

"So she could have done it," said Bethancourt reflectively.

"The sleeping tablets rather point to her."

"Yes," said Bethancourt, "but it's very circumstantial, especially now that we know there was an unattended bottle of them at the farmhouse. Almost anyone could have got hold of the pills while they were visiting the Bensons. Or it might be someone else's prescription altogether—although it's not a common medication."

"You just like to complicate things," said Gibbons. "It's barely possible that someone else connected to the case had access to Seconal, but it's extremely unlikely."

"True." Bethancourt smoked for a moment in silence, his hazel eyes thoughtful. "What bothers me, though, is that there's still no motive. To me, that means there's something we haven't discovered."

"We haven't begun to investigate Miss Bonnar," Gibbons reminded him. "Perhaps something will turn up there."

"Perhaps, but you must admit nothing springs readily to mind."

"Besides," said Gibbons, "motive's the last thing to consider. Means and opportunity first—that's the rule."

"Which Joan Bonnar had," said Bethancourt. "Only everyone claims she and Bingham were very happy together, and even if they'd had a row, she'd hardly murder him just to keep him from telling the tabloids about their affair."

"There may have been something else," said Gibbons, sneaking another look toward the kitchen. He had finished the rolls.

"Bingham," continued Bethancourt, "might have been going to see his daughter or his business partner rather than Joan. Neither of them, so far as we know, have access to Seconal, though one can make a case for them both having motives. On the other hand, someone from the village had access to the tablets, but no motive we can come up with, and no reason to meet Bingham in London."

"Why stick to London?" said Gibbons sarcastically, while he signaled for another pint. "We've never succeeded in tracing his car—he might have gone anywhere."

"He told Peg Eberhart he was off to London."

"Yes, just as he always did when he was going to see Joan Bonnar. Now that we know that, there's no reason to suppose otherwise."

A gleam had appeared in Bethancourt's eye. "You're right there," he said. "If in fact he wasn't going to meet her, then he must have had a reason for lying to Peg Eberhart."

"Oh, very well, have it your way," said Gibbons. "He wasn't meeting Joan, he was meeting Leandra Tothill, with whom he'd also been having an affair. But Leandra has gotten the wind up, and is afraid he'll tell someone. So she pinches the Seconal at the farmhouse and feeds it to Bingham mixed up in some whisky. He dies, and she drives him back to his cottage, arranges him in the sitting room, and then rides home on her bicycle which she has earlier stashed behind the hedge. There you are—motive and opportunity together."

"That's really very fine, Jack," said Bethancourt admiringly. "I'd never thought of Mrs. Tothill."

"She's a very unlikely suspect," said Gibbons. "Oh, look, here comes the food."

Gibbons applied himself industriously to his steak and mushrooms and parsley new potatoes, listening with only half an ear as Bethancourt returned to their discussion.

"In any case, all I'm saying is that it's difficult to think of a motive for Joan Bonnar," said Bethancourt. "Unless," he added, struck by a thought, "she had somehow lost all her money and had already secretly married Bingham."

Gibbons snorted to show his opinion of this theory.

"True," said Bethancourt sadly. "It doesn't work at all."

He ate a piece of beef and was silent for several moments while Gibbons demolished his potatoes and most of the rest of his steak. Bethancourt, eating in a more leisurely manner, suddenly paused with his fork in midair.

"You said the press agent was with her that night?"

Gibbons nodded. "Watkinson is his name."

"Perhaps . . ." Bethancourt chewed ruminatively for a moment. "Perhaps it was an accident after all. Listen to this, Jack. Bingham doesn't know about the Sunday interview and on impulse he decides to spend the evening with her. He arrives at her townhouse, finds her still out, and settles down to wait. Only he's got a headache and mistakes the sleeping tablets for aspirin. Anyway, he takes them by accident and dies. Joan comes in with Watkinson and finds him. She assumes it's a heart attack—anyone would—and explains the situation to Watkinson, who sees no reason she should be stuck with the bad publicity that is sure to result. It's the kind of thing a press agent would think of. He moves the body back to Chipping Chedding, possibly with her help. But when there's a murder investigation, they decide they'd better come clean about the affair after all, since the police will be bound to find out sooner or later. Only they don't want to confess to moving the body because they know that will result in a criminal charge."

Gibbons, having finished his meal, was willing to consider this. "It's possible," he said slowly. "There's only the one point about how and why Bingham took the tablets."

"Oh, no," groaned Bethancourt. "I'd forgotten the damn tablets in Bingham's cottage. A theory's no good unless it accounts for that."

"Unless Joan realized he had taken the tablets."

But Bethancourt was shaking his head. "In that case, she would have said she'd lent him some. And anyway, how would she know? If you have a boyfriend with a bad heart and you come home to find him dead, you assume it's a heart attack. You don't go rifling through your medicine cabinet to see if any of your pills are missing."

"Put like that," said Gibbons, "I have to agree."

Bethancourt had gone back to his supper. "I forgot to ask," he said. "What did Eve want this evening?"

He glanced up at his friend, but Gibbons showed no sensitivity about the subject, and Bethancourt breathed a sigh of relief.

"She only wanted to ask about Joan Bonnar," answered Gibbons. He raised a hand for the waiter. "I wonder what they've got left for pudding," he said.

He had a choice between bread pudding and chocolate cake, and opted for the pudding. Bethancourt ordered coffee and then leaned back and lit an after-dinner cigarette, exhaling with a sigh of deep comfort and satisfaction.

"Are you going to the funeral tomorrow?" he asked.

"No," answered Gibbons. "I was surprised to hear you were. Or was that just an impulsive effort to cheer Eve up?"

Bethancourt grinned. "I'm not that nice," he said. "No, Astley-Cooper is panting to go, and I said I'd accompany him. Besides, I haven't seen Joan Bonnar yet."

Gibbons raised a brow. "I don't see what you expect to find out from her in the middle of a funeral."

"Nothing," said Bethancourt. "I just want to see how she behaves."

"If you can see anything at all," said Gibbons. "That funeral's going to be a three-ring circus."

Bethancourt waved this away. "It will be an event," he said. "I imagine everyone in Chipping Chedding will turn out for it."

"No doubt," said Gibbons with a shrug and turned his attention to his dessert, which was just arriving.

CHAPTER

ibbons's prediction of a circus was not far wrong. Bethancourt reflected on it as he stood beside Astley-Cooper the next morning. The church was packed. People who would ordinarily never have come to Charlie Bingham's funeral had come because he was murdered. Others who would not have turned out for a mere murder had come because Joan Bonnar would be there. The media was represented in full, and there were large numbers of people who simply could not be gotten into the church and were milling about outside, waiting for the coffin to make its final journey to the grave. Some of the younger people had even climbed the trees at the churchyard's edge to ensure themselves a better view, and every man jack of the local police had been enlisted to try to control the crowds and deal with the parking and traffic problems.

The vicar had abandoned his tweed jacket and threadbare worn cassock for the appropriate vestments and appeared perfectly calm, going about the service as if it were any ordinary funeral. In the front pew, Leandra Tothill stood beside Eve Bingham, her dark gray coat making a poor showing alongside Eve's elegant black Chanel suit. The strain was showing badly in Eve's face and in the tense way she held herself; Leandra's concerned eyes frequently strayed to her. Eve, however, gazed fixedly ahead at the vicar and the coffin. He stood behind.

On her other side stood a large, pleasant-faced man in a dark gray suit, whom Bethancourt had identified as Andrew Sealingham. Beside him was a small, vivacious-looking woman who was obviously his wife. Christopher Macklin was not present.

The pallbearers occupied the other front pew; Bethancourt knew only two of them. Steve Eberhart, the vet, was the tallest of them and looked solemn but at ease. In contrast, James Benson's face was strained and nervous, the result, no doubt, of being without the support of either his sister or Martha Potts.

They were not far off, however. In the pew behind the pallbearers, Julie Benson and Mrs. Potts flanked Joan Bonnar. She had dressed carefully in a matching dress and coat of dark navy wool. On the collar of the coat was a small diamond-and-sapphire brooch; Bethancourt wondered if Bingham had given it to her. She was rigidly in control of herself, although her eyes were suspiciously bright at times. Mrs. Potts, on the other hand, let a few tears fall unashamedly; she wore a black outfit of ancient vintage. Julie had solved the whole problem of funeral wear by donning a dark brown coat and keeping it well-buttoned up. Her only emotion was mild distaste whenever her mother reached out for her.

There was no sign of Derek Towser, but Peg Eberhart stood on Bethancourt's other side. Her eyes were also full of tears, although the majority of her attention was taken up with keeping the baby in her arms quiet. Bethancourt, who had a young nephew, assisted as best he could by fishing various distractions out of Peg's capacious black patent leather purse, which was apparently standing in for the usual nappy bag.

Eventually, the vicar stopped speaking and the pallbearers moved forward. At the back of the church there was an indecorous commotion as some of the onlookers tried to get out first in order to have a good place at the graveside. The vicar raised his voice and put a firm stop to that, stating in no uncertain terms that the funeral procession would go first, followed by the orderly emptying of the pews. The ushers moved up to support this view, and Eve shot the vicar a grateful look.

The slow procession moved forward. Outside, the police were valiantly keeping the crowds back, leaving open a path from the church door to the graveyard. They had done their best to keep people out of the churchyard, but they could do nothing once the people from the church started filing in and others flooded after them. Soon the graveyard was jammed with a milling throng, all in search of some way to get a glimpse of the action. Several of them climbed up on gravestones to peer curiously over the heads of their fellows.

This was nothing new to Joan Bonnar. Her face was set and she paid no attention whatsoever to the interlopers. Astley-Cooper, however, was looking nervous as he and Bethancourt attempted to protect Peg Eberhart and her son from the worst of the crush around the gravesite. Others were also looking wary, their attention distracted from the vicar, who was saying a prayer from his station at the head of the grave.

The lowering of the coffin into the deep, squared hole roused everyone's attention again. Eve Bingham stared at it, tears slipping silently down her waxen cheeks. She had a single rose clutched tightly against her chest, and once the coffin was lowered, she stepped forward and tossed the rose in after it. She stood gazing down into the grave for a long moment, making no attempt to wipe her tears away. When at last she turned away, the vicar and his wife came up on either side of her.

Bethancourt had lost sight of Joan Bonnar in the crush, but he saw her come forward after Eve had passed. She, too, held a flower, and she brought it to her lips before casting it into the grave with a beautifully dramatic gesture. Bethancourt did not think the gesture was deliberate; it came naturally to her.

Various other people began to file past the grave, but Bethancourt turned away with Astley-Cooper and Peg Eberhart.

"Are you going on to the vicarage?" Astley-Cooper asked her.

She nodded, shifting the baby from one arm to the other. "I'm meeting Steve there," she said. "We can't stay long—Steve has to drop me back at the cottage and change before he goes on his rounds."

"Let me carry the baby for you," offered Bethancourt.

"Thanks," said Peg gratefully, handing over her offspring. "I didn't want to bring his usual baby carrier or anything—they're such bright, cheerful colors."

The Tothills, at Eve's request, were hosting the after-funeral gathering, with Constable Stikes on guard at the door to ensure that only those who had actually known Bingham were admitted. Most of the crowd was now slowly dispersing, preparing to create fresh traffic problems for the police to deal with. The media had congregated at the vicarage gate to get shots of the bereaved daughter and the grieving film star.

Eve had already passed into the house with the Tothills, but Joan Bonnar was only just approaching, accompanied by Mrs. Potts and a thin, gray-haired man whom Bethancourt thought must be the press agent, Watkinson. This was confirmed by the way he guided a silent Miss Bonnar past the media and their questions with practiced ease. The twins were nowhere to be seen.

It was unfortunate that several onlookers saw her enter. They immediately assumed that the vicarage was Miss Bonnar's country retreat and began chipping bits off the fence for souvenirs and climbing into the garden in search of more. Constable Stikes put a stop to this desecration while endeavoring to keep one eye on the front door, which was instantly attacked by a couple of reporters. Stikes turned back to prevent their entry, thus giving the souvenir hunters the opportunity to sneak around the back. The situation was getting out of hand when a second constable, involved in trying to get the cars unparked and moving, noticed the trouble and went to help. He succeeded in evicting the rest of Miss Bonnar's fans from the vicarage garden while Stikes maintained her guard at the door and equably watched the traffic situation deteriorate rapidly. As Bethancourt followed Peg into the vicarage, horns were beginning to sound frantically, and Inspector Adams of the traffic division was running up with fire in his eyes.

Inside the front hall of the vicarage, they met Leandra, evidently posted there as a second guard on the door. She welcomed them and pointed them toward the drawing room.

"Eve's not down yet," she said, "but Richard's in there serving coffee."

There was already quite a crowd in the drawing room. Peg found her husband and Bethancourt returned the son and heir to his father. Then he followed Astley-Cooper toward where the vicar was handing out coffee behind a table loaded with small savories and fancy cakes. They complimented him on the service and Tothill shrugged.

"It went off as well as could be expected under the circumstances," he said, pouring out. "Here you are, then. Cream and sugar down at that end."

They moved off.

"I wish Miss Bingham would come down," said Astley-Cooper. "I'd like to offer my condolences and get to a pub or something."

Bethancourt nodded absently and glanced about the room. His eye fell on Andrew Sealingham, Bingham's business partner, standing not far away. His genial features were set in appropriately sober lines and he had his eye on the door. His wife was not in evidence. Bethancourt eased over until he was standing next to him.

"Very sad, all this," he said casually.

Sealingham turned to look at him. "Yes, indeed," he agreed. He eyed Bethancourt quizzically, noting the tailor-made gray suit and silk tie. "I suppose you met Charlie down here?" he asked doubtfully.

"Actually," confessed Bethancourt, "I didn't know him. But my girlfriend knows Eve, and I happened to be staying down here with friends, so I thought I'd push along and offer condolences. Were you a very old friend of his?"

"Yes," answered Sealingham. "We were in business together and very close. I hadn't seen as much of him in recent years, of course, but we still wanted to come."

"Then you must know his daughter, too."

"Oh, yes." Sealingham looked a little uncomfortable. "To tell the truth," he said, lowering his voice, "I barely recognized her—she was still a girl when I last saw her and now she looks the way I remember her mother. My wife and I thought perhaps Evie could use a bit of support at a time like this, but it's difficult to know what to say to a young woman you only knew as a child."

Bethancourt sympathized and added that Eve seemed to be bearing up well. "It must be doubly hard for her," he said, "knowing he was murdered."

"Quite," said Sealingham and frowned. "I really can't understand that, you know," he added. "Charlie could be a bit eccentric, but he was always very well-liked. He had a certain charm. I can't imagine how anyone could have hated him enough to kill him."

"Well," said Bethancourt, "you said you hadn't seen much of him lately. Perhaps he'd changed."

"No, no." Sealingham shook his head. "He stopped with us for a weekend when he returned to England, and he was still just the same. Characters like Charlie don't change much, they just get more so as they age. You're still a young man, but you'll find as you get older that it's true."

Bethancourt assented to this and said that it was certainly all very mysterious.

"That it is. Ah, here's my wife. Annie, dear, this young man is a friend of Evie's. I'm sorry, I didn't catch your name?"

"Phillip Bethancourt," he said, reaching to shake hands.

"Andrew Sealingham and my wife, Ann."

Ann smiled. "Such a pity about Charlie," she said. "I do wish now we'd made more of an effort when he came back, but of course we thought there'd be plenty of time to fit him back into our lives."

"If he'd taken up my offer of an office down at the plant, we might have seen more of him," said Sealingham.

"Offices were never Charlie's thing, dear."

"No, m'dear, you're right there."

They began to reminisce, and Bethancourt listened to stories of the old days while his eyes watched the room. Leandra had come in from the hall and made her way to her husband. She murmured in his ear and then Tothill nodded and moved away, his wife taking his place behind the coffee urn. Bethancourt, having finished his coffee, excused himself to the Sealinghams and edged his way back to the refreshment table.

"Hello," said Leandra. "Can I get you a refill?"

"Yes, please," said Bethancourt, handing over his cup. "How is Eve doing?"

Leandra sighed. "She's pulled herself together," she replied, "but I think she's rather dreading coming down. I've sent Richard up to escort her."

"I thought she bore up wonderfully," said Bethancourt.

"She did, for the most part," said Leandra. "But she came all to pieces when she saw the coffin actually going in. They often do," she confided. "It's the dreadful finality, I always think. Oh, here she is."

Eve moved mechanically, the vicar at her elbow, but she seemed in control of herself again. Tothill steered her over to a chair, while Leandra excused herself to Bethancourt and brought over a cup of coffee, murmuring into Eve's ear as she handed it to her. Eve smiled and thanked her, taking a careful sip.

"I think you've met the Eberharts," came the vicar's voice, as the vet and his family came over to offer condolences.

"Yes, of course," said Eve. "Thank you so much for acting as pall-bearer, Mr. Eberhart . . ."

She had herself in hand now, thought Bethancourt, and was taking refuge in formality.

"So sorry . . ." Peg Eberhart was saying, ". . . very fond of Charlie . . ."

Bethancourt had said that this sort of thing was really meant for the bereaved, so that they could let their loved ones go amid the company and sympathy of friends, to ease them over the loss, and that was true. But none of these people were Eve Bingham's friends and so it became an ordeal. He wondered why she had agreed to go through with it. After all, she would never see any of these people again; if they thought she was a barbarian for leaving them at the graveside, why should it matter to her? He could understand her having a desire to do right by her father, though it was rather out of character for the persona she presented to the rest of the world, but he was also aware that a murderess might have thought it would be suspicious not to do the usual thing.

He turned to find Leandra back behind the coffee urn.

"She'll do now," she told him in a low voice.

"I'm rather surprised she wanted to go through all this at all," said Bethancourt. "I mean, it's not as if she knows most of these people."

"I was surprised myself," said Leandra, "but Richard said she wanted to do it for her father, to show respect, I suppose. Richard said she seemed quite anxious all along that everything should be just as if she and Charlie had lived here for years. Oh, look—there's the Eberharts off. I must go and see that everyone's lining up nicely. Excuse me."

Bethancourt nodded and moved to a vantage point by the fireplace. He slid his coffee onto the mantel and lit a cigarette. The vicar was introducing someone else to Eve, and she was saying something about a wreath. Hovering on the edge of this conversation was Joan Bonnar. She was alone now; Watkinson had disappeared and Mrs. Potts was chatting on the far side of the room with a plump woman in a purple dress whom Bethancourt did not recognize. As Eve was saying thank you for coming, Joan straightened, automatically smoothing her skirt, and approached. A moment ago she had been biting her lip, but now she appeared quite sure of herself.

"Ah, Miss Bonnar," said Tothill, a smile belying the uneasy look in his eyes. "I'm sure you've heard of Miss Bonnar, Eve."

"Of course," said Eve steadily, holding out a hand.

"I'm very sorry about Charlie, Miss Bingham," said Joan. "As you may know, I was . . . very fond of him myself. It's a great pity we should meet under these circumstances—I had once rather looked forward to our meeting."

Eve met her eyes, pausing for a moment. Then she said, "I'm sorry for you, too. You were probably closer to him these days than I was."

"I was there," said Joan simply, "but it was you who were always in his thoughts."

"Thank you," said Eve, barely audible.

Joan inclined her head. She reached out and touched Eve's shoulder and then turned away. Eve followed her with her eyes, even while Tothill was introducing someone else.

"There you are, Phillip," said Astley-Cooper. "Let's move up, shall we, so we can get it over with? At least you've met the girl before."

"Yes," agreed Bethancourt dryly, flinging his cigarette into the fireplace. "I met her while questioning her as to her whereabouts at the time of her father's murder."

"Oh, come," said Astley-Cooper. "You said yourself you're branded in her mind as Marla's boyfriend. Besides, she wouldn't hold it against you." He chuckled. "She certainly didn't hold it against Gibbons."

Bethancourt eyed him suspiciously. "Did Marla tell you that?" he asked.

"Of course. She's very amusing, that girl of yours, Phillip."

"Very. I wouldn't let that story get about, Clarence. It wouldn't do Jack any good if it did."

"My dear chap, who would I tell?" Wounded innocence suffused Astley-Cooper's features.

"The whole of Chipping Chedding, probably," muttered Bethancourt under his breath. "Come along—we can pay our respects now."

While the sedate pace of life in Chipping Chedding was being disrupted, Gibbons and Carmichael were driving to London. They had been at the farmhouse earlier that morning, and were comparing notes as Gibbons guided the police Rover down the A40.

"So Watkinson confirmed what we thought?" asked Carmichael.

"What you thought, yes, sir," answered Gibbons. "On the night of the murder, he stopped off at the Indian restaurant while Miss Bonnar went on to the house. In all, he thought it was about fifteen or twenty minutes before he joined her there."

Carmichael grunted. "Plenty of time for her to drag Bingham's body into the bedroom if she needed to. Unless, of course, she enlisted Watkinson's help."

"I almost think she didn't, sir," said Gibbons. "Not unless Watkinson is as good an actor as his client. I've never seen a man so unconcerned about a police investigation into his movements."

"Far more worried about our interest in Miss Bonnar, eh?"

"Oh, yes. Much more worried, sir."

Indeed, as Watkinson had begun to realize, with mounting horror, that Joan Bonnar was a major suspect in the death of Charles Bingham, he had frequently broken off his litany of his own actions to interject a denial that she could have had anything to do with it. This reached a pinnacle in his last statement, in which he tried to amend his earlier testimony that he had left the house at about 9:45, by claiming that in fact he might have stayed later; he really couldn't be sure of the time. Gibbons paid no attention to this at all.

"Of course," Gibbons continued, "he hasn't an alibi after he left Miss Bonnar that night, so I could be wrong. And he says he returned to her house at about half ten the next morning, in time to meet the magazine interviewer, who was due at eleven. He said Miss Bonnar's agent—I forget her name—was already there when he arrived."

"Emily Redston," supplied Carmichael, consulting his notes. "That tallies with what Miss Bonnar told me. Her agent arrived at about nine, and Watkinson left her a bit before ten the night before, after which she rang Bingham, got no answer, and went to bed."

"Did you find out who else knew about her and Bingham?" asked Gibbons.

"Yes, but there weren't many," answered Carmichael. "Just the housekeeper at the house in town, one of Bingham's archaeologist friends and his wife, and Dame Sarah Kelling."

"Well, that figures," said Gibbons. "At least, one always hears Joan Bonnar and Sarah Kelling are the best of friends. Only doesn't it strike you as odd, sir, that if Miss Bonnar and Bingham planned to be married, they were still keeping their relationship a secret from nearly everyone?"

Carmichael shrugged. "I asked about that," he said. "Miss Bonnar said that they were waiting until after Bingham had told his daughter. It seems he wanted to do it in person, but somehow hadn't yet arranged to go to Paris. Miss Bonnar claimed to have urged him, in their last conversation, to get on with it, and warned him it would only be matter of time before the media got hold of the news and Eve found out that way. He apparently agreed to ring Eve this week and make arrangements to see her."

"I suppose that does make sense," said Gibbons. "That he would want to tell Eve first, I mean. And we all know how easy it is to put things off."

Carmichael nodded and they fell silent for a space as the miles sped away beneath them.

"I think," said Carmichael in a little bit, "I'll have Mathers get a warrant and find out if any chemists in Sealingham's neighborhood have been filling prescriptions for Seconal lately."

Gibbons was surprised. "But surely the Seconal came from Miss Bonnar?" he asked.

"Well, it never does to make assumptions," said Carmichael slowly. "And to tell the truth, I'm a bit troubled by one thing: Miss Bonnar denied that it was in any way possible that she might have left some of her sleeping tablets in Bingham's cottage. If she murdered him and left the tablets there to account for the drug being in his system, you'd expect her to at least leave the door open on that. But she was as positive about it today as she was when we first asked her."

"I see, sir," said Gibbons thoughtfully. "I hadn't thought of that. In fact, I had been thinking Bingham's death might still have been an accident."

"So was I," agreed Carmichael ruefully. "Once we knew Joan Bonnar was his girlfriend, and that she had Seconal in her possession, it all looked so obvious. She arrives home, finds her fiancé dead and panics about the publicity—or Watkinson panics for her. Anyway, they move the body to try to keep her name out of it. The natural thing would be for her to assume Bingham had died of a heart attack, but it was possible she realized he had taken the Seconal. In the first case, the tablets we found in his cottage would have been some she had left there herself for her own use; in the second, they would have been planted there in case an autopsy was performed. But either way, Miss Bonnar would have to admit to the possibility that she had at some time left her tablets there."

Gibbons absorbed this in silence for several moments. "She might," he said finally, "have killed him deliberately and left the tablets to lend verisimilitude to the idea that his death was accidental and occurred at his home. But now that theory's been exploded, she's decided it's best to deny having left any tablets there, thinking that will tend to exonerate her. Which," he added, "it does."

Carmichael sighed. "I'd thought of that," he admitted. "Still, it never does to be too sure. It would be an enormous coincidence to find another prescription for Seconal in this case, but, well, such things have been known to happen. Look at poor Cratchett and the Banks case."

"Oh, yes—that *was* pretty awful."

"And I've no intention of letting it happen to me," said Carmichael firmly. "As yet, we have no evidence that Bingham was ever in London that Sunday. You had better go along today and do a house-to-house of the square, see if anyone can put Bingham or his car there on the Sunday. You can interview the housekeeper, too. I'll get on to that archaeologist—he's in Egypt now, so it will have to be by phone—and speak to Sarah Kelling, see if their description of the relationship tallies with what the Bensons and Martha Potts told us. And I'll speak to the cast and crew at Miss Bonnar's current production—they will probably have noticed any recent change in her mood. And then we can all spend the evening looking at traffic photos and CCTV footage to see if we can place Bingham's car in town."

"Yes, sir," said Gibbons resignedly. It wasn't as if he hadn't seen the traffic photos coming.

Carmichael paused and then heaved a deep sigh. "Frankly, Gibbons," he said, "at this moment, I think Joan Bonnar murdered her fiancé. But I don't think we'll ever prove it."

As the last light of the sun faded from the October sky, Gibbons made his way across Wardour Square toward Joan Bonnar's London home. It had taken most of the day to complete the house-to-house, despite the fact that one side of the square was undergoing renovations and therefore had no one in residence at the time. The renovations also provided a wealth of extra parking, making it far more likely that

Bingham—if he had indeed visited his fiancée—would have found space to leave his car in the square.

This had initially heartened Gibbons, and he had started the house-to-house in high hopes that one of Joan Bonnar's neighbors might have seen the old Morris. But although many of those he interviewed had recognized his description of the car, no one could remember if they had seen it last Sunday. With reluctance, he admitted to himself that this was not surprising, considering it would have been dark by the time Bingham reached Wardour Square.

The closest Gibbons had come to witnesses were the two teenage daughters who lived on the corner of the square nearest the renovations. At about seven o'clock that Sunday, they had gone out to a film, and they had seen an old, battered car parked a little ways down the block. Unfortunately, they could not identify the make of the car; Gibbons received the impression that they would be unable to distinguish between a Ford and a Rolls-Royce. They thought the car they had seen was a dark blue. Asked if it mightn't have been green, they agreed that it could have been. It was dark, they explained. If the car had still been there when they returned home, they hadn't noticed it.

As far as solid evidence went, the day had been a complete washout, and he did not expect much from the upcoming interview with Joan Bonnar's housekeeper.

Mary Calthorp did not live-in, but she kept regular hours at the house, and had perforce been taken into the actress's confidence regarding Bingham. Like Martha Potts and the Bensons, she had believed them to be a happy couple.

"They were comfortable together," she said. "It wasn't a grand passion—personally, I think as one grows older, one loses the capacity for that—but they suited each other."

Her phrasing struck Gibbons.

"Suited each other?" he asked. "They were from very different worlds."

"Yes," admitted Mary, "but that was just why they got on together so well. I've been with Miss Bonnar a number of years, and she lives the kind of life you would expect: all up in the clouds, if you take my meaning. What she's wanted for some time is someone who could give her ties to reality, and Mr. Bingham did that. And at the same time, he was a very intelligent gentleman, who could grasp what her world was all about." Mary smiled. "And of course he was very clever, very amusing. He had a wonderfully active mind for a man his age; he kept Miss Bonnar amused."

From her expression, Gibbons gathered Miss Bonnar had not been the only one to find Bingham entertaining.

"That's very well put," he said. "But you haven't said what you think she did for him."

Mary tilted her head to one side. "I didn't know him well," she said, considering. "But if I had to guess, I would have thought she gave him a place here, in England, I mean. You said they were from two different worlds, but he'd left his behind, you see. He needed to make a life here for himself, and Miss Bonnar provided that."

"But what if he had decided he didn't want to live in her world?" asked Gibbons.

Mary shook her head. "I saw no sign of that," she said firmly.

All in all, it did not sound to Gibbons like the kind of situation someone—even a histrionic actress—would murder for. He sighed as he thanked Mary Calthorp and took his leave. She could tell him nothing more; she had not been present that Sunday evening and could say only that she had found nothing out of order when she had arrived at work on the Monday morning.

Gibbons paused once he had left the house, pulling out his mobile and checking for messages. He had kept in touch with Carmichael all day, but there was another message from the chief inspector waiting for him. Gibbons pressed the speed dial as he made his way out of the square.

"There you are, lad," said Carmichael. "Have you done yet?"

"Just finished, sir," Gibbons answered. "The housekeeper said much the same as your archaeologist."

"It's only to be expected," said Carmichael. "I've finally got in touch with Dame Sarah, and she's waiting at her house now. If you've finished, I thought you might like to come with me. It's not every day we get to interview someone famous."

"Thank you, sir," said Gibbons, much pleased. "I would like to come. As you say, I won't likely get the chance to meet her again."

"Good, good," said Carmichael. "You can meet me there, then, and we'll go in together. That would be best, I think."

It was Dame Sarah herself who admitted them to the flat she kept as a pied-à-terre, having, as she told them, got rid of her London house some years ago when she and her husband began to spend the bulk of their time in Buckinghamshire.

"It was always wanting something doing to it," she said with a laugh, as she led them down the hall to the sitting room. "The town house, I mean. It got to be quite tedious, always having to drive in to speak to roofers, or masons, or plumbers. So we sold it and got this nice little flat, which does us very well. Here we are. Greg, this is Chief Inspector Carmichael and Sergeant Gibbons. My husband, Greg Evanston."

Sarah Kelling and Joan Bonnar had begun their careers within a few years of each other, both stunning the theater world with their ingénue performances and rocketing thereafter into the top ranks of their profession, but unlike her friend, Sarah's personal life had not kept pace with the tempestuousness of her acting. She had married early, just after her stunning success at eighteen as Juliet, divorced quietly three years later, and married again at about thirty, this time to a doctor. They had raised two children together and, by all reports, got on famously, despite the strains and separations occasioned by Sarah's career.

She sat beside him now on the couch, leaving the armchairs for the detectives. Dame Sarah had never been as beautiful as Joan Bon-

207

nar, but her elfin face with its over-large pale green eyes was mesmer-
izing, even now, when she was nearing sixty. She cocked her head, like
an alert bird, and regarded them curiously, while her husband sat at
his ease, emitting the assured air of the medical professional.

"You've come to ask about Joan, of course," said Dame Sarah.

"Yes, ma'am," answered Carmichael, settling himself into his chair
and glancing around. The room was well-proportioned and money
had been spent on its furnishings, but it was comfortable rather than
ornate, and there was nothing in it to suggest that one of its occupants
was a renowned actress.

Carmichael cleared his throat and returned his attention to his
hosts. "I assume you've spoken to Miss Bonnar since she received the
sad news?" he asked.

Dame Sarah nodded. "Yes, several times, by phone. I offered to
come to the funeral this morning, but she said better not, it would be
too much jam for the press as it was, and there was Charlie's daughter
to consider after all."

"Of course," said Carmichael. "I understand you had only recently
learned of her relationship with Charles Bingham?"

"Oh, I knew quite some time ago," said Sarah. "One could hardly
miss the difference in her, could one?"

She looked at her husband, who nodded. "At least, you couldn't,"
he said. "I don't know if I would have noticed myself."

Sarah smiled. "Even you remarked on how even-tempered she'd
been of late," she said.

"Well, yes, but I didn't twig the reason."

"So when did she tell you?" asked Carmichael.

"Oh, sometime at the beginning of last summer. I asked, actually,
because I knew there was someone. Mind, we never let on to Charlie
that we'd known for so long; it was understood that we wouldn't."

"Ah," said Carmichael. "And why was that?"

Dame Sarah frowned while Evanston smiled broadly.

"Because," he said, "it is very difficult to explain to ordinary people that their friends may not be as trustworthy as yours. We went through that bit ourselves, didn't we, Sarah?"

Sarah sighed. "Oh, yes." She turned her eyes back on Carmichael. "It sounds dreadful," she said, "but it's quite true. You never know how people will deal with fame until they do it. Naturally Joan felt quite confident in telling Greg and me, because we'd kept her secrets in the past, just as she had ours."

"I see," said Carmichael, nodding. "So, although you knew about the relationship, you didn't actually meet Mr. Bingham until recently?"

"That's right. It was about a month ago, I think. They came to our house in Bucks for dinner, and it was a great success. We both quite liked Charlie, didn't we, dear?"

"Oh, yes." Evanston nodded. "He was a very amusing chap—we were both very sorry when we heard the news, for our own sake as well as Joan's. We'd been looking forward to seeing him again."

"And how would you describe their relationship?" asked Carmichael.

"To tell the truth," said Sarah confidingly, "I was desperately hoping we would like Charlie once we did meet him, because he was so clearly good for Joan. Quite soon after she began seeing him, she seemed to settle down into a placid sort of serenity, if you know what I mean. Very unlike Joan, it was, but just what she needed. I think she'd been very lonely ever since Gene died."

"She was hardly placid or serene while Gene was alive," protested Evanston.

"Oh, no," agreed Sarah. "They loved each other quite madly, but they weren't at all good for each other. But he did leave an enormous hole in her life when he went."

Carmichael exchanged a brief glance with Gibbons before asking, "So would you say that she and Mr. Bingham were quietly happy together?"

Sarah nodded at once. "Yes, that describes it very well," she said, and Evanston concurred.

It was the same thing they had heard from all their other witnesses, and Carmichael sighed a little as he proceeded with his questioning. As a situation for murder, it was not very promising.

Evanston and Dame Sarah had little more light to shed; they had only met Bingham that once, though there had been plans for him and Joan to come out to Bucks over Sunday and Monday next. They had both been in America last week, and so had missed the news of Bingham's death, only hearing of it when they returned on Saturday.

Dame Sarah volunteered that she had spoken to Joan just before leaving for the States; her friend had complained about not having the time to see Bingham last week, but had been looking forward to their plans together over this weekend, and to their trip to Buckinghamshire next week. Sarah had noticed nothing amiss.

"And so say all of us," muttered Carmichael as he and Gibbons left. "I told you, didn't I, that's just what all the theater people said, once I managed to track them down this afternoon? That Miss Bonnar had been very cheery and pleasant all through their rehearsals as well as after the production went up, and no one had noticed any change in her over the last few weeks or days."

"Well," said Gibbons, "she is an actress, after all, sir. Perhaps she was just putting up a good front."

Carmichael merely snorted.

"Here," he said, "I can't stand the thought of those traffic photos without a good meal inside me. Let's splurge, shall we, Gibbons? My treat—there's a very nice little restaurant 'round over this way, if I remember rightly."

Gibbons, no more eager for the traffic photos than his superior, agreed with enthusiasm.

Richard Tothill was back in his old cassock and brown tweed jacket. With his wife he stood at the edge of the graveyard, surveying the wreckage. They had seen a drained, exhausted Eve Bingham off once the last guests had left, and had then set to clearing away the leftover cakes and biscuits and doing the washing up. Now they stood ready to tidy up the churchyard.

Bingham's grave had been filled in and covered over with fresh turves by the sexton, but he had had no time, he explained, to clear up the litter. He had sounded quite aggrieved about it, and the vicar had decided that the wisest course might be for him to lend a hand himself. That, of course, was before he had actually seen the graveyard.

It was amazing how much litter a crowd could leave behind, but it was not only that. The grass was trampled and dug up in places, the gravel of the path was spread everywhere but where it belonged, and, worst of all, two of the oldest gravestones had been toppled by people attempting to stand on them.

"I can see what Harry meant," said Tothill, referring to the sexton.

"Well," said Leandra, sighing, "if we pick up the litter, Harry will probably do the rest. We'd better make a start."

She produced a large plastic bin bag and moved forward purposefully. "God," she said, bending to collect several cigarette ends, "I'll be glad when this is over."

"It's more or less over," said Tothill, following her example. "Eve is leaving tomorrow or next day, and then things will begin to settle down."

Leandra shook her head. "No," she said, "it won't be over 'til they find out who killed Charlie. If they ever do," she added glumly, pitching an empty soda can with unnecessary force into the bag.

Tothill sat back on his heels and gazed at her, thinking, as always, how lovely she was, even stooping in an old brown coat to pick up garbage. He was a sensitive man and, as his wife's happiness meant a great deal to him, he naturally paid attention to her thoughts and feelings. He could not protect her from feeling sorrow at Charlie's death, any more than she could protect him, but for the first time he began to sense that the tragedy had affected her more deeply. They had both liked Charlie and he did not think Leandra felt the loss more than himself, but she seemed more troubled by the manner of the man's death. She had, now he considered it, been on edge ever since they had heard it was murder. That was terrible, of course, the more so in a small village like this, but in truth Tothill did not think it very likely that any of the villagers had murdered gregarious, well-liked Charlie. Perhaps, he thought, still gazing at his wife, women were more sensitive to any kind of violence.

"Richard," said Leandra sharply, "we will never get on if we don't both work at it."

"I'm sorry," he apologized, moving into action again. "I was thinking about how charming you look. Have I mentioned today that I love you?"

She laughed at him. "I would be better pleased if you would prove it by helping me pick this stuff up. Talk is cheap, you know."

"Righto," he said, tossing a chewing gum wrapper into the bag.

The weather was turning colder. Bethancourt tightened the belt of his cashmere coat as he stood in the gardens of Stutely Manor and peered about in search of his dog. They had stayed out in the wooded hills rather later than Bethancourt had intended and it had grown dark by the time they had reached the gardens, making it easy for Cerberus to slip off to investigate an interesting scent without his master noticing until it was too late.

Bethancourt sighed and began to whistle when he was interrupted by the ringing of his mobile phone. He dug it out of his pocket and examined the number on the back-lit screen, flicking the phone on at once when he recognized Gibbons's number.

"What cheer?" he asked, hoping for news.

"Not much," came the answer. "Carmichael decided we needed a decent meal if we were going to spend the night searching through traffic photos, so we're waiting for a table. He decided to ring his wife and I said I'd ring you."

"I'm glad I rate so high," said Bethancourt, "but I'm sorry about the traffic pictures. There was nothing new, then?"

"Nothing," affirmed Gibbons in gloomy tones. "Nobody could place the Morris in the square that night, and everyone we've talked to all day long has agreed with the Benson twins and Mrs. Potts: Joan and Charlie were a very quiet, happy couple."

Bethancourt considered this as he lit a cigarette. "That's somehow not what I'd expected," he said slowly. "Still," he added more cheerfully, "outsiders never know everything that goes on in a relationship."

Gibbons snorted. "That does me a lot of good," he said. "That just breaks the case wide open, that does."

"Well, it's true," said Bethancourt, rather hurt.

"It may be, but it's also unprovable," Gibbons said, and then sighed. "Sorry," he said. "I'm tired and hungry, that's all. Oh, look, there's the waiter. Sir? Yes, yes, we're just coming."

"You'd better ring off," said Bethancourt. "Have a good meal."

"Yes, thanks. Sir, the table's ready . . . no, I'll get that—"

The phone went dead in Bethancourt's hand.

He replaced it in his pocket thoughtfully, and blew a long stream of smoke out into the chill evening air. He had been thinking to himself earlier that the Bensons and Martha Potts were unreliable witnesses where Joan Bonnar was concerned, and that it was entirely possible that her relationship with Bingham had begun to go sour. He had known of other cases where the decision to marry had ultimately resulted in a decision to break up. But Gibbons's report shed new light on that theory: was it truly reasonable to suspect several different witnesses who all said the same thing? And despite what he had told his friend, was it any more reasonable to suppose that no hint of a trouble so deep that it had led to murder had come to anyone's notice?

Bethancourt smoked pensively, hardly noticing that his fingers were becoming chilled as he paced slowly up and back along the gravel path. It was possible, he supposed, that Bingham had attempted to back out of the marriage. In someone sufficiently egotistical, pride could be a powerful motivator, and for all the turbulence of her previous affairs, Joan Bonnar had always been the one who left the men in her life, not the other way around.

The trouble with that theory was that he could not come up with a time when Bingham could have told Joan of his doubts. If it had occurred the weekend before his death, why should he then have gone to see her—in a cheery mood, according to Peg Eberhart—the next Sunday? And if he had made up his mind to tell her on the day he died, it was ridiculous to suppose Joan Bonnar would have resorted to her sedative to do away with him on the spur of the moment. Quite apart from the difficulty of administration, poison was not the weapon of choice for a *crime passionel*.

He sighed and ground his cigarette out beneath his heel. He did not think the massive quantities of beer he had imbibed with Astley-Cooper after the funeral were doing his thinking processes any good. Or possibly, he thought with more confidence, there was something they were missing.

Along the rear facade of the manor, the outdoor lights went on, momentarily blinding him, just as Cerberus came bounding up, panting happily. Looking down, Bethancourt could just make out that the dog had found a patch of mud somewhere; his paws were leaving a black trail behind him.

"Clarence will never let you into the house like that, old boy," Bethancourt told the dog, who wagged his tail. "You'll have to have a paddle in the fountain to clean you off. Come on, let's get in."

All was quiet at the old farmhouse. Watkinson had returned to town that afternoon, but Joan had elected to stay on. Dinner had been a strained and silent meal, with Joan looking red-eyed and wan, and the twins unusually quiet. There was a feeling in the air that once again Joan's unrestrained love affairs had brought unwelcome upheaval into their lives. Joan herself was not insensitive to this and retired up-

214

stairs after dinner with a bottle of whisky. The irritant of her presence removed, Mrs. Potts was determined not to let Julie and James continue to sulk. She cleared the dishes away and left the washing up 'til later. Instead, she retraced her steps to the study where the twins were whispering together on the sofa.

"How about a game of Scrabble?" she asked, smiling cheerfully.

They glanced at each other.

"It's not a bad idea," said Julie slowly.

"All right," said James. "I'll get out the board."

They settled around the old card table, while James produced a dictionary and a pad and pencil.

"There we are," he said, pulling out a chair. "All set."

"That's right," said Mrs. Potts, shaking the bag vigorously before selecting her tiles. "This is just what I wanted after all the fuss today— a nice, quiet evening."

"She'll have to go back tomorrow," said Julie, "and then things will get back to normal."

"I just hope she doesn't volunteer me to drive her," said James.

"I doubt that," said Mrs. Potts calmly. "You know your mother likes to drive—always has. Are you ready yet, Julie?"

"Mmm." Julie shifted a tile and then looked up at them, a pleased twinkle in her eye. "I'm ready," she said, and laid out all her tiles on the board.

"Oh, God," said James. "Not a seven-letter word first thing. I can't stand it."

Julie merely giggled and looked triumphant.

" 'Loiters,'" spelled out Mrs. Potts resignedly, taking up her pencil and adding the fifty-point bonus to the total. It was a discouraging start to the game, especially since Julie usually won anyway, but Mrs. Potts didn't care. It was the first time in days that she had seen either of the twins look so cheerful.

Gibbons arrived home very late and in a thoroughly depressed mood. He had been rather looking forward to getting a pint at his local pub before retiring, but it was long past closing by the time they finally found a photo of Bingham's Morris and he was allowed to go home. They now had proof that Bingham had been in London on the day of his death, and in the general neighborhood of Joan Bonnar's town house. It did not feel like much of a triumph.

His flat was a small one, but he had bought some new furniture for it over the past summer, when he had thought it would not be long before he would have a different kind of life awaiting his return from a long day's work. That he would have had a larger, more comfortable home was not among his foremost regrets, but at times like this, even that loss loomed large, perhaps because it was an easier one to deal with than the remembrance of the woman he had once thought would be here to welcome him.

He tried, as he did most every night, to put all that out of his mind. He removed his jacket and hung it up carefully, as if domestic tidiness might make up for complete failure as a detective and as a man. He switched on the standing lamp beside his armchair and was just on the point of sitting down when he remembered that there was a nearly full carton of butter-pecan ice cream in the freezer. Armed with this and a spoon, he returned to the sitting room and switched on the television, flicking through the channels until he found a rugby game in progress. Gibbons did not much care for rugby—football and cricket were his games—but he watched the game doggedly until its finish. By that time, the ice cream was gone.

He turned off the television and went to bed, where he lay awake in the darkness, ferociously trying to think of ways in which to further their investigation. As he finally began to drift toward sleep, his subconscious took over and suggested a solution that, while not practical, at least enabled him to drop off. It had to do with finding a bloodstained knife in Joan Bonnar's town house.

Chief Inspector Carmichael, being unconcerned with promotion—

in fact, retirement was not so very far down the road these days—and being much more accustomed to difficult cases, spent a pleasant evening with his wife. He had missed her while he was in Chipping Chedding; he found he missed her more of late when he had to go away. Still, there was no denying that she was fast asleep by his side long before he himself succeeded in turning his mind off and settling down for the night.

Bethancourt, having thoroughly muddied the water in the Stutely Manor fountain in the process of cleaning his dog's paws, ate a substantial English meal with Astley-Cooper and discussed the wool market. After supper, they ventured out to the Sheep's Head pub, where they continued their discussion, now joined by various worthies, and Bethancourt, in a leisurely way, began to pick the burrs out of Cerberus's coat. All in all, Bethancourt enjoyed the evening very much, and was understandably reluctant to break his mood when Gibbons rang to fill him in on the lack of progress in the case. He sought his bed early afterward, taking a book to read himself to sleep, which he did quite shortly in a very contented frame of mind. It is always nice to have various interests and to be able to keep them separate in one's mind.

CHAPTER

At 10:15 the next morning Constable Stikes was sorting through the messages on her desk in the Stow-on-the-Wold police station, trying to pick up the threads of her usual routine, which the Bingham murder had thrown into chaos. She had been somewhat miffed at the revelation of Joan Bonnar as Bingham's girlfriend after she had put in so much work on compiling a reasonable list of tourists whom Bingham might have been dating. It was also annoying that the idea of Joan Bonnar had never once occurred to her, even though she had been well aware of the fact that the star had been spending more time than usual in Chipping Chedding over the past few months.

The investigation apparently having been shifted firmly to London, Stikes had dealt as best she could with the chaos of the funeral yesterday and with the rash of petty thievery which broke out in its aftermath, and had earmarked today for a return to normal. She was a bit late starting, owing to a broken alarm clock, but she felt all the better for the extra hour's sleep and there was, as it turned out, nothing urgent awaiting her.

She was just deciding on a schedule for the day when she was interrupted by a call from James Benson up at the old farmhouse. He sounded quite distracted, but Stikes put that down to the fact that his sister was probably standing at his shoulder, putting in her own ideas every time he paused for breath. Everyone in Chipping Chedding knew who wore the trousers at the old farmhouse.

Gradually, however, Benson's message become clear. His mother was missing—they had searched everywhere and couldn't find her, and her car was still there. Stikes said she would come at once and rang off, all thoughts of a normal day fleeing from her mind. As she ran for her car, she pulled out the number for Detective Chief Inspector Carmichael and punched it into her mobile phone.

At 10:25, Gibbons was cooling his heels in Emily Redston's office. The secretary had been very apologetic—Mrs. Redston had missed her train, but would take the next one and be in the office by eleven, probably a little sooner. Gibbons had decided to wait. He was making small talk with the secretary when his mobile rang, and he excused himself to answer it.

"I'm glad I caught you," said Carmichael. "Have you finished with the Redston woman?"

"No, sir," replied Gibbons. "She's running late. She should be in by eleven, though, and I thought I'd wait."

"We can send O'Leary to see her," said Carmichael gruffly. "I've had a call from Chipping Chedding. Joan Bonnar's gone missing. No, you stay there. I'll get the Rover out and pick you up on the way. Meet me in the street in fifteen minutes."

Carmichael rang off.

"Something up?" asked the secretary brightly.

"Yes," answered Gibbons. "I'm afraid I'll have to go. Someone else will be along to see Mrs. Redston later."

He was already dialing Stutely Manor as he made his way out the door.

Bethancourt was sitting in the dining room, sipping his second cup of black coffee and reading the paper. Astley-Cooper looked as if he had a bit of a hangover, but had eaten a prodigious portion of bacon and eggs nonetheless, and some color was returning to his face. Bethancourt, who never ate breakfast, was toying with the idea of a slice of toast when the telephone rang. Astley-Cooper went to answer it, returning in a moment to say it was Gibbons.

"I don't know what this country is coming to," said Bethancourt, setting aside the paper. "Anybody would think that policemen should be hard at work by half ten in the morning, not making personal phone calls."

Astley-Cooper giggled. "Maybe he has news," he said hopefully and Bethancourt went out to the phone.

Gibbons did not reply to his inquiry after his welfare.

"Joan Bonnar's disappeared," he announced.

"Really?" said Bethancourt, startled. "When?"

"This morning, presumably," said Gibbons. "I don't know anything about it yet, but I thought I'd let you know. Carmichael and I are starting down at once."

"All right," said Bethancourt. "I'll go over and see you there, if she hasn't turned up before then."

Once he had heard the news, Astley-Cooper insisted on accompanying his guest to the old farmhouse, an idea which Bethancourt embraced as guaranteeing his entrance to the house. After all, there was no very good reason for Martha Potts or the Bensons to welcome his presence, but they could hardly turn away Astley-Cooper.

Mrs. Potts opened the door to them.

"Hello, Martha," said Astley-Cooper. "We heard you were having a spot of trouble and thought we'd pop 'round to see if there was anything we could do. You remember Phillip, don't you?"

"Yes, of course, come in. Is it all over the village, then? Constable Stikes only just arrived herself."

"No," answered Bethancourt, "I don't imagine everyone will have heard yet. Sergeant Gibbons rang me—he and the chief inspector are on their way from London."

"Well, come on through—though I don't know as there's anything to be done. We're waiting for the police at the moment."

"Have you looked for her?" asked Astley-Cooper. "If her car's here, she can't have gone far."

"We've been searching since breakfast," said Mrs. Potts, leading them down the hall toward the sitting room. "That's when we missed her. She was drinking last night, so I wasn't surprised when she wasn't down to breakfast, but once we'd finished, I thought I'd better see if she wanted coffee in her room. Only the room was empty when I went up." She spread her hands, pausing in the hall outside the sitting room door. "I wasn't alarmed at first. I told the twins and they went out to see if she was at her car or had gone to the stables. When we couldn't find her in any of the obvious places, Julie thought perhaps she'd gone down to Charlie's cottage. So I rang Peg Eberhart, but she hadn't seen her and said the cottage was still locked up. That was when we began to worry. We looked all over the house, and then rang Constable Stikes." She turned and opened the door. "Julie and James are in here."

The twins were perched on a windowsill, looking out, while the constable stood in a corner, talking on the phone. She raised a brow at them, while the twins turned to see who had come.

"Oh," said Julie, "I thought you were more police."

"No, it's only us," said Astley-Cooper.

"Clarence and Phillip have come along to help," said Mrs. Potts.

James scowled. "I don't know what anybody can do," he said gloomily.

"She's just disappeared," said Julie. "Her car's here and so are all of ours, and none of the horses are out, yet she's nowhere to be found. Something must have happened to her, although I can't think what."

Bethancourt privately thought it more likely that Miss Bonnar had fled, though he was surprised. He had really not thought her guilty.

"When did you last see her?" he asked.

"Last night after supper," said Julie. "At about nine o'clock or so."

"Mrs. Potts said she had been drinking?"

"Oh, yes," said James. "She took the bottle up with her—we all saw her—and most of it's gone this morning."

"Then," said Astley-Cooper, "she might have disappeared at any time during the night."

"Did she take a coat or anything?" asked Bethancourt. "It was chilly last night."

"Yes, her coat's gone," replied Julie. "And a pair of flat shoes. I'm not sure what else she was wearing—she always brought a lot of clothes."

"Well," said Bethancourt, "if she was a bit tipsy and went for a walk at night, she may easily have fallen and broken a leg or something." He had no faith at all in this theory, but he could hardly tell them he thought their mother was a murderer. And however bad it looked, it was entirely possible that an accident had occurred.

"We thought of that," said Julie impatiently. "James walked down to Charlie's cottage earlier—it seemed the most likely place for her to have gone on foot."

"I kept a sharp lookout," said James, "but there was no sign of her."

Constable Stikes had rung off, and now walked over to join them.

"Cheltenham are sending a search team," she said. "I'm going to go down to the road to be sure they don't miss the turn. I've been explaining the lay of the land to the sergeant in charge, and he's already organizing his men as they come. We'll find her, never worry."

"Thanks so much," said Julie. "We appreciate all you're doing. Look here, do you think the police could leave a man at the road to prevent the press coming up? They'll be swarming all over, otherwise."

Stikes nodded. "I'd already mentioned it to the sergeant," she answered. "Let me go down and meet them now."

They were all silent once she had left them.

"Well," said Astley-Cooper in a moment, "you know, she mightn't have gone anywhere in particular."

Everyone looked at him, confused.

"I mean," he said, "she could have just taken a walk. You know, when you can't sleep at night and think a breath of fresh air might help."

"Yes," said Julie thoughtfully, "I suppose that's possible." She looked at her brother. "I would have thought, if that were the case, she'd just take a turn around the garden, and we've checked there. But she might have gone along the path instead."

"The path?" asked Bethancourt.

"It leads out to the lake—it's a favorite walk of all of ours," explained James.

"It's also how one walks to the cottages," said Mrs. Potts, frowning, "and James has already been along there."

"But I didn't look around the lake itself," said James. "It didn't occur to me. I had my eyes on the path, thinking if she had fallen, she would be somewhere along it."

"It's a chance," said Julie, standing up. "I'll go look myself. I'll take one of the horses—I shall go quicker that way. Do you want to come, James?"

Her brother shook his head. "No," he said. "I'll wait here with Marty for the police."

"You'll want someone along," said Bethancourt. "In case you find her, I mean. I could go with you, if you like."

Julie shot him a suspicious look. "I don't know," she answered. "Can you ride? Really ride, I mean. My horses are tender-mouthed and I intend they should stay that way."

"I can ride, actually," said Bethancourt.

"Phillip plays polo," said Astley-Cooper helpfully.

This seemed to mollify her, and she led Bethancourt out to the back door, where she paused to don a jacket and a pair of Wellingtons, glancing at his trousers as she did so.

"You're going to ruin those flannels," she remarked.

"That's all right," he replied, smiling at her. "All in a good cause."

Like many women before her, she melted beneath that smile and looked away. "Well, it's very good of you," she said. "Let's get on then."

The stable lay beyond the kitchen garden, a desolate place at this time of year. Julie walked briskly through it, and entered the stable through a door into the tack room. She paused here, biting her lip anxiously for a moment, and then said, "I suppose you can ride Storm. That's his gear there."

Bethancourt gathered up the saddle and bridle from their hooks and followed her into the stable proper.

"Storm's the gray there," she said, pointing with her chin. "He's the steadiest of the lot."

"Right," said Bethancourt, hanging the saddle over the half-door and reaching out to make friends with the horse. He was aware, as he tacked up, of Julie's critical eye on him, but she made no objections and appeared to be somewhat reassured by his practiced movements. Still, she watched him carefully as he mounted and gathered up his reins. Apparently he passed inspection on this score, for she turned her own mount and pointed.

"The lake's that way," she said.

"May I suggest," said Bethancourt, bringing Storm up beside her, "that we ride several yards to one side of the path?"

"Why?"

"If we don't find her, the police may want to look for footprints."

224

"Oh," she said, biting her lip again. "I hadn't thought of that. Very well."

On horseback, the lake was only a few minutes away. After the first few yards, Julie ceased to watch Bethancourt's every move, having evidently made up her mind that Storm was safe in his hands. Bethancourt was very glad he had not been bluffing when he said he could ride; he could hardly imagine her reaction had his abilities been found wanting.

They rode at a brisk trot, topping the little hill that lay between the house and the lake. The well-worn track of the path led down the hill and straight to the water's edge. At the shore, it forked, leading along the bank in either direction and at last into the trees, which crowded along the lake's farther shore.

There was no sign of a figure huddled on the ground on the open expanse, but the grass between the path and the water had not been mown and grew thick and tall, and Bethancourt supposed someone could lay quite hidden in it.

Julie was moving on down the slope.

"There's no point in looking here," she said. "James has already been over this part." She pointed off to the left. "That's the path to the cottages," she said. "We want to go to the right. Do you see that rock over there?"

Bethancourt squinted through his glasses. Not quite halfway around the lake was a large boulder sticking up from the grass.

"I see it," he said.

"Well, that's the end of the usual walk. The rock's more comfortable to sit on than you'd think, and we moor the rowboat there, too."

"Boat?" asked Bethancourt.

"Oh, Mother wouldn't have taken that," said Julie, laughing. "It's only a creaky old rowboat and she hated it. You can't see it from here because the rock's in the way."

They reached the lakeshore and slowed the horses to a walk, keeping their eyes on the ground as they followed the water's curve. When they came to the rock, Julie drew up.

"Nothing," she said, clearly disappointed.

Bethancourt was examining the boulder. It was larger than it had looked from a distance and would be easy enough to clamber onto. In the side facing the lake there was a sort of shelf, where he presumed one would sit, and from there the rock sloped down toward the water. A ring had been driven into the rock a couple of feet below the shelf and it was to this that the boat was tied up. There was less than a foot of soggy earth between the base of the boulder and the water, and from his vantage on horseback, he could see footprints marked there, though whose they were and when they had been made was beyond his ability to determine.

Queasily, he began to entertain another scenario that had nothing to do with criminals fleeing.

"Is the water very deep here?" he asked Julie.

She shrugged, still despondent. "It's deep enough for the boat," she answered. "Close to the shore here, it's about up to my waist, but farther out it's deeper." She frowned. "But it's ridiculous to suppose Mother went for a midnight swim in mid October."

"Of course not," said Bethancourt. "I was only curious."

Julie was looking off into the trees.

"I suppose," she said dubiously, "she might have gone on from here. The path goes on into the wood."

Bethancourt thought this highly unlikely, though he did not like to say so. Woods are not encouraging places at night, and he could not see a woman with a few drinks inside her and in an unhappy frame of mind seeking them out. But he said, "We might as well check while we're here. It won't do any harm."

Julie nodded and clucked to her horse.

Beyond the boulder, the path was less well-defined, straying gradually away from the shore, and climbing up a rise into the trees.

"There's really two paths here," Julie said as they entered the trees. "One's very steep and runs back to the lake, but we can't get the horses up there, and I can't think Mother would have gone that way in any case. It's not a very good path."

"What's the other one?"

"It goes up the hill to a little glade. We sometimes have picnics there in the summer."

The ride beneath the trees was a pleasant one, and Bethancourt did not bother too much about looking for someone in distress in the underbrush. In another five or ten minutes they reached the glade, which was indeed an agreeable spot for a picnic. However, it was not large and there was quite obviously no one lying about in it. Julie, who had stood up in her stirrups as they approached, slumped back down.

"Oh damn," she said. "I did so hope . . . well, never mind."

"The police will have dogs, I expect," said Bethancourt. "They'll have a better chance of finding her."

She gave him a wary look. "I suppose," she said, "you think the same as the police—that she murdered Charlie and ran off during the night. That's why I wanted to come myself, because I knew they wouldn't really look."

"Not at all," said Bethancourt stoutly if untruthfully. Then another thought occurred to him as they turned the horses for home. "Tell me, Julie," he said, "what would have happened if you had got up this morning and found a note saying she'd gone back to London? If she had packed a bag and taken her car?"

Julie threw him a withering glance. "I'd have thought she'd gone back to London."

"But you wouldn't have rung her up or anything?"

"No, of course not. Why should I?"

The queasy feeling was returning to Bethancourt's stomach. If Joan Bonnar had truly decided to flee, it was inexplicable that she should not have written a note, ensuring that she would not be missed until she failed to turn up at the theater tonight. It would have given her all day to get out of the country, rather than having the search instigated directly after breakfast. Even if she had left earlier, after dinner last night, and her family were covering up for her, it still made no sense to let the search start so early.

That left why she had gone out at all during the night.

"Julie," he said, "did your mother have any mail or telephone calls yesterday?"

She looked at him blankly. "Some people sent notes saying they were sorry about Charlie," she answered. "And I think she took several calls from various friends in the afternoon. Why?"

"I only wondered if she could have made an appointment with anyone—however, it has just occurred to me that she could have done that at the funeral."

Julie was frowning. "An appointment? For the middle of the night?"

"She might have slipped out shortly after she had gone upstairs."

"I suppose she might," said Julie doubtfully. "The sitting room door was open, and I think we would have heard her coming down the stairs, but it's true we weren't particularly listening. If she was quiet, we might not have heard her. But even if she did go out then, why can't we find her now?"

To this Bethancourt had no answer, or at least none he wanted to give, and they rode back to the stables in silence.

CHAPTER

*B*y the time Carmichael and Gibbons arrived, the police search had begun, in a somewhat desultory fashion. It was clear to Bethancourt that they thought their prime suspect had fled, and that they were wasting their time searching for her here. In addition, the dogs were having difficulty picking up the scent, owing to its having rained the night before, and to the fact that Miss Bonnar had taken a walk after returning from the funeral, so that when the dogs did find a scent in the garden, it led them back to the house.

Bethancourt had left Astley-Cooper in the house with the family and gone out to smoke in his car and await the detectives' arrival. He greeted them as the Rover pulled up in the drive, and Gibbons thought his friend looked unwontedly somber.

"There you are." Carmichael took stock as he emerged from the car, noting the police vehicles. "I take it the search is under way?"

"Such as it is," said Bethancourt. "They think she's done a bunk."

Carmichael gave him a shrewd look.

"And you don't?" he asked.

"I did," admitted Bethancourt. "But she didn't take her car or leave a note. If she had, she wouldn't have been missed 'til this evening, at the theater."

"Well, well," said Carmichael, digesting this. "On the other hand, people do sometimes panic and do very stupid things."

"I think you ought to take a look at the lake," said Bethancourt. "It's a favorite family walk and there are a good set of footprints down there. I couldn't tell much about them, but you'll know. And, of course, the lake itself is wonderfully handy for disposing of dead bodies."

"Is that what you think happened?" asked Gibbons.

"It seems an awfully tempting idea, doesn't it?"

"We'll have a look," said Carmichael. "Are the family all in the house?"

"Yes—they're drinking tea in the sitting room with Clarence."

"Then they'll keep. Where is this lake?"

Bethancourt led the way, taking them around the side of the house and out into the fields beyond. Carmichael gazed appreciatively at the landscape as they went.

"It's pretty here," he said. He was thinking of moving to the country when he retired—the real country, not just the suburbs. He had saved a little money since the children had left home and, while he wasn't sure what his pension would stretch to, he thought they ought to be able to afford something, even if it was small. And then his wife could go in for her gardening in earnest and he, well, he could mow the lawn.

He sighed and returned to the present as they topped the rise and met up with part of the search party, who were eager to report that they had had no luck so far.

"Keep at it," Carmichael told them. "I'm just going down to have a look at the lake."

"The lake, sir?" said the sergeant doubtfully. "We haven't got that far yet."

"No matter," said Carmichael genially. "Carry on."

They went on down the hill, Carmichael squinting at the lake as they approached it. The detectives paid close attention to the path as Bethancourt led them around to the boulder.

"Look there," said Gibbons, pointing to a damp patch of ground just to the left of the track. "That's a man's shoe there—a number nine or so, I think."

"Hmm, yes," said Carmichael, who was bent over a different section of the path. "And here's a woman's flat shoe, I think—she seems to have slipped a little."

They examined the whole of the path running along the lake to the boulder. The man's footprint did not recur, but the woman's could be discerned in several places. There was one particularly clear print by the boulder itself.

"These were certainly made within the last twenty-four hours," pronounced Carmichael, turning his attention to the rock itself, but there was nothing obvious to see on its rough surface. "Well," he said, straightening, "someone walked down here recently, and it might well have been Joan Bonnar." He turned to gaze out over the lake. "And she might well have gone into the water."

"If she's near the rock," put in Bethancourt, "Jack could wade in and have a look—Julie Benson says it's fairly shallow there."

Gibbons glared at him.

"You didn't do any looking yourself, did you?" asked Carmichael suspiciously.

"No, sir. Certainly not."

Carmichael nodded and was silent a little. "I see what you're thinking," he said at last. "The idea would have been to make it look like she came out here by herself and sat on the rock. Yes, I think we might have a look."

"I'll run back to the house," offered Bethancourt, "and rustle up some towels and blankets."

"Please do," said Gibbons, eyeing the water resignedly. "I think, sir, if you don't mind, it would be better if I stripped off."

"Of course," said Carmichael. "I'm sorry to let you in for this, Gibbons, but there's no denying I'm a bit past it for this sort of thing. And we do want to find out as quickly as possible if there's anything to be investigated here or not. No, wait a minute, lad. We don't want you catching cold. Wait 'til Bethancourt comes back with the towels."

Bethancourt was not long. When he appeared on the horizon, his arms full of towels and blankets, Gibbons shrugged out of his jacket and pulled his sweater over his head. He glanced longingly at the little rowboat, but he knew that it would have to be examined by a forensics team. By the time Bethancourt rejoined them, Gibbons was standing shivering in his underwear. The sun promptly went behind a cloud.

He pushed through the grass on the far side of the boulder in order to avoid the footprints and tested the water with his toe. It was very cold. Behind him, he heard Carmichael asking Bethancourt what he had told them at the house.

"Just that you had decided to have a look at the lake as a precaution, and that they should stay put. And I nabbed a bottle of brandy, too, Jack."

Gibbons grunted, wading cautiously out into the water. The bottom was muddy, and sloped off suddenly, landing him in water up to his waist. He gasped with the cold and took a moment to steady himself. Then he began to wade along, making for the water directly before the boulder, his feet catching in the weeds. The water was very murky; he could not see his lower legs, and there was an eerie sensation in feeling his way along, waiting for his toes to touch something other than mud and rocks.

"All right, lad?" asked Carmichael from the bank.

"Yes. It's slow going."

He kept on, searching the lake bottom with his feet before taking another step. There were rocks here, covered with moss and slippery, but their rough touch could not possibly be mistaken for a body, not even by toes going numb with cold.

He was coming up on the rope that moored the rowboat and he eyed it with disfavor. He was going to have to submerge to get under it.

And then, all at once, his toes touched something soft. Sternly, he repressed an urge to clamber out of the water at once, and sought for a firm foothold. He bent, reaching down with his hands, and groped until his searching fingers closed on the soft thing, identifying it at once as the corner of some heavy material. His heart hammering, he reached out farther, touched the rough surface of a rock and then, beyond it, something cold and smooth and firm. He let go at once and stood up.

"Are you all right, Jack?" came Bethancourt's voice, concerned.

"Yes," croaked Gibbons. He turned and began to wade back as quickly as he could, anxious to be out of the water which held such horrors. "Yes, there's something there."

He floundered a bit and then he was at the shore, scrambling in the mud while Bethancourt and Carmichael reached down for him, their hands warm on his cold skin. He felt the coarse grass beneath his feet, and Bethancourt flung a towel over his shoulders. He clutched it to him, shivering.

"Here, lad," said Carmichael, uncorking the brandy. "Have a swallow of this."

Gibbons took the bottle gratefully, feeling the liquor burn its way into his stomach. Bethancourt had got another towel and was vigorously drying his back.

"Better get out of those wet pants," he said.

Gibbons, normally a modest man, made no protest. The material was cold and clammy and he felt as though his testicles had contracted to the size of two marbles. Bethancourt gave him a towel to put around his waist and rubbed his legs with another towel. He seemed to have brought the entire linen closet.

"So you found her?" asked Carmichael, handing over the brandy again as Gibbons's teeth began to chatter.

"I found someone, sir," he managed. "I didn't bother ducking under to look since the water was so murky."

"You did well. All right, I'll call a forensics team out and call off the search. You get dressed as quick as you can. I'll send one of the local boys down to stand guard so you can get into the house and warm up."

"That's it, then," said Bethancourt as Carmichael strode away. "I was so hoping I was wrong."

Gibbons was struggling into his trousers. "It might still be an accident," he said. "As murder, it doesn't fit very well with the rest of what we've got."

Bethancourt merely snorted. He lit a cigarette and glanced at his friend. "You're still shivering, Jack," he said. "Get your shoes on so we can get back to the house."

"We have to wait for one of the constables to come," pointed out Gibbons, sitting on the grass to don his shoes and socks. "Here, give me another swig of that brandy."

Bethancourt handed him the bottle. "Here," he said, "have this blanket around you."

"Thanks." Gibbons took a deep swallow and rose, pacing in an effort to warm up. "Where's Cerberus?" he asked suddenly.

"I left him at Stutely Manor," said Bethancourt, "not knowing what I'd find here. I'm glad I did; he would almost certainly have found those footprints before I did and walked all over them."

"Yes, the chief inspector would have been annoyed about that."

"I didn't find out when the Bensons and Mrs. Potts went to bed last night," said Bethancourt. "It might have been one of them—easy to suggest a walk."

"You forget," said Gibbons, turning and pacing back, "all three of them have alibis for Bingham's murder."

"Yes, isn't that suspicious?"

Gibbons laughed.

"Well," said Bethancourt, a trifle impatiently, "what do you think happened?"

"I don't know," answered Gibbons. He rubbed his arms in an effort to stop shivering, and walked briskly in a circle. "We haven't enough information to base any kind of hypothesis on yet. We don't even know for certain that the corpse is Joan Bonnar."

"Oh, really," said Bethancourt. "The Cotswolds are hardly burgeoning with corpses. Who else could it be?"

"Derek Towser, for instance," said Gibbons. "He might have been out late last night and happened on Miss Bonnar making an escape."

Bethancourt snorted again.

"Or," added Gibbons, turning to walk widdershins about his friend, "granting that it is Joan Bonnar, it might be suicide. She must certainly have been feeling very low if she was innocent. And even if she was guilty, she might have bitterly regretted what she'd done."

"If it were suicide, I should have expected her to do it at Bingham's cottage."

"This place may have had significance you don't know about," said Gibbons. "He could have proposed to her here, for example."

"That's true," said Bethancourt. "Jack, you're making me dizzy. Can't you stand still?"

"I'm still cold," retorted Gibbons, continuing to pace. "The feeling is only just coming back to my toes."

"Well, for heaven's sake, let's just walk up and back. This circling is making me nauseous."

"There's another possibility," said Gibbons, obligingly veering into a straight path. "It could be that Joan did come out for a walk, and met the murderer. There might have been a struggle."

"A struggle?"

"Yes, and the murderer slipped, striking his head on that rock.

Joan saw he was dead and panicked, knowing she's already suspected of Bingham's murder. So she tips him into the lake and flees. How's that for a hypothesis?" He grinned up at his friend.

Bethancourt regarded him pityingly. "That brandy has gone straight to your head," he said.

Gibbons started to reply and then checked himself. "Look," he said, "here comes the constable with some scene-of-the-crime tape. Let's head back."

When they arrived at the house, they found Astley-Cooper sitting alone in the kitchen.

"I thought I'd better take myself off," he explained. "It didn't seem the thing, somehow, to stay on once I'd said how sorry I was. Besides, Chief Inspector Carmichael came in and clearly wanted me out of it."

"Is he with the Bensons and Mrs. Potts now?" asked Gibbons.

"That's right." Astley-Cooper shot him a concerned look. "You look chilled to the bone, Jack."

"He had to go into the lake," said Bethancourt, while Gibbons drew a chair up before the electric fire set in the hearth and turned on all four bars.

"Well, luckily I've got water on the boil," said Astley-Cooper cheerfully. "I was going to make some tea and I filled the kettle in case anyone else should want some. Here, take off your shoes."

Gibbons stared at him. "You must be mad," he said. "I've only just got the feeling back in my feet."

But Astley-Cooper was bustling around the kitchen. Out of the pantry he hauled a large basin and dropped it on the floor at Gibbons's feet. "Put your feet in that," he ordered. "I know what I'm doing—there's only one way to take the chill off."

While Gibbons reluctantly divested himself of his shoes and socks, Astley-Cooper poured boiling water into the basin and added a judicious amount of cool water from the tap. "Stick 'em in there," he said. "I'll have the tea ready in a moment, and you drink it as hot as you can."

Bethancourt sat at the table and watched the proceedings with some amusement. It worked, as Astley-Cooper had said it would; in a few minutes Gibbons had thrown off the blanket he had kept wrapped about his shoulders and declared he was feeling positively overheated.

While his subordinate was warming up, Carmichael was finding out what he could from the family. The Bensons were subdued and pale, Mrs. Potts much more volubly aghast. Carmichael took them carefully through their movements on the evening before, mentally comparing what they told him with what Bethancourt had reported them saying earlier. There was, so far as he could see, no divergence.

After some discussion, they agreed that their game of Scrabble had finished at about ten thirty. The Bensons had put the game away while Mrs. Potts went to the kitchen to wash up. The twins had joined her there, and James had made cocoa, which they had drank when Mrs. Potts was done with the dishes. It had been about eleven thirty when they had gone up to bed.

"A rather late evening, wasn't it?" asked Carmichael.

"Yes," said Mrs. Potts. "We usually eat earlier, but Miss Bonnar doesn't like to dine before eight, so when she's here, things get a little late."

"All the same," said Julie, "we usually turn in by ten. But what with Charlie's funeral yesterday, we were all feeling a little restless."

"Funerals often have that effect," agreed Carmichael. "When you went up, you noticed nothing amiss upstairs? Was your mother's door closed?"

"Oh, yes," said Mrs. Potts. "And it still was this morning."

"You didn't hear her moving about or anything?"

They all shook their heads.

"All right. So you were in here, and then went to the kitchen. None of you left the house?"

"Oh," said Julie, looking abashed. "I did. I forgot. I went over to the stables to check on the horses—I always do."

237

"When would that have been?" asked Carmichael.

"When James and I went to the kitchen, so it must have been about ten forty-five."

"And you would have returned by what time?"

"Oh, before eleven," she answered. "It doesn't take long. I just ran across and back, and found James making cocoa when I came in."

"I see. Now then, I'd like to ask you about Miss Bonnar's mood last night. How did she seem to you?"

Mrs. Potts answered, looking at him suspiciously, as if this might be a trick question. "She was depressed and unhappy. I mean, she'd just been to her fiancé's funeral."

"Of course," said Carmichael soothingly. "I was looking for something beyond that. Did she say anything, for instance, about her future plans? Or make reference to any particular person?"

They were all silent for a moment, thinking. Then Mrs. Potts said, "Really, she was very quiet. Unusually so. I can't remember that she said much more than "Pass the salt," at supper."

"That's right," said Julie. "We spoke about the funeral I remember—you know, what a nice epitaph the vicar had given and such like—but she hardly said anything at all."

Carmichael nodded. "Do you think it possible," he asked, "that she had anything on her mind besides Mr. Bingham's death?"

They glanced at each other, unsure.

"Well," said Mrs. Potts, shrugging, "there's really no way of telling, is there? We expected her to be feeling down, and she was. I didn't think further, myself."

With this Carmichael had to be content. If Joan Bonnar had been contemplating either suicide or a meeting with a murderer, she had given no clear indication of it to her family. He thanked them and rose.

"I'll just collect my sergeant and have a look at her bedroom," he said. "I'll be back after my team gets here and recovers the body."

Mrs. Potts made a little sound and put her hand over her mouth. Julie and James just looked depressed.

Bethancourt would have liked to see the dead woman's bedroom, but felt he could hardly leave Astley-Cooper alone in the kitchen. After all, if he was horning in on the detectives' turf, there was no obvious reason that Astley-Cooper should not do the same. So he stayed behind, settling in with a cigarette and a cup of tea, and told his eager host all about the discovery of the body.

In time, the detectives returned, carrying an empty whisky glass, a half-empty bottle, and a container of prescription tablets, all encased in evidence bags. These they stored in the boot of the police Rover, and then hung about outside, awaiting the arrival of forensics.

They appeared in due course, accompanied by a medical team and a diver, and everyone trooped back out to the lake. Bethancourt and Astley-Cooper hovered on the fringes of the activity while the men set to work collecting evidence, and the diver went in to examine the body while the doctor waited impatiently on the shore. Some of the men donned wading boots and entered the water at a little distance from the boulder in order to bring up the corpse. They went carefully and slowly, spreading the water with their hands, while the diver, having shot several pictures with an underwater camera, waited for them to make their way over to him.

"She's right here," he said, stooping.

"I can't see a thing."

"Feel for it."

"You get 'round that end, Jeff."

One man slipped and fell with a splash, cursing.

"Clumsy lout."

"Damned rocks are slippery."

"Yes, and the water's cold. All right, now, better take her out this way."

"Everybody stand firm and pass her along. We'll do better that way."

"Here she comes."

"Don't lift her so high—let the water float her."

A sodden patch of black cashmere broke from the surface and was

239

eased along, past the boulder and toward the grass. The men, wet and shivering now, moved carefully, easing the corpse along. Two of them scrambled out onto the shore and crouched down at the ready, the water streaming off them and soaking the earth.

"All right. Easy now. Lift all together."

The black cloth rose again, molding itself to a woman's form, crowned with golden hair which was darkened to brown by the wet. With a slow, sucking sound the lake gave up its prize.

"Gently now."

"Roll her this way a little."

"Have you got her, Dan?"

"Yes, it's all right. Just push a bit."

"There!"

The men on the shore drew back, breathing harshly. Those in the water began to climb out, one of them lingering long enough to heave up the trailing end of the black coat and throw it over the body. It landed with a loud splat.

The body lay facedown on the shore, shrouded in soaked black cashmere, the white legs curving lifelessly from beneath the fabric. The doctor bent to examine the head, searching expertly with his fingertips amid the wet locks of hair. He muttered to himself and then, with the ease of long practice, grasped a shoulder and flipped the body onto its back. He examined the forehead and temple and then felt down the length of the corpse.

"Well?" asked Carmichael, standing over him.

"Looks like she drowned," said the doctor, still on his knees. "I won't know for sure, of course, until I get her back. No other obvious injury. Do you want to get her fingerprints before I take her?"

"Yes, that and the shoes," answered Carmichael, beckoning to one of the forensics team.

"Shoes?" said the doctor. "Oh, I see. Footprints."

His hands already encased in rubber gloves, Carmichael himself carefully worked the shoes off. They were flat, leather shoes, olive-colored like the weeds in the water. Carmichael dropped the first one into a plastic bag produced by Gibbons; the left shoe, however, he held flat on his outstretched palm.

"Let's have a little confirmation," he said.

He moved to the other side of the boulder and bent over the clear footprint in the earth there. The shoe in his hand fit into it perfectly. He looked up at Gibbons.

"That's it then," he said. "She walked here herself."

It was late afternoon by the time they were ready to leave the farm-house. Carmichael paused as they emerged from the house, mar-shalling his thoughts.

"We'd best see what our other suspects were doing last night," he told Gibbons. "Though it could all be for naught—this might turn out to be suicide, or even an accident, in the end."

"Yes, sir," said Gibbons, unlocking the Rover. "To Derek Towser's cottage, then?"

"Yes. No one seems to have seen him today." Carmichael glanced about as he went to the passenger door. "Where's Bethancourt, then? The body put him off?"

"No, sir," said Gibbons. "At least, it didn't affect his appetite. He went off with Astley-Cooper to have lunch."

Carmichael grimaced. "I'd have liked some lunch myself," he said.

"So would I, sir," said Gibbons feelingly as he got into the car.

There was no answer at Derek Towser's cottage, but just as they were returning to the car, the artist drove up. He pulled in behind them and leaned out of the window, his head adorned with a shapeless felt hat.

"Looking for me?" he called cheerfully.

Carmichael, who had been in the midst of cursing elusive sus-pects, changed gears smoothly.

"Yes, indeed," he said. "I'm Detective Chief Inspector Carmichael, and I've one or two questions for you."

"Righto," said Towser, climbing out of his car, and nodding to Gibbons. "Come on in."

He unlocked the cottage door, ushering them into the studio.

"There's nowhere to sit in here," he said apologetically to Carmichael, "but if you'll come through to the kitchen . . ."

"That's quite all right," said Carmichael. "This won't take but a minute. We're only interested, if you'll be so good, in your movements last night and early this morning. Starting at about nine o'clock yesterday evening."

Towser sobered immediately. "Last night?" he repeated. "Has something happened?"

"Yes, sir, I'm afraid it has. If you could tell me—"

"But what's going on?"

Carmichael remained impassive. "I'd prefer to hear about your movements first, sir, if you don't mind."

"I do bloody well mind."

Carmichael did not reply. He merely stared back at Towser until the young man averted his gaze.

"I expect," he said moodily, "you'll tell me afterward?"

"I don't see why not," replied Carmichael levelly. "You're bound to hear before the day is out."

"Well . . ." Towser pulled off his hat and ran a hand through his hair. "Very well, then," he said grudgingly. "At about nine last night, Eve Bingham stopped by for a drink. Actually, I think it might have been a bit earlier. She stayed until some time after ten, perhaps ten fifteen. I went for a short walk after she left, came back, did up the dishes, and went to bed."

"And this morning?"

"I was up early, left the house by seven or so. I drove over to Mr. Kellam's farm and settled in to do a painting of his barn. That's where I've just come from—the painting's in the back of the car if you'd like to see it."

242

"Not just at the moment, sir," said Carmichael. "You say you took a brief walk after Miss Bingham left you last night? Where did you go?"

"Up toward the lake." Towser jerked his head. "There's a path out back. I wanted to clear my head, on account of having to get up early today."

Carmichael's eyes gleamed, and he let his gaze fall to Towser's feet, as if mentally estimating their size.

"Exactly how far did you go, sir? Did you walk along the lake?"

Towser looked suspicious. "For a little ways," he admitted warily.

"Up along to that boulder on the far side?"

Towser shook his head. "Not that far. I stopped when I got to the path to the farmhouse and turned back."

"But you could see the boulder?"

"I expect I could have, if I'd looked. Although it was pretty dark—in fact, it started to drizzle just as I turned back—so perhaps not."

"And you saw no one else?"

"No, of course not. The Bensons and Martha go to bed early, and they're the only ones who walk around there." He looked alarmed. "Did one of them drown?"

"No," answered Carmichael. "But Joan Bonnar was found dead there this morning."

Towser's eyes widened. "Joan Bonnar? She's dead?"

"Yes, sir. Are you certain you didn't see her? She was wearing a dark coat, but her hair would have been light."

Towser shook his head, still stunned by the news. "No," he said. "I didn't see anyone."

"And what time was it you were there?" asked Carmichael. "If you went for your walk directly after Miss Bingham left—"

"I expect it was about half ten," said Towser hastily. "Ten thirty when I reached the lake, I mean. I can't put it closer than that."

"Very good. And can I ask what shoes you were wearing last night?"

"Shoes?" echoed Towser, staring wildly. "Why, the ones I'm wearing now, I suppose. Yes, I must have been."

They all looked down at the black leather trainers, which had seen better days.

"But what happened?" asked Towser. "Did she take the boat out or something?"

"We don't know yet," answered Carmichael. "Mr. Towser, it would help us enormously if we could take your shoes with us. You'd have them back by tomorrow or the next day," he added persuasively.

For a moment, Towser merely gaped at him. Then realization dawned and he said slowly, "I see. You've found footprints, haven't you?"

"One footprint," agreed Carmichael. "It's very likely yours, according to your account of your walk, but you must see that we have to absolutely eliminate the possibility that it belongs to someone else."

"Yes, I see." Towser was thoughtful, staring down at his feet. "You can do that, I expect?" he asked. "I mean, you can tell the difference, even if someone else was there and wearing trainers like these?"

"Oh, yes," said Carmichael confidently. "Yours aren't new by any means—there will be a pattern of wear on the soles. No one else could match that."

"Well," said Towser uncertainly. "Well, all right, then." He sat down abruptly on the stool before the easel and began pulling off the shoes. "I may be a fool," he said, "but it seems to me to be more suspicious not to let you have them than the other way about. I will get them back?" he added, rising and holding them out. "They're the most comfortable shoes I've got."

"As soon as we can," promised Carmichael, taking his prize. "Thank you very much, Mr. Towser. And thank you for your time."

Despite this triumph, Carmichael was in no very good mood as they returned to the cars.

"I expect we'd better get on to Eve Bingham," he said with a sigh as he settled himself in the passenger seat. "Frankly, even if she killed her father, I can't imagine why she should want to do away with Joan Bonnar, but it never does to skip things."

"Yes, sir," said Gibbons, starting up the car.

Carmichael frowned and gazed out the window.

"I want the pathologist's report," he said peevishly. "I want to know whether this was suicide or not."

Gibbons wisely said nothing.

In the end, they found Eve Bingham closer to hand than they had expected. As they rounded the curve in the road, they saw a brown lorry parked in front of Bingham's cottage, with two men loading crates into it. Gibbons slowed at once, looking at his superior.

"If the removal men are here, sir," he offered, "Eve Bingham should be as well."

"Yes, yes," said Carmichael impatiently. "Pull up behind them."

They found Eve Bingham in the sitting room, hands on her hips, watching a burly man marking a box. She turned as they entered, and then hesitated as she saw who had come.

"Hello, Miss Bingham," said Gibbons. "This is Detective Chief Inspector Carmichael."

She held out a hand. "Chief Inspector," she said, her glance straying back to the movers almost at once. "What can I do for you?"

"We just wanted to check on your movements last night and this morning," said Carmichael.

She swung back to him, giving a short bark of brittle laughter.

"Surely," she said, "you don't suspect me of helping my father's murderer to escape?"

Carmichael only smiled. "Then you've heard of Miss Bonnar's disappearance?"

She nodded. "Mrs. Eberhart mentioned it."

"Well then," said Carmichael, "you'll understand that we are anxious to be certain that she disappeared of her own free will."

Eve's expression showed that she thought anything else highly improbable, but she shrugged and reeled off a sparse description of her

245

evening. It coincided with Towser's account, except that she thought it had been nearer ten when she left his house.

"And afterward?"

"I came back here to finish. I suppose I came away about twelve."

Her account of the morning was even less interesting. She had slept in until about eleven, breakfasted in the hotel dining room, and then come here to supervise the move. Her air said clearly that she wished they'd let her get on with the job.

"Mrs. Eberhart saw me arrive this morning," she added, her eyes drifting impatiently toward the huge bear of a man who was hefting a teakwood chest experimentally. She refocused her attention abruptly on Carmichael. "Will that do, Chief Inspector? You can see it's not a very convenient time."

"No, but there's no help for it," said Carmichael agreeably. "Were you planning to return to Paris yourself?"

"Of course," she said shortly. "As soon as may be. I will, of course, notify you when I do."

"Yes, do that. In the meantime, you might be interested to know that we've found Miss Bonnar."

"You have?" Her eyes narrowed.

"Yes. She was in the lake—quite dead. Good day, Miss."

Eve turned a little pale, her eyes following him as he turned away. Then she looked at Gibbons, as if for confirmation.

"I'm afraid it's true," he said, shrugging.

"But—" Eve broke off and bit her lip even while Gibbons paused, on the verge of following Carmichael out. Then Eve shook her head and without another word she turned away to deal with a removal man hovering in the background.

Having enjoyed a large lunch at Stutely Manor, Bethancourt was eager to rejoin the detectives, while Astley-Cooper was just as eager to spread the news.

"I'll just run down to the vicarage," he announced. "Someone should really let the vicar know. And perhaps I'll stop for a pint on my way back. Sure you don't want to come, Phillip?"

Bethancourt hesitated, wondering if the Tothills might have any insight to offer.

"Well," he said, "perhaps I'll stop at the vicarage with you. I'd like to speak to the Tothills. But then I think I had better go in search of Jack and the chief inspector."

"Very well, very well," said Astley-Cooper, pleased. "You can follow me down to the village."

Leandra Tothill was washing her kitchen floor. For this pursuit she had donned an ancient, moth-eaten sweater that was rather too tight for her. Bethancourt, peering in through the glass over Astley-Cooper's shoulder, paused to admire the shape of her bosom, which the sweater delineated quite nicely. With Marla as a standard, few women seemed to be worth pausing for, but Leandra Tothill was one of them.

Astley-Cooper tapped politely on the door and she looked up, smiling as she put aside her mop and moved to let them in.

"Hullo," she said, smiling at them and reaching down her hand to pet Cerberus. "Do come in—you're a welcome distraction."

Astley-Cooper hesitated. "We don't want to muck up the floor," he said. "We could go 'round to the front."

"No, no," she said, pushing an unruly curl off her forehead. "I've only done that half. Just keep to this side—that's it."

Bethancourt called his dog to heel, a command Cerberus was uncharacteristically slow to obey; he remained with his head pressed against Leandra's side.

"Good Lord," said Bethancourt, taken aback by his pet's disobedience. "I said heel, Cerberus."

Leandra laughed as this time Cerberus obeyed, casting a look of deep reproach at his master as he did so.

"Muck up her clean floor and see how well she likes you then," muttered Bethancourt to his pet as they followed Astley-Cooper down the hall and into a small parlor Bethancourt had not seen before.

"Has something happened?" asked Leandra, looking from one to the other of them eagerly. "You haven't found who killed Charlie, have you?"

"No," said Bethancourt, "I'm afraid that's not it."

"Oh." Her face fell and she began to stroke Cerberus again automatically. "I rather thought you might be coming to summon Richard to counsel the criminal."

Astley-Cooper, who a short time ago had seemed so eager to disseminate the news, looked sad. "I wish so," he said, "but instead we're the bearers of bad tidings, Lee. There's been another death."

Leandra went very still, her hand frozen on Cerberus's head. Her eyes were frightened. "Who?" she whispered.

"Joan Bonnar," said Astley-Cooper.

"We don't know," added Bethancourt hastily, "that it was murder. But under the circumstances, the police are treating it as a suspicious death."

"Dear God, how awful. The poor Bensons and Martha." The phone began to ring in the next room, and the sound roused her from her shock. "That's probably them," she said. "I'll just answer it—you two go on and break the news to Richard. He's in his study."

They followed her into the passage where she motioned them on as she picked up the receiver. "Hello? . . . Oh, it's you . . . No, not just at the moment . . ."

They left her voice behind and went to knock on the study door.

Tothill was seated at his desk. As usual, he wore his cassock, but in deference to the slight chill in the room, he had donned an orange pullover which looked even more incongruous than the tweed jacket.

He was poring over a ledger book and a shoe box full of receipts stood at his elbow. The expression on his face was one of harassment.

"Hello," he said, looking rather pleased to be interrupted. "I've been going over the parish books. I'm afraid I'm not terribly methodical and my churchwarden nearly had my head off last night. Kept me closeted in here 'til all hours."

Astley-Cooper sympathized and sat down while Bethancourt drew up a second chair.

"I've come to break some rather bad news," he said.

Tothill looked anxious.

"It's about Joan Bonnar," Astley-Cooper continued.

Tothill, to Bethancourt's eye, relaxed just a trifle. Joan, after all, was not one of his parishioners.

"I heard this morning she'd gone missing," he said.

"The police found her this afternoon. She's dead."

Tothill had seen it coming. He sighed deeply and leaned back in his chair.

"How?" he asked. "Was it—was it another murder?"

Astley-Cooper explained. About halfway through, Leandra came in. She looked agitated, but seated herself calmly enough on the arm of her husband's chair. He put an arm about her and her hand fell to hold his.

"False alarm," she said. "It was only Derek Towser, also ringing to give us the news. He said she was drowned?"

Obligingly, Astley-Cooper began his story again. When he had finished, Tothill sighed again and Leandra's hand tightened on his.

"I'd better go out there and see if there's anything I can do. Not that there is," he added gloomily.

Leandra smiled at him and ran a hand through her hair. "No," she said, "but people like to have you rally 'round. It'll make Martha feel better anyhow."

"I suppose it will. Normally, I'd contact the undertakers first, but of course in this case they won't be wanted for sometime. And besides, I don't know what arrangements may have been made. Miss Bonnar might have wished to be buried in London."

"You could still offer to talk to whichever funeral parlor it is," said Leandra. "Only do take off that jumper before you go. I don't think orange is quite the thing somehow."

Tothill looked down at himself as if surprised to find he was wearing orange, and Bethancourt stifled a laugh.

But he was thoughtful as he and Astley-Cooper left Tothill to get on with the business of being the vicar and made their way toward the pub. He had hoped that this new development might strike some chord in the minds of those who had known Bingham best, but the look in Tothill's eyes had been bewilderment. Oddly, his wife's eyes had betrayed fear, but fear of what he could not tell.

It was past midnight and raining steadily. The temperature had dropped and, in deference to this, Astley-Cooper had set a blazing fire going in the huge, seventeenth-century fireplace. Like everything else in the house, the fireplace's ornamental hood was a fine example of its period, but this particular piece of antiquity did not appear to depress its owner, possibly because it was in fine repair.

"Draws beautifully," he said, patting the hood affectionately. "You can get a really good fire going in there."

Bethancourt and Gibbons grunted assents. They had already pushed their chairs back several feet from the heat of the blaze, while Cerberus had removed himself to the far side of the room.

"And," added Astley-Cooper triumphantly, "it never needs anything doing to it, beyond having the chimney sweep in once in a while. But you have to do that with any chimney, even the most modern ones."

They duly admired the functionality of the fireplace, while their host slipped back to his seat and promptly began to doze.

Gibbons felt rather like dozing himself. He had recovered from his earlier immersion in the lake, but it had been a very long day and between the fire and the whisky, it was all he could do to keep his eyes open. Yawning, he made an effort to rouse himself, sitting up straighter and sipping at his drink.

"What it really comes down to," said Bethancourt, "is whether we think she was murdered or not. And, if not, do we think she killed Bingham?"

Gibbons yawned again. "There's nothing to go on," he said. "I told you about the autopsy: she was drunk, had taken a couple of her sedatives, and she drowned. She died somewhere between ten and eleven thirty. The accident scenario is probably the simplest explanation."

Bethancourt narrowed his eyes. "The accident scenario," he said dubiously, "being the one where she was miserable, and when the whisky didn't put her to sleep, she took her tablets on top of that. They would take a few minutes to work, and she grew impatient when she didn't drop off at once and decided to go for a walk. However, by the time she reached the lake, the tablets were making her drowsy at last, so she sat on the rock, passed out, and fell into the water. It doesn't seem very likely to me. What does Carmichael say?"

"He doesn't like it. He says it's by far the most reasonable explanation, along with the idea that Bingham took a sedative by accident in her London house, and she and Watkinson panicked and moved the body, but he doesn't like it. Neither do I."

"Ah." Astley-Cooper came to suddenly with a grunt. He blinked at them. "So you think she was drugged on purpose, like Charlie?"

"That would make Martha Potts the prime suspect," said Bethancourt. "Her alibi isn't really very good: her sister on the one hand, and the Benson twins on the other. And it's perfectly obvious they'd lie themselves black in the face for her, especially if they truly believed her innocent."

"Don't be an ass, Phillip," said Astley-Cooper. "Why on earth should Martha Potts do anything of the kind?"

Bethancourt lit a cigarette and exhaled the smoke lazily. "Possibly she had an affair with Bingham before he met Joan Bonnar. Last bid for love and all that."

"Oh, really." Astley-Cooper swallowed half his drink in annoyance and then coughed miserably.

"She could have taken the tablets herself and still have been murdered," pointed out Gibbons helpfully. "After all, she walked down there herself—the liquor and drugs clearly hadn't made her that woozy. Derek Towser by his own admission was walking there. Possibly he'd made an appointment with her, or it might have been just accident. Either way, they talk, and she lets something slip which alarms him. Very likely something she doesn't realize the importance of, but which to Towser is the death knoll. So he tips her into the lake, and she's too drunk to save herself. It doesn't take long to drown," he added reflectively. "I remember another case, an accident. There was a party of very drunken people who decided to have a late-night swim to cap off their evening. They were having a grand old time, throwing each other into the pool, splashing about and so on. One young man was so drunk, he got turned around in the water and drowned. The others never noticed until it was too late."

The room was quiet. Astley-Cooper had fallen asleep again during this recital. Bethancourt pitched his cigarette end into the fireplace and rested his fair head against the back of the chair, staring into the flames.

"That's a very sad story," he said at last.

"Yes, it was rather pathetic. They were all so bedraggled, and half of them still hadn't any clothes on when we got there. They were just shivering around in towels."

"I'm rather sorry you told me," said Bethancourt. "And sorry you had to see it, of course."

Gibbons shrugged. "Part of the job."

"Yes, I suppose so. It must make you wonder why you went in for it in the first place, though."

"Because it's mostly interesting, I'm good at it, and it has a future," replied Gibbons. "The more interesting question is why you do it. You needn't if you didn't want to."

Bethancourt was silent for a space. He lit another cigarette, sipped his drink, and then said, "Curiosity, mostly, I expect. I like figuring things out about people. And because it's your job and I like thinking things out with you. And also, I suppose . . ." His voice trailed off.

"Also what?" asked Gibbons.

Bethancourt inhaled deeply and then watched the smoke escape in the firelight. "There's something real about it," he said. "Something very basic."

"Yes," said Gibbons after a moment. "I know what you mean."

They were quiet then, each occupied with his own thoughts, watching the fire with an abstracted air. Then the bottom log gave way with a crack and shower of sparks, waking both Astley-Cooper and the dog. Cerberus circled and lay down at his master's feet, while Astley-Cooper, who clearly had no recollection of being asleep, said firmly, "Of course. Not that I think Derek Towser did it, either, mind you. It could have been anyone. What about the daughter?"

"Substitute Eve Bingham in the Derek Towser scenario," said Gibbons. "It would work equally well."

Astley-Cooper nodded, looking a little confused since he hadn't heard most of the Derek Towser scenario.

"Or put in the twins," said Bethancourt suddenly.

"They have an alibi for Bingham's murder," Gibbons reminded him.

"And she was their mother!" spluttered Astley-Cooper.

"Perhaps Bingham's death really was an accident," said Bethancourt, ignoring his host.

Gibbons raised a brow. "Surely," he said, "Joan Bonnar's death is more likely to be the accidental one."

"Yes, yes—you're right." Bethancourt subsided.

Astley-Cooper had risen and was prodding at the logs with the poker.

"I don't think I'll put on another one," he said, glancing at the clock. "It's going well enough and it's after one."

To this his overheated guests readily agreed. Astley-Cooper patted the hood fondly again, reached for the bottle, and topped up everyone's drinks. Then he settled back into his chair and began to doze off again.

"What about Bingham's partner?" asked Bethancourt.

"Andrew Sealingham? Apart from the fact that he had no possible reason to want Joan Bonnar dead, he's got an alibi of sorts. He went to a film with his wife. We haven't actually checked at the cinema, but he seems a very unlikely suspect."

Bethancourt nodded.

Gibbons stretched his legs out before him and settled back into his chair. "What about you, Phillip?" he asked. "You never said how you felt about the idea of an accident."

"I think it's rot," Bethancourt replied. "It just doesn't feel right. For one thing, she smoked, didn't she?"

Gibbons glanced at his friend curiously. "Yes, she did," he said. "What has that got to do with anything?"

"Well, it's possible that, being drunk, she forgot to take her cigarettes along when she decided to go for a walk," said Bethancourt. "But I don't believe she settled down on that rock without them. She'd want a cigarette then. I mean, as a rule one smokes more when one's been drinking."

Gibbons eyed the ashtray. "You do, anyhow," he said, and yawned.

"I know it's a small thing," said Bethancourt, "and probably easily explained away. But, given everything else, it's just another little piece that doesn't quite fit."

Gibbons merely grunted agreement. He was very nearly reclining in his chair by now, and his blue eyes were sleepy.

Bethancourt smoked in silence for a moment, watching the flickering flames, turning over ideas in his mind.

"Of course," he said in a moment, "if Joan was a threat to Bingham's killer, it must have been because of something he told her, or possibly something he left at her house. Are you searching the London house tomorrow, Jack?"

There was no answer. Bethancourt turned to look at his friend and found him fast asleep. Smiling a little, he turned back to the fire and finished the last of his whisky. Cerberus, who had not had his before-bed outing, looked up hopefully.

"There's something," Bethancourt said to the dog, "that we still don't know about this case."

Cerberus wagged his tail.

CHAPTER

nconsciously, Martha Potts's right hand felt for her left ring finger, and then stopped when there was no signet ring there. She sighed at herself. It was a nervous habit, she knew, but she missed it when the ring wasn't there, the more so when she was upset about anything. She really must remember to ask her sister if she'd found it.

There was a knock at the kitchen door and she frowned. The police had barricaded off the end of the drive that morning, but she supposed that by now an energetic reporter might have found his way across the fields. She went to the door with a stern look, out of temper, and more than ready to heave newsmen off the premises herself.

But it was Phillip Bethancourt and his beautiful dog who stood on the step, Bethancourt smiling charmingly and apologizing for barging in while the dog waved his tail gently.

"That's all right," she said, opening the door. "Come in and have a cuppa. I thought you might be a reporter," she added, to explain her first, inhospitable expression.

"Awful nuisances," he said, seating himself at the butcher-block counter. "I expect you're used to it?"

"Not really," she answered, getting out a second mug for him and plucking the cozy off the teapot. "They've left us alone down here for the most part—except, of course, when Mr. Sinclair died."

Bethancourt beamed at her. "That's just what I've come to ask you about," he said.

She looked surprised. "About Mr. Sinclair's death?" she asked, handing him his cup and settling herself on the stool beside him.

"Yes. Miss Bonnar came down here after she heard the news, didn't she?"

Mrs. Potts nodded. "She stayed for almost a fortnight."

"And what did she do?"

"Carried on, mostly." She shrugged.

"But, I mean, did she stay in her room, wander about the house? Did she eat her meals?"

"Oh." Mrs. Potts thought back. "She ate virtually nothing for the first few days, I remember that. Locked herself in her room and cried for days straight, she did. Didn't sleep, either, but she drank a good bit. Self-indulgence, I thought it, but I have to say when the starting date for her new film came, she packed her bags and went off to Spain just as she was supposed to. And she was good in the film, too. We all liked it. *The Daughter,* it was."

Bethancourt nodded. "But she didn't go for walks while she was here?"

"Lord, no. She was terrified of reporters—" Mrs. Potts stopped in midsentence and stared at him. "I see what you're trying to do," she said in a moment. "You're trying to make out she was murdered."

Bethancourt had removed his glasses and was rubbing the bridge of his nose. "No," he answered. "I'm trying to get at the truth."

Mrs. Potts sat silent for a moment, looking down at her hands. "Well," she said slowly, "it's true that after Mr. Sinclair died, Miss Bonnar wasn't traipsing over the fields. But it's also true that this time wasn't so bad. She cried a bit, but she wasn't locked in her room sobbing for days on end. And she ate her dinner Monday night. Maybe not as much as she would have normally, but she got a fair bit down."

"Yes, I see." He replaced his glassed and sipped at his tea. "Tell me something else," he said. "When I was out searching with Julie yesterday, she mentioned her mother was not a great walker. Do you remember her being troubled at any other time and going for walks to work it out?"

She shook her head. "She went for walks, certainly, but mostly, as I remember, when it was a fine day or when one of us was going." She paused, her hands fumbling together in her lap, and then sighed. "You do think she was murdered, don't you?"

"Yes," said Bethancourt frankly, "I do. But I'm not out to prove anything that isn't true. I could be wrong and what you've just told me proves nothing. Whatever her usual habits, she might still have gone for a walk that night. I gather you do think I'm wrong?"

"I don't know." She sighed again. "I want you to be wrong. It's the twins, you see. They've had to suffer so much from her notoriety. It isn't easy, you know, being the child of someone famous. I don't want there to be another scandal over her death. But," and she straightened up on her stool, "if she was murdered, well, of course there's no help for it."

Bethancourt was still unsure how far she would go to spare her darling twins another uproar. He mulled it over as he returned to the car, pausing to light a cigarette and then looking up when he heard a horse approaching.

"Hello." Julie Benson waved from the back of a gray gelding.

"Hello," said Bethancourt. "It's my old friend Smoke, isn't it?" He came around the side of the Jaguar to pat the horse's neck while Julie swung down.

"Yes," she said, "it is. I was just bringing him in when I saw the car. I rather thought it was yours. Anything up?"

"No, not really," he replied. "Just a question for Mrs. Potts." He smiled at her. "I suppose I might ask you as well, if you wouldn't mind."

"Not at all. What is it?"

"Did your mother often take walks to sort things out? You said yesterday she wasn't a great walker."

"Nor was she." Julie frowned for a moment and began thoughtfully pulling off her gloves. "Mother did take walks, of course," she said. "It would be silly to have a place like this and never go out in it. But, to tell you the truth, I can't recollect what sort of mood she was in when she took them. I suppose, when she did go off by herself, I was just glad to have her out of the way. Mother can be—could be—very draining on a person."

"Yes, I can see that," said Bethancourt sympathetically. He hesitated, but the conversation did not seem to be distressing her. "What about after Mr. Sinclair died?"

Julie wrinkled her nose. "Oh, she was in fine form then. Mostly she kept to her room while the rest of us crept around the house like mice, trying not to disturb her." She paused. "I do remember one night," she said slowly. "I had woken up and gone to the loo, and as I passed my bedroom window, I thought I saw a light in the garden. I thought it was one of those reporters, but when I looked out, I found it was Mother, just sitting on the bench and smoking. I must have seen the flame when she lit her cigarette." She looked up at him doubtfully. "That's not the same as walking all the way to the lake, of course. The bench is quite close to the house."

"But it does show that she sometimes went out on a night when she was troubled," said Bethancourt. "Was this very late?"

Julie shrugged. "I don't know. I had been asleep, so it was after eleven or so, but I couldn't tell you now how long after it was."

"No, of course not," said Bethancourt. "Well, thanks very much. That's very helpful. I'd better push along now."

He turned to open the back door of the car for Cerberus.

"It was nice seeing you again," she said, backing the horse a few paces. "I wanted to say, Smoke here is just fine after yesterday. You really are a very good rider."

"Thank you. Praise from Sir Hubert . . ."

He smiled back at her as he got into the car.

She blushed a little and hesitated. "Er . . ."

"Yes?" he asked.

"I was wondering . . . it's silly, really."

"What's silly?"

"Well, I was wondering how long you'd known that model."

He was surprised. "Marla? I've been seeing her for almost a year now. Why?"

"Oh, nothing," she said hurriedly, staring down at her boots. "I was just wondering, that's all. Are you still staying with Astley-Cooper?"

"That's right," said Bethancourt.

"Well, I'll see you about then," she said, turning the horse toward the barn.

Bethancourt started the engine, looking after her and frowning a little. She could not possibly imagine that a man whose taste ran to fashion models would ever be interested in her. But to a man of his experience, there was also no mistaking the look in her eyes. He sighed as he guided the car down the drive.

Derek Towser had awakened later than his wont. The sky was clearing as he made himself coffee, but he elected not to go out. He didn't think he could concentrate.

He took his coffee into the studio and stood contemplating the painting on the easel. He had thought to put some finishing touches on it today, but he didn't even pick up a brush. He knew he wasn't really seeing the painting. He wandered back to the kitchen.

Scotland Yard was as good as their word. When he heard the knock on the door, he knew that was what he had been waiting for, though he hadn't admitted it to himself. His heart was beating absurdly fast as he went to let the police in.

Detective Chief Inspector Carmichael was alone on the doorstep.

"Good morning, sir," he said cheerfully. "I've brought your shoes."

"Thank you, Chief Inspector," said Towser, taking charge of the package the detective held out. "I hardly expected them back so soon."

Carmichael smiled. "Oh, the lab's very quick these days," he said. "They've made the casts and done all the comparisons. I thought you might like to know how we did with them."

Towser swallowed. "Yes," he managed, "yes, I would."

Carmichael was still smiling. "It was your footprint, without a doubt."

"Ah." It was what he had been dreading, and he wasn't sure how to react. "My footprint."

"Yes, indeed," said Carmichael. "Thank you very much for lending us the shoes, sir. You have helped the police with their inquiry."

He turned to go.

"Wait," said Towser desperately. "Wait a moment, Chief Inspector."

Carmichael turned back, one bushy eyebrow raised in question.

"What happens now?"

"Nothing, for the moment."

"Nothing?" Towser was astounded.

"Nothing," replied Carmichael firmly. "Mr. Towser, it is not illegal in this country to take an evening walk by a lake which adjoins the property you are renting."

"No, of course not," said Towser.

"Good day, then. No doubt we will be speaking again in the next few days."

Carmichael smiled again and turned back to his car.

Towser stared after him, still clutching his shoes.

❧ ❧ ❧

"There we are then," said Carmichael with a satisfied smile as he got back into the car. "That's got the wind up him good and proper, that has."

"Yes, sir," said Gibbons, letting in the clutch while his superior busied himself with his safety belt. "I hope it stirs something up," he added.

"Well, you never can tell, lad," said Carmichael, settling into his seat and fishing for a cigar. "It was an opportunity, and worth taking in my opinion. Towser panicking because he believes we think he's guilty of two murders may do nothing more than add to the village gossip mill. But sometimes, when people think the police have their minds made up, they get careless, or at least less wary."

"Then you don't think there's any chance left that Towser *is* guilty?" asked Gibbons.

Carmichael's eyes narrowed as he brought out his lighter. "He certainly *could* have done it," he said. "He's had every opportunity to get at that Seconal, but we've never found a motive for him to want Bingham dead, much less Joan Bonnar. No, as far as she's concerned, it's the crowd up at the old farmhouse who may have motive."

Gibbons was silent for a moment. "The problem," he said, "is that we know Bingham's death was a suspicious one because we know the body was moved afterward. But Joan Bonnar's death may well have been accidental—if it weren't for her connection with Bingham, we'd probably not be looking into it at all."

Carmichael frowned and then sighed. "Too true, lad," he said. "It's only my instincts that say something is badly amiss. And I could be wrong—heaven knows it's happened before—but on the other hand, I don't like to ignore a hunch." He put down his window with a thoughtful look on his face, and bent his head to light his cigar. In between puffs, he added, "I want at least to know if Joan Bonnar had given her children or their dragon of a nanny cause to want her dead recently—if she had changed her will, or anything like that."

"I'd like to know, too," admitted Gibbons. "But it doesn't do to forget that the Bensons and Mrs. Potts all have alibis for Bingham's death."

"Ah, well," said Carmichael, flicking his lighter shut with a click, and settling back in his seat. "Martha Potts's alibi isn't a very good one, and we never looked too closely at the Bensons', not knowing at the time that their mother was engaged to a murder victim. We mustn't let a little thing like an alibi trouble us, Gibbons."

His sergeant laughed and Carmichael grinned at him as he blew out a stream of smoke.

"We'll see where we're at once we've spoken to all these people to-day," he added more practically. "Has the superintendent got that search warrant in hand yet?"

"He said he'd have it by this afternoon," said Gibbons. "I've arranged for a team of scene-of-the-crime officers to be ready."

"Good, good. If everything's ready when we arrive, you can go with the SOCKOs and oversee the search, and I'll keep your appointment with Miss Bonnar's agent."

"Yes, sir," said Gibbons, and, turning onto the A40, put his foot down on the accelerator.

Bethancourt, returning from the Benson farm, stopped in the village at the tobacconist's. As he emerged from the shop, his attention was caught by a white Rolls-Royce proceeding apace down the High Street. It slowed as it came abreast of him, and then swerved abruptly over to the curb, narrowly missing the right front bumper of his Jaguar.

"Hullo," he said, somewhat startled.

Eve Bingham leaned across the passenger seat and he obligingly stepped to the window.

"I've decided to stay on here until after the Bonnar inquest," she announced.

"That's good," he said, nonetheless rather surprised. She looked tired, he thought. Her face was pale and beneath the dark blue eyes there were circles. More than tired, he decided, she looked unhappy, as if she had lost the strength to battle further with life.

"It's Wednesday," he said impulsively. "Choir practice night, you know. Why don't you come 'round with me tonight and listen to it?"

She smiled grimly and shook her head. "And have the whole village staring at me, wondering if I'm a murderer? You're a brave man, Phillip, but I don't think I'm up to it."

"Nonsense," he said. "They'll all be busy singing. You don't have to come to the pub afterward, you know, if you don't want to. And we'll be sitting at the back, so that I can smuggle the dog in."

She bit her lip, hesitating. "Very well," she said abruptly. "I'll meet you at the church at—what time?"

"Seven o'clock," he answered, smiling at her. "You'll see, Eve. It will do you good to get out."

She laughed mirthlessly. "Christ," she said. "My first big night out since I got here and I'm going to the village church to listen to hymns. Would anyone have believed it? If this gets back to Paris, I'm finished."

"Your reputation is safe with me," Bethancourt promised. "I'll see you tonight."

She nodded and eased the Rolls back into the street.

Bethancourt gazed after her for a moment, pulling a cigarette from the fresh packet he had bought and tapping it absently on the back of his hand. Then he shook his head.

"I'm probably a fool," he said, and bent to shield his lighter flame from the breeze.

CHAPTER

16

Joan Bonnar's solicitor was a hearty, rotund man whom Carmichael found tediously self-important. Mark Smith, Esq., did his best to give the impression that his famous client could barely make a dinner reservation without consulting him. After several minutes of persistent questioning, however, Carmichael elicited the information that in fact Mark Smith, Esq., had not spoken to Miss Bonnar since she had signed the contracts for her current play back at the beginning of June. Certainly she had never spoken to him about changing her will.

But, thought Carmichael, at the beginning of June, she had only known Charles Bingham for a month or so and would hardly have been thinking of marriage. He tried to come at the problem from a different angle.

"But if she had thought, for some reason, of altering her bequests," he said, "would you have expected her to be in touch at once? I mean, was she generally efficient about such things? Or was she more apt to put a thing off until the last moment?"

Smith gave a smug little smile. "Artistic people are often a bit lax about their business affairs, Chief Inspector." He said this as though it were an original thought, and one that would probably surprise Carmichael. The detective suppressed a sigh and kept a neutral expression on his face. "However," Smith continued, "Joan was better than many of her peers. If she had made up her mind to change her will, I should have expected to hear from her within a week or two. In fact, it would really be more likely that she would have rung me to get my advice about the changes before she made up her mind."

Carmichael ignored that last sentence; it was all of a piece with how Smith wanted his relationship with Joan Bonnar to be seen, and Carmichael doubted very much that it was true.

"What about if she contemplated marrying again?" he asked. "She'd have to update her will then?"

"There would, of course, have to be a new will in that case," answered Smith. "The marriage would nullify the old one. But the provisions in it wouldn't necessarily change. Joan didn't alter her bequests when she married Daniel Mitchum, although of course there was a prenuptial agreement then."

"And when she married Eugene Sinclair?" asked Carmichael.

Smith waved a hand, as if Joan's two marriages to Sinclair were of no importance. "I was not acting for Joan at that time," he said. "Her affairs were in the hands of our then-senior partner, who has since retired. I expect I could find out, if you wished."

"Yes, that might be helpful," said Carmichael thoughtfully. "I'd also like to know if there were prenuptial agreements on those occasions and, if so, how they differed from the last one."

Smith made a note. "I'll have my junior research it and ring you," he said.

"Thank you very much," said Carmichael, reflecting that, if the man was annoying, he was also being quite helpful in his way. "I think that only leaves the terms of the will itself. Could you outline the basics for me?"

"Certainly, certainly," said Smith. "It's not a difficult document at all. There are several bequests to the charities she favored, as well as provisions for both Martha Potts and Mary Calthorp to receive their salaries until their deaths, even after their retirements. But the bulk of the estate—and we are talking quite a sizeable amount here, Chief Inspector—goes to her children, as you would expect."

Carmichael nodded. He had indeed expected it, but it did nothing to help make a case against the Bensons, or anyone else for that matter.

Suppressing yet another sigh, he thanked the solicitor one more time and rose to take his leave.

Once outside the office, he switched his mobile back on, and it obliged him by ringing almost as soon as he had returned it to his pocket.

"There you are, sir," came Gibbons's voice. His sergeant sounded almost cheerful. "How was the solicitor?"

"All negative," growled Carmichael. "Although he was helpful enough, I must say. Did you find out anything from the agent?"

"No," admitted Gibbons. "She's quite overcome, and is certain Joan would never have committed suicide. But what I rang to say, sir, is that the search warrant's come through. I'm on my way to meet the SOCKOs at the town house now."

"Excellent," said Carmichael, trying to sound enthusiastic, although in truth he expected little if anything would come of the search. "I'll leave that to you, Gibbons, and go on with the interviews myself. Ring me if you find anything."

"Certainly, sir," said Gibbons.

Carmichael rang off, sighed, and hailed a taxi to take him to Dame Sarah's flat.

Marla rang when she returned from Paris that afternoon, the more eager to tell Bethancourt what she had discovered about Eve and her father as it tended to exonerate Eve. Nevertheless, there was an odd undertone to the conversation that Bethancourt could not quite define; it was almost as if Marla were angry with him. But that could hardly be possible; they had not seen each other in three days and had parted before that on the best of terms.

"I did my best," said Marla, "but there wasn't a lot to find out, really. It seems that while her father was in town, Eve dropped out of all the doings to spend time with him. There was an evening at the theater, but aside from that only Catherine met him."

"Catherine?"

"Yes, Catherine DeLorre—the wine heiress. She went to dinner with Eve and her father one night. I could tell she wasn't sure what to make of Charlie, but she said quite definitely that Eve was very proud of her father. Hung on his every word, and kept touching him as if she couldn't believe he was real. 'Affectionate,' Catherine said."

"So apparently they were getting on like a house on fire."

"They were that night, at any rate. God only knows how they spent the rest of the time. Still, it does tend to show that she was fond of him rather than the reverse, don't you think?"

"I do. That's brilliant, Marla. You've been a great help."

"And," she continued, "what with all the rest of the hoopla, I really think Eve's out of it."

"It does look like it," admitted Bethancourt. "You've heard about Joan Bonnar, then?"

"Of course I heard," said Marla impatiently. "The BBC's new motto is 'All Joan Bonnar, all the time.' I'm sick to death of Joan Bonnar."

"Oh," said Bethancourt, a little nonplussed. "Well," he said, rallying, "did you want to come back here? Eve's staying on until after the Bonnar inquest—"

"I don't think so," she interrupted him. "In fact, I had rather thought you would be back here by now."

Bethancourt hastily ransacked his memory, but he could think of nothing he had said which might have given her this impression.

"But, love," he said, "you knew things might not be finished here."

"I can't really see what more there is to do out there," she said. "And there is Drew's party tomorrow night."

Bethancourt was silent a moment. He had entirely forgotten the party and knew he could not admit it. Moreover, he could, on the instant, think of no possible way of telling her he did not intend going that would not result in a terrific blowup.

"But that's tomorrow night," he said, rather desperately.

Marla's tone warmed immediately. "Then you are coming back?"

"Of course," said Bethancourt. There was really nothing else he could think of to say. It was obvious to him that, having convinced herself Eve was not a murderer, Marla's interest in the case had evaporated. "I'll drive down in the morning," he continued, thinking he might as well be hung for a sheep as a lamb, "and we can have lunch and go to that costume exhibit at the V and A."

"That would be lovely," she purred, instantly appeased. "We could come back afterward and have champagne at my flat. Before we dressed for the party, you know."

He knew what she meant by that and felt a pang of regret that he wouldn't be there.

"I'd love that," he said. "Look, darling, I promised to take Clarence to choir practice, so I had better go now. I'll see you tomorrow then."

"Lovely," she said. "Until tomorrow."

Bethancourt rang off and tried not to think about the fireworks he would have to face in the morning when he rang her to say he wasn't coming.

"Dear God, but this is a mess."

Gibbons swiveled around and found Carmichael surveying the SOCKOs as they took Joan Bonnar's town house apart, piece by piece.

"Sir?" he asked. "I didn't realize you'd arrived."

"Yes, I'm here," growled Carmichael, glaring at a perfectly innocent technician who was dusting the television for prints. "All Joan Bonnar's friends and acquaintances agree that she would never have killed herself. She might, they admit, in the stress of the moment, have taken too many pills while she was drunk." He snorted. "I've spent all day finding that out, Gibbons, and somehow I don't think it was worth it."

Gibbons hid a sigh; he didn't think it was worth it, either.

"As if," continued Carmichael, "I ever thought the bloody woman had topped herself to start with."

"Nor that it was accidental?" asked Gibbons, though he fancied he knew the answer.

Carmichael snorted. "I was willing," he said, "to believe that Bingham's death was accidental, however difficult it was to account for how he had ingested those tablets without meaning to, but I'm damned if I'll swallow two accidents in the same case. Don't tell me you think it's possible, Gibbons."

"No, sir," agreed Gibbons. "There are too many little pieces that don't fit."

"And no evidence of what really happened," grumbled Carmichael. "And none, I'll be bound, to be found here," he added, glaring at the room.

"We're very nearly done here, sir," Gibbons said, trying to sound cheerful. "I've been going over her diary. She's made notations of some of her dates with Bingham, using his initials, but that doesn't tell us much."

"It tells us she wasn't lying when she said she was his girlfriend," said Carmichael sarcastically.

"Yes, sir," replied Gibbons in as neutral a voice as he could manage.

"Take no notice of me, lad," said Carmichael, heaving a deep sigh. "I'm in a foul mood. I don't mind dotting my i's and crossing my t's, but I do hate a pure waste of time. And I'm much mistaken if we're going to net anything here. The answer is in Chipping Chedding, though I'm damned if I can find a way to prove it." He shook his head, as if trying to rid himself of his mood. "What I need," he said, "is a quiet night at home with Mrs. Carmichael. Let's have an evening off, Gibbons—it'll do us both a world of good, and we can drive back to the Cotswolds first thing in the morning."

Gibbons did not think his empty flat would do much for his state of mind, but he agreed respectfully nonetheless, and added, "I can finish up here, sir, if you'd like to get on. As you say, we aren't likely to find much."

"That's uncommonly good of you, lad," said Carmichael. "I appreciate it."

Gibbons grinned at him. "It's all to my good to let Mrs. Carmichael put you in a better mood," he said, and elicited a laugh.

"She'll have her hands full tonight," said Carmichael ruefully. "Right, then. I'll take the car and pick you up at nine."

Gibbons nodded and watched his superior wend his way back out, the thought of an evening spent with his wife already easing the tense lines of his shoulders.

Gibbons himself turned back to Joan Bonnar's diary with a sigh, feeling unaccountably depressed.

Cerberus was sniffing leisurely at the porch while his master leaned against the doorjamb, smoking. From the stone walls of the church came the muted sound of singing, accompanied by the faint bellows of the organ. Bethancourt threw down his cigarette and trod on it carefully. He held his watch up to catch the faint light from a lancet window. Seven fifteen. He would wait a few more minutes.

In another moment, the Rolls-Royce, gleaming whitely in the dark, came up and rolled to a stop on the verge. Bethancourt watched as the headlamps and motor died, and then stepped forward as Eve emerged.

"Good evening," he said. "I'm glad you came."

"I'm not sure I am," she replied. "But you're right—I needed to get out."

Calling to Cerberus, he ushered her inside and stood politely while she sank into one of the back pews.

"Cerberus," he whispered, motioning as he seated himself, and the dog lay down obediently in the nave.

They were lost in the shadows where they sat, eyes focused on the lights in the choir stall where Leandra was leading the choristers in song.

"God," whispered Eve, "I haven't been in church since I was a kid." She looked around her, following the vaulted shadows into the dim recesses of the ceiling. "It makes me feel, well, as if I were a little girl again." She did not sound as if she were enjoying the feeling.

"I like old churches," Bethancourt whispered back. "And simple pleasures, like listening to a village choir practice. It makes a nice change."

She nodded doubtfully and was silent.

Choir practice lasted until nine. About halfway through, the watchers slipped out for a smoke on the church steps.

"Having fun?" asked Bethancourt optimistically.

Eve drew on her cigarette and smiled at him. "Not bad," she said. "They're quite good, actually, and it's entertainment of a sort, anyway."

"Ever do much singing yourself?"

"At school," she answered. "Not much since then—unless you count the shower."

"Me, too," said Bethancourt. "I'm a great shower singer."

He happily caroled the opening bars of "Greensleeves" as a demonstration and Eve laughed at him.

"Is *that* what you sing in the shower?" she asked scornfully.

"It seemed appropriate to the setting," said Bethancourt, desisting. "So, do you think you'll come on to the pub? It's quite a social occasion in Chipping Chedding, Wednesday nights at the pub."

"Pubs were never my thing. I don't even like beer."

"They have other things to drink. Don't tell me you don't like a fine, single-malt scotch."

"Sometimes," she answered. "But martinis or wine are more my taste."

"I like an occasional martini myself," said Bethancourt. "I'm sure they can make them at the pub. They get an awful lot of tourists here during the summer, you know."

But she shook her head. "I really don't think so," she said. "It's kind of you, but no. I really don't feel like making one of a merry party."

"Well, you can always change your mind later," said Bethancourt, flicking his cigarette out into the street. "Shall we go back in? It's getting chilly out here."

"Yes, let's."

After the practice, Bethancourt saw Eve out to her car while everyone else was still milling about in the nave, bidding good night to those who were not going on to the pub.

"Sure you won't come?" he asked her as he held the door open for her.

"No," she answered. "This was nice, though. Thank you for asking me."

"Thank you for coming."

He closed the door and stood back, watching as she pulled away. When he turned back, he found Leandra Tothill coming toward him. People were beginning to file out into the porch, adjusting their coats before moving off toward the car park.

"Hullo," he said, smiling. "It sounded splendid tonight."

"Thank you," said Leandra, bending to pet Cerberus. She glanced over her shoulder and then said in a low tone, "I want to talk to you about something."

Bethancourt raised an eyebrow. "I'm at your service," he said.

"Not here. Can we—"

"There you are," called Astley-Cooper, trotting down the steps. "We were in fine form tonight, don't you think? Did Eve enjoy it?"

"Very much," answered Bethancourt. "I tried to persuade her to come on to the pub, but she didn't feel up to it."

"Where's Richard?" asked Leandra, looking back toward the church.

"He's coming—someone lost a scarf, I think. Oh, good night, Mrs. Collins."

"Dear me," said Leandra. "Phillip, I think Cerberus has something caught in his coat."

"Probably a burr," said Bethancourt gloomily. "He's been picking them up all over the place."

"No," she said, "it seems sticky." She crouched down to look more closely. "It's chewing gum, I think."

"Good Lord," said Bethancourt, crouching beside her. "Where is it?"

"Just here." She caught his eyes with hers. "It'll have to be cut out. We can just stop at the house and I'll grab some scissors. That way it won't get any worse."

"All right," said Bethancourt, straightening. "Thank you." He looked at her speculatively.

"Here we are," said the vicar, emerging at last. "All accounted for. Shall we wend our way pub-wards?"

"Phillip and I are going to stop at the house," said his wife. "There's some gum in Cerberus's coat. But you go on, and we'll be along directly."

They parted from the others as they strolled down the lane, and Leandra led the way into the vicarage kitchen. She flicked on the lights, placing her handbag on the table, and Bethancourt saw that her hands were trembling. She stood very still by the table, staring down at her purse.

"What's up?" asked Bethancourt mildly.

"I was thinking," she said slowly, not looking at him, "you're not really the police, are you? I mean, if I told you something, you wouldn't necessarily have to tell anyone else."

"That would depend," he said, "on what it was."

"But if it wasn't important . . ."

He leaned back against the counter. "You might as well tell me now," he said, not unsympathetically. "You've shown your hand, you see. Even if you don't say another word, I'll know you're hiding something. If you tell me now, perhaps it won't be important, and I can forget it straightaway—although I warn you, that seems unlikely to me. But if you don't tell me, I shall have to try to find out what it is. Which I would not do alone."

"Yes, I see that," she said miserably. She took a deep breath and ventured a glance at him. She saw only a fair-haired young man, perfectly calm, who looked at her kindly through his glasses. Her eyes roved over his angular frame as if searching for something in him that she could trust. At last she sighed and said, "That Sunday night when Charlie was killed, I went to the pub. I often stop in on Sundays while Richard's off playing chess. Derek Towser was there and we got to talking about his work. He suggested I go over to his place and look at some of his paintings. So I did."

"You left the pub separately," said Bethancourt tonelessly. "You left ten minutes or so before he did."

"That's true," she answered. "You know the rumors about him. I felt if I was seen to be going off to his cottage alone with him, no one would ever believe it had been to look at pictures."

Bethancourt was surprised to find he did believe it. He had some experience in being deceived by women—beautiful women, he had noticed, generally appeared to be better at it—but although the woman before him was certainly beautiful, she did not, to his eye, appear deceptive.

But on the other hand, it was ludicrous to think that any village vicar's wife would not have realized the impropriety of such a visit.

"Does your husband know?" he asked.

"That's the awkward part," she answered, her eyes on her handbag once again. "I didn't tell him. I—I knew I shouldn't have gone, you see, and I really couldn't bear to have him reproach me about it."

"I see," said Bethancourt, realization striking him. "You didn't stop to think how it would look. Not until you were there and Towser actually tried it on."

Leandra flushed and looked away.

"No, no," she said. "Derek wouldn't do something like that."

This time Bethancourt did not believe her, although he understood now how it had happened. A friendly drink and a discussion about art had contrived to remind her of the bohemian life she had once enjoyed before her marriage. Probably she had not been aware of missing her old life, so delighted was she with the new; Bethancourt remembered once asking her if she missed London and the way she had evaded a reply. But the invitation to recapture that life, if only for an evening, had proved irresistible to her. She had likely not realized her mistake until Towser had made his move. That, of course, had brought her to her senses and shown her just how far she had strayed from her proper path.

He looked at her, standing there and watching him, waiting to see if he would accept this story, too proud to admit she was ashamed of her transgression or to protest how deeply she loved her husband, and how she would do almost anything to keep from hurting him. Anything but let an innocent man be arrested for murder.

"And now," he said, dropping the subject, "Towser has had the fear of God put into him by my Scotland Yard friends, and is begging you to come forward."

She nodded. "I thought I could tell you, and you could keep it to yourself unless it looked like the police were really going to arrest him."

"That might be entirely possible," he replied. "But let's get things straight first. What time did you arrive and when did you leave?"

She was relieved to deal with the mundane. "It must have been a quarter to seven when I got there, perhaps a little after that. I meant to stay only a short while, but we were chatting and I lost track of time. It was past ten when I left. I was worried that Richard might get home before me and be concerned, so I borrowed Derek's bicycle."

"Oh, Lord," said Bethancourt, the light dawning. "Don't tell me—you had a puncture just outside Bingham's cottage."

She looked surprised. "Yes," she said. "How did you know?"

"We found some nails in the road, and the marks of a bicycle just inside the hedge."

"Oh. I never thought you'd know about the bike. But you're right, of course, and it was very inconvenient. I hadn't time to take the thing back, and it would have taken years to walk it home, so I just shoved it behind the hedge and went on. I rang Derek when I got in to tell him where it was, and I suppose he went and got it the next morning."

"But why," asked Bethancourt, "didn't Towser simply drive you back if you were concerned about the time?"

She looked surprised that he should ask. "It was only just after closing time at the pub," she said. "Everyone would have been on their way home—someone would have been sure to see us."

"Ah, yes, of course," said Bethancourt. "I was forgetting—it was Sunday and early closing. Oh, by the way, while you were stowing the bicycle, did you notice if Bingham's car was there?"

"Oh, yes. It was there and his lights were on. I didn't think anything of it at the time, of course, beyond being careful he didn't see me."

"Of course." Bethancourt glanced at his watch. "We had better be getting on," he said, "or tongues will be wagging about us. It might tarnish your reputation in Chipping Chedding, but Marla would have my head if she ever heard about it."

She smiled at him. "Thank you," she said, laying a hand on his arm. "You are very understanding. And you won't say anything?"

"Not unless I must," he answered. "And I doubt it will come to that. Cerberus, time to go, boy."

On the short walk to the Deer and Hounds, he tried to recapture the casual air of their previous encounters, and partly succeeded, encouraging her to talk about music. Inwardly, he was so astonished by her confession that he found it difficult to concentrate on her replies to his questions.

It preoccupied him all evening, as he sat by Astley-Cooper's side and watched the Tothills together. They still struck him as one of the happiest couples he had ever seen.

And perhaps, he thought to himself, they were. If he had learned anything in his study of human nature, it was that people were complicated, and more than capable of feeling two quite different things at the same time. Leandra might be head over heels in love with her husband, delighted with the life they were building together, and yet still be capable of regret over what she had given up.

In any case, decided Bethancourt, it was none of his business. If things came to a head, the only story Gibbons was going to hear from him was one about a woman concerned for her reputation who had gone to look at some art.

Gibbons, having gone to dinner with some of the SOCKOs after they had finished at Joan Bonnar's house, reached his own flat at about half nine to find a message from Carmichael awaiting him. The chief inspector did not sound as if his mood was much improved from earlier in the evening and Gibbons sighed as he dialed Carmichael's home number.

"Good, you got my message," grunted Carmichael when he came on the line. "We're not starting for Chipping Chedding in the morning after all."

Gibbons's hopes would have risen if Carmichael's tone had not been so dour. "Has something happened, sir?" he asked.

"Something's happened, right enough," agreed Carmichael. "Assistant Commissioner MacDougal's got his knickers in a twist is what's happened. He's decided there's nothing for it but to hold a full-bore press conference tomorrow afternoon and, since he knows nothing about the Bonnar case, he wants to meet with me and Superintendent Lugan at noon tomorrow so we can fill him in."

"I see, sir," said Gibbons sympathetically.

"It's lucky for us MacDougal's morning is already booked solid or you and I'd be down at the Yard this minute. As it is, I think we'd better start early. I want all my ducks in a row before I walk in there."

"Of course," said Gibbons. "What time would you like to meet?"

"Eight will do, I think," replied Carmichael. He sighed heavily. "I don't like bringing in the higher-ups so early, Gibbons. It only complicates things."

"I suppose there's no help for it with a celebrity like Joan Bonnar," said Gibbons.

"No, and I should have seen this coming. The press office's been on to me every chance they get—it was only a matter of time before the AC got dragged in. Well, there's nothing for it but to do our best. I'll see you in the morning, lad."

"Yes, sir," said Gibbons. "Good night."

He went to bed that night feeling, for once in his life, actually grateful that he was not the lead detective on a case. He did not think the AC was going to have a very high opinion of their reasons for believing Joan Bonnar had been murdered.

CHAPTER

ethancourt's outlook the next morning was decidedly gloomy. He had had a terrific row on the phone with Marla just after breakfast, which left him uncertain that he still had a girlfriend at all. He had not had any new thoughts about the case, and today it appeared to him to be unsolvable.

The day outside was not encouraging; it was gray and rainy, a typical late-autumn day. Bethancourt stared out at it through the very fine bay window of Stutely Manor while he waited for Gibbons to ring. The detectives were due back this morning, but it was nearly noon now and Bethancourt had heard nothing. He smoked moodily, watched the rain, and began to feel that Astley-Cooper might have a point about architectural features praised for being a fine example of their period; their very fineness could be quite irritating.

He answered the phone when at last it rang like a tiger pouncing on its prey.

"I hate this case," stated Gibbons unequivocally. "I don't know what really happened, I shall probably never know what really happened, and I shall still be a detective sergeant when I'm sixty."

Bethancourt's spirits immediately plummeted further. "There was nothing in Joan Bonnar's town house?"

"Nothing to do with the case," responded Gibbons. "We've accomplished nothing really since we left, and now we're stuck here until the assistant commissioner's had his press conference. Although," he added, "I don't know what there is to get back for—we've got no leads that I can see."

"Stuck?" asked Bethancourt, surprised. "You're not ringing from the village?"

"No, I'm at the Yard. I'm sorry I forgot to let you know, but the AC decided last night that he wanted to know all about the case so he could appease the press this afternoon. Carmichael's just gone off to meet him."

"That sounds rather grim," said Bethancourt.

"It is, to hear him tell it," said Gibbons. "You haven't got anything, have you?"

"No," said Bethancourt. "Well, at least nothing important. Marla got back from Paris yesterday and says Eve's friends report she and her father appeared to be on very affectionate terms when he visited her on his way to England last year. I took Eve out last night," he added.

"You did what?"

"I got Eve to come to choir practice last night. I thought she needed cheering up."

"It's nice to have you on a case," said Gibbons sarcastically. "I can always count on you to take care of details—we wouldn't want a murder suspect getting depressed."

"Well, I suppose I also thought that if I got to know her a little better—oh, never mind. Nothing came of it, and anyhow, it wouldn't prove anything. People quite often go insane over just one thing and are perfectly normal in all other respects."

"Like me," said Gibbons. "I've gone insane over this case."

"At least you don't have to worry about redheads thirsting after your blood."

"Marla?"

"Got it in one," said Bethancourt gloomily.

"Angry about your taking Eve around last night?"

"Well, no," admitted Bethancourt. "Actually, I haven't told her about that. She's angry because I sort of gave her the impression I would drive back to London today."

"I didn't know you had planned to go back," said Gibbons, surprised.

"I didn't."

Gibbons was confused. "Then why did Marla think you were going to?"

"I expect it was because I told her I would," said Bethancourt despondently. "I had to say something, and, frankly, nothing else occurred to me at the time. I meant," he added, "to think of some way of appeasing her when I did tell her I wasn't coming, but, well, I never did."

"Dear God."

"She's not speaking to me," continued Bethancourt. "After she'd finished her tirade and hung up on me, I tried to ring her back. She hung up on me again."

"Did you try more than once?"

"Yes. Same result. Then she just stopped answering—probably unplugged the phone."

"Well," said Gibbons, "I don't know as there's much to keep you there; we seem to have struck a dead end. You could probably come back and try to make it up to her. By the time you get here, she may have cooled off a bit."

"Maybe," said Bethancourt doubtfully. "When's the inquest?"

"On Saturday. We'll get it adjourned, of course, but I can't see that we'll have much more for them when it comes up again."

"No," agreed Bethancourt with a sigh.

There was a long, dispirited silence.

"So," said Bethancourt at last, trying to recover a positive attitude, "are you coming back here today?"

"After the press conference, Carmichael says," answered Gibbons. "I've got no notion what he plans to do once we arrive," he added glumly.

"Well, why don't you come 'round here for dinner if you're free?" suggested Bethancourt. "It's Clarence's night to cook, and I'm sure he'd be pleased if you joined us."

In truth, Bethancourt did not much relish the prospect of facing one of Astley-Cooper's elaborate creations alone.

"Thanks," said Gibbons, a little surprised by the invitation. "If nothing comes up, I'd love to come."

"Then turn up 'round six or sevenish—and do ring if anything happens."

"You, too," said Gibbons. "After all, you're the one who's Johnny-on-the-spot at the moment."

"Righto," said Bethancourt, and rang off. He lit yet another cigarette, glanced balefully out at the rain, and went to tell Astley-Cooper he would have an additional guest for dinner.

"I feel guilty saying it," said the vicar, "but I've never been so relieved in my life as when Julie Benson told me her mother had already arranged to be buried in London, next to Eugene Sinclair. After Charlie's funeral, I was really dreading the idea of having to preside over Joan Bonnar's interment."

He was ensconced on the couch with his wife, enjoying an after-dinner cup of coffee before she went off to the Women's Institute meeting and he was called to the Parish Council meeting.

"Well, I don't think you ought to feel guilty the least bit," said Leandra. "One's got to be practical, dearest, and Joan Bonnar's funeral would have been ten times worse than Charlie's." She paused, setting down her cup, and asked, "How are they up at the farmhouse?"

"Pretty well, really," Tothill responded. "Julie and James are dreading the funeral and all the media, but they're bearing up remarkably well otherwise. And Martha's keeping herself busy fussing over them—oh, and she's rather upset about that ring of hers. Apparently it wasn't at her sister's after all."

Leandra frowned. "But I thought Derek Towser had it," she said. "In fact, I'm sure he mentioned finding it a few days ago."

"Really?" said Tothill, surprised. "Well, I expect he forgot to return it in all the excitement. I'll just ring Martha before I go off and let her know he has it. She'll be glad to get it back—she was really distressed to think it might have gone for good." He chuckled. "Remember the Sunday before last, when she dropped it in the collection plate? Made a noise quite unlike a coin, but she never noticed."

"That's right," said his wife, smiling. "I think it was James who fished it back out when the plate got to him. She was quite surprised when he handed it back. Looked at her finger as if she couldn't believe it wasn't still there."

"That's what's so amusing," said Tothill. "The fact that she's always losing it and yet is always surprised to find it gone."

The clock on the mantelpiece chimed softly and Tothill hurriedly drained his coffee cup.

"I'd better be off," he said. "You'd better, too."

"Yes," said Leandra. "I'll just clear away the coffee things while you call Martha."

"Very well."

But she sat still after he had left her. She heard his voice in the next room, evidently speaking to James. She did not really want to go to the meeting tonight, a sentiment that was not helped by the weather. The rain seemed to have tapered off, but it was still a dank, dismal sort of evening, not at all a good time for venturing out to be plagued by everyone's suspicions and questions about the latest celebrity murder.

She sighed and thought of dear Charlie Bingham. She had missed him last night at the pub; in fact, she had noticed that she seemed to miss him more, rather than less, as time went on. He would have enjoyed Martha dropping her ring in the collection plate, but of course that had been the Sunday that he died, and they had never had the chance to tell him of it.

In the next room, Tothill was saying good-bye. Rousing herself, Leandra leaned forward to place the coffee mugs and spoons on the tray, and then stopped all at once, turning pale as a thought struck her.

"That was James," said the vicar, coming back in. "He said he'd pass the message on to Martha. Why, what is it, my dear? You look upset."

"I just—that is, I can't believe . . ." She shook her head firmly and began to busy herself with the coffee things. "It's nothing," she said, "I'll tell you later—you'll be late if you don't get off at once."

"I know, I know," he replied. He reached out to embrace her gently and she rested her head on his shoulder. "Oh dear," he said regretfully in another moment, "I really must go."

"I'm right behind you," said his wife, lifting her face up to be kissed. "I'll just take care of these things and then go."

"All right, darling." He kissed her tenderly. "I'll see you tonight."

"Tonight," she echoed, squeezing his hand.

After he had gone, she carried the tray into the kitchen and stood indecisively for a moment. Outside, she heard the car start up and slowly move off; Tothill was a cautious driver. She shook her head as if to clear it, and then moved toward the phone.

As Bethancourt had anticipated, Astley-Cooper was thrilled to have an extra guest on whom to test his culinary skills. He stood with Gibbons in the ancient kitchen, watching while their host tried to skin a chicken with a large carving knife.

"What's he doing?" whispered Gibbons.

285

"It's going to be *poularde a la D'albufera*," replied Bethancourt placidly. He glanced at his watch. "If we're lucky, it should be done by midnight."

"But it's only seven thirty."

"Have some cheese and biscuits," advised Bethancourt. His mood had improved since the afternoon, and he was watching Astley-Cooper with an air of amusement.

"Now for the breast," said that gentleman cheerfully. "I just slice it carefully off the ribs."

This apparently was easier said than done. Bethancourt and Gibbons watched, fascinated, as he attacked the bird, awkwardly chopping off bits of the breast meat. "It gets cut up later, anyway," he said.

"Of course," murmured Bethancourt.

"Here," said Astley-Cooper, waving a strip of breast meat at them. "Can you bring the marinade over? It's there in that dish."

Bethancourt looked at the dish on the sideboard. "It doesn't have anything in it," he said.

"Oh dear," said Astley-Cooper, not at all deterred. "Could you just empty that can of truffles into it then? And just a splash of port and cognac? Oh, and I think you need to chop up a shallot."

Bethancourt pushed up his sleeves while Astley-Cooper returned to the chicken. Gibbons munched cheese and biscuits and admired the massive fireplace.

"There," said Astley-Cooper, after several moments of silent struggle with the chicken breast. "Now for the shears." He set to work with them, happily sawing at the rib bones.

"Good lord," muttered Gibbons. He edged his way over to where Bethancourt was competently chopping shallots. "What's he doing?" he asked again.

"According to the recipe," said Bethancourt instructively, "*poularde a la D'albufera* is traditionally served as a half-boned chicken. It makes carving at the table easier, you see."

"Carving isn't all that difficult," said Gibbons, watching Astley-Cooper's ministrations.

"The breast meat also picks up additional flavor from the stuffing," went on Bethancourt serenely. "Actually, I think my mother served something like it once and it was really very nice. At least," he added, glancing at his host doubtfully, "I think it was."

Astley-Cooper appeared to have hit a snag in removing the breastbone from the carcass. He was still working with the shears, but his enthusiasm had abated, and he kept casting quizzical glances at the instructions in his cookbook.

He was muttering to himself and peering uncertainly at the badly mauled chicken when the sound of the telephone reached their ears.

"Ah!" he said brightly, abandoning the shears. "I'll just answer that—could be Mullet about the sheep."

He returned in a moment, however, to announce that it was Derek Towser, asking for Bethancourt.

Behind his glasses, there was a gleam of interest in Bethancourt's eyes. "Very well," he said, wiping his hands. "I've finished your marinade, Clarence."

Derek Towser sounded agitated.

"Is that you, Phillip?" he asked. "I've rung you because I know Leandra spoke to you, but really I think it should be the police."

"What's happened?" asked Bethancourt.

"I've just got home to find the place ransacked, with Leandra's bicycle out front and no sign of her. She must have walked in on a burglar. I don't know what to do—I should ring the police, but I promised her I wouldn't. Can you come?"

"Yes," said Bethancourt, thoroughly alarmed. "But I'm afraid the police will have to come into it now. Jack Gibbons is here and he knows it's you on the phone. We'll be right over."

"Thank God."

Bethancourt rang off and hastily made his way back to the

kitchen. Knowing Gibbons would not welcome Astley-Cooper's help, he kept his voice deliberately cheerful as he caught Gibbons's eye and said, "Jack and I will have to step out for a moment, Clarence. You carry on, and we'll be right back."

"Wha—?" said Astley-Cooper, swiveling round. "Why? What's happened?"

Bethancourt waved aside his questions, already retreating. "We'll tell you all about it over dinner," he said. "Cerberus, come, lad."

Gibbons, who had taken his warning from the look in Bethancourt's eyes, slipped out after him.

"What is it?" he asked in a low voice as Bethancourt led the way out of the house.

"Towser just arrived home, expecting to meet Leandra Tothill there. Her bicycle's out front, but there's no sign of her and apparently his cottage has been searched. I've no idea what it's all about, but it sounded bad to me."

"So it does," replied Gibbons, frowning and reaching for his mobile. "I'd better ring Carmichael—he was cadging a lift back from Stow with PC Stikes, but I don't know whether they've left yet or not."

"Do you want to take the Jaguar or the Rover?" asked Bethancourt, pausing outside the front door.

"I'd better drive," said Gibbons, dialing. "The Rover."

He spoke with Carmichael while he settled himself in the driver's seat and Bethancourt put Cerberus in the back.

"Carmichael and Stikes are on their way from Stow," said Gibbons, punching off his phone and starting up the car. He let in the clutch and took off with a spray of gravel. "Bloody hell. I had given up on the Towser angle. My God, Phillip, you don't think Leandra knew something and he's killed her for it? This could all be a blind on his part."

"No," answered Bethancourt. "You see, Jack, Leandra had given Towser an alibi for Bingham's murder."

"What?" Gibbons jerked his attention from the road and stared at his friend.

Succinctly, Bethancourt outlined what Leandra had told him, stressing the fact that she had gone to Towser's merely to look at pictures. Gibbons frowned.

"And you weren't going to tell me this?" he demanded.

"I was going to," answered Bethancourt, not entirely truthfully. "It just didn't seem very pertinent." They rounded a curve, the Rover swinging into the middle of the road, and Bethancourt grabbed the armrest. On either side, the trees rushed by like the wind. "The point is, if she was telling the truth, Towser's out of it."

Gibbons was silent for a moment. "We thought he was out of it anyway," he said. "He's still a very dark horse. And yet—if Leandra lied for some reason to protect him and decided to go back on her story, well, that doesn't look very good for him, does it?"

"No. Though, as you say, it's a rather remote possibility."

They fell silent as they swept through the village, barely slackening speed, and then began to climb the hill that led to the cottages.

Towser looked almost frantic. He threw open the door before they were out of the car and motioned them inside. The studio did not look unduly disturbed, although the drawers of the taboret had been turned out, their contents scattered on the floor by the easel. Cerberus moved to investigate it all, apparently picking up an interesting scent.

"I've no idea what's going on," said Towser, wild-eyed. "You've got to believe that, Sergeant. This is all mad."

"Just start at the beginning," said Gibbons, soothingly. "You were expecting Mrs. Tothill to come by?"

"Yes, yes." Towser ran a hand through his hair. "She rang earlier, about Martha's ring. She was quite upset, said I mustn't on any account give it back, and perhaps we could say I had found it. She was coming up to talk it over and decide the best thing to do."

"But you weren't here when she arrived?" asked Gibbons, resisting the urge to ask about the ring. The important thing now was Leandra.

"No," replied Towser. "Steve Eberhart rang just before she did. He had an emergency call out to the Whitley farm and couldn't get his car to go. I said I'd drive him over. I told Leandra that, but that it shouldn't take long and I'd leave the door open for her. It did take a little longer than I'd thought," he added. "I was gone for a good forty-five minutes altogether, and I told Leandra I'd be back in half an hour. Steve only had to give this cow a shot as it turned out, and he asked if I'd wait and bring him back. I couldn't very well refuse."

"No, of course not," said Gibbons, glancing about the room. "Have you looked for Mrs. Tothill? Checked the other rooms?"

"Yes, yes." Towser was impatient. "I've even checked the garden, but she's nowhere. And why would she have left without her bicycle, or without leaving me a note? Something's happened to her."

Gibbons privately agreed.

"Jack," interrupted Bethancourt. "Come look at this."

Bethancourt had gone to see what Cerberus found so interesting on the floor and now he beckoned his friend over urgently.

"It looks like a smear of blood to me," he said, pointing and holding his dog back from the spot.

Gibbons frowned and bent to examine it, careful not to touch the slight stain. "It does," he agreed, "but we'll have to wait for forensics to be sure. Anyway, it's a fresh stain."

"Blood?" echoed Towser, alarmed.

Bethancourt looked up at him. "You mentioned Mrs. Potts's signet ring," he said. "What does that have to do with anything?"

"It was the night Leandra was here," answered Towser. "The night Charlie died. Leandra took my bicycle to go home and got a puncture just by his place. When she got off to look at the tire, she found Martha's ring there on the ground. She picked it up and gave it to me the next time we saw each other to give back. You see, there was always the chance Martha would remember where she'd dropped it, and then Leandra would have to explain how she'd happened to be in Charlie's driveway. Only after she gave it to me, I forgot all about it."

Gibbons nodded. "But what made Mrs. Tothill change her mind tonight and tell you to keep the ring?"

Towser spread his hands helplessly. "I'm not sure," he replied. "She said something about a collection plate, but that meant nothing to me."

Bethancourt, however, started and stared at him, drawing Gibbons's attention.

"What is it, Phillip?" he asked.

"The collection plate," echoed Bethancourt. "Mrs. Potts dropped her ring into it and didn't notice. James had to fish it out for her when the plate got to him."

"So?" demanded Gibbons.

"I think—yes, I'm sure—it was the Sunday of Bingham's death," said Bethancourt.

"When Mrs. Potts went straight off to visit her sister," Gibbons finished the thought. He turned back to Towser. "Mrs. Tothill didn't say anything about that? About Mrs. Potts?"

Towser was looking confused. "No," he answered. "Leandra's main point was that we should have to hand the ring over to the police and whether or not we could say I had found it instead of her. I wasn't sure I liked that idea, and we agreed she should come 'round and talk it over. Here it is," he added, pulling a gold signet ring out of his pocket. "I went to look for it after Leandra rang because I couldn't remember what I'd done with it. You'd best take it now, I expect."

Gibbons accepted the ring automatically, while Bethancourt asked, "So Mrs. Potts doesn't know you have it?" There was a kind of desperation in his voice.

"Well, I'm not sure," said Towser. "Leandra did say something about her coming to get it."

The sick feeling in Bethancourt's stomach got worse.

Gibbons was looking at his watch, calculating. "So Mrs. Tothill spoke to you, what, at about six thirty?"

"About that, I suppose," answered Towser.

"And you arrived back here at seven twenty or so?"

Towser nodded silently.

"Then they can't have left very long before that," said Bethancourt.

"No," agreed Gibbons. "Let's go—we might catch them up. Where's this path to the lake, Mr. Towser?"

"At the bottom of the garden," he replied, looking puzzled. "But surely you don't think Martha would have—"

"If there was a car, it's hopeless," said Bethancourt, nevertheless making for the back door.

"But there mightn't have been one," said Gibbons. "People stick to what they usually do. I'll fetch the torch from the car and meet you."

Bethancourt nodded, moving into the kitchen and flinging open the back door there. Cerberus bounded ahead of him into the garden while his master fumbled for the outdoor lamp switch.

"Here," said Towser, who had followed him, and flicked it on.

It illuminated a small, mostly untended garden. There was a short stretch of lawn beyond it, hemmed in by the trees. Cerberus had paused at the edge of it, but, seeing his master following, he returned to nosing the grass before trotting confidently toward the trees.

"Where's he going?" asked Towser, producing his own torch.

Bethancourt merely shrugged and started after his pet, though the thought hovered in his mind that Cerberus had taken to Leandra in quite an extraordinary way for a normally aloof dog.

Gibbons came after them, flashing the beam of a far more powerful torch than Towser's. He started at a run for the trees, Bethancourt and Towser following behind.

Beneath the boughs it was dark and the path, though clear and broad, was hardly smooth and they were forced to slacken their pace.

"Leandra!" called out Bethancourt, though it seemed futile, and behind him Towser echoed the call.

"That's odd," muttered Bethancourt, struck by a sudden thought, but in the next moment he forgot it as the path ahead of them split in two, one direction leading downhill where the twinkling of lights could just be made out between the trees, the other leading upward in the dark. In the lead, Cerberus had paused, but before they caught him up, he turned into the right-hand way.

"That's the way to the lake," gasped Towser. "The other path leads down to the cottages—you can see the Eberharts' lights."

They followed the great dog, the light from the torches bouncing as they moved along at the best speed they could manage, the sheen of the dog's fur moving in and out of the light with every jolting step.

"If we're right," panted Bethancourt to Gibbons, "she can't have gone far. Leandra Tothill's not a large woman, but she's no tiny thing, either."

Gibbons only grunted and called out again, bellowing Leandra's name into the dark, though none of them really believed she would answer.

And then suddenly Cerberus was gone, between one bounce of the light and the next, and they all stumbled to a halt.

"There!" cried Gibbons, flashing his torch about and catching the white of the dog's coat.

They surged ahead again, off the path to the right, crashing through the bracken to where Cerberus stood beneath a large oak, his tail waving like a beacon. Beside him lay the still form of Leandra Tothill. Gibbons fell to his knees beside her at once, feeling for a pulse, with Bethancourt and Towser hovering over him. And as they stood there, silent except for their labored breathing, they heard the sound of running footsteps somewhere ahead in the distance.

Gibbons leapt to his feet.

"Ring for an ambulance, Phillip," he shouted as he ran off in pursuit.

Bethancourt took his place beside Leandra, nearly falling to his knees in relief.

"Thank God," whispered Towser behind him, and Bethancourt thought he was crying.

He fumbled out his mobile and dialed 999, while with his other hand he felt for the reassuring pulse in Leandra's throat. When he had finished giving directions, he sat back on his heels, gently stroking the hair out of Leandra's face in the light from Towser's torch.

"You'd better go back," he said, "and wait for them. They'll need someone to show them the way out here."

"But that will leave you without a light," objected Towser.

"I'll be all right," answered Bethancourt. "I don't need light to stand guard here. Go on."

"Very well," said Towser. He hesitated. "She is all right, isn't she?" he asked.

"Her pulse seems strong," replied Bethancourt. "She's been knocked on the head, I think—I got blood on my fingers when I was moving her hair. But the sooner the paramedics can see to her, the better."

"Yes, of course," said Towser, and turned abruptly away.

Bethancourt settled himself on the ground and called to his dog, who was trying to apply the universal canine remedy for all ills—licking. Cerberus obeyed, coming to lie down beside his master, who reached out to fondle his ears.

"Good lad," he said.

Behind him, he heard Towser's retreating footsteps, and then quiet descended. Thoughts flickered through his brain. He remembered what had struck him as odd earlier, a memory of searching for Joan Bonnar through the woods with Julie Benson, who had never once called out for her mother though she had appeared frantic enough to find her. And then there was the signet ring, Marla surrounded by admirers in the Deer and Hounds while he stood by her side, and lastly he thought of the whereabouts of everyone on the Sunday of Bingham's death, working through each of the villagers in turn.

He had not, up until then, particularly noticed the chill of the evening, but as he sat there in the dark, he found he was growing increasingly uncomfortable, and the thought occurred to him that lying on the damp ground could hardly be good for a traumatized body. He stripped off his jacket and laid it over Leandra and then urged Cerberus to lay down close to her. He moved to her other side and took her hands in his, noticing how cold they felt.

It seemed an age before anyone came, and when he first heard the sounds of someone approaching, it was not reassuring, coming as it did from the direction of the lake. But in the next instant a light swept over him and Gibbons's voice called, "Phillip? Are you there?"

"Here," he shouted, and the light turned in his direction.

"I couldn't remember how far along it was," said Gibbons, turning off the path to join him.

"Did you—?"

"No, I lost them," answered Gibbons ruefully. "I've been up to the old farmhouse, but no one's answering the door there. One of the cars is gone, but I'm sure I would have heard it start up as I came along, so likely it was gone before. Our culprit is either still out here somewhere, or else hiding in the house. How's Mrs. Tothill doing?"

"Cold," answered Bethancourt. "I wish they'd come."

"Here, take my jacket, too. They should be along soon now."

Gibbons shrugged out of his jacket and while Bethancourt tucked it around Leandra, he bent to feel for the pulse again, his fingers finding the place on the throat far more quickly than Bethancourt's had earlier.

"Still regular," he grunted, and played his torch over her still form.

"I think it's a head wound," offered Bethancourt. "Here, by her temple."

Gibbons's light found the spot. "That's nasty," he said. "I don't think we'd better try to move her—I don't know much about head wounds, and I wouldn't like to take the chance of making it worse. She hasn't shown any sign of waking up, has she?"

Bethancourt shook his head. "No," he answered.

Gibbons sighed and, straightening, leaned back against the tree.

"I've been thinking," said Bethancourt, gently rubbing Leandra's hands between his own. "I'm not sure Mrs. Potts is our killer after all."

"I've been thinking the same thing," agreed Gibbons. "She looks a sturdy specimen and all, but she's also well past fifty—I can't see her dragging Mrs. Tothill all this way and then successfully sprinting off into the night. Although," he added, "I can't say I've worked out how Bingham's murder was done."

"I think I have," said Bethancourt. "I was remembering that first night we were here, when Marla and I went to the pub with Clarence and the rest of the choir. Half the village had turned out and they made a terrific fuss over Marla. We were standing at the bar together and I remember thinking that no one would ever remember I had even been there."

"I see what you're thinking," began Gibbons, but he was cut off by the sound of his mobile ringing. He dug it out of his pocket and consulted the display. "It's Carmichael," he said, and answered promptly.

"Gibbons here . . . yes, sir, I'm fine . . . no, I lost them, sir. I'm back with Mrs. Tothill now. . . . Well, sir, we could do with that ambulance—it's damned cold out here on the ground . . ."

Bethancourt stopped listening; he thought Leandra had stirred and he bent over her.

"Leandra?" he said hopefully, but she did not reply.

Gibbons was rapidly filling in the chief inspector on the events of the evening and their conclusions. In a few moments he rang off and turned back to Bethancourt.

"Carmichael's going up to the farmhouse himself," announced Gibbons. "He and Constable Stikes have just arrived at Towser's. Stikes will bring the paramedics up as soon as they come."

"Just let it be soon," said Bethancourt.

It was, in fact, not very much longer. Stikes and Towser led the way up the path with powerful torches, and Bethancourt and Gibbons gave way to the three paramedics, who examined Leandra briskly and transferred her to a stretcher, replacing the men's jackets with blankets.

"How is she?" Gibbons asked them.

"I think she'll do," answered one of the paramedics cautiously. "No telling until the doctor sees her, of course. You did quite right to try to keep her warm without moving her—that's a very nasty crack on the head she's got."

They lifted the stretcher and started back, Towser leading the way while Stikes hung back to have a word with Gibbons. Bethancourt followed last of all, with Cerberus at his side. He reached down to pat the dog while he pulled his mobile from his pocket and rang Stutely Manor.

"Ah, Phillip, there you are," said Astley-Cooper cheerfully. "The chicken's not done yet, but I'll have it in the oven directly."

Bethancourt, who felt as if an age had passed since they had left the manor, was surprised to find that the evening was still relatively young.

"You'd better leave the bird," he told Astley-Cooper. "I need you to find Reverend Tothill and drive him to hospital."

"Hospital?" asked Astley-Cooper, confused. "Is he ill?"

"No, but his wife's on her way there now," answered Bethancourt. "She was attacked tonight, Clarence. The paramedics seem to think she'll be all right, but she's unconscious."

"God above," whispered Astley-Cooper. "What is happening to us all? You've got to get to the bottom of it, Phillip. We can't go on much longer like this."

"I think we're almost there," said Bethancourt grimly. "You'll find the vicar, then? I don't know where he is, although I suspect he's not at the vicarage."

"Oh, I know where he is," replied Astley-Cooper. "It's the Parish Council meeting tonight. I'll run right over and give him the news, make sure he's all right. I'll speak to you later, Phillip."

"Thank you, Clarence," said Bethancourt, and rang off.

Ahead of him, Stikes appeared to be giving Gibbons directions to someplace, which he was attempting to note down as they walked, the constable shining her torch on his notebook. Bethancourt felt emotionally and mentally spent; he was still not certain of exactly how everything had come to pass, but his brain refused to process any further information. They had saved Leandra Tothill. He clung to that single, most important fact as he trailed along in the dark.

As soon as they emerged from the trees, he paused and lit a cigarette, which he had been wanting badly for some time, but which he had not liked to do for fear of further contaminating a crime scene over which they had already run roughshod.

"Hurry up, Phillip," called Gibbons. "Or aren't you coming?"

Bethancourt eyed his friend, who appeared alert and ready for action rather than spent.

"Yes," he said, "I'm coming. Where are we going?"

"To Stow, of course," answered Gibbons. "Haven't you been listening?"

"I was ringing Clarence," said Bethancourt. "He's going to fetch the vicar to the hospital."

Constable Stikes started and looked faintly guilty. "Thank you for thinking of that, sir," she said. "I should have done it myself."

"You just get yourself up to the farmhouse as soon as you can, Constable," said Gibbons.

"The minute the forensics team arrives, sir," Stikes promised.

"Right, then," said Gibbons, turning away. "Come along, Phillip. We've got to be off."

Bethancourt, still unsure of where they were going or why, but unwilling to be left behind, followed his friend out to the Rover and ushered Cerberus into the back of the car before settling himself in the passenger seat. Gibbons, starting up the engine, was already on the phone to Carmichael.

"I'm on my way, sir," he reported. "The constable seems to have set everything up, and she's given me directions . . ." He tugged his notebook out of his jacket pocket and tossed it in Bethancourt's lap. "At the back," he whispered. "What? No, nothing, sir . . ."

Bethancourt adjusted his glasses and flipped open the notebook, turning to the back as directed. He peered at the writing there, tilting the page so the light from the dashboard fell on it.

"I can't read this," he announced as Gibbons rang off. "It's in shorthand."

"Hell, I forgot," said Gibbons. "Give it here."

Bethancourt handed it back. "So we're going back to Stow?" he asked. "What for?"

"To break the Bensons' alibi," replied Gibbons, stepping on the accelerator as he reached the A-road.

Carmichael sat on the front steps of the farmhouse and bent his head to light a cigar. The evening was chilly, but he could see the stars peeking out from between the clouds that hovered overhead and the air was fresh and clean. In his heavy coat, he was not uncomfortable, and he had resigned himself to a bit of a wait.

In a few minutes, he heard the sound of a car coming up the drive, but he did not stir, almost certain it was merely Constable Stikes returning, and this was borne out in another moment as her Ford appeared and drew up neatly beside the other two cars already parked beside the house.

"Everything all right, sir?" Stikes asked as she emerged.

"Perfectly quiet, Constable," answered Carmichael. "Come have a seat. Have forensics arrived then?"

"Yes, sir." Stikes walked over and seated herself on the step beside him. "They've got it well in hand down at Towser's cottage, and he's shown them the path up to the lake and where they found Mrs. Tothill. Oh, and Constable Evans rang, sir. He's at the hospital, looking after her. He'll report back as soon as she comes to and says anything."

"Good, good," said Carmichael, and puffed on his cigar while the constable fidgeted beside him. He glanced at her between puffs and asked, "So what do you think, Constable? Is Sergeant Gibbons right?"

Stikes sighed. "He must be, sir, particularly if he's certain whoever he was chasing didn't leave in the car that's missing." She pointed at the two vehicles parked beside her own. "That sporty model is James Benson's and the BMW next it is his sister's. The one that's missing, the Volvo estate wagon, is the general run-about car and the one Mrs. Potts uses."

"So you deduce she's the one who's absent."

"That's right, sir. Mind you, either or both of the Bensons might be with her—they often take the Volvo when they all go out together—but if either of the twins had gone out without Mrs. Potts, they would have used their own cars."

Carmichael nodded. "And do you think all three of them were in it together?"

Stikes hesitated. "I don't know, sir," she said reluctantly. "The only thing I'm certain of is that James didn't act alone. He hasn't the gumption or the brains to think it all out for himself. And he'd do whatever Julie or Mrs. Potts told him to. It's either all three of them, or the Bensons together."

"But not Mrs. Potts alone, despite the evidence of her ring?"

"As for the signet ring, sir," said Stikes, "Mrs. Potts is always losing it—and there's no denying the Bensons are the likeliest people to have found it. It seems far more likely to me that Mrs. Potts lost it somewhere before she left for her sister's that Sunday and Julie or James picked it up and pocketed it to give back when she returned."

"And then it would have fallen out of the pocket while they were moving Bingham's body." Carmichael nodded. "And do you agree with Gibbons that Mrs. Potts couldn't have carried Mrs. Tothill so far? You're about the same height and build as she is."

"It seems very unlikely, sir." Stikes considered a moment. "I think I could just have managed it," she added.

"But she's twenty years older," said Carmichael.

"Exactly, sir. I think the sergeant is right—it must have been James Benson he was chasing." She shook her head. "What I can't understand is why any of them should want to kill Mr. Bingham."

"Neither do I, Constable," said Carmichael, blowing out a stream of smoke and carefully rolling the ash off his cigar against the step. "But I have one or two ideas. We'll get to the bottom of it, never fear."

They fell silent then for a space, the countryside laying dark and silent all around them.

The same question was plaguing Gibbons as he parked the Rover along the High Street in Lower Oddington.

"It would seem to me," he said, swinging open the car door, "that killing Joan Bonnar would have done well enough. And I'll swear they weren't lying when they claimed to have no antipathy toward Bingham."

"I'll take your word for that," agreed Bethancourt. "And since Bingham didn't need money, there was no need for Joan to alter her bequests. In light of that, it does seem unreasonable for the Bensons to have murdered Bingham. It gained them nothing."

He let Cerberus out of the back while Gibbons leaned into the car to retrieve the envelope of photos they had picked up from the local newspaper editor in Stow-on-the-Wold. The editor was well-acquainted with Constable Stikes and had been happy to let her Scotland Yard colleague have several pictures of the Benson twins, taken at various local events over the years. He had even found one of Julie Benson at a charity ball, when she had worn her hair down. It was five or six years old, but she had not changed very much in that time, and it was still a good likeness.

A lot of people in the area apparently liked to start their weekend early, and the Kestrel pub was crowded, its dining room doing a brisk business. They had to wait several minutes at the bar before the landlord could attend to them. He proved just how good his memory for a face was by recognizing Gibbons straightaway.

"Well, you've had a lot on your plate since I saw you last," he said, raising an eyebrow. "You know, this is generally a quiet part of the country—not much goes on in the usual way of things."

Gibbons grinned at him. "And I wouldn't be here if these were ordinary times," he said. "No, thank you—we haven't time for a pint tonight. I just want to know if you still remember that couple we talked about the other day."

"Well enough," said the landlord, shrugging. "I haven't seen them again, if that's what you want to know."

"No, this time I have pictures," said Gibbons, producing them from the envelope.

The landlord identified Julie Benson at once, but he took longer over the pictures of her brother, considering several of them carefully before he said, "I don't think this is the man. I didn't see as much of him as I did the girl, but the man that was here was blonder and heavier than this fellow, and, well, rounder in his features if you know what I mean."

Gibbons assured him that he did, and thanked him as he gathered up the photos and took his leave.

"That's it then," he said to Bethancourt as they emerged from the pub. "I'll wager if we can discover which innocent friend of the Bensons was here that night with Julie, the landlord will pick him out for us."

Bethancourt agreed, but he frowned as they started back for the car. "But doesn't it strike you as odd," he said, "that they arranged such an elaborate alibi for Bingham's murder, and yet had virtually none at all for their mother's death?"

"It is odd," admitted Gibbons, and sighed. "We're still missing something, Phillip. I can't think what, but it doesn't all quite tie together."

"It's almost as if Joan Bonnar's murder was done on the spur of the moment," continued Bethancourt. "Like an afterthought."

"Can murder ever be undertaken as an afterthought?" asked Gibbons. "I really don't think so."

"I didn't mean that it was one," retorted Bethancourt. "Just that it seems that way from the outside. We've agreed that their mother's murder had to be the more important one."

"And they might have brought that one off, if it had occurred alone," said Gibbons. "Even now, there's not much evidence to say it wasn't an accident."

Bethancourt seemed about to agree, when he suddenly stopped dead and said, "Dear God. Of course. It would explain everything."

"What?" demanded Gibbons.

"If Bingham's death was an accident," said Bethancourt. "Jack, supposing it was Joan who was supposed to die that night? The Bensons have their alibi ready—and, mind you, it's for the time after Joan arrived home, not for the time of Bingham's death—and the likelihood is that it will be taken for a tragic accident anyway."

"Only," said Gibbons slowly, working it out, "Bingham drives up to see Joan on impulse and drinks the whisky meant for her. And, with his weak heart, instead of merely knocking him out, it kills him. It does make sense, Phillip."

"I think it does," said Bethancourt with satisfaction.

"Let me ring Carmichael," said Gibbons, pulling out his mobile as they resumed their walk to the car. "I hope the Bensons haven't turned up yet."

They had not. Constable Stikes, growing chilly, had risen and begun to pace while she spoke with her counterpart at the hospital. He was reporting that Mrs. Tothill had been taken in to the operating theatre, that the doctors were still optimistic about her prognosis, but that it was unlikely she would recover consciousness until morning. Her husband had arrived and was sitting in the waiting room with Clarence Astley-Cooper.

Having absorbed this information, Stikes rang off and turned back to the chief inspector, who had taken a call of his own while she had been speaking with Constable Evans. His cigar was clamped between his teeth, and his eyes were narrowed under his bushy brows while he articulated a series of grunts, culminating at last in the words, "Very good, Gibbons, I agree. What? No, wait a moment." He looked up at Stikes and asked, "What's the word from the hospital?"

"Mrs. Tothill is in surgery, sir," replied Stikes. "They still think she'll be all right in the end, but they're not expecting her to wake up until morning."

Carmichael nodded and spoke into his phone. "You might as well come back, Gibbons," he said. "I can't see what more we can do tonight, and Mrs. Tothill is still out at the hospital. All right then."

He rang off, and said with satisfaction, "Well, Constable, you'll be pleased to know that alibi's gone south. There's still a bit more to be done there, but I think I'm safe in saying there's no longer an obstacle to our theory."

"That's good news, sir," said Stikes.

Carmichael squinted at his watch. "What is it, coming up to ten? Surely if Mrs. Potts's outing is a legitimate one, she ought to be back soon."

"I should think so, sir," answered Stikes. She did not know whether to hope that Mrs. Potts was indeed involved in the crimes, which would at least prevent her from having her heart broken when she realized what the twins had been up to, or to hope that the woman was innocent. Stikes had always liked Mrs. Potts.

"You might as well check 'round the back again, Constable," said Carmichael. "See if there's been any change there. We'll wait it out a while longer, at least until my sergeant returns, but then I'm thinking of calling it a day."

"Yes, sir," said Stikes. She retrieved her torch from the step and was about to set off when she paused, hearing a car coming up the drive.

"Ah," sad Carmichael, rising with a grunt. "That must be her. We'll see what she has to say about the whereabouts of the Bensons."

In another moment, headlamps swept over them as the Volvo Estate pulled up before the house, coming to a stop beside the other cars.

"Is that you, Constable?" came Mrs. Potts's voice as the engine died and the passenger door swung open. She climbed out of the car a moment before a second figure emerged from the driver's side.

"It's the chief inspector, too," said Julie Benson. "Has something happened?"

Carmichael watched their faces as they came forward into the light from the door lamp. "There's been a spot of bother down at Mr. Towser's cottage," he affirmed. "Have you both been out long?"

"We've been to a film," answered Mrs. Potts. "The new Hugh Grant one—I thought it would help take our minds off our troubles."

Carmichael's eyes strayed toward the car. "Mr. Benson isn't with you?" he asked.

Julie laughed. "No, James isn't much for romantic comedies," she answered. "He stayed home and watched a DVD."

"He doesn't answer the door," said Carmichael.

Mrs. Potts looked alarmed and moved at once toward the door, digging in her bag for a key. "His car's here," she said. "I can't think . . ."

"Perhaps he went for a walk," suggested Julie. "It's a nice night out."

"Perhaps," said Mrs. Potts uneasily as she unlocked the door and flicked on the hall lights. "James! James, are you here?"

There was no answer at first as they all moved into the house, but then a voice came down the stairs.

"Coming, Marty."

"Oh, thank God." Mrs. Potts sagged in relief against the hall table.

"Marty, are you all right?" asked Julie, coming to her side.

"Yes, yes, dear. It's just that, with your mother and Charlie, well, never mind. It was silly of me to be worried."

Julie, Carmichael noticed, did not appear much relieved. She patted Mrs. Potts's shoulder with true affection, but her eyes were tense as they turned toward the stairs and her brother.

"Hullo, all," said James, coming down slowly. "Didn't realize the police were here. Is something up?"

"You haven't been answering your door, sir," said Carmichael, genially enough. "The constable and I have been trying to raise someone here for some time."

"Oh, sorry," said James. "I'm afraid I fell asleep upstairs. Marty and Julie will tell you, I'm a sound sleeper when I go off. Can sleep through most anything. I must not have heard the door. Were you looking for me?"

He was wearing slippers, and had a thick robe tossed over his shirt and trousers, but his hair appeared recently brushed and there was no sign of sleep in his eyes.

Carmichael opened his mouth to reply, and then hesitated, a sudden thought occurring to him. He glanced at Constable Stikes, praying she would not queer the pitch he was about to try; he wished Gibbons had returned in time. His sergeant would always follow his lead.

"I wasn't looking for you in particular, sir," he said to James. "It was actually Mrs. Potts I was hoping to have a word with." He turned back to her, one eye on Stikes, but she behaved beautifully, her face remaining impassive.

Mrs. Potts was regarding him alertly. "With me?" she asked. "What is it?"

"On the Sunday of Mr. Bingham's death," said Carmichael, a little ponderously, "I understand you went to church with the Bensons here, returned here to the house, and, after a meal, drove straight off to Somerset. Is that correct?"

Mrs. Potts looked surprised. "Why, yes," she said. "That's right."

"You did not, then, stop by Mr. Bingham's cottage?"

While Mrs. Potts denied this, Carmichael, out of the corner of his eye, saw James was desperately trying to communicate something silently to his sister. Her face remained set and tense.

"But I also understand," continued Carmichael, "that you had your signet ring at the service, but subsequently lost it later that day?"

Mrs. Potts appeared amazed that her ring should be of interest to the police. "Yes," she answered. "I don't know where it's gone to." A sudden light appeared in her eyes. "Are you saying you found it, Chief Inspector?"

"Yes, Mrs. Potts, we have," said Carmichael.

She smiled broadly, obviously pleased, while Julie at her side stiffened.

"That's a great relief to my mind," said Mrs. Potts. "I'm always losing it, I admit, but I usually find it again right away. Thank you so much, Chief Inspector. May I have it back now?"

"I'm afraid not," said Carmichael. "You see, it was found in the drive of Mr. Bingham's cottage on the Sunday night, while you were supposedly at your sister's."

"Supposedly?" Mrs. Potts frowned, trying to work this out. Slowly, her expression changed. "But you can't think that I—"

"You've just denied you were there on Sunday," said Carmichael.

"Well, I wasn't—"

"She could have dropped it there anytime," broke in James.

Carmichael raised an eyebrow. "When?" he demanded. "She had it at church that Sunday. The ring was found that night."

"Charlie probably found it himself somewhere," said Julie. "No doubt it dropped out of his pocket while he was getting in or out of his car. That would explain it."

"But Mr. Bingham did not leave his cottage that day until he went to London," replied Carmichael. "And that was after Mrs. Potts had supposedly left for Somerset. No, I'm afraid the conclusion is inescapable: Mrs. Potts was at that house sometime on Sunday, very likely after dark."

Mrs. Potts was looking stunned.

"No," said Julie. Her eyes were desperate. "Wait a moment, how do you know Marty had the ring in church? She probably lost it earlier."

Mrs. Potts roused herself. "No, Julie," she said gently, "I know I had it that morning. It was the day I dropped it in the collection plate, remember?"

"Oh, that." Julie gave a short laugh. It had a hint of hysteria in it. "No, you're wrong, Marty, that was the Sunday before. Isn't that right, James?"

"Of course," he replied at once. "I remember it perfectly."

Mrs. Potts hesitated, a puzzled frown on her face. "No," she said, half to herself, "I'm certain it was that Sunday . . ."

"So are several other people who noticed the incident," said Carmichael sternly. "Mrs. Martha Potts, I am arresting you on suspicion of murder."

"No!" cried out James before Carmichael could continue with the formal words of the caution. "Julie, do something. You can't let them take Marty! You can't!"

"I'm afraid there's nothing your sister can do, Mr. Benson," said Carmichael.

"But it wasn't Marty," James protested. "It was me. I dropped the damn ring—"

"James, shut up!" said Julie urgently.

"I dropped it, I say," shouted James, his deeper voice drowning out that of his sister's. "I found it in the car after Marty had gone and put it in my pocket. She must have lost it on the drive back from church. I thought I had it safe, but it must have dropped out when I was trying to get Charlie out of the car. Oh, God, we never meant to hurt Charlie—"

Julie was still shouting at him to be quiet, not to be a fool. Mrs.

308

Potts had smiled indulgently at his first words, but the smile had faded from her face now and there was a growing horror in her eyes. Constable Stikes was doing her best to remain impassive, but her eyes had widened in surprise as James went on.

Carmichael was smiling very slightly.

"We?" he said coolly. "Who do you mean by 'we,' Mr. Benson?"

"No one," James replied, stricken. "There's no one else. Marty had nothing to do with it, it was I who killed Charlie. I didn't mean to . . ."

Mrs. Potts was staring at him. "It can't be true," she whispered, horror-struck. "Why would you even think of—Oh, God, not your mother, too . . ."

Her eyes sought Julie's, as if for comfort, but Julie looked away, and Mrs. Potts gasped and grabbed at the edge of the table. "Dear heavens," she murmured. "Julie, tell me you knew nothing about this. Tell me!"

"Of course not," said Julie shortly, but she did not look at her.

"But of course she knew," said Carmichael relentlessly. "If she hadn't, she would have no reason to lie and claim Mr. Benson was with her that night."

Julie pressed her lips together tightly, but the way in which Mrs. Potts put a hand over her mouth showed whom she believed.

"How could you even think such a thing?" she said brokenly.

"I'm very sorry," Carmichael told her as he moved to take James's arm and give him the caution. At his nod, Stikes did the same with Julie, while Mrs. Potts shook her head in shock, her haunted gaze going from one to the other of the twins, as though they were changing before her eyes.

CHAPTER

18

Astley-Cooper rolled down the window of his Range
Rover and leaned his face into the cold, damp wind
that blew into the car.

"Almost there," he muttered to himself.

It was the very wee hours of the morning and he was tired. He had
felt obligated to wait with Tothill until Leandra came out of the operating theatre; it had seemed the only decent thing to do.

"She's going to be fine," the surgeon had told them, standing wearily
in the hallway, still in his scrubs. "The blow she sustained to her head
did result in some slight bleeding into her brain. We hoped that might
resolve of its own accord, but in the end it was necessary to relieve the
pressure before it did any damage. It all went very well, and she'll be
right as rain when she wakes up, beyond having a beast of a headache."

"Oh, splendid," Astley-Cooper had said. "Good man."

"Can I see her?" asked Tothill anxiously.

"They haven't brought her down yet," replied the surgeon, glancing at the clock. "They'll watch over her for a bit before they shift her

to a room, but it will be several hours before she wakes up. The best thing you can do is go home, get a bit of sleep, and come back in the morning."

Tothill had refused this excellent advice. He had contained himself quite well during the hours they had waited, praying quietly at times, but otherwise remaining still and responding reasonably to whatever cheering remarks Astley-Cooper thought to make. He was nonetheless distraught for all that, as the quiver in his voice showed.

"I think I might as well stay for a bit," he had said. "At least until they bring Leandra down and I can see her. I'll never sleep before then, anyhow. But you should certainly go home, Clarence. You've been too patient as it is, waiting with me all this while."

Though by that time Astley-Cooper had been longing for his bed, he had not been able to leave his friend sitting alone in the sterility of the hospital waiting room. Privately, he had been rather touched by such devotion, although of course it was not how he had been brought up. His parents had been of the old school, and if it had been his mother in that hospital bed, his father would have stiffened his upper lip, gone home as advised; and at least pretended to sleep even if it gave him an ulcer. Which, Astley-Cooper reflected, he had indeed suffered from at the end.

So he had stayed with Tothill until Leandra was brought back to her room, still unconscious, with a bandage on her head, and dark circles beneath her eyes. By that time, the young constable stationed there had left, saying he would return in the morning to collect Mrs. Tothill's statement, but they were not to worry: the chief inspector had arrested the guilty parties, so Leandra would be safe now.

It was then, while the vicar moved a chair up by the bed and settled himself beside his wife, taking her limp hand in his, that Astley-Cooper had crept away and at last driven himself back to Stutely Manor and his well-deserved bed.

As he turned the car into the drive, he began to shiver in the breeze from the open window.

"Overtired," he mumbled to himself, but he did not close the window; the bracing wind was all that was keeping him awake. He wondered if Bethancourt had come in yet, though in truth he rather suspected his houseguest had long since returned and gone to bed. And yet, tired as he was, he would have welcomed a full explanation of the night's events. He had got hold of Bethancourt once during the long wait, but all he had gathered from that was a confused story about Martha's ring and the fact that the Bensons had been arrested. Why either of them should have attacked Leandra, he still could not imagine. Neither could the vicar, who seemed principally confused over why his wife had not been at the Women's Institute meeting, but Bethancourt had not mentioned the WI at all. In fact, thought Astley-Cooper, he was still not sure exactly where Leandra had been attacked, or how they had come to find her.

The gabled front of Stutely Manor was dark against the star-studded night sky as he came up the drive and pulled to a halt, and he was very grateful to see it. He did not bother with putting the car away, simply getting out and heading straight for the front door.

Someone had left a light on for him in the hall, but otherwise the manor was dark and hushed, speaking of a household long since gone to their rest. Even Whiff had fallen asleep waiting for him, and lifted his head blearily as he heard his master enter. Pulling off his gloves, Astley-Cooper saw that Bethancourt's coat was among those hung on the coatrack and was conscious of a certain disappointment that his curiosity would go unsatisfied.

"It's probably for the best," he told the dog. "If he did start telling me, I'd no doubt fall asleep before he'd finished. I'm all in."

Sighing, he added his coat to the rack and trotted off to his own bed where, despite his curiosity, he was soon fast asleep.

≫ ≫ ≫

Gibbons yawned hugely as he sat before his computer late the next morning. He stole a look at his watch, but the minute hand did not seem to have moved any closer to noon since the last time he had looked. And he could not possibly expect Carmichael to return and sweep him off to lunch until at half twelve at the earliest. He sighed, took a sip of coffee to revive himself, and returned his attention to the chief constable's report, yawning again as he did so.

He and Carmichael had been up most of the night, persuading James Benson to make a statement while his sister sat mute in a separate room, refusing to say a word until her solicitor arrived. They had not got to bed until well after three, but neither of them had thought of sleeping in. They were eager to tie up the loose ends of the case and prepare their reports.

Accordingly, they had been on the road to Stow-on-the-Wold by nine the next morning. By eleven they had found and interviewed the unsuspecting friend who had had drinks with Julie Benson the night of Bingham's murder, gone on to have his photograph identified by the landlord of the pub in Lower Oddington, and arranged for both men to come in to sign statements later in the afternoon.

Afterward, Carmichael had decided to run out to the old farmhouse to see how forensics were coming along.

"It would be nice," he had said, "if we could find even a scintilla of physical evidence."

Gibbons agreed and had offered to drive his superior, but instead had been relegated to make a start on the chief constable's report. This he had done, but he was finding it much more difficult to keep awake sitting at Constable Stikes's desk than it had been when he was more actively engaged, and his mind kept straying to thoughts of Bethancourt, whom he had not heard from all morning and who was presumably sleeping in. He was just turning back to the computer when his mobile rang and, hoping for more good news from Carmichael, he answered it quickly.

But instead it was Eve Bingham.

"Sergeant Gibbons?" she said.

"Speaking," he replied, a little discomfited. In the press of events, he had forgotten her existence, much less her status as onetime suspect.

Her voice was hesitant. "I've just heard that you made an arrest last night. Is that true?"

"Yes, miss," said Gibbons. "Quite true. The Bensons are presently in custody."

He thought he heard a little sigh escape her before she said, "You believe they killed my father?"

"Yes," he answered. "I think there's no doubt of it, Miss Bingham. James Benson confessed last night."

There was a long pause in which Gibbons searched for something comforting to say and found no words.

"Thank you, Sergeant," she said at last. "In that case, I wish to inform you that I will be leaving for Paris this evening. I believe the police wished to be informed of my movements?"

Her tone now was cool and Gibbons grimaced.

"No, need, Miss," he said politely, "not now the case has been concluded."

Despite the lateness of the hour at which he had retired, Astley-Cooper woke at seven, his accustomed time. He felt quite bleary, but knowing that further pursuit of sleep was hopeless, he rose and made ready to face the day. He was irked to discover, when he emerged from his bedroom, that Bethancourt was still asleep and showed no signs of stirring. While he ate his breakfast, he considered waking his guest, but decided in the end against it, as being somewhat inhospitable.

"Will Mr. Bethancourt be wanting breakfast this morning?" asked Mrs. Cummins, looking in from the kitchen. "I only ask, sir, as I've noticed he doesn't seem to eat in the mornings, only having coffee."

"True," agreed Astley-Cooper, who had noticed the same thing.

"No, just get a pot of coffee ready for him. I'd better run back to hospital and make certain the Tothills are all right, but I should be back for lunch. Tell young Bethancourt that when he comes down, will you?"

Mrs. Cummins agreed to relay this message, and Astley-Cooper bustled off, sincerely hoping that Bethancourt would give him the whole story at lunch.

At the hospital, he found Leandra awake and picking at the breakfast she had been served. She smiled wanly up at him.

"I have a terrific headache," she confided. "It doesn't do much for one's appetite."

"Haven't they given you anything for it?" asked Astley-Cooper.

Leandra sighed. "Yes, they have," she answered. "It doesn't seem to help very much. Where's Richard?"

Astley-Cooper looked around. He had assumed, when he had not found the vicar at the bedside, that Tothill was off procuring his own breakfast, and said so.

"No," said Leandra. "He was here when I first woke up last night. It's all a bit hazy now, though I believe I cried all over him, but the nurse says he left soon after I went back to sleep." She frowned. "I don't know what time that was—perhaps it was later than I'd realized."

"Probably," said Astley-Cooper. She looked so confused, he did not like to tell her that her encounter with her husband had occurred sometime after four A.M. "I'm sure he's still asleep," he said instead. "He was awfully worried last night. I'll stop by the vicarage on my way home and wake him up—he'd want to be here if he knew you were up. Are you feeling all right apart from the headache?"

Astley-Cooper settled himself in the visitor's chair and prepared to be sympathetic. It was always difficult, he had found, to carry on much of a conversation with people in the hospital, but they seemed to like the company. On this occasion, however, he was rather unsure of what to say. Could he refer to the events of last night without upsetting her? And, if not, what else was there to talk about? Should he tell her about his effort to make *poularde a la D'albufera* or was that too mundane a topic?

His dilemma was cut short by the appearance of Constable Evans, who had returned to take Mrs. Tothill's statement, always assuming she remembered anything.

Leandra frowned. "I remember rather more than I'd like to," she said.

Evans smiled sympathetically and turned to Astley-Cooper. "Then if you wouldn't mind giving us a moment, sir?" he asked.

"Not at all," said Astley-Cooper, rising and collecting his coat. "I'll just run over to the village, Leandra, and let Richard know you're awake."

He made good his escape, rather relieved at not having to bear the burden of cheering her up alone. It was, he told himself, her husband she wanted in any case, and he would do best by supplying him as promptly as possible.

Bethancourt did not wake until almost eleven, being a man who liked his eight hours of sleep a night, and who seldom had cause to deny himself in this. When at last he rose, found himself eyed pleadingly by his dog, and hurried to bathe and dress so that he could venture downstairs and let his pet out. Mrs. Cummins delivered Astley-Cooper's message with the coffee, and Bethancourt assured her he would be at lunch, feeling rather badly that his host had had to wait so long for an explanation of the night's events.

But one o'clock came and went without Astley-Cooper's arrival.

"Shall I hold lunch, sir?" asked Mrs. Cummins. "He hasn't rung to say he wouldn't be here."

"Does he usually?" asked Bethancourt.

"Oh, yes, sir. He's a very considerate man, is Mr. Astley-Cooper."

"Then we'd better wait," said Bethancourt, a little reluctantly since he was unusually hungry. "He's probably just running a bit late."

316

He was over half an hour late in the end, and did not seem pleased when he did arrive.

"I want my lunch," he declared peevishly as he divested himself of his coat. "Lunch and an explanation. What on earth happened last night?"

"I'm very sorry," said Bethancourt soothingly, following his host into the dining room. "I never meant to run off like that, but events rather overtook me. Here, would you like me to open the wine?"

"Please," said Astley-Cooper, seating himself. "I find I'm just a little tired after staying at the hospital so late last night. Oh, there you are, Mrs. Cummins. Yes, we're quite ready. So, Phillip, what *did* happen last night? Why in heaven's name should the Bensons want to attack Leandra?"

"Because of Mrs. Potts's ring," answered Bethancourt, pouring. "I thought I told you that last night."

"You did," muttered Astley-Cooper. "It didn't make any sense then, either."

"Well—Ah, roast mutton! That smells very good."

"It does indeed," agreed Astley-Cooper. "Thank you very much, Mrs. Cummins, that's excellent. Here, Phillip, help yourself."

"Cheers," said Bethancourt, spearing a thick slice of mutton. "I haven't really eaten since lunch yesterday."

"I missed dinner myself," said Astley-Cooper, helping himself in turn. "Unless one counts that dreadful sandwich at the hospital last night."

"The sandwiches are just as bad at the police station," said Bethancourt, applying gravy with a liberal hand, and handing the boat to Astley-Cooper.

For the next few moments they applied themselves to their food in silence, but then Astley-Cooper glanced at his guest and demanded,

"Well? What *did* happen last night?"

Bethancourt, swallowing, made haste to explain the night's events while he ate.

"If only Mrs. Tothill had stopped to think," he ended up, "she would have realized Mrs. Potts could never have managed Bingham's murder alone, which naturally makes the Bensons spring to mind. But as it was, she thought James was innocent, and there was no harm in asking if they had all happened to stop by Bingham's on the way home from church that Sunday. And that made James panic."

"So he struck Leandra over the head and dragged her off—where?" asked Astley-Cooper incredulously. "What on earth did he think he was doing? You can't mean to say that he intended to murder her, too?"

"Well," said Bethancourt, "he admitted he thought of simply dumping her in the lake, but wasn't at all sure he could face it. He realized he'd made a terrible mistake as soon as he'd knocked her out, you see, but couldn't think what to do next. What he really wanted was to talk to Julie, but she had her mobile turned off while she was at the cinema. So he carried Mrs. Tothill off just to give himself time. When he heard us coming along behind him, he dragged Leandra off the path a few feet in the hope we wouldn't stumble over her, and then took off for home as fast as he could."

Astley-Cooper shook his head, sighing, and fed himself an enormous bite of mutton and gravy. He was thoughtful as he chewed and at last asked, "Did James tell you why they wanted to kill their mother to start with?"

"In part," answered Bethancourt, pausing with a forkful of peas poised. "Though I imagine Julie would have been more forthcoming had she chosen to speak. They've always hated her, but of course they didn't have to see much of her, and they had their own place, here in the village, where they weren't known only as Joan Bonnar's children. But Joan was planning to marry Bingham and come back to live in the farmhouse the Bensons had always considered theirs. Her presence here would totally disrupt their lives, not to mention the fact that they were rather afraid it would be suggested that they should move into Bingham's cottage."

"It's quite a nice cottage," said Astley-Cooper. "Georgian, you know. Never needs much doing to it."

"Yes, but it's tiny compared to the farmhouse and, anyway, it's the farmhouse that's been their home all these years. And," he added, "to top it off, they, like everyone else, still believed Bingham had no real money. In that case, their mother would be sure to settle something on him, perhaps quite a lot, and that would cut into the Bensons' inheritance."

Astley-Cooper nodded, chewing slowly, and looking rather pained. "That's—that's rather awful," he said. "I quite realize she wasn't much of a parent to them—it was remarked on in the village at the time, when they were young yet—but, still, there was a relationship there. She did provide for them, and handsomely, too. All those horses of Julie's, and the cars . . ." His voice trailed off and he shook his head, taking another large bite of potato.

They were silent again, giving their attention to their meal, until at last Astley-Cooper paused to savor a mouthful of wine and leaned back in his chair, saying, "It's an odd way to murder someone. Did they expect the whisky and drugs to kill their victims?"

"No," answered Bethancourt, sipping his own wine. "That part of the plot was actually based on an incident from several years ago, after Eugene Sinclair's death. Apparently there was a morning on which Julie went to wake her mother and was unable to rouse her due to the amounts of alcohol and sedatives Joan had taken the night before. When they decided their mother had to die, Julie remembered that and used it to devise a plan to make the murder look like an accident. The original idea was what they eventually did do, which was to drug her while she was here, at the farmhouse, and then drown her in the lake. But they seized their chance when the opportunity presented itself."

Astley-Cooper nodded understanding. "The weekend when she wasn't seeing Charlie. Only he went up to visit her unexpectedly. I suppose he got at the whisky before Joan came home?"

"That's right," said Bethancourt. "James drove up to town while Joan was at that interview and substituted the doctored bottle of scotch for the one in Joan's house. He was then supposed to wait and watch for Joan's return, but he was feeling nervous without Julie by his side, and went off to a pub to have a drink to calm himself down."

"No wonder," muttered Astley-Cooper. "I should have needed several drinks, myself."

"I suppose it was natural," agreed Bethancourt. "If, that is, one can say anything about the business is natural. Anyway, once he did return, nearly the first thing he saw was Bingham's car parked in the square. He was horrified and raced in to switch the scotch bottles back, only to find Bingham was already dead. He rang Julie at once, of course, and she had the wits to see that they couldn't possibly kill off their mother and her fiancé all in one evening, and decided to try to make Bingham's death look natural. She had James replace the drugged whisky, and drive Bingham back to Chipping Chedding in his own car. You know the rest."

Astley-Cooper finished the last bite of his mutton and leaned back with a well-satisfied air, wineglass in hand.

"I'm surprised," he said, "that they dared to try again after that."

"James didn't want to," said Bethancourt. "He'd had a bad fright, but Julie, having been on the verge of getting rid of her mother, couldn't stand to wait. She switched the whisky bottles that night and presented James with a fait accompli. He nearly balked, but in the end she talked him into it and together they got their mother downstairs and trundled her down to the lake in a wheelbarrow. They tipped Joan into the water and that was that."

Astley-Cooper shuddered. "That's very cold-blooded," he said. "Quite awful."

"Murder," said Bethancourt grimly, "usually is."

"It makes me quite ill to think of," said Astley-Cooper, resting a hand on his abdomen.

"Probably you've eaten too much," said Bethancourt, finishing his own prodigious portion and washing it down with the last of his wine. He refilled his glass carefully and topped up his host's for good measure.

"Thank you," said Astley-Cooper absently, taking a sip. He ruminated silently for a moment, turning it all over in his mind. Then he sighed deeply.

"Well," he said, "it's good to have it all cleared up at last, although knowing the truth is almost as unsettling as the uncertainty. And at least you were quick enough to save Leandra."

"Thank God for that," said Bethancourt, lighting a cigarette. "How is she, by the way? Awake, I gather, since she gave a statement to Constable Evans this morning."

"Oh, yes, she's awake," said Astley-Cooper gloomily. "She probably wishes she wasn't."

"Why?" asked Bethancourt, concerned. "I didn't think she was that badly hurt."

"Well, she has a pretty nasty headache, I gather."

"Oh," said Bethancourt, rather at a loss. "A bad patient, is she?"

"No, no. I don't think you could say that." Astley-Cooper darted a look at his guest. "I thought you said you knew," he went on, obviously uncomfortable.

Bethancourt frowned. "Knew what?" he asked.

"Well, you know . . . about Leandra and Towser."

"I know she was up at his cottage the night Bingham died," said Bethancourt. "Is that what you're on about?"

"Well, yes," said Astley-Cooper. He added indignantly, "You needn't pretend it was all innocent for my sake."

"But it was," protested Bethancourt.

Astley-Cooper just shook his head, looking very somber, and Bethancourt experienced a wave of doubt.

"At least, I thought it was," he amended. "I was nearly certain of it. What makes you think they actually slept together?"

Astley-Cooper flinched at this bald description, but retorted, "What on earth else would they have been doing?"

"Well," said Bethancourt, tapping his cigarette on the edge of the ashtray, "they might have been looking at Towser's paintings. Did Mrs. Tothill tell you differently?"

Astley-Cooper shook his head. "Of course not," he replied, "but apparently she confessed to Richard when she came to in the hospital. He's not taking it well."

"Oh, dear," murmured Bethancourt, an anxious frown appearing between his brows.

"I don't think," continued Astley-Cooper, "Leandra remembers what she told him last night. When I was at the hospital she was asking after him as if there was not the least thing wrong in the world."

Bethancourt raised an eyebrow, faith in his own perceptions returning.

"So," Astley-Cooper went on, "I stopped by the vicarage to wake Richard up and send him back to the hospital, only I found he hadn't been to sleep. He was just sitting in his study, looking all hag-ridden, and muttering about how he didn't know how he'd get on without her."

"That's not good," said Bethancourt. "But did you find out what she actually said to him? There's an enormous difference between confessing to infidelity and confessing to an indiscretion."

"I don't know what she said, but Richard seemed to have no doubt about it." Astley-Cooper sighed heavily. "It took me some time to make sense of it all—it was as if he were in shock and couldn't put two words together. But when I suggested he should go back to the hospital and talk to her, he flatly refused. Said he couldn't stand to see her." Astley-Cooper paused and took a healthy swallow of wine.

Bethancourt, remembering the joy the Tothills had always seemed to take in each other, drank deeply as well.

"Last night in the hospital," said Astley-Cooper after a moment, "we were both praying like mad while we waited for word. And when we heard she was all right, Richard went on praying, this time in thanksgiving."

"That's natural enough," said Bethancourt.

"Yes, indeed," said Astley-Cooper. "But this morning he wasn't praying at all. I even suggested it, Phillip—that he pray for guidance, you know—and he only shook his head. I'm terribly afraid he's lost his faith as well as his wife."

"He hasn't lost his wife," objected Bethancourt. "He's casting her off—it's quite a different thing. Did you try the bit about forgiveness and turning the other cheek?"

Astley-Cooper nodded glumly. "It didn't work," he said. "Nothing I said made any difference. I'm not sure he was really listening." He hesitated and then went on, "I rang the hospital on my way here and left a message to say Richard wouldn't be coming, that there had been a parish emergency. I didn't want Leandra to fret, and I *did* want my lunch. And I wasn't sure what to do. I thought she might take it better coming from a female friend, but I don't like to spread this about the village—Richard might come around. Really, she should have family with her, but I've no idea how to get in touch with her sister or her parents."

Bethancourt considered this, swirling the last swallow of wine in the bottom of his glass.

"Getting hold of her people shouldn't be a problem," he said. "The vicar no doubt has their telephone numbers. And I think you're right not to spread this about the village. Frankly, Clarence, I remain un-convinced that actual, physical infidelity took place."

"What other kind is there?" asked Astley-Cooper.

Bethancourt sighed. "You'd be surprised," he said. "In any case, there's no need for the entire village to be privy to the intimate details of their marriage. Bad for morale and all that."

Astley-Cooper agreed, but then looked discouraged. "I expect that leaves me with the job of telling Leandra," he said gloomily. "I can't possibly put her off until her people can get here."

"Well, I don't know about that," said Bethancourt, taking pity on his host. "I can quite see how awkward it would be for both of you. The news might come better from a relative stranger, like me."

Astley-Cooper looked up hopefully. "Do you think so?" he said.

"It's bound to be a bit of an awkward scene," replied Bethancourt, "and at least this way, she won't be reminded of it every time she sees you—always assuming things work out in the end. I'll go along to the vicarage with you and help wrestle the phone numbers out of the reverend. Then, once you've rung Mrs. Tothill's people, I'll trot off to the hospital while you stay and try and talk Tothill 'round."

Astley-Cooper looked greatly relieved. "Bless you, Phillip," he said. "I was really dreading that. I don't mind admitting that this kind of thing isn't my line of country at all, not at all. I suppose," he added doubtfully, "you're quite sure Leandra didn't, er . . ."

Bethancourt shrugged. "Even if I'm wrong," he said, "I still think they ought to try and reconcile. If I ever saw two people who were meant for each other, it's the Tothills. It would be a pity for them to lose that because of a single mistake, however large."

"Do you really?" asked Astley-Cooper, apparently heartened by this sentiment. "I must say, I've been thinking the same thing, but of course I can't really imagine how Richard feels. I suppose with Marla, you've got a much better grasp of these affairs."

Bethancourt laughed and Astley-Cooper, realizing the implications of the way he had expressed himself, reddened.

"I didn't mean," he said, "that Marla would ever . . . that is . . ."

"It's all right, Clarence," said Bethancourt, still amused. He had, in fact, certain suspicions about what might have gone on during one or two of Marla's out-of-town photo shoots, but he had never inquired too particularly into the matter. He still thought that the wisest course. "Though of course Marla and I are not the same thing at all," he said. "She's only my girlfriend, not my wife, and she's been that for less than a year. If she was unfaithful, it would be ridiculous to suppose I could feel the same sense of betrayal as the vicar."

"Well, yes, certainly," agreed Astley-Cooper. "But it does give you a different viewpoint, as does your age. I sometimes think," he added reflectively, "that we older people are too set against change. It's a natural instinct, to want to keep things the way you're comfortable with them. But it's not always the best thing, and one does have to guard against it. I'm very glad to have the opinion of someone younger."

"I'm happy to give it," said Bethancourt. "Oh, here's Mrs. Cummins with the coffee."

No one answered Astley-Cooper's knocking at the kitchen door of the vicarage. Undaunted, he opened it himself and stepped inside.

"Richard's probably still in his study," he told Bethancourt, leading the way. "That's where I found him this morning. I let myself in thinking he was still asleep, you see, and meaning to wake him. Richard!" he called out as they made their way down the hall. "It's Clarence again."

Tothill was, as Astley-Cooper had said, still sitting listlessly at his desk, and it was obvious from his rumpled appearance and drawn expression that he had neither slept nor washed. His eyes, as he turned to look up at them, had a desperate, lost look in their depths.

"Oh, hullo," he said, but it came out as more of a croak and he tried to clear his throat, appearing slightly embarrassed to see Bethancourt.

Pushed to one side of the desk was half a bottle of Bell's and an empty glass, but Bethancourt, viewing the vicar with an experienced eye, did not think the man was very drunk. He seemed, as Astley-Cooper had said, to be in shock.

"I'm afraid I rather seem to have fallen apart," said Tothill, running a hand down his creased cassock. "Very odd, really. I'm usually quite good in a crisis, Clarence here will tell you . . ."

"Yes, indeed," said Astley-Cooper with forced cheerfulness.

"But they're not usually your own crises, are they?" said Bethancourt, sitting down in the chair meant for parishioners and signaling to Cerberus to lie down at his side.

"Er, no, I suppose not," muttered Tothill, apparently a little discomforted by this evidence of Bethancourt's intention to stay.

Bethancourt and Astley-Cooper exchanged a look.

"We've come," said Astley-Cooper, "to get the numbers of Leandra's sister and mother from you. You must have them written down somewhere, I expect?"

Tothill flinched at the mention of his wife's name, but he nodded, looking a little confused.

"I've got them in the address book," he said. "But why do you want to ring them?"

"We thought someone ought to go and sit with her," answered Bethancourt, lighting a cigarette. "She is in hospital, after all, and she's had a very nasty experience."

"Oh. Oh . . ."

"And of course," he continued, "she'll want someone with her when she finds out you're leaving her—she's bound to be upset, and what with the trauma she's already undergone, well, a family member seemed best."

Tothill stared blankly at him.

"Where's this address book, Richard?" asked Astley-Cooper.

"What? Oh, in here . . ."

Tothill opened the desk drawer and pulled out a black, leather-bound book, which Astley-Cooper took from him, flipping through the pages.

"Ah, yes, here we are," he murmured to himself, holding the book at arm's length and squinting at the page. "I thought that was the name . . . I'll just nip into the parlor and ring from there, shall I?" he added, looking up again. "Be back in a moment, Richard."

"Yes, of course," said the vicar vaguely. "Yes, I should have rung them myself. I never thought . . ."

His voice trailed off as Astley-Cooper disappeared and with an effort he brought his eyes back to the relative stranger sitting opposite him.

"I expect you're not thinking quite straight at the moment," said Bethancourt kindly. "What you want is a wash and a bite to eat and a nap. You'll have a better perspective on things after that."

Tothill rubbed a hand over his face. "Maybe," he muttered, unconvinced. And then, with sudden bitterness, "You can't know how it feels."

"No, of course not," said Bethancourt, still sympathetic. "But all those things would do anyone who's had a shock good."

"It's been a shock, right enough," said the vicar. He had hunched his shoulders and was staring down into his lap. "I thought I knew her," he muttered, so low that Bethancourt could barely make out the words. "I thought we knew each other. I trusted her completely—how could she? And I loved her so much . . ."

"As she does you," said Bethancourt.

"She can't. Not the same way," said Tothill flatly.

"Of course she does," said Bethancourt, a little impatiently. "And, yes, I know I've never been married. But I have been unfaithful, and it never has anything to do with how I feel about my girlfriend. It has to do with the madness of the moment, and being too weak to resist temptation at that moment, on that night."

"I wouldn't know," snapped Tothill, a spasm of pain flashing across his face.

"No, I expect not," said Bethancourt. "But that doesn't make it untrue."

Tothill merely shook his head mutely, not as though he were denying Bethancourt's words, but as if he simply could not cope with the subject.

"Look here," said Bethancourt. "I know we don't know each other terribly well, so it's impertinent of me to pry into your affairs, but are you really quite sure Mrs. Tothill said she committed adultery?"

Tothill stared at him as if he had gone mad.

"What in God's name do you think I'm so upset about?" he demanded.

"It's just," persisted Bethancourt, "that I was so entirely sure what she was feeling guilty about was forgetting her position as vicar's wife and going off to Towser's by herself."

Tothill looked outraged. "And I don't expect you're ever wrong about people, are you?" he snapped, but then immediately shook his head. "I'm sorry, I'm sorry," he muttered. "I didn't mean that. I don't seem to be thinking very clearly just now."

"Of course not," said Bethancourt. "Nobody could without any food or sleep or anything. Ah, here's Clarence."

"All set," said Astley-Cooper, coming back in and replacing the address book in the desk. "I spoke to the sister, who's coming on at once. She said it would be best if I let her tell her parents, so I agreed."

"Then I'd better push off," said Bethancourt, rising. He glanced at Astley-Cooper and made a slight motion with his head.

"Right," said Astley-Cooper. "I'll just see you out, shall I? Be back in a moment, Richard."

Tothill waved vaguely.

"He seemed quite sure of himself," said Astley-Cooper in hushed tones once they had reached the kitchen.

"Yes," said Bethancourt, who was having further qualms about his own opinion. "But even so, it may not be hopeless. Try to get him to bathe or at least eat something—something plain," he added hastily, remembering the *poularde a la D'albufera*. "A scrambled egg and some toast, perhaps."

"I can do that," said Astley-Cooper. "But what he really needs is sleep. I was thinking—do you think Dr. Cross might give him something? He'd be safe enough with the secret, anyway; doctors are always keeping things quiet."

"I don't see why not," said Bethancourt. "If you can't persuade him to lie down, have the doctor in by all means. I'd better go now. Cerberus, come."

Bethancourt made his way back to the car and lit a cigarette as he settled himself in the driver's seat. He was conscious of a deep reluctance to get on with his self-imposed task, but he quashed the feeling firmly and drove off, albeit at a very moderate speed, for the hospital.

Gibbons, emerging from his room at the pub that evening, found his mobile ringing and answered it hopefully. He had not heard from Bethancourt since before dinner.

"Hullo," said his friend, and he sounded tired. "What are you doing?"

"Just heading down to the pub for a pint," answered Gibbons. "Where are you?"

"I'm leaving the hospital," answered Bethancourt. "I'll meet you— I could do with a drink."

"I'll order you a scotch, shall I?"

"By all means," said Bethancourt. "Cheers."

Gibbons had drunk half a pint by the time Bethancourt arrived and sought out the corner table Gibbons had procured for them.

"There you are," said Gibbons, reaching out to pet Cerberus. "I've got your drink here."

"Thanks," said Bethancourt, slumping into a chair and taking up his glass at once. He savored a large swallow of the amber liquid and then sighed. "That's better," he said.

"Long day?" asked Gibbons.

"Long and painful and endless," replied Bethancourt, stretching out his legs and lighting a cigarette. "How was yours?"

"Pretty long," said Gibbons, "but there's an end in sight. The evidence has been rolling in nicely all day, and Carmichael and I have very nearly finished the chief constable's report. Carmichael's meeting with him tomorrow morning before the inquest, and once that's over we'll be off home."

"Home," echoed Bethancourt. "That sounds nice."

"But what have you been doing all day?" asked Gibbons. "Why were you at the hospital so long? Mrs. Tothill's not worse, is she?"

"It all depends on what you mean by that," responded Bethancourt. "The nurses assure me she's healing up very well, but her spirits have definitely plummeted. Here, you might as well hear the story."

Leaning forward and lowering his voice, Bethancourt briefly related the origin of the Tothills' woes.

Gibbons was greatly surprised.

"Well," he said thoughtfully, when Bethancourt had done, "well, I never would have imagined. To tell the truth," he added, looking rather embarrassed, "I was rather jealous of the Tothills. I mean, they seemed so happy together, and I kept thinking that if only Annette and I . . . well, never mind. I was wrong, wasn't I? Mrs. Tothill turned out to be no better in the end."

"That all depends on who you ask," replied Bethancourt. "She claims she's innocent of any such thing."

"Well, she would, wouldn't she?"

Bethancourt eyed his friend. He had been thinking that this case had at last succeeded in distracting Gibbons from his heartache over Annette Berowne. Certainly Gibbons's spirits had improved since he had come to the Cotswolds, and he had seemed to be completely focused on the matter in hand, but that last remark clearly showed that not all the wounds were yet healed. Still, thought Bethancourt encouragingly, Gibbons seemed to be over the worst of it.

"I actually believe her," said Bethancourt mildly, earning a startled look from his friend. "I'm as certain as I can be," he added, "that my belief is not founded on a desire not to be proved wrong."

Gibbons grinned at him. "Wouldn't blame you if it was," he said. "But, honestly, Phillip, how can you look at the fact that she went secretly and alone to Towser's cottage, stayed there for some hours, and say you think it was an innocent visit?"

"Several things really," answered Bethancourt. "For one, you should have seen her face when I told her the vicar believed she had been unfaithful. Astounded doesn't begin to cover it."

"She was probably astounded that he hadn't believed her when she said she hadn't."

"But that's just the point," said Bethancourt. "She never told him she hadn't slept with Towser—from her point of view she didn't need to because such a thing was unthinkable. Her sin—and one she takes seriously, by the way—was one of indiscretion. It was very wrong for the vicar's wife to accept an invitation from a man of a certain reputation to visit him alone, and she knew it was wrong when she did it. At the time, she no doubt convinced herself that no one but the most hide-bound would mistake her intentions, but that was debunked when Towser actually tried it on with her."

Gibbons mulled this over for a moment in silence. "Oh, hell, Phillip," he said at last. "You can always make the most impossible things sound quite reasonable."

Bethancourt smiled. "And I can believe six of them before breakfast," he said. "But I truly do think I'm right in this case. For another thing, look at the Tothills before all this happened: I don't think I've ever seen two people so crazy about each other."

"I'll give you that," said Gibbons. "I believe I said as much before."

"Well, I find it difficult to believe that a woman so in love with her husband would even want Towser. Yes, he's a remarkably handsome man, but he's no more handsome than she is beautiful. And by all accounts, she's had his like often enough before her marriage—it's not as if he would be a novelty for her. I just don't see where the temptation lies."

Gibbons rubbed his chin. "There's something in that," he agreed. "When I was with Annette, it's not as though I stopped noticing other women, or even stopped admiring them. But I wouldn't have gone home with any of them. I wouldn't have wanted to. I'd much rather be with Annette."

He sounded wistful and Bethancourt winced inwardly.

"Exactly," he said aloud. "And men's libidos are notoriously more active than women's."

"Well," sighed Gibbons, "I expect you're probably right, you usually are about things like this. God knows," he added bitterly, "you were right about Annette."

"I never said—" began Bethancourt, but Gibbons waved him to silence.

"I know you didn't," he said. "I still knew how you felt. Never mind," he continued, exhibiting a welcome, to Bethancourt's mind, refusal to dwell on his heartbreak. "The one I feel sorry for," he said, "is Mrs. Potts. I don't know as she'll ever get over it."

"Did her sister turn up?" asked Bethancourt.

"Arrived this afternoon," said Gibbons. "Mrs. Winslow," he nodded toward the landlord's wife, who presently stood behind the bar, "had gone up to keep an eye on her this morning. She said she couldn't get Mrs. Potts to eat any lunch, but that she did seem glad to see her sister. Mrs. Winslow had a quiet word with her when she arrived, and says she seems well able to cope. She was talking—the sister, I mean—about getting Mrs. Potts right away, possibly even taking their usual vacation now instead of in the summer. Apparently they usually just go down to Cornwall, but they had been thinking about doing something a little more exciting this year, like going to the Greek islands. Mrs. Kimmel thinks something like that might be just the thing to help Mrs. Potts over the worst of it."

Bethancourt privately thought that even the glory of Mediterranean islands would hardly be enough to soothe Mrs. Potts's spirit, but he said, "She's probably right. A change of scene will help—although I should save the islands until the trial comes up. Otherwise Mrs. Potts will feel it's her duty to go and sit in court everyday, and that will be pure torture for her. There will be a trial, I expect?"

"It looks like it," agreed Gibbons. "We never did get a word out of Julie Benson last night, except to deny everything. James was distressed enough to give us the story and some telling details, but he's busy recanting everything today. That won't make much difference in the end, we recorded everything, but Julie will be a closer thing. We've only got James's word for it that she was involved at all."

"But she gave him an alibi," objected Bethancourt. "And she must have driven him back to London to get his car that night."

"Oh, she admits to all that," said Gibbons. "Only she claims that she had no notion what he'd been up to. Said he rang her saying he'd got into a spot of trouble with his car, and could she keep quiet about it and drive him back to town. She says naturally she did as he asked, never thinking there was anything seriously wrong."

"I doubt she'll get that past a jury," said Bethancourt, taking another deep swallow of scotch.

"Well, I rather doubt it, too," said Gibbons. "The more so as we've found absolutely no one who knows them who thinks James could have done it all on his own. And *somebody* walked down to the lake in Joan Bonnar's shoes because we found a clear print. It certainly couldn't have been James; his feet are twice the size. And it wasn't Joan herself because James claims that Joan was completely unconscious and he rolled her down there in a wheelbarrow."

Bethancourt shrugged. "Again, there's only his word."

Gibbons grinned at him. "That's where you're wrong," he said. "Forensics found the wheelbarrow out in the stable and they've pulled three blond hairs and four black fibers out of it. They're busy matching them to Joan Bonnar's hair and coat this moment."

"Oh, well done," said Bethancourt. "That ties it up nicely, don't you think?"

"I do," said Gibbons, still grinning. His tired eyes gleamed with satisfaction and he raised his glass before he drank. "Here's to it."

"Hear, hear," said Bethancourt, lifting his own glass and knocking back the last of his whisky.

"Want another?" asked Gibbons.

"No, I'd better get back to the manor and see how Astley-Cooper's evening went."

333

"He was with the vicar?"

"That's right," said Bethancourt. "He wasn't doing very well, last I heard—Reverend Tothill, I mean, not Clarence."

Gibbons frowned. "I take it he doesn't share your opinion of his wife's innocence?"

"He didn't," answered Bethancourt. "But I haven't spoken to Clarence since I rang to assure him Mrs. Tothill denies ever confessing to infidelity, much less committing it. Obviously, the vicar wasn't immediately taken with the idea since he didn't sprint off to hospital on the spot, but Clarence may have talked him 'round since."

"Well, I hope they work it out," said Gibbons, swallowing the last of his beer. "Speaking of relationships, how is Marla?"

"Still not speaking to me," replied Bethancourt with a sigh. "Any reconciliation there will have to wait until I get back to London, I'm afraid."

"You'll talk her 'round," said Gibbons confidently.

"I'm glad you're so sure," muttered Bethancourt.

"You always do," pointed out Gibbons, pushing aside his empty glass. "Well, I had best get back to the chief constable's report."

"Yes, and I had better get on. Cerberus, come, lad."

They parted amiably at the door of the pub.

"I'll ring you tomorrow once I've got Carmichael safely ensconced with the chief constable," said Gibbons.

"Right," said Bethancourt. "And I'll see you back in town."

Gibbons paused on the point of turning away.

"You're coming back soon then?" he asked.

"I'd better if I want to have a girlfriend," said Bethancourt wryly.

Gibbons laughed and bade him good night.

Astley-Cooper was just arriving home himself when Bethancourt reached Stutely Manor. He looked tired, but his mood was giddy.

334

"There you are," he said, smiling at Bethancourt. "Hullo, Cerberus, old lad. Now, Whiff, don't be jealous."

"Have you just come in?" asked Bethancourt, divesting himself of his coat.

"Yes, just this moment." Astley-Cooper regarded the hall fondly, his eyes travelling over the linen fold paneling. "I must say, it's nice to be home." He looked back at Bethancourt. "I was just heading down to the kitchen," he said. "I'm feeling a bit peckish, and there's plenty of cold mutton left. And some apple tart. Would you like some?"

"Absolutely," said Bethancourt happily. "I had to make do with another of those hospital sandwiches for dinner."

"Poor boy," said Astley-Cooper. "Come along then. Did Leandra's family arrive?"

"Her sister did," replied Bethancourt. "And her parents are due in tomorrow morning. How's the vicar doing?"

"A bit better, I think," said Astley-Cooper. "I finally got him bedded down with one of Dr. Cross's pills. It put him out like a light. Oh, look, Mrs. Cummins has got some of that bread I like so much. Shall we make sandwiches?"

"By all means," said Bethancourt, eyeing the bread greedily. "Shall I get the mutton out?"

"Yes—and see if there's any lettuce, would you? There should be onion . . ."

"Do you want mustard?"

"Oh, yes, certainly, we must have mustard. There's a knife in that drawer if you'd like to slice the mutton. Was Leandra very distressed when Richard didn't come 'round?"

"Well, the news didn't come at a very good time," said Bethancourt, carving mutton. "The poor woman already had a head wound, and was still having nasty flashbacks about last night. She cried and they had to give her a sedative."

"Oh, dear," said Astley-Cooper. He had found a bread knife and was slicing thick slabs of bread from the loaf. "I was rather afraid of that."

"Why didn't Tothill turn up?" asked Bethancourt. "I mean, after I'd told you Mrs. Tothill claimed it was a misunderstanding. Did he not believe her?"

"He did at first," said Astley-Cooper, laying aside the bread knife. "One could see the hope dawning in his eyes. But then he turned all fatalistic and decided she had probably lied to you since she would never admit such a thing to a stranger. I take it you still believe she's telling the truth?"

"I do," said Bethancourt firmly. "Did you put the mustard on?"

"Yes, it's all ready, and I've sliced the onion, too. There, that makes a fine sandwich."

"Do you honestly think there's any chance the vicar will come around? In time to win her back, I mean."

Astley-Cooper was startled. "Win her back?" he echoed. "What-ever do you mean, Phillip?"

"I mean," said Bethancourt, grimly slicing the sandwiches, "that after the first shock, Mrs. Tothill is decidedly upset with her husband for leaping to the conclusion that she had been unfaithful to him, and her trust in him is eroding with every passing moment in which he fails to appear at her bedside. Her sister," he added, "was not best pleased, either."

"Oh, dear," said Astley-Cooper again, shaking his head. "I can only say I've never seen Richard behave this way before. This whole business seems to have hit him where he lives, so to speak."

"Indeed," agreed Bethancourt.

"Yes, I quite lost my temper with him—here are the plates, and do you want a beer? I thought I'd have one."

"Cheers, that'll do very well."

"Shall we just sit at the table here?"

They settled themselves with their sandwiches and took their first bites.

"Heaven," murmured Bethancourt, washing down his mouthful with a deep draught of beer. "This was an excellent idea, Clarence."

"I've been looking forward to it all evening," admitted Astley-Cooper. "Now, what was I saying?"

"Losing your temper with Reverend Tothill."

"Oh, yes, yes." Astley-Cooper nodded. "I was doing a great deal more listening than talking, you understand, but then Richard happened to say something about the sanctity of the marriage vows. So I said, 'Well, if they're so sacred, I don't see why her breaking one of them gives you leave to break any of the others. You did vow to take her for better or worse, you know.' And he fell silent at once and seemed to actually be thinking. Which I thought was very good because I don't believe he's been doing much of that. Thinking, I mean."

"No," agreed Bethancourt, chewing industriously. "And in any case, she *hasn't* broken her vows, so he has even less reason to break his. There must be some way to convince him."

Astley-Cooper took a thoughtful bite of his sandwich. "Half his complaint is that he can't go on without her," he said slowly. "In truth, I think he'd eventually take her back even if she had betrayed him. I knew him, you know, before he was married, when he first came here. He's always been quite a practical chap—I liked that about him right away, while everyone else was still complaining about how young he was. This has been a great shock to him, but he'll come to his senses once he's had time to think it all over. At the moment, though, it's rather as if his favorite dog has bitten him and he can't quite believe it's happened."

"If half his complaint is that he can't go on without her," said Bethancourt around a mouthful of mutton, "he should be relieved to realize he doesn't need to."

"As you say," agreed Astley-Cooper. "And I'm sure I hope he comes around by morning. I tell you, it's very difficult being the man's only confidant. I'm not at all suited to it, really."

"Well, you'll have some help tomorrow," said Bethancourt. "Apparently the vicar is quite close to his father-in-law, and he'll be arriving in the morning."

"That's true," said Astley-Cooper, cheering slightly. "Richard lost his own father while he was still in his teens, you know, so he was glad to be adopted by Leandra's. Yes, I daresay Michael will sort it all out."

Bethancourt, finishing the last of his sandwich, could not help wishing that someone would take this much interest in reconciling him and Marla. But he pushed that thought aside; Marla was always more impressed by actions than she was by words, and there was no action he could take until he returned to London.

"I was thinking of going back tomorrow afternoon," he told Astley-Cooper. "If you think you can cope, that is."

"My dear boy," said Astley-Cooper, "you must do exactly as you like. You've been a tower of strength through all this upset and I don't mind admitting to you that I'm not awfully fond of houseguests as a rule, but I've enjoyed your company thoroughly. You must come back sometime when no one has been murdered or anything unpleasant like that."

Bethancourt laughed. "By all means," he said. "I'd like that very much."

"Because," added Astley-Cooper, "Chipping Chedding is normally a very quiet, ordinary sort of place. Prettier than most, but quite ordinary otherwise. I don't feel you've got at all a proper impression of us on this visit."

"I don't know, Clarence," said Bethancourt. "Some places and people show their best side in adversity. I'd say Chipping Chedding was that sort of place."

"Very good of you to say," said Astley-Cooper, beaming, but in the next moment his smile had become a yawn.

"Oh, excuse me," he said. "Perhaps it's time for bed, what do you think?"

"I'm with you there," replied Bethancourt.

They left their plates and bottles for Mrs. Cummins to clean up, and mounted the beautiful Jacobean staircase, whose newel posts were considered a particularly fine example of their period.

EPILOGUE

*G*ood God," said Marla, as she entered her sitting room.

On the table to her right was an arrangement of two dozen red roses, received that morning, and around her throat was a jade necklace which had arrived from Asprey's the day before. Bethancourt had been back in town for almost a week, and although she had yet to speak to him, the evidence of his return was all around her. Presents had arrived with regularity, always accompanied by romantic notes (mostly plagiarized from the great poets). There was a new silk scarf in her drawer, and a framed charcoal sketch of her face was propped up on her desk. She couldn't imagine who he had found to do that in such a hurry. In the kitchen was a box of her favorite chocolates, also accompanied by flowers.

But none of this was what attracted her attention now. She thought she had heard some noise from the street, and the cause of this was now apparent. Outside her window, which was tightly closed against the inclement October weather, Bethancourt was standing on the fire escape. Behind him, pressed up against the railings, was another man with a guitar who was accompanying Bethancourt while he sang "Greensleeves" in a quite passable voice.

Marla simply stared at him for a moment. She toyed briefly with the idea of leaving the flat by the back entrance, but she knew she had been relenting in any case, and in another moment she began to giggle. She crossed to the window and opened it.

". . . and who but my lady Greensleeves?" Bethancourt sang at her.

"How on earth did you get out there?" she demanded.

"I bribed the woman downstairs," he responded. "Are you tired of 'Greensleeves'? I wasn't sure how well you could hear through the window."

Marla squinted out in the darkness at the man behind Bethancourt, who was still playing the tune.

"Who is that?" she asked.

"This is Jim, a friend of mine's younger brother." Jim smiled and nodded as he continued to play. "He's at university and is an aficionado of English folk music. Perhaps," he added to Jim, "we had better go on to the next one. She doesn't seem too taken with 'Greensleeves.'"

"I think," said Marla, "you had better come in. It's going to rain."

Bethancourt bowed. "My lady," he said, "we had not hoped for so great an honor."

"Oh, yes, you did," she said, standing aside as they climbed in. She paused while Jim politely closed the window behind him. "The necklace is beautiful, Phillip," she said softly.

He shrugged. "Less than you deserve after the disgraceful way I behaved," he answered, but he eyed the necklace as he spoke. It had not come cheap, nor had the roses or the scarf, and even Jim had had to be bribed before he would consent to drag his guitar out on a damp night and spend his evening perched on a fire escape. No one, Bethancourt reflected, seemed to believe in romantic love anymore.

"Excuse me," said Jim, "but if we've finished playing, I think I'd better get on. It was very nice to meet you, Marla."

"Delighted," said Marla vaguely, while Bethancourt thanked his musician and ushered him swiftly out the door. As he turned back, he found Marla standing close beside him, a smile playing about the corners of her perfect mouth.

"Phillip," she said, "I think I've decided to forgive you."

"Have you, Marla?" he replied. "I'm awfully glad."

But his last words were lost as she reached to kiss him. And as he gathered her into his arms, he decided that winning her back had not really been so expensive after all.